Also by Chrissie Manby

Flatmates
Second Prize
Deep Heat
Lizzie Jordan's Secret Life
Running Away From Richard
Getting Personal
Seven Sunny Days
Girl Meets Ape
Ready Or Not?
The Matchbreaker
Marrying for Money
Spa Wars
Crazy in Love
Getting Over Mr Right
Kate's Wedding
What I Did On My Holidays
Writing for Love (ebook only)
A Proper Family Holiday

About the author

Chrissie Manby is the author of eighteen romantic
comedy novels and a guide for aspiring writers,
Writing for Love. She was nominated for the Melissa
Nathan Award for Comedy Romance in 2011 for
Getting Over Mr Right.
Raised in Gloucester, Chrissie now lives in London.

You can follow her on
Twitter www.twitter.com/chrissiemanby
or visit her website to find out more
www.chrissiemanby.com.

CHRISSIE MANBY

A PROPER FAMILY CHRISTMAS

HODDER

First published in Great Britain in 2014 by Hodder & Stoughton
An Hachette UK company

1

Copyright © Chrissie Manby 2014

A CIP catalogue record for this title is available from the British Library

Paperback ISBN 978 0 340 99276 0
Ebook ISBN 978 1 444 70934 6

Typeset in Sabon MT by Palimpsest Book Production Limited,
Falkirk, Stirlingshire

Printed and bound by Clays Ltd, St Ives plc

Hodder & Stoughton policy is to use papers that are natural, renewable and
recyclable products and made from wood grown in sustainable forests. The
logging and manufacturing processes are expected to conform to the
environmental regulations of the country of origin.

Hodder & Stoughton Ltd
338 Euston Road
London NW1 3BH

www.hodder.co.uk

To Mum and Dad

Prologue

December 1971

A week before Christmas, in a tiny bedsit in a little town in Essex, a young woman carefully wrapped her Christmas gifts.

The list of people she had to buy for that year wasn't long. She didn't need to get anything for her mother or father. She had no siblings. She had no boyfriend. She hadn't been in town long enough to have any real friends. In fact, there was just one person she wanted to remember. But that one person on her Christmas list was more precious to her than anyone else in the world. That person's name was Daisy.

The young woman wrapped the small pink teddy bear with infinite precision, finishing the package with a ribbon. She placed it on the table alongside the baby blanket and the white romper suit and the rattle shaped like a heart. She had chosen them all so carefully, spending more than she could afford to buy the very best.

As it was, she had no idea whether the gifts would ever reach their intended recipient. Having wrapped each one in Christmas paper, she put them into a cardboard box that she addressed to an anonymous office. It would be up to someone she didn't know whether the gifts were passed on to Daisy's new family. It would be up to Daisy's new family whether the teddy bear made it under their Christmas tree.

A nagging voice in the young woman's head reminded her she might be wasting her time but her heart could not let this moment pass unmarked. It was Daisy's first Christmas. What mother wouldn't want her child to have a gift?

'But you're not her mother any more,' said the little voice. 'She's someone else's baby now.'

Five days later, the box full of gifts arrived at a smart Victorian mansion in the countryside near Warwick. The lady of the house thanked the postman and carried the box into the kitchen. She opened it with a sigh. She recognised at once the girlish handwriting on the gifts' colourful labels. Reading the messages brought tears to her eyes. Taking a deep breath, she tore off the wrapping paper and regarded the contents. She held the tiny romper suit, which was already much too small.

'I can take all this to the charity shop,' said her husband, when he found her crying over the pathetic little pile. 'Someone will be glad to receive them.'

'No,' said the lady. 'Not everything. We should at least hang on to this.'

She put the little pink teddy bear beneath the Christmas tree, on top of a mountain of presents from new grandparents, godparents and friends. Though she would never know whom it had come from, the baby would keep that teddy bear close by her entire life.

Chapter One

Annabel Buchanan

December, last year

Everything about Annabel Buchanan breathed entitlement. From the way she looked, with her pearls peeking out from the collar of a crisp white shirt under a V-necked cashmere sweater, to the way she walked, shoulders back and head high as though balancing an invisible book. She had a way of gaining the attention and assistance of everyone she came across, from baristas to barons. Her voice was clear and commanding and spoke of an ancestry peppered with generals and admirals. Her manners were never less than impeccable. She was a firm favourite for chairing committees and sitting on councils and organising village fetes. Though she and her husband had only recently moved into the Great House in Little Bissingden, you would have thought her to the manor born.

The ladies of Little Bissingden looked to Annabel when it came to all matters of taste and etiquette, which was why Annabel was horrified when, on a shopping trip to London, her daughter emerged from the changing room in Peter Jones in a dress that looked like a sweet wrapper. It was certainly about the same size as a piece of foil from a Ferrero Rocher. Annabel winced.

'Darling,' she said to Isabella – Izzy – her only child. 'Isn't that just a little bit common?'

'Common? Mum!' Izzy pouted. At sixteen years old, the only criteria she had when it came to choosing a dress was that one of her friends already owned something just like it. 'Jessica's got one,' was her defence now.

'Which just about proves my point,' said Annabel. Jessica was not one of Annabel's favourites among Izzy's private-school friends. She was the original 'bad influence'.

Annabel sent her daughter back into the dressing room to try on the classic little black dress she had picked out for her instead. They were searching for a dress for the Little Bissingden Christmas Ball. It was especially important that the Buchanan family make a collectively classy impression that year as Annabel was hoping to host the ball at the Great House in twelve months' time.

Izzy reappeared in the black dress, which was suitably demure and elegant. It very nearly reached to her knees.

'Perfect,' said Annabel. 'You look like a young Inès de la Fressange.'

'Who's that?' Izzy wrinkled her nose.

'Someone with a lot more class than your friend Jessica. Or her mother. That's who.'

'Class isn't the only thing that matters, Mum,' said Izzy with a world-weary sigh. 'You act like anyone who doesn't speak like you isn't worth knowing.'

Annabel smiled at her daughter in a way that said, 'one day you'll learn', absolutely unaware as she did so that the universe was lining up a few lessons of its own.

But for now, Annabel Buchanan was set for a perfect Christmas. She'd got her daughter in modest black velvet and had an organic bird for the big day, picked up from a butcher in Mayfair. Well worth the drive from the Midlands.

Later that evening, turning into the driveway of the Jacobean pile she now called home, Annabel was struck once again by the incredible beauty of the place. She would never get bored of driving her car down the long, tree-lined driveway that opened on to the most exquisite house Annabel had ever seen. She had known from the first moment she saw the Great House – on a mini-break fifteen years earlier – that one day she would live there. Richard took a little longer to be persuaded. He baulked at the thought of maintaining a listed building. He didn't understand why they needed something so big. There were only three of them, after all. But Annabel had told him he could have his own wine cellar. That was all Richard needed to hear.

They had been at the Great House for just over two years now. The renovation was almost complete. Annabel had overseen much of the refurbishment herself, stripping out the previous owner's ridiculous Essex-style fittings and replacing them with National Trust tones and carefully curated antiques inherited from both Annabel's and Richard's families. The interior designer who had assisted had asked whether the Buchanans would allow their finished home to be photographed for *Architectural Digest*. Annabel was delighted. Richard asked if the magazine would pay.

The cost of the renovation had become a small bone of contention. It was true that the original estimate of costs had more than doubled and it had taken twice as long as it should have done. But it was worth every penny to have created such a showpiece. The perfect family should have the perfect home. And money was really no object for the Buchanans.

Back from the shopping trip to London, Annabel decanted eight bags from the back of her Porsche Cayenne into the hallway. Izzy was sulking, having been refused a trolley dash round H&M because Annabel wanted to beat the traffic. While Izzy went straight to her bedroom, Annabel headed into the kitchen. She flicked on the Nespresso machine, which coordinated perfectly with the Smallbone of Devizes cabinets. The cleaning lady had arranged a pile of post neatly next to the fruit bowl.

As the Nespresso maker gurgled away in its corner, Annabel filleted envelopes. Bills went straight into a pile for her husband. A society wedding invitation was placed for high visibility on the shelf above the Aga. A leaflet about local council elections went straight into the bin (Annabel and Richard would be voting for their friends). A flyer from Harrods announcing a ten-per-cent-off day for black card holders was also filed in the rubbish. Christmas cards from suitably impressive senders joined the wedding invitation as Annabel wondered briefly whether the tinsel along the edge of the shelf was *de trop*. That was Richard's doing, of course. The mix of metallic green, red and gold clashed horribly with the kitchen colour scheme.

The rest of the house was decorated for the season in suitably tasteful style. There were three Christmas trees. One in the stairwell in the hallway, dressed in silver and white. That one was almost twelve feet high. Another stood in the corner of the dining room – a mere nine footer with blue baubles. The third, and most spec-tacular, was in the 'great room' with its double-height ceiling and inglenook fireplace, which was where the family would gather to open their presents on Christmas Day. The perfectly shaped Norwegian fir was dressed in silver and gold.

Annabel carried her coffee into the great room now and took a moment to look at her handiwork. The coordinated decorations. The beautifully wrapped presents beneath the tree. The glow of the logs in the fireplace. It was like a page from a glossy magazine. The only hint of whimsy was the old teddy bear, wearing a tattered tutu sewn by Annabel's mother Sarah some forty years earlier, which always took the place of the traditional fairy on top of the tree.

Yes, the scene was set for another perfect family Christmas.

Chapter Two

Ronnie Benson

Five months later

The very last thing you expect when you wake up on a British May bank holiday weekend is that the sun will be shining. The good citizens of Coventry certainly hadn't expected it. Neither had the BBC weatherman who had assured the people of the Midlands on the previous evening's news that the Bank Holiday weekend would be 'business as usual'. That is to say, it would be grey at best. Likely wet. With a fifty-two per cent chance of a hurricane.

Well, he was wrong.

Ronnie Benson squinted at her alarm clock. Then she squinted at the window. Was that actual sunlight coming in through the curtains? It couldn't be.

'Sun's shining,' she told her partner Mark with a tone of some surprise.

'Won't last,' said Mark, turning over his pillow and settling down to sleep through it.

'Get up, you lazy sod,' said Ronnie. 'It's your turn to make the kids' breakfast.'

'They're not up yet,' said Mark.

'Yes they are,' said Ronnie. 'Listen.'

She put her finger to Mark's lips so that he could concentrate on the sound floating up the stairs. The unmistakable strains of the *SpongeBob SquarePants* theme tune. That meant their six-year-old son Jack was up for sure.

Mark groaned.

'Five more minutes,' he pleaded.

But Ronnie prodded him until he slithered out from beneath the duvet and walked like a zombie towards the bedroom door. Just as he got there, Ronnie said, 'If it's going to be a nice day, we should go out, don't you think?'

Mark turned to look at her as though she had suggested that he take this sunny day as the perfect opportunity to repaint the whole front of the house. With a toothbrush.

'Go out?' he echoed.

'Yes. To Warwick Castle or something.'

'We always go to Warwick Castle.'

'Then somewhere different. Kenilworth? Stratford? I don't know. But we should go somewhere. Look at it, Mark. This might be the only good weather we get all year.'

Mark had to concede that Ronnie was probably right about that. 'OK,' he said. 'We'll go on a trip.'

'Good. We'll take a picnic. I'll call Mum and Dad and see if they want to come with us.'

Ronnie's mother made fantastic picnics. Having her parents tagging along was worthwhile for that alone, but Ronnie also knew that her mother would appreciate time with her grandchildren and vice versa. Especially on such a lovely day.

Mark nodded.

'So, if you could just make sure that Jack has a bath and that Sophie knows she's not going out with her friends . . .' Ronnie issued more instructions. 'There's a white wash to go on. The dishwasher needs unloading. Oh, and a cup of tea would be lovely.'

'Yes, Ma'am.'

Mark gave her a brief salute before he headed downstairs. Once the door was closed behind him, Ronnie turned her own pillow over to find the cool side and sank back down for another forty winks.

Jacqui and Dave, Ronnie's parents, were delighted to be asked along for the ride. Of course, they would have to bring Ronnie's grandfather too. Bill, now eighty-five and not entirely in possession of all his marbles, could not be left on his own.

Granddad Bill was a handful. While at Ronnie's house Mark made sure his son was washed and tried to persuade Sophie that a day spent with her family would not 'ruin her life', Jacqui had to help her father-in-law, Bill, bathe and dress. He used to take great care of his appearance. These days, he insisted on wearing the same Coventry City FC shirt every day. On his feet he wore carpet slippers, which he said were the only shoes that didn't hurt his feet.

All the same, even without the complication of choosing an outfit, it took almost an hour to get Bill out of his bedroom and into his favourite chair in the kitchen. Then there was a picnic to be made. While Jacqui was dressing Bill, Dave went to the supermarket and came back with French bread and a rotisserie chicken. Jacqui made quick work of the chicken, turning it into sandwich filling. She knew her grandson Jack would be delighted. Neither she nor Dave could remember if Sophie was a vegetarian that week.

She can eat the bread, was Ronnie's response to Jacqui's worried text on the subject.

It was eleven o'clock before the whole family was ready for their big day out but amazingly, the weather was holding. If anything, it was shaping up to be too hot. Jacqui and Dave drove to Ronnie's house for a quick conference over coffee before they set off. They'd yet to decide where to go. Warwick and Kenilworth castles were both well loved but way too familiar. Jack wanted to go anywhere else he might pretend to be a knight. Sophie pronounced every suggestion 'lame' and made it clear that she would rather stay at home, basking in the glow from her computer screen.

It was Jacqui who came up with the suggestion of the fete at Little Bissingden.

'One of the girls at work went last year. She said it was good fun. Lots of things for the kiddies.'

Sophie rolled her eyes.

'And you don't have to pay to get in.'

Ronnie was sold. The Little Bissingden fete it was. They piled back into two cars (Jack insisted on travelling with his grandparents) and headed for the small village that put on a very English extravaganza each year.

Jack was delighted by the old-fashioned entertainments. He threw his all into 'whack the rat' and forced his father on to the greasy pole. Jacqui and Ronnie enjoyed watching the local children give a display of country dancing. Dave found a beer tent for Bill. 'He needs to be in the shade,' was Dave's flawless reasoning. Even Sophie seemed to be having a reasonably good time. She took a fiver she had wheedled out of her dad and toured the nick-nack stalls. She bought a bracelet made out of an old fork, melted and then twisted into a circle. It suited her 'emo' aesthetic.

But what everyone, at least the women, looked forward to most of all was the guided tour of the village's Great House. From the outside, the place looked like something from a novel. The gardens were beautiful too. There was even a small maze. Mark paid two quid and took Jack round it. Meanwhile Jacqui and Ronnie were just itching to get a look at the inside of the house itself. To see, as Jacqui put it, 'how the other half lives'.

Having conquered the maze in minutes, Jack and his father would have been happy to carry on trying to win at 'whack the rat' but as the appointed time for the guided tour drew near, the bank holiday weather finally returned to form and the skies above Little Bissingden darkened. Sensing that the rain would arrive at any moment, Ronnie and Jacqui insisted that everyone in their family go round the house.

'But what about Bill?' Mark asked. 'We won't be able to get his wheelchair in there. I'll stay with him in the beer tent.'

'That's all right, Mark,' said Dave. 'I'll stay with Bill.'

'No, really, I'm happy to,' Mark tried. 'You want to look round the house.'

'I don't want to deprive you . . .' said Dave.

Ronnie made the executive decision. She told Mark, 'You're coming with me. You might find it interesting. Might give you some ideas on how to do our kitchen.'

'If we win the Euromillions. I don't need any ideas,' said Mark. 'We're having whatever I can lay my hands on. I told you.'

Ronnie pouted. Mark was a kitchen fitter and the fact that Ronnie would be getting other people's offcuts rather than the bespoke kitchen of her dreams was a sore point. She dreaded having to live with some stranger's plain white cupboards and dark grey worktops instead of the classic country-style kitchen she preferred.

Ronnie cheered up a little when Jack tucked his small hand into hers and said, 'I'm coming with you, Mummy. Do you think they've got a dungeon?' Her smile faded again when Jack's father answered.

'Almost certainly. That's what all those posh types like to do of a Saturday evening, isn't it? Go down into the dungeon for a nice bit of spanking.'

'Spanking's not nice,' said Jack quite vehemently. 'You're not supposed to spank people. You're supposed to give them a "time out".'

Jack's school was very keen on making sure its pupils knew their rights with regard to corporal punishment.

'For heaven's sake, Mark,' Ronnie scolded.

'Just having a laugh,' said Mark.

Sophie rolled her eyes extravagantly. 'Don't think about entering *Britain's Got Talent* as a stand-up, will you, Dad?'

So, Jacqui, Ronnie, Mark and the children joined the queue for the tour, which started at the Great House's 'scullery' entrance. At the appointed hour, the lady of the manor appeared at the door. She was wearing an elegant tea dress that might have been pinched from the set of *Downtown Abbey*. Ronnie couldn't immediately work out how old the woman was, but she was definitely younger than Ronnie had expected and she felt a stab of envy at the thought. Somehow it was harder to take the idea that people had so much more than she did when they seemed to be her contemporaries.

'Welcome, welcome,' the woman said. 'I'm Annabel Buchanan and I'm so glad you could all make it here today.' Her smile sank a little as she did a headcount of the crowd that had gathered to see her home. 'Gosh, there are a few more of you than I expected. I suppose it's because of the weather. Never mind. You're all *very* welcome. Please come on in.'

Annabel Buchanan stood to one side to let her visitors pass.

'I'd be grateful if you could all do your best to really, really *properly* wipe your feet on the mat before you step into the boot room. Some of the floors in the older parts of the house are very, very delicate and we'd like to keep them dry.'

As the rain started to fall, Ronnie pushed little Jack ahead of her. Eager as he was to get a look at the dungeon, Jack neglected to wipe his feet. Ronnie caught Annabel Buchanan frowning as Jack realised his error and dutifully stepped back onto the mat and did a comic shuffle. Stuck-up bitch, thought Ronnie. It wasn't as though she would be cleaning her own floor anyway. Ronnie gave her own shoes a desultory wipe on the enormous doormat that led into the boot room. Boot room! She was rewarded with a tight smile.

'Of course, in the house's heyday, this would have been the back door,' Annabel Buchanan began once everyone was inside and squashed into the vestibule with its carefully arranged rows of Hunter wellies, pristine Barbours and unusually clean dog basket.

'Bet it still is the back door and all,' Ronnie whispered to her mother. 'Can't have plebs like us coming in the front, can she?'

'Ssssh,' Jacqui hissed at her. 'She's been good enough to open her house.'

'Not much point having a house like this if you can't show it off, is there?' Ronnie commented.

'Ssssh,' said Jacqui again. 'I want to hear what she's saying. I'm interested in the history. Imagine what kind of a family must once have lived here.'

'I think I know what kind of family lives here now,' said Ronnie.

Chapter Three

Izzy

Izzy Buchanan had been dreading the village fete for months. As far as she was concerned, it was the very worst day of the year. She hated the stupid stalls selling cheap old crap and the way all the adults in the village pretended to be having so much fun on the greasy pole. The funniest thing about it was when someone fell off and broke an arm. But she especially hated the fact that this year her family home was going to be one of the attractions. What on earth were her parents thinking of? For what seemed like weeks before the fete, Izzy's mother had followed her round the house, nagging her every time she so much as looked as though she was going to put her school bag down in the wrong place.

'We are going to be on display!' her mother had shrieked when she opened the bedroom door that morning to bring Izzy her wake-up tea.

'Not my room,' said Izzy. 'You never said anyone would be coming into *my* room.'

'What are you talking about, Isabella?'

She was always 'Isabella' when she'd done something wrong.

'I've told you a hundred times. Your window . . .' said Annabel, pointing to the casement. 'People will want to see it. That's the only reason some of these people will have come.'

Ah yes. The window. While her mother bustled around the room collecting up dirty laundry, Izzy ran her fingers over the ancient stone ledge. This was what all the fuss was about. Izzy defied anyone who hadn't been told the story to know that there was anything special about her bedroom window at all, but apparently there was. There on the sill was a small group of scratch marks. They were very faint. All but invisible. But they were part of *history*. For Izzy's bedroom had once belonged to a couple of far more notable teenagers. During the civil war, the Great House, then a royalist stronghold, had played host to the young princes, the future Charles II and his brother James. They had left behind their initials scored in the stone.

'Your room holds an important part of British heritage,' Izzy's mother reminded her. 'There will be people here who have travelled to Little Bissingden specifically for the chance to see that windowsill. The least you can do is make sure that it's not strewn with nail varnish bottles.'

Strewn? There was *one* nail-varnish bottle on the windowsill. Just one. But Izzy knew her mother was not one to let the facts stand in the way of a good piece of hyperbole.

Having gathered up an armful of socks, T-shirts and the jeans that Izzy had been intending to wear that morning, Annabel left and closed the door loudly behind her.

Sitting up to drink her tea and prepare for the inevitable cleaning session ahead, Izzy was sorely tempted to cover the princes' scratches with some graffiti of her own, rendered in her favourite nail varnish. That would teach her mother a lesson about showing off to total randoms.

But, of course, after another lecture, delivered with

a plate of toast and Marmite half an hour later, Izzy bent to her mother's will and tidied up her bedroom. She swept her loose make-up into a drawer and found a place for those discarded clothes her mother hadn't already picked up in the wardrobe (as opposed to the 'floor-drobe'). She put books back on to the shelves and straightened her prized pile of *Elle* magazines. Last of all, she locked her secret diary into the real safe beneath her bed, along with her small collection of genuine Tiffany jewellery (mostly charms and earrings. Birthday gifts from her parents, grandparents and godparents over the years) and her real Cartier watch (her sixteenth birthday present).

'Nothing will go missing,' her mother had promised her. But Izzy did not like the look of the people her mother was intending to let walk all over their house. The fete always attracted a dodgy crowd. That was the problem with not charging an entry fee. Later that day, Izzy peeped out from behind her curtains to watch them gathering by the back door. Far from coming to the Great House to see the princely graffiti, they had probably come to case the joint to plan for a later burglary.

Izzy focused her disdain on one girl in the queue in particular. The girl was about Izzy's age but could not have been more different from the privileged daughters of the rich and famous who attended Izzy's private day school. She was dressed in the emo style that the least popular girls in Izzy's class seemed to favour, as they tried to turn the fact that they were oddballs into something to be proud of. Like it was a style choice rather than a total lack of fashion sense.

Anyway, the girl in the queue for the house tour was doing the very worst kind of emo. Emo on the cheap. She'd probably picked it all up on a market stall. Despite frequently lecturing her mother on her snobby class politics, Izzy was not immune to making the same kind of social judgements herself. The girl glanced up in the direction of Izzy's window, as though she sensed that someone was watching her. Izzy stepped back into the room so that she couldn't be seen.

'Chav,' she muttered.

Izzy checked the combination on the safe one more time, then she slipped out of her bedroom and down the back stairs into the utility room, which was the one room that her mother had promised no one would see. Her father was already in there. He'd arranged a couple of deckchairs in front of the washing machine as though he were intending to watch a delicates' cycle.

'All right, Izzy-Wizzy,' said Richard.

'Dad, don't call me that,' said Izzy, as she plopped down into the deckchair beside him.

Richard offered her a biscuit. 'How long do you think this is going to take?'

'Knowing Mum, she'll waffle on for days.'

'Good job I've got the weekend FT then.'

Izzy tapped on the screen of her iPad and brought up the e-book app.

'Reading a book?' her father asked. 'Not more vampires, I hope.'

'French existentialism,' said Izzy, flatly.

'Really?'

'No. Not really.'

'Shame. Thought I might be getting my money's worth out of that school of yours at last.'

Chapter Four

Annabel

Though she'd been a little disconcerted to see the number and type of people who had massed at her door, Annabel was very much enjoying giving her visitors the grand tour. She had spent a great deal of time working on the content of the visit. The research she had done into the history of the house was worthy of a dissertation. So much had happened within the imposing walls of the place she liked to call home. Fortunes had been made and lost. Great men had been born and died in the blackened oak four-poster bed that still occupied the second bedroom. Great women had strolled in the Italianate garden.

'So, these are, like, your ancestors?' asked a mousy little woman from Birmingham as Annabel swept her arm to take in the portraits that lined the main staircase. There were faces from all centuries, right back to the Jacobean family who had commissioned the place to mark their new-found wealth. Annabel had bought some of them from the house's previous owner, who had kept them in the barn. Others she had tracked down at auction.

'No,' said Annabel. 'They're not my ancestors, exactly, but I suppose you could say I've adopted them since I became the chatelaine of the house.'

'Oh. I'm surprised,' said Brummie Mouse. 'Because you look a lot like that one.'

Brummie Mouse pointed at the portrait of Mary Cavanagh, who had been mistress of the Great House in the sixteenth century. It wasn't an entirely flattering comparison. Mary Cavanagh had a pinched and weary look to her patrician face. When the Buchanan family first moved into the house, Izzy had proclaimed that she was frightened by all the portraits, but especially Mary's. She nicknamed her 'The Witch'.

Annabel's smile wavered just a little but she soon recovered and carried on. 'Even though we've changed the house in a great many ways, I can still feel the echoes of the people who went before. They're in the walls. They're in the furniture. In many ways, I feel a greater kinship with them than I feel with my real family.'

'That's a strange thing to say,' said a largish woman, who sounded like she was from Coventry, loud enough for Annabel to hear.

'Not everyone is as close as we are,' whispered the woman's companion, who was probably her mother. They had a similar build.

'If you think I look like Mary Cavanagh, then I'm very pleased,' Annabel continued. 'She was an unusually well-educated woman for her time. She wrote a book regarding the emancipation of the poor; a rare achievement for a woman in those days. I like to think that if she were around today, we would have a lot in common.'

'They do share a nose,' the Coventry woman muttered.

Annabel gritted her teeth. 'OK, everybody. We're going upstairs. Do be careful not to knock into the paintings as you come up.'

The little boy who hadn't wiped his feet took the stairs two at a time. The portraits obviously didn't interest him but he seemed keen to get a closer look at the suit of armour on the landing.

As the rest of the visitors streamed by him – they were going up another flight – the boy lingered in awe. It was quite charming, the look on his face. His hand hovered in front of the armoured mannequin's breastplate.

'Jack! Don't touch,' the child's mother – the woman from Coventry – screeched and yanked his hand away. 'How many times do I have to tell you?'

Annabel gave the boy a consoling smile.

The tour group followed her up another two staircases and squeezed on to the narrow galleried landing at the very top of the house. Fortunately, there was no armour to be monkeyed with here.

'And now,' said Annabel, 'the most important room in the house.' She turned to indicate a closed door.

Unlike the rest of the house, the door to this room hinted that something other than *Architectural Digest*-style perfection lay behind. A brightly coloured nameplate announced that this was 'Izzy's room'.

'Ladies and gentlemen, you'll have to excuse the mess.'

Chapter Five

Sophie

Sophie Benson-Edwards' bedroom back in Coventry was the smallest room in the house. Somehow her brother Jack had ended up with a bigger room. Their mother Ronnie had made the decision. She said that Jack had more crap: toys and train sets and the like, which she was not going to have downstairs in the lounge. The only way to contain Jack's junk was to make sure that his bedroom was big enough to play in.

Most of the time, Sophie was fine with that. Her bedroom was tiny but it overlooked the street in front of the house, which was useful now she was going out with Harrison Collerick. Whenever Sophie was grounded, which was often, Harrison would stand in the bus shelter across the road so that she could see him in real life while they BBMd each other frantically. It was real Romeo and Juliet stuff.

But this girl's bedroom was something else. While Annabel Buchanan explained the historical signifi-cance of a few dull scratches on the windowsill, Sophie made an inventory of everything Annabel's daughter had that Sophie could only dream of. The room was huge, for a start. It contained an actual four-poster bed. A modern one, though. Not like the freaky old beds with all the carving in the rooms on the floor below. No way would Sophie sleep in one of those. The woman giving the tour said people had been born and died in them, like that was a good thing.

As well as the amazing bed, there was an armchair by the window. On the big oak desk in the corner were an iPod and a laptop. Sophie was ready to vomit with envy when she saw the fantastic music system. Above the fireplace – yes, the room was big enough to have a fireplace – was a flat-screen television almost as big as the one in the lounge back at the Bensons' house.

Annabel Buchanan's tale of the two princes and the civil war went right over Sophie's head as the teenager let her eyes wander over the photographic montage on the wall over the desk. Sophie wondered which of the girls in those photos was the owner of this room. She decided it must be the brunette who appeared in at least seventy per cent of the snaps. Boy, did she seem to have the ideal life. She was pictured on tropical beaches of the kind that Sophie had only ever seen in adverts, at the top of the Empire State Building, riding a pony. She was pictured skiing, sailing, snorkelling and sipping a brightly coloured drink with an umbrella in it at some swanky beach club. At fifteen and a half years old, Sophie had never been abroad. Her parents couldn't even afford for her to go on the school trip to Germany. Sophie was suddenly embarrassed that she'd never set foot on a plane while this girl had obviously seen the world.

'Any questions?' Annabel asked.

Like a group of shy schoolchildren, the people on the tour just smiled and shook their heads. Except for Jack. Sophie cringed when she saw that her little brother had put his hand up. What would he come out with this time?

'Yes, young man?'

'I was told we would see a dungeon. I haven't seen one yet.'

'Well,' said Annabel. 'We'll have to put that right. I think there might be something to interest you as we make our way back to the boot room and out into the fresh air. Everybody ready? Follow me.'

Annabel Buchanan started to usher her guests back out into the corridor. As the other visitors wandered off, Sophie lingered in the bedroom for as long as she could, imagining how different her life could have been if *her* parents owned the Great House. She let her fingers drift over a dress that hung from the wardrobe door, forgotten in Izzy's last-minute tidying spree. It was made by All Saints. Sophie could only dream of owning anything from All Saints. It must have cost two hundred quid. The label was still hanging on it. Sophie was about to pull it out of the neckline so that she could take a look at the price when she heard someone behind her. She turned round. It was the girl in the photographs.

'Ahem,' said the girl. 'If you wouldn't mind stepping out of my room. This part of the house is now closed to the general public.'

Izzy Buchanan smiled but never in a million years could anyone have mistaken the smile for a friendly one. Sophie certainly didn't.

'Sorry.' Sophie stepped out past her. 'I was just looking at . . .'

Sophie gestured back towards the windowsill and the scratches that she hadn't bothered to examine at all.

'Yeah, right,' said Izzy, physically barging Sophie as she took repossession of her room. 'Chav,' she muttered under her breath.

'Excuse me?' said Sophie.

'Nothing,' said Izzy.

'I thought I heard you say something.'

'I didn't say anything. I was just clearing my throat.'

'Good,' said Sophie, setting her face in a scowl.

The rich girl blushed. Rude cow. She wasn't quite so tough as she seemed. She slammed the door shut in Sophie's face. Sophie heard the sound of a bolt being thrown to make sure she stayed out.

'Money clearly doesn't buy manners,' Sophie hissed through the closed bedroom door.

Chapter Six

Jack

Sophie's little brother Jack had been working hard at being good. Apart from when he thought about touching the suit of armour on the way up the stairs, he had kept his hands by his sides at all times, just as he always did when he was following his mum through the tableware department of John Lewis in Solihull. Whenever they had to go through the glass displays, Jack would actually cross his arms in front of himself and tuck his hands into his armpits to ensure his safe passage. Sometimes, he would even hold his breath. Who knew if those crystal glasses would withstand a hearty sigh? It only became a problem if his mum wanted to take a closer look at something. Once, when she was looking for a wedding anniversary present for Grandma and Granddad, Ronnie did stop to look at a glass fruit bowl and Jack had to hold his breath for so long that he started to feel faint. Eventually, he had to take an enormous gasp that made everybody turn and stare.

'What are you doing?' Ronnie asked him.

Jack explained his stringent safety measures.

'You doughnut,' said Ronnie, ruffling his hair. 'You can't *blow* anything over. I just don't want you to touch anything.'

Family legend had it that Sophie had once touched a glass paperweight shaped like a bird. She knocked it off a shelf, it broke, and Ronnie had to buy the shattered thing. It cost fifty pounds. Fifty pounds! The whole family had to eat toast for a month.

So Jack was extra careful at the Great House. But the armour was so tempting. Jack's imagination was well and truly fired up. Had that suit of armour gone into battle on the back of a brave prince? The size of the suit was particularly intriguing. It was so small. Jack imagined himself inside it.

Meanwhile, the lady of the house was bringing them back down the stairs very slowly. She was talking about the staircase itself, this time, explaining that it had been carved from solid oak and incorporated the emblems of the family who had the house built. Some of the emblems hinted at a dark past, of a fortune made in battle. But there were touches of humour in there too.

'Perhaps,' said the lady, 'one of you children will be the first to spot the tiny mouse, modelled on the beloved pet mouse of the little girl of the house.' She gestured back up the stairs to a portrait of a sickly-looking young miss, who held a small white mouse in her hand. 'Come on. First person to spot it is the winner.'

Jack was more interested in the armour. And what luck! Somehow, just by following his mother, he had come to find himself right next to the ancient knight again. While the other children in the tour group dutifully sought out the rodent in the bannisters, Jack's focus was entirely behind them. He examined the sword that hung from the armoured dummy's belt. Was it a real sword? Had it ever been used to run someone through?

As the other children looked for the mouse, Jack suddenly had the idea that he was standing in front of his best chance to get the sort of supernatural powers that made Doctor Who so unbeatable. If he could touch the tip of his sonic screwdriver to the tip of the sword, then surely there would be a transfer of energy. He would be invincible. Thomas, the boy at school who had made much of Jack's second year there a misery, would never be able to bully him again.

Slowly, silently, Jack drew his sonic screwdriver from his pocket. His parents and grandmother were focused on the bannisters. Jack lifted the plastic screwdriver towards the sword. His little heart beat wildly, as though a bolt of lightning might jump between sword and screwdriver and send him flying through the air. This was a dangerous enterprise. A Hollywood-style voiceover started to play in Jack's head. *No one knew this was the moment when Jack Benson-Edwards would be transformed from ordinary boy to super space knight.*

Jack jabbed his sonic screwdriver towards the pommel of the sword, but he missed and instead his jab hit the body of the dummy.

Crash.

The mannequin plunged forward, sending the closest members of the tour group jumping out of the way in horror. Jack narrowly missed being flattened.

'Jack!'

His mother didn't even have to look.

'Heavens!' said Annabel Buchanan.

'For crying out loud!' Ronnie wailed.

Jack cowered by the toppled dummy with his fingers in his mouth as Ronnie knelt down to inspect him.

'Is anybody hurt?' asked Annabel, though it was clear from the strained tone of her voice that what she really wanted to ask was 'Is anything broken?'.

Mark and Jacqui joined Ronnie and between them they set the mannequin upright. Jack's eyes were wide with fear. Was he going to be in trouble? Was that dent in the chest-piece a new one? How much was it going to cost them to replace the precious antique? If a glass bird cost fifty pounds, then a suit of armour must be four hundred million pounds at least! Jack wouldn't get any Christmas or birthday presents for the next twenty years.

Ronnie grabbed him by the top of the arm and held him tightly to keep him from causing any more damage.

'What the hell were you doing?' she hissed.

Jack had no time to explain.

Annabel Buchanan reached them and smiled.

'No harm done,' she said. 'The errant knight will live to ride again. I'm sure he must have suffered much worse on the battlefield.'

'Will I have to pay for it?' Jack asked.

'Goodness, no,' said Annabel. 'Nothing has been broken. And accidents will happen.'

Jack felt a sudden rush of love towards the kindly lady.

'Is this your family armour?' Ronnie asked.

'If only. It's from a *brocante* in Provence,' said Annabel. 'My husband's idea. A little *blague*.'

Ronnie and Jack were none the wiser.

'As long as your little boy is OK.'

'He's fine,' said Ronnie. 'And he's going to hang on to my hand from now on, aren't you, Jack?'

Jack nodded. He still couldn't quite believe he'd got away with it. Maybe the armour had worked some magic after all.

Just a few minutes later, the Bensons regrouped outside the Great House's back door. Sophie couldn't wait to get outside. Not only had that brush with the girl who lived in the house upset her, Jack had managed to embarrass the family in front of everybody. Again.

After the accident with the armour, Annabel Buchanan seemed as keen to see them go as the Bensons were to leave. The rest of the tour was definitely rushed. They seemed to skip most of the rooms on the ground floor and there was no dungeon viewing. Once her guests had filed out, Annabel stood in the doorway with her hands on the frame, as though physically barring re-entry. She didn't even take her hands off the frame to wave them off. She just shouted, 'Goodbye everybody. It's been an absolute pleasure to meet you all.'

She could not have sounded less sincere.

Sophie and Jack led the sprint to the beer tent, where Dave and Bill were helping to double the fete's takings by buying up the last few bottles of Spitfire.

'Has Dave been looking after you, Bill?' Jacqui asked.

'He's been wonderful. I've had a packet of crisps and three bottles of Spitfire. I've won the bloody lottery.'

Jack climbed on to Bill's knees and started to tell the story of the suit of armour. Bill assured him that he had actually been wearing a suit of armour when he landed on the Normandy beaches.

'No, you didn't,' said Jack. 'They didn't have armour in *your* war.'

'That's where you're wrong. It was an invisible suit,' said Bill. 'None of those Nazi bullets got me, did they?'

Jack forgot all about the armour in the Great House as Granddad Bill reprised the story of his experience of the Second World War, in which he had apparently fought underage. It was an interesting story – a true hero's tale – but on the thousandth hearing it lost some of its charm and the ever-changing details made some people wonder if it was even true. The adults quickly returned to talking about the present day.

'Nice house?' Dave asked his wife and daughter.

'Lovely. But I wouldn't want to live there,' said Jacqui. 'Imagine all that dusting.'

'I don't suppose for one moment that woman does her own dusting,' said Ronnie.

'No. I suppose you're right,' Jacqui agreed. 'Lucky for some. Oh look, the sun's come out again. Shall we go and have another look round the fete while Dave and Bill finish their pints?'

'Can't we just go home now?' Sophie asked.

'But I didn't get to see the dungeon!' Jack cried. 'Can we go back and ask the lady to let us see it now?'

Jacqui and Ronnie shared a look.

'I don't suppose Lady Muck will ever want to have us lot back in her house again.'

Chapter Seven

Izzy

'You behaved appallingly today,' Annabel shouted when Izzy came back downstairs. 'You were supposed to be helping me to make people welcome, instead you couldn't have been more surly if you'd tried. Everybody noticed it.'

'When you say "everybody", you mean your stupid friends from the WI. Just because you want to climb your way up the social ladder, doesn't mean that I have to help you. This is my home too. You let complete strangers into my room. What if something had been stolen?'

'Nothing was stolen.'

'There was a girl hanging around after you showed them the princes' graffiti. She looked like she was going to steal something.'

'Do you realise what you're saying? That's a very serious accusation to make.'

'Yes. And it's true. It was stupid of you to open the house up. If we get burgled in the next few weeks, you'll know exactly why.'

'You're being unbearable,' said Annabel. 'You've been lucky enough to have everything a person could want your whole life. I don't suppose that girl you're accusing of being a thief has had half the privileges that you have.'

'Sure, Mum. I could see the way you looked at those people. You were thinking exactly the same as me. You're such a hypocrite.'

'I most certainly am not,' Annabel protested.

'You're as glad to see the back of those people as I am.'

'I know I am,' said Richard, as he emerged from an afternoon in front of the washing machine.

After supper, Izzy was only too happy to go back to her room. She took the dress from the wardrobe door and checked it for dirty fingermarks. She couldn't see any but she shuddered at the thought of that strange girl actually touching it. Before she got into bed, Izzy checked her room over one more time. There was a chewing-gum wrapper on the floor by the window. Izzy was about to march downstairs and present it to her mother as evidence of the kind of behaviour she had allowed into the house when she remembered that it was her own. She'd discarded it herself. Somehow that made her even angrier. She scrunched the wrapper up and pitched it at the bin, missing it by a metre.

Izzy loved her parents but if there was one thing that drove her completely nuts, it was the way her mother was so concerned with appearances while at the same time denying she was a snob. As far as Izzy was concerned, if you had class, which she was certain she did, you didn't have to be any particular way. You were just yourself. Trying too hard was what made people look naff.

Izzy was determined that she would never, ever toady up to anyone like her mother did. Opening the house to the general public was the final straw. Why did she have to do that? Why did she feel the need to show off? Sometimes it was as though her mum didn't think she was good enough. It was weird.

But Izzy wasn't in the business of worrying too much

about her mother's mental health. Instead she went online to give her best friends, Jessica, Chloe and Gina, the complete low-down on the dreadful day.

Jessica and Chloe were already in virtual conversation.

We've got to go to a festival, Jessica wrote. *To celebrate the end of our GCSEs. Either SummerBox or Glastonbury. Chloe's parents have already agreed and mine are bound to say yes once I've told them yours are OK with everything too.*

I wouldn't hold your breath. God knows what my parents will say, replied Izzy. *I'm in trouble for being surly in front of the WI.*

Ha! It will be fine. Here's how it works, Jessica explained. *You tell them that my parents have already said 'yes' and I'll tell mine that yours have done the same. It doesn't have to be true. But then they'll both say 'yes' and it will be sorted anyway. Genius, eh? We're going to a festival. It's going to be awesome.*

Brilliant, Izzy had to agree.

Chapter Eight

Sophie

Back in Coventry, Sophie Benson-Edwards (though her parents weren't married, they had double-barrelled her name) sat in her bedroom, looking at the sheaf of paperwork that school had sent home regarding that term's big trip. The German class trip to Berlin. Sophie liked German. Her German teacher was gentle and kind. But that wasn't the real reason she wanted to go on the school trip. The real reason was that her boyfriend, Harrison Collerick, would be going.

Sophie had been 'going out' with Harrison Collerick since the start of year ten. Not that they had ever really 'gone out'. Going out consisted of walking home from school together and spending the weekends hanging out in a gang in the centre of town, with a bunch of other kids from their year. All Sophie wanted was some time with her boyfriend when she knew her parents couldn't suddenly appear.

The trip to Germany was the talk of the class. Students who had attended on previous occasions claimed that it was the wildest school excursion you could go on. Everyone knew that the German teachers – single Miss Johannson and very-married Mr Stott – were in love with each other and used the trip as a sort of clandestine mini-break. While they were busy canoodling, the schoolkids could run wild. Alcohol was easy to come by. German shopkeepers never asked for ID. Two kids from the previous year even claimed to have got into a bondage club.

But Sophie's parents said she couldn't go. They didn't have the money.

When she relayed the news to him, Harrison assured Sophie that if she didn't come on the trip, it wouldn't make a difference to their relationship, but Skyler, who was Sophie's 'best friend', said that Sophie was really opening herself up to danger by staying home. All that temptation. German girls were supposed to be really beautiful.

So, Sophie said she would go on the trip. She forged her mother's signature on the consent form and made excuses for her parents' absence at the meetings parents were supposed to attend ahead of the departure. She took in the photographs and identification she needed to be included on the group passport. Yes, for the past two months, Sophie had been pretending that she was going to go to Germany, in the vain hope that her wishful thinking would become a reality. Her parents would find the money somehow. Her dad was always playing the lottery. Just a little win would do.

But now it was too late. The trip left on Friday and Sophie did not have the money. When she got back to school after the bank holiday, Sophie had to admit to Miss Johannson that she would not be joining the party. It was so unfair. That girl in the Great House at Little Bissingden probably never had to give money a second thought.

On the appointed day, everyone who was going on the German trip came to school in their casual clothes. Those pupils who weren't going to be on the trip had to come in wearing uniform. There were just three in Sophie's class who wouldn't be going. Sophie herself. Nathan (who was going to a family wedding that weekend). And Shelley Tibbetts. Shelley Tibbetts had been the butt of everyone's jokes since they arrived at the school almost five years before.

Sophie went to the library as her peers piled on to two coaches for the overnight boat trip to Hamburg. Seeing Skyler primping herself earlier that day, Sophie had silently wished her 'best friend' a dose of seasickness.

To make things worse, not going on the school trip didn't mean there wasn't work to be done. Sophie's form teacher reminded her that GCSEs were now less than a year away. Sophie should use this quiet time, without the distraction of her friends, to make real progress with her coursework. It was a rare opportunity to have the one-to-one attention of the teachers.

It was not the kind of opportunity Sophie could appreciate when she thought about her classmates, creating memories that would always exclude her.

Sophie sulked for the rest of the day. When Ronnie asked what was wrong that evening, Sophie reminded her that the rest of the class were on their way to Germany.

'Bloody stupid arranging trips that cost so much money,' Ronnie said. 'You'll be able to go to Berlin when you're grown up and earning your own cash.'

'That's not the same,' said Sophie.

'I never got to go to Berlin,' said Ronnie.

'You weren't taking German.'

'Well, I've got some news that will cheer you up,' said Ronnie, as the family sat down to dinner.

Sophie dug her fingers into her thighs. If her mother chose that moment to announce that they had won the lottery, Sophie would definitely scream. But they hadn't won the lottery.

'You know that Grandma is sixty this year,' Ronnie continued.

'That's really old,' said Jack.

'Yes, well, don't go saying that to Grandma. Anyway, she and Granddad have been saving up for a holiday at the end of August. And they want us to go with them!'

Sophie's heart sank. They went on holiday with the grandparents every year as it was. And every year they went to the same place: the campsite near Littlehampton where Granddad Bill had bought a static caravan about a million years before. It was horrible, that van was. It was nowhere near big enough for the whole family and it still smelled of the cigars the previous owner liked to smoke.

'Whoop-di-do,' said Sophie.

'Hang on,' said Ronnie. 'I haven't told you where it is yet.'

'Surprise me,' said Sophie.

'Lanzarote. We're going to Lanzarote. All of us.'

'Where's Lanza-*rotty*?' Jack asked.

'It's an island off the coast of Africa but it's actually part of Spain.'

'Is it?' asked Mark.

'Yes,' said Ronnie. 'Actually, it is. And we're going to be staying in a resort with three swimming pools.'

'Hooray!' Jack was over the moon but then it didn't take much to make Jack happy. A packet of Haribo. An episode of *Harry Hill's TV Burp*. Their great-grandfather's toxic farts.

'Swimming pools! Swimming pools!' Jack chanted.

'Will I have to share a room with Jack?' Sophie asked.

'We'll have to sort that out with Grandma.'

'I didn't get to go to Germany,' Sophie reminded her parents.

'We'll see what we can do,' said Mark.

'It's going to be lovely,' said Ronnie. 'A proper family holiday.'

Sophie cheered up just a little.

But the following day, Skyler texted from Berlin. Apparently Harrison was missing Sophie badly. Skyler was taking it upon herself to keep him from getting too sad. Just a little later, Sophie got a text from another friend, saying that Skyler and Harrison had been spotted making out in the youth hostel.

A holiday in Lanzarote didn't seem like such a big deal any more. Sophie's life was still rubbish. She would never be as lucky as the girl in the Great House.

Chapter Nine

Izzy

A couple of weeks after the fete, Izzy sat her GCSEs. It was a tense time for all the family, though no one doubted that Izzy would do well. She had always been academic. As a small child she raced through all the reading programmes, achieving a reading age of twelve when she was still only seven years old. She'd been accepted at her first choice secondary school. And now she was on target to pass into the sixth form there with no problem whatsoever. After that, good A levels and a great university place were practically a formality.

So, when Izzy's parents said that she would be entitled to a special treat if she got good GCSE results, Izzy was not in the least bit superstitious about planning what that treat might be long before the results came in. She knew exactly what she wanted. She wanted to go to a festival with Jessica and the others.

Izzy presented a compelling case. The festival she and the girls had chosen was one of the cheaper ones, an event called SummerBox. It was relatively nearby. Just over the border in Northamptonshire. The bands that were headlining would attract a sedate crowd (positively square, said Izzy. Like her dad's favourite Coldplay). And *everyone else* was going. Jessica and Gina and Chloe and . . .

'Pleeeeease!'

Izzy tipped her head to one side and put on her most appealing look. She could tell that her father was softening but her mother . . .

'I don't think you should go,' said Annabel. 'You're only sixteen.'

'Seventeen in October,' Izzy pointed out. 'And sixteen's not young. I could get married if I felt like it.'

'Not without our permission,' Richard reminded her.

'Look, everyone else is going. *Everyone*. To celebrate the end of our exams. I'll be the only person who didn't get to go and when everyone's back at school in September, I'll be left out. They'll all be talking about it and I won't be able to join in.'

'Hardly a terrible hardship,' said Annabel.

'You don't understand,' Izzy wailed. 'Please! I'll never ask for anything else again.'

'You've asked for at least five things since breakfast,' Annabel pointed out. 'Is this festival instead of or as well as that concert in London?'

'Mum,' said Izzy. 'That's unfair. You said I could go to that concert ages ago. Don't you remember?'

Izzy wasn't really surprised her mother didn't remember. Izzy had asked her about it while they were on holiday in Turkey for the Easter break. Unusually, Annabel got completely wasted on cocktails. It was a night that Richard referred to often, because apparently Annabel had jumped on him and ravished him like she used to when they first got together. The thought made Izzy sick. She stuck her fingers in her ears whenever her parents alluded to it. But at the time she had taken advantage of Annabel's inebriated state and the subsequent hangover to wangle all sorts of concessions.

Anyway, the argument as to whether or not Izzy should go to a festival continued, with Izzy getting more and more irate as her parents raised more and more concerns. There were all sorts of things for a parent to worry about. And not just the usual drink, drugs and sex.

'The weather will be awful and you might end up with trench foot,' suggested Richard. 'No laughing matter, trench foot. Nearly cost us the First World War.'

'Dad!' Izzy wailed. This was no time for joking. Izzy needed to know as soon as possible. Yes, it was technically true that she might yet be revealed to have failed all her exams but that wasn't really likely, was it? Meanwhile the festival tickets went on sale first thing on Friday morning. They would be sold out within an hour. If Izzy was going to stand any chance of being there, she had to have her parents' 'yes' now.

Eventually, Izzy could bear it no longer. She stormed off to the sanctuary of her bedroom, and then she crept back downstairs to listen surreptitiously through the kitchen door.

'What do you think?' Richard asked.

'Well, Jessica's mother said she would drive them there. She says it's not like Glastonbury. It's a fraction of the size. The security is very tight. Lots of middle-class families go. They even take their toddlers. And Chloe's parents, the Greenwoods, live nearby and have agreed to be on standby overnight. So if the girls get into any trouble whatsoever, they can call Kerry Greenwood and she'll be there within ten minutes.'

'And technically this is for her exam results, so if she doesn't actually get the results we're expecting, she has to forego her birthday present instead.'

'Yes,' Annabel agreed.

'Her mock exam results were pretty good though,' said Richard.

'They were,' said Annabel.

'And she worked very hard for the real ones.'

'She certainly spent enough time on her computer. Let's hope it wasn't all on Facebook.'

'And it will give us a weekend to ourselves,' Richard added. That was clearly the clincher for him.

'All right,' said Annabel. 'Are we going to tell her now or should we wait until she's posted about how miserable and unfair we are online?'

Izzy burst into the room.

'Tell me now!' she said.

Chapter Ten

Annabel

Izzy was beside herself with happiness when Annabel and Richard told her she could go to the festival after all. Of course she understood that if she failed her exams, it would have to be her birthday present, she told them. And *of course* she would not abuse their trust in her. She knew how important it was that she made them both proud. There would be no alcohol. No drugs. And no allowing boys to stay overnight in the tent. Not even platonically. She also promised that she would call her parents at eleven o'clock each night so that they could gauge whether she had stuck to her promise about the booze.

'This is very important,' said Annabel. 'We are doing this against our better judgement, but we understand that it's important for you to have your independence. And because you're so nearly officially an adult, we know you'll do your best to act like one.'

'Of course!'

Izzy beamed. She hopped from foot to foot as Annabel wound up her lecture, then dashed straight upstairs to announce the good news to her virtual world.

Annabel couldn't help feeling warmed by her daughter's excitement. Now she was a teenager, there wasn't much that put such a big smile on Izzy's face.

'I'll need some new stuff,' Izzy said at dinner. 'Festival clothes. Wellies. Things like that. Can I have them for my birthday? Only early?'

Richard and Annabel shared a look. Richard gave a small nod.

'Well, I suppose you can always use wellies.'

Annabel took Izzy into London the following weekend. They stayed in the flat Richard used as a pied-à-terre when work was especially busy and shopped for festival gear up and down Kensington High Street. At least, thought Annabel, she could be sure that Izzy wouldn't get cold if the weekend was nippy or wet, as it was almost certainly bound to be in the middle of June. She piled thermals and extra-thick socks into the shopping basket, while Izzy searched for hippy vest tops that cost £29 a pop even though they looked as though they had been thrown together for pennies.

'You're going to be cold,' Annabel warned her. 'I don't want you to spend the weekend wearing crop tops and ending up with a chill.'

'I know,' said Izzy, then, echoing the words of her grandmother, Sarah, which Annabel had seamlessly incorporated into her own maternal mantra: 'You've got to keep your kidneys *lagged*.'

'You think it's funny,' said Annabel. 'You won't be laughing if you end up unwell.'

'No chance of that in these,' said Izzy, holding up a pair of thermal leggings in disgust. She put them back on the shelf.

'You're taking them,' said Annabel, picking them up again. 'You're going prepared.'

'It's a festival, Mum, not a girl-guide camp.'

'All the more reason to make sure you've got the right equipment.'

The day of the festival arrived. Izzy was up early for once. Annabel made her an enormous breakfast, as though Izzy wouldn't be able to find any food at all until she was next at home. Izzy happily scarfed her way through a stack of pancakes. Annabel was delighted.

Jessica's mother, Jodie, arrived in her Range Rover at two o'clock, as arranged. Jodie had picked up Gina en route to the Buchanans' house. They would be picking up Chloe Greenwood on the way.

The car was already full to bursting with Jessica and Gina's camping equipment.

'Anyone would think they were going to the Arctic Circle,' said Richard. 'In my day, we'd have a rucksack and a rolled-up sleeping bag.'

'Yes, well. It's not your day any more,' said Annabel. 'I'm glad to see they're going to be properly equipped.'

Jodie agreed. 'It cost a fortune but I told Jessica she's got to do the Duke of Edinburgh's Award scheme next year anyway. It'll look good on her uni applications.'

Jessica rolled her eyes at Izzy.

'Excellent idea,' said Annabel. 'You'd better get used to camping, Izzy.'

Leander, the Buchanan family's twenty-month-old Labrador (Izzy's fifteenth birthday present), was keen to go along too. He tried to jump into the back of the Range Rover but was bounced straight back out again when he landed on a foam mattress.

'Come on, Leander,' said Richard. 'Not this time.'

At last, Richard and Annabel stood on the step of the Great House to wave their daughter off. Annabel did her best to plaster on a happy smile but she couldn't help sniffing a little. Her daughter going to a festival! It was hardly a rite of passage on a par with starting school but Annabel suddenly felt almost as tearful as she had done that momentous day. Must be hormones, she thought.

'At some point,' said Richard, 'we have to accept that Izzy's growing up. She's making her own way in the world. It's a good thing. Besides Jessica, Gina and Chloe are all very sensible girls. They'll look after each other.'

'Who are you trying to convince,' Annabel asked. 'Me or yourself?'

Richard laughed. 'Mostly me, I think. But let's make the most of it,' he said. 'We've got the house to ourselves.'

Richard took Annabel by the hand and gave her what could only be described as 'the eye'. It was a ridiculous expression, which seemed to belong to someone much older. Annabel swatted him with her hand.

'Shall I open the wine?' he asked.

Actually, Annabel found she wasn't really in the mood for wine that afternoon. Richard pulled a bottle of her favourite Provençal rosé out of the fridge. Ordinarily, just one sniff of it would transport Annabel back to the south of France and the villa they loved so much they'd rented it three years in a row. They would have gone back again that year but some other lucky family beat them to it.

That day, however, Annabel wasn't in a Provençal sort of mood. In fact, she recoiled from the liquid in the glass.

'Is this off?' she asked Richard.

'It's perfect,' he said, taking another sniff to be sure.

'Really? It smells musty to me.'

Richard picked up his glass and stuck his nose deep

inside. He inhaled deeply. Then he took a sip and swished it around his mouth. 'It tastes just fine but I am willing to bow to your greater powers of smell. You're always telling me that a woman's sense of smell is even better than a dog's. Isn't that right, Leander?'

Leander wagged his tail. He agreed with anything Richard said.

Annabel picked up her glass and gamely took another sip but it still tasted horrible. If anything it was worse than she'd first thought. She asked Richard to open a bottle of white instead. He picked a Chardonnay. That too tasted slightly weird but Annabel metaphorically held her nose and drank it. She thought briefly about an article she'd read that said that a woman's sense of smell changes dramatically at the menopause. She'd been a bit anxious about getting older lately but she was still only forty-three, for heaven's sake. It couldn't be the menopause. She knocked back the glass to prove it to herself.

'Mmmm,' she said. 'Delicious.'

Annabel and Richard took the bottle of Chardonnay into the garden. It was a beautiful afternoon. Against all the odds, the weather was set to be good for the whole weekend, so at least they wouldn't have to worry about Izzy sitting around in wet clothes and coming home with pneumonia.

At five o'clock, Izzy texted to confirm that the girls had arrived at the venue and found a place to pitch the tent. At half past seven, she called Richard and had him talk her and Jessica through how to put the tent up. At eight o'clock, they reported that the 'nice Radley guys' in the tent next door had helped them and they now had a roof for the night.

'See,' said Richard to Annabel. 'Radley boys.' He

knew Izzy was referring to Radley the public school. 'You get a much better class of layabout at SummerBox.'

'When I was at university,' said Annabel, 'Radley boys had a reputation for fighting.'

Richard frowned. 'Well, as long as they're defending Izzy's honour.'

He picked up the bottle for a top-up but discovered it was empty. 'I'll get another,' he said.

'Are you sure you should?' Annabel asked him.

Richard had recently started taking medication for high blood pressure and was supposed to be making 'lifestyle' changes too, including losing weight and cutting back on the booze. Annabel was supposed to be helping him but Richard mostly perceived her efforts as nagging so that evening, she let it slide and Richard fetched another bottle from the kitchen. They were being naughty but this was a one-off. They had the house to themselves without their eye-rolling, deep-sighing teen. Bliss.

'It's going to be like this all the time in the not too distant future,' said Annabel.

'What? Sunny?' asked Richard. 'I wouldn't bet on it.'

'I mean, it'll be just you and me, when Izzy's gone off to university. You and me and our beautiful house. Just the two of us. Alone.'

Annabel studied Richard's face for a reaction. She was mightily relieved to see him smile. He raised his glass in her direction.

'I for one can't wait,' he said. 'Here's to an empty nest and a second honeymoon.'

Annabel felt herself melting inside, just as she used to all those years ago whenever she heard Richard's old Mini pull up outside the flat she shared with two other girls on the Cowley Road. She still loved him every bit as much as she had always done. With Richard, she felt safe and happy. He treated her like a real princess.

They'd met at Oxford. It was Trinity term of Annabel's first year. She had gone down to the river with some friends to watch the boat races of Eights Week. Richard was visiting a friend in the boat club. He was in his third year at Cambridge, studying law. They hit it off right away. That summer they met again at a house party in London.

For the next two years, Annabel spent her weekends going up to London or having Richard visit her in Oxford. At first her parents warned her that she shouldn't waste her college years on a long-distance relationship, but Annabel knew it would be no waste and her parents Sarah and Humfrey soon came to agree with her.

They got married very young by today's standards. Annabel was just twenty-two and Richard was twenty-four. But there was something very lovely about having married her first real boyfriend. Lots of Annabel's friends had married total randoms out of desperation when they got into their late thirties. Some of them had definitely 'settled'. It was hard to combine your life with someone else's when you were both so used to doing your own thing. When you married young, you grew together, like two trees in a topiary display, leaning towards each other gradually to make the perfect arch. That was how it felt for Annabel with Richard.

Annabel wished such a love for her daughter. She wished for her daughter such a lovely, peaceful, charmed life.

Chapter Eleven

Izzy

While her parents sipped Chardonnay in the beautiful surroundings of their country garden, Izzy was chucking back cider in a tent with a view of the Portaloos. Of course, the four girls' parents had forbidden them from taking any alcohol with them to the festival. Jessica's mother Jodie had gone so far as to check the girls' rucksacks as she was dropping them off at the gate. She proudly reported that fact via text to the parents of the other three girls: No alcohol on them and the stewards have assured me they won't be served without ID.

Of course, none of the parents actually believed that meant the girls wouldn't get their hands on a single drink all weekend, but they all sincerely hoped it would limit the amount they could find and thus lessen the chances of any of them ending up with alcohol poisoning.

But they had not reckoned on their daughters' resourcefulness. Jessica had been secretly dating a lifeguard from the swimming pool where she trained with the county team every morning before school. The lifeguard was called Saul. He was twenty years old and he too would be attending the festival. Saul was taking a two-man tent, in which Jessica would be joining him. Saul would also be bringing alcohol. And lots of it. Earlier that week, Jessica had the other girls chip in fifty quid a head for supplies. Saul duly arrived with ten bottles of supermarket cider and more than a hundred small bottles of beer picked up in France by his wheeler-dealer brother. He would buy more as they needed it. Of course, he had ID.

They started on the cider.

It wasn't so bad. Izzy was more used to drinking than her parents imagined. All those social evenings the Buchanans hosted at the Great House had formed part of her training. While Annabel and Richard were getting quietly sozzled with their guests, Izzy would hang out in the kitchen with the village kids Annabel hired as waiting staff, knocking back the dregs of the champagne Annabel always served as an aperitif.

And whenever Izzy visited Jessica, they always found something to drink at her house. Jessica's parents kept an especially well-stocked booze cabinet. It wasn't that Jessica's parents actually let their daughter and her friend have free rein. They still had to steal it. Izzy and Jessica stuck to the clear drinks: vodka and gin, and topped up the bottles with plain water so that Jessica's parents never noticed the levels going down, though Jessica's mother often accused Jessica's father of serving short measures when he made her a G and T.

Anyway, Izzy Buchanan could hold her drink. She liked the way it made her feel. Almost as soon as she had her first sip she wasn't shy any more. She could talk to anyone. When she went to the Portaloo and saw her reflection in the smeary unbreakable plastic-coated mirror, she even liked the way it made her look. That slight flush to her apple cheeks. Her pupils wide and dark. She felt sexy in a rock-chick way like a younger Daisy Lowe. It made her happy.

But Jessica's boyfriend Saul hadn't just brought the alcohol. He'd brought along weed as well. Izzy helped him to roll a supply of joints that would last all weekend. She was proud of her ability to roll cigarettes. She had spent plenty of time practising in her bedroom when her mother thought she was revising.

Saul nodded with pleasure when he saw Izzy's joints lined up like a row of soldiers.

'Respect,' he said. 'You make the best rollies out of anyone I know.'

Izzy glowed with pride until she caught Jessica giving her a slightly disapproving look. Jessica didn't like anyone impressing Saul except her. Jessica took her long blonde hair out of its clip and shook it so that it cascaded over her shoulders. Izzy couldn't compete with that. She had inherited her hair from her mother's side of the family. There was plenty of it but it was fine and dead straight and definitely not blonde.

Jessica held her hand out towards her boyfriend.

'You going to let me have one of those?' she asked, nodding towards the joints. 'That *Izzy-Wizzy* has rolled so nicely.'

Izzy winced at the use of her old nickname.

'Whatever you want, babe,' said Saul. Though he was four years older than Jessica, there was no mistaking who was boss.

On that first day, there weren't any bands the girls desperately wanted to see until The Twilight, who wouldn't be playing until ten o'clock on the main stage. So as the sun went down, the girls and Saul and a couple of guys Saul knew just lolled around outside the girls' tent, drinking cider and eating Pringles and smoking half the joints Izzy had rolled.

Izzy lay back on the grass and looked up at the purple sky.

'I am, like, totally at peace with the world,' she said. 'I am at one with the earth. I think I can actually feel it spinning beneath me.'

Jessica lay back alongside her.

'Yeah,' she said. 'You can. You can totally feel the earth moving.'

Saul lay down on top of Jessica.

'You're not supposed to feel it moving without me,' he said.

Izzy glanced across at her friend. Saul was kissing her. Jessica stretched her arms above her head in joyous abandon. Izzy felt a momentary stab of envy. She wanted someone to love her the way Saul loved Jessica. Perhaps she would meet someone that weekend. It wasn't impossible. Fixing her gaze on the sky again, Izzy had the strangest feeling that something momentous was going to happen.

Chapter Twelve

Annabel

The following morning, Annabel awoke with the worst hangover of her life. It was a beautiful morning, but the sun just seemed offensive. When Richard opened the bedroom curtains, Annabel wailed in pain as though she were a vampire and he had just opened the lid of her coffin in full daylight.

'Bit of a headache?' Richard asked her.

'Er, duh!' said Annabel. 'I feel bloody awful. How much did we have? And how come you're so full of the joys of spring? How come you're not in agony too?'

'I remembered to drink a glass of water before I went to sleep,' said Richard. 'I got one for you too.'

The glass, still full, was on Annabel's bedside table. Richard sat down on the bed beside Annabel and handed it to her now.

'Want me to get you some Nurofen?'

'Please,' she said.

Richard returned with the tablets.

'If your daughter could have seen you last night. Rolling drunk, making advances.'

Annabel swatted at Richard with her hand. Then she picked up her phone and immediately checked to see if Izzy had texted, as promised. Izzy had sent her last text at one in the morning, claiming that she was going to sleep. That was unlikely to have been true. But as

Annabel held the phone in her hand, Izzy texted again, saying that she was up and off in search of a bacon butty. The very words made Annabel salivate. She quickly texted Izzy back: That's great, darling, but don't forget to try to eat some vegetables this weekend if you can find them.

'Vegetables!' Richard laughed when he saw what Annabel had written. 'The only greens she'll see all weekend is weed.'

'Don't say that,' said Annabel.

Richard made breakfast. A fry-up. Something else, if he listened to his GP, he should be giving up for the sake of his cardiovascular health. But Richard made the best breakfasts in the world and ordinarily when she smelled the bacon, Annabel couldn't wait to tuck in. She didn't fancy it that morning, however, even though it had seemed a great idea when Izzy texted about that bacon sarnie.

'I think this is the worst hangover I have ever had,' she said when Richard placed a plate before her. 'In fact, it's so bad—' She got up from the table and made a dash for the guest cloakroom, where she heaved over the toilet bowl. Nothing came up but she didn't trust herself to keep anything down. So Richard shared her breakfast with a very grateful Leander, who was on course to be the fattest Labrador in the county. They really must walk him more often. Richard needed to get more exercise too.

A couple of hours later, Annabel made herself some toast and after eating that she felt much better. The weather was great again so they set deckchairs in the garden and lounged there all day, listening to the sort of music that would have had Izzy rolling her eyes. It was just like when they were first married and had all the time in the world for each other.

For just a moment, Annabel felt slightly guilty that she missed Izzy far less than she expected. She was worrying about her far less than she had thought she would too. She was having a wonderful time.

Chapter Thirteen

Izzy

Izzy too was having a wonderful time. She went with Saul to find breakfast. Jessica and the other girls weren't awake.

Izzy liked Saul more and more. He told Izzy that she was his favourite of Jessica's friends. She was adventurous but she didn't make a big deal about it, he elaborated. Like when he asked her to roll all those joints. The other girls would have been shrieking and making out like he was trying to send them straight to jail, but Izzy just got on with it. She didn't draw attention to herself. She may only have been sixteen but she acted as though she was a whole lot older. More sophisticated.

'Do I? Do I really?' Izzy wanted to squeak. She wanted to hear Saul tell her she was sophisticated again, but she guessed that wouldn't be cool in the least, so instead she just nodded and said, 'Thanks, Saul.'

At the catering van, Saul borrowed forty quid off Izzy to buy breakfast for the whole gang. He got two bacon butties for himself. Izzy had two as well. One to eat right then, before they were even three steps away from the van, and one to eat with everyone else later on. When Izzy got tomato ketchup on the side of her mouth, Saul gently brushed it away with his thumb. He looked into Izzy's eyes as he did it and she felt her insides liquefy. He looked at Jessica like that all the time. Lucky cow.

Izzy gave him a quavering smile in return. It didn't mean anything. She had to remember that. Saul was her best friend's boyfriend. Izzy made a point of talking to anyone but Saul for the rest of the morning. But later on Saul drew her into a conversation he was having with Jessica.

It was about drugs. Saul didn't just want to drink beer and cider and smoke Izzy's perfectly rolled joints all weekend. To him, the festival would only really get going when they took some ecstasy. Jessica wasn't having it.

'Well, I'm not doing it,' she said.

'What? Because your mum told you not to?' Saul teased.

'Not because of anything my mum said,' Jessica told him. 'Because I don't want to. Smoking weed is one thing but when you take tablets, you don't know what you're getting. And I'm not stupid enough to take that risk. Though you obviously are.'

'There's nothing wrong with these,' said Saul, pulling a small plastic bag of pills from a pocket in his poacher's jacket. 'I've been buying off the same guy for years.'

'And who does he buy them from?' Jessica asked.

'He always gets them from the same place. I've never had any trouble. He just wouldn't give me the dodgy shit. Though there was this one time . . .' Saul began to chuckle at the very thought of the story. 'There were these kids here last year. A bunch of stuck-up gits from Eton. They swaggered over, all full of it, like they were in *Breaking Bad*. They had wads of cash. Big thick bricks of it like you see in gangster films. They asked Josh what he was selling. Didn't even try to haggle on the price. And he sent them off with a handful of his girlfriend's aspirin, for her migraines, like. The best bit was . . .' The memory was so amusing to Saul that he could barely get the next part of the story out. He lay on his back on the floor, trying hard to keep the hilarity in, holding on to his stomach.

'What was the best bit?' asked Jessica. She did not look amused in the least.

'The best bit was, they were completely taken in by it. They had a tent about fifty metres from us and all night long they were dancing and giggling and falling over like they were completely out of their heads. The next morning, they even came by our tent and asked if we had some more, because it was the best ecstasy they'd ever taken in their lives.'

Saul slapped his thighs.

'Fucking idiots. It was aspirin. Aspirin! And they were totally off their heads. *The power of suggestion.*' Saul waggled his fingers in a stage magician's gesture. 'Josh says he's brought a whole load of aspirin with him this year in case those dicks turn up again.'

'And how can you be sure he hasn't given you aspirin too?' Jessica asked.

'I'm not that stupid,' said Saul.

'I'll check for you,' said Izzy. 'If it's aspirin, it should be printed on each one,' she added, though she didn't know that for sure. Saul handed the tablets over and she peered at them closely through the clear plastic.

'What if one of those kids had been allergic to aspirin?' Jessica carried on.

'You can't go to prison for selling someone something they could buy over the counter in Boots,' said Saul.

'That's not the point,' said Jessica. 'The point is, when you buy drugs you don't know what you're getting. You just don't. And that's why I won't touch anything like that.'

'When did you get to be so dull?' said Saul. If he meant it to come out gently, as a joke, it didn't.

Jessica's eyes flashed with anger.

'I'm not dull. I just don't want to take anything and I don't want you to take anything either. I care about you. I don't want you to die.'

Saul snorted.

'You sound like that drug talk we got at school. No one's gonna die, babe. Banning drugs is just another part of the conspiracy to keep the ordinary man down. If drugs were legal, they wouldn't generate so much cash. And arms sales.'

'Why do you even want to be involved with something that leads to arms sales?' Jessica asked. 'You're an idiot.'

'And that's your old man talking,' said Saul.

Evidently, Jessica's parents weren't terribly keen on her beau, which is why she had told them that Saul would be surfing in Cornwall that weekend. He wouldn't be anywhere near the festival. She'd promised on her life.

'Maybe Dad's right,' Jessica said.

Jessica got up and walked off. Gina and Chloe followed her, leaving only Izzy with the boys. Saul shrugged his shoulders.

'Aren't you going to go after her?' Izzy asked.

'Time of the month,' said Saul. 'She always gets like this. She'll calm down eventually. I'm not going to let her ruin my night.'

'I don't think these are aspirin,' said Izzy, handing back the pills Saul had given her to inspect.

He nodded his thanks.

Izzy felt torn. On the one hand, she probably should be with her best friend, offering the kind of sisterly support she usually would in these circumstances. But lately she'd been feeling that Jessica hadn't been quite so supportive of her. She'd been snippy and unkind about all sorts of things, belittling her and calling her 'Izzy-Wizzy' in front of people whose respect Izzy valued. Perhaps they were drifting apart. Izzy wanted to stay here with Saul. Right now, he was paying her all the attention she craved. And Jessica was overreacting. Just because she didn't want to take any ecstasy didn't mean she had to give Saul and the others a lecture. They were adults. They could make their own decisions.

Now Izzy made the decision not to run after her bestie, like they were starring in some Disney made-for-TV movie about high school friends. She wasn't Jessica's Siamese twin. She could make her own choices. Instead, Izzy sank back on to the cushions next to Saul. His leg was brushing against hers. She could feel the heat through her jeans. Saul was rolling another joint, hopelessly. Izzy asked him if she could help.

'Yeah. You're the best at this,' he said.

Izzy deftly manoeuvred the rolling paper between her thin fingers to make a tight little tube of tobacco and the last of the weed. She licked the edge of the paper to make it stick. She fixed her eyes on Saul's while she did it. He looked straight back at her.

'You're a top girl, Izzy. You're different,' he said.

'Yeah.'

Chapter Fourteen

Annabel

Back in the garden at the Great House, Annabel and Richard were enjoying a bottle of prosecco in the last of the sun. Well, Richard was enjoying it. Annabel thought the prosecco tasted like licking zinc. Anyway, the conversation had moved, as it always seemed to, on to the subject of their daughter. They were both proud of her and enjoyed these moments, when it was just the two of them in private conversation, when they could reminisce and brag without worrying about boring their company. They were their daughter's biggest fans.

'I worry about Jessica though,' said Annabel. 'She's not the kind of friend I would have chosen for Izzy. She cares so much about what she looks like. She dresses like she's auditioning for *TOWIE* and she doesn't seem terribly sensible. I wish Izzy wouldn't just follow what Jessica does all the time.'

'But those other girls. Gina and Chloe. They're very sensible,' said Richard. 'And so is Izzy. The thing is, the more we try to discourage her from hanging out with girls like that, the greater appeal they'll hold.'

'Well, I suppose Jessica is doing all right at school. And her mother, while she isn't the sort of person I would choose to have around, does seem to be very caring.'

'We should have them over,' said Richard. 'Jessica's parents. What are their names? Jodie and—'

'No way! You'd spend the whole evening looking at her cleavage.'

'Perhaps they're swingers,' said Richard. 'Perhaps we could reinstate the swingers' evenings here.'

The rumour in the village was that the previous owner of the Great House had used it as a venue for wild sex parties. He'd imported hookers from Russia especially.

'There were no swingers' evenings here,' said Annabel. 'That's just envy talking. He never invited anyone from the village to the house and so they made up all that ridiculous nonsense about swingers' parties to get their own back.'

'We never invite anyone from the village here. I wonder what they say about us,' Richard mused.

'I invite people from the village here all the time,' Annabel protested.

'In your role as Lady Bountiful.'

'I think I did my part this year. I let God-only-knows-who traipse all over the house. That family . . .' Annabel shuddered. 'The ones with the little boy who knocked over the suit of armour.'

'Our family heirloom!' Richard exclaimed, laughing at the very thought of it. The armour from the French junk shop. 'Thank goodness it was OK.'

'I know, but why couldn't they just keep their child under control? They were feral. Next year, I want you to do the tour with me. You can bring up the rear. Make sure no one is hanging about. Like that girl Izzy claims she caught in her room.'

'You're doing it again next year?' Richard frowned. 'Do we have to?'

'Yes,' said Annabel. 'We do.'

'Anything for you, my love.' Richard planted a kiss on Annabel's neck and started to growl lasciviously.

'Richard,' said Annabel. 'Remember your blood pressure!'

Then Izzy texted. I hope you're behaving yourselves!

Chapter Fifteen

Izzy

Just after Izzy texted her parents, she finally got a text from Jessica. Jessica said that she and the other girls were going to watch Creepers on the main stage and Izzy should meet them there.

'Is that from Jess?' Saul asked when Izzy got the text.

'Yeah.'

'Is she still in a mood?'

'I think so. She says she's going to watch Creepers.'

'Are you going to meet her?'

Izzy shrugged. 'I don't think so. I don't really like Creepers,' she added.

That was a lie. Izzy loved the band. She'd been looking forward to seeing them enormously. But earlier that day, she'd heard Saul say he thought they were *derivative*, the kind of band you got into if you weren't old enough to know what was really good. She didn't want Saul to think she didn't know good music when she heard it. So she was going to miss a live show by her heroes.

'I'd rather stay here and listen to the didgeridoo,' she claimed.

A man three tents down had been playing the didgeridoo non-stop for what seemed like hours. Just two notes. Over and over and over. He could only have found that kind of stamina on drugs. Izzy secretly wished he would shut up but Saul claimed that the noise of the ancient instrument connected with the human soul at its very deepest level. He insisted that Izzy lie on the ground and feel the spiritual vibrations.

'Yeah,' she said. 'I totally get what you mean.'

Really she just felt dizzy from all the cider and the weed.

Saul had been waiting for the right moment to take a tablet. There was no point taking one when you were in the wrong mood, he explained. The reason why people had bad experiences with drugs wasn't because of the drugs but because of their own brain chemistry. If you were in a bad place to begin with, then the drugs could only take you to a worse one. If you were in a good place, however, you'd have the time of your life. And, as they listened to the didgeridoo, Saul said he was now getting towards that good place. Arguing with Jessica had put him into a bad mood but having talked to Izzy he was feeling much better. Together with the ancient rhythms of Australia, she had brought him back to that buzzed state he spent most of his life trying to achieve.

Izzy was flattered.

Saul dug in his jacket pocket for the little plastic bag.

'So are you going to have one?' he asked, as he shook some pills out. He held his hand out towards her. There were two tablets in his palm. Izzy stared at them. If she was honest, she had rather hoped this moment wouldn't come.

'Perhaps I could take half?' Izzy suggested.

'No, you don't want to do that,' Saul told her. 'If you only take half, you can end up having a really bad time.'

'Really?' Izzy wasn't sure how that made sense but Saul certainly had more experience of ecstasy than she did. She took him at his word. Still she hesitated. She started to say 'I don't know . . .'

'I'll be with you the whole time,' he said. 'I'll look after you.'

Then Saul got a text from Jessica: Since you can't be arsed to come and find me, you can consider us over, it said. And tell Izzy-Wizzy she can fuck off too.

Saul gave a bark of a laugh and showed Izzy the text.

Fuck off? Izzy-Wizzy? Izzy would ordinarily have been mortified to get a text like that from her friend, but in the gathering dark, buzzing from the booze and the marijuana, with Saul beside her, she instead saw it as a crack in the door to a different life. Saul was single now. She was single too. Jessica wasn't talking to her. She might as well have some real fun.

'I'll take one,' she said, delicately picking one of the two tablets out of Saul's hand. Saul smiled. Izzy popped the pill straight into her mouth.

Chapter Sixteen

Annabel

Annabel and Richard had let their guards down. They had allowed themselves to believe that on the basis of Izzy's first successful night away from home in a tent, her second would be equally uneventful. There was little reason why they needed to be on alert. Thus the bottle of prosecco was followed by a bottle of red, so that when the phone call came, at three in the morning, neither one of them was in a fit state to drive.

'It's Kerry. Chloe's mum. We're at the hospital. Izzy's been taken unwell.'

While they waited for a taxi, Annabel and Richard had plenty of time to sober up. Annabel kept in constant contact with Kerry Greenwood while Richard kept his line free for a call from one of the doctors at the hospital itself.

No one seemed to know for sure what had happened. Chloe Greenwood and the other two girls were fine. They'd got back to the tent after watching a band and found Izzy just lying there.

'I just thought she was asleep at first,' Chloe cried in the background while her mother talked to Annabel. 'But then she started having a fit.'

Apparently, the St John Ambulance team covering the festival that weekend were on the scene within minutes. But whatever was ailing Izzy seemed to be beyond their capabilities. Izzy was hurried to the nearest general hospital.

'Annabel,' Kerry's voice dropped to a whisper. 'Jessica thinks that Izzy might have taken something. She thinks she had some sort of drug.'

'Impossible,' Annabel muttered as the cab sped them cross-country towards Northampton. 'She wouldn't do that. She promised she wouldn't do that.'

Annabel refused to entertain the possibility that her daughter might have taken ecstasy even when they got to the hospital and were whisked straight to the ICU. She told the doctors who met them there that they were barking up the wrong tree. They should be testing for some kind of virus. Might not meningitis cause the symptoms Izzy was experiencing? Why weren't they testing for that?

There was no time for a debate. The ICU team just stuck to protocol and went through their usual routines. Izzy was semi-conscious with a temperature of forty degrees. She'd had another series of convulsions in the ambulance on the way to the hospital. Her heart rate was too high. The clinical team were working hard to establish some stability before anyone even started to think about how Izzy had got into such a state.

Annabel tried to get closer to her daughter.

'You're going to need to stay out of the way,' she was told.

Thank goodness Richard was the kind of person who was calm under pressure. While Annabel made desperate phone calls to her mother and fielded other calls from Jessica and Gina's mums, Richard had the difficult conversations with the doctors and filled out paperwork and gave signatures when asked. He refused to go down the 'worst-case scenario' route that always seemed to beckon to Annabel. Izzy would be fine. They just had to let the hospital staff do their jobs. They didn't seem panicked so Richard and Annabel shouldn't panic either.

Annabel got off the phone to her mother and fell sobbing into her husband's arms. He stroked her hair.

'She's going to be all right,' Richard said. 'You know our little girl. She's a fighter. She gets it from you.'

But they had a long night ahead of them.

Chapter Seventeen

The Buchanans

While Richard and Annabel could do nothing but wait, the medics battled to save Izzy's life.

It had happened like this. After taking one of Saul's tablets, Izzy had gone dancing. At first she felt exactly as Saul had promised she would, as though the volume had been turned up on the world. Music was louder; colours were brighter. She had never felt so happy to be alive. A little later Saul persuaded her to take another pill. And another. But the joy of Izzy's first ecstasy experience was to be short-lived. Within an hour of taking the third dose, she'd suffered a rare reaction to one of the ingredients in the tablet. Perhaps the MDMA itself. Perhaps any one of a hundred contaminants the drug dealers had used to bring the cost of making the tablets down. Those pills contained ingredients even wise-guy Saul had never heard of. Suddenly Izzy was unable to control her body temperature. She hadn't been drinking enough water anyway. She was already dehydrated from all the cider she'd had that day. She got too hot. She started boiling on the inside. Her organs couldn't cope.

As the Buchanans sat in the waiting room, a television they couldn't turn off kept them company. There was an item on the local news. 'A Midlands schoolgirl,' said the presenter, 'attending the SummerBox music festival was taken to hospital in Northampton earlier this evening. It's believed that she may have suffered an extreme reaction to the drug ecstasy, which has been known to cause overheating and acute organ failure. A hospital spokesperson described her as being in a stable but critical condition.'

Then the newsreader was on to the next story. Noisy neighbours had forced an elderly pensioner out of her home. She was planning to sue the council for having failed to protect her from emotional distress. Then there was a segment about a local school choir that had made it to the national finals of a singing competition.

Life was going on.

All night long, the ward was busy. The night shift made no concessions to the late hour, bustling around every bit as noisily as their day-shift counterparts. Vital signs were taken every hour on the hour. Izzy's blood and urine were tested. The presence of MDMA, amphetamine and benzylpiperazine was confirmed.

Annabel and Richard looked to every hospital worker who entered Izzy's room for the slightest indication that the situation might be improving. They even asked a cleaner what he thought. No one would tell them anything without a doctor's approval, though the cleaner said that he had seen another kid in the exact same position the previous year and that kid had pulled through.

'Woke up asking for chocolate milk,' the cleaner added.

Annabel and Richard fell upon the cleaner's anecdote as though it was a consultant's report. But the comfort didn't last long. Izzy was attached to half a dozen drips and a frightening array of monitoring machines. She was still barely conscious. She didn't speak.

Whenever she could get close enough, Annabel held Izzy's hand and talked to her. She reminded her of the funny things she'd said as a small child. She told her that Jessica, Gina and Chloe were all keen to know when she woke up. Annabel talked and talked and talked while the plastic bags hanging from the drip stands emptied themselves into Izzy's tainted bloodstream, flushing out whatever was ailing her. More medics came and went, taking measurements and consulting screens.

As dawn began to break, Annabel convinced herself that Izzy was starting to look better. Her skin was pinker, wasn't it? Annabel showed Richard Izzy's hand. 'Look, you can see it in her nails. Her circulation is coming back.'

Richard wanted to believe it too

Annabel's mother Sarah arrived around half eight, having started driving from Hertfordshire as soon as it was light. There was no one else to come. Annabel's father and Richard's parents had all unfortunately passed away. Sarah burst into tears the moment she saw her daughter at her granddaughter's bedside.

'I promised myself I wouldn't cry,' she snorted into Richard's swiftly proffered handkerchief. 'Oh, Izzy! Oh, Annabel. What on earth happened?'

Izzy still wouldn't wake up. She'd been sedated so that the medics could do their work. More blood was taken. More tests.

Jessica came to visit at about ten o'clock. Her mother Jodie was with her. As soon as her mother was out of earshot at the coffee machine, Jessica began to tell her side of the story. She was distraught. She was full of guilt.

'I told her not to, Mrs Buchanan. Saul was trying to get us all to take them but I told him I wouldn't and he called me a baby and me and Gina and Chloe walked off. I thought Izzy would come with us. But she didn't. Even then, I didn't think she'd be persuaded to take anything. She was always the sensible one.'

Richard wrapped his arm round Jessica's shoulders and Annabel did her best to assure the girl that it really wasn't her fault. Though inside Annabel was blaming everyone. For once, ironically, Izzy hadn't blindly followed her friend. But if Jessica hadn't been allowed to run so wild, she wouldn't have got mixed up with Saul in the first place. And if Jessica hadn't been seeing Saul, Izzy would never have met him. He wouldn't have offered her those drugs. She would be getting ready to come home right now. Tired and dirty, perhaps, but not ill. Not on the verge of death.

But most of all, Annabel blamed herself.

'We should never have let her go,' she said over and over again.

'We had to let her go at some point,' said Richard. 'She's nearly seventeen. She's almost an adult.'

'Now she might not make it to being an adult!' Annabel wailed.

'She will,' Richard insisted. 'She's a fighter.'

Jessica was starting to look awkward. 'I've got to go,' she said. 'Will you text me to let me know what happens? I'll come and see her later.'

'Of course,' said Richard.

Annabel was too busy crying to say 'goodbye'. Jessica touched her on the arm. 'I'm sorry,' she said. 'I should have protected her.'

'No,' said Annabel. 'I should.'

By that afternoon, the waiting room was full of Izzy's friends. A steady stream of schoolgirls arrived with flowers they weren't allowed to leave. They couldn't get close to Izzy either. Still Jessica returned with her iPad and showed Annabel Izzy's Facebook page, which was already full of tributes.

Get well soon babe.

Cant beleev whats happened hun.

Were all thinking of u.

Annabel knew that Jessica was trying to cheer her up by showing her just how many people had been moved to make a comment, but she found it horribly disconcerting. One poster, who clearly hadn't been keeping up to speed with developments, had actually written 'RIP'. Annabel asked Jessica to make a Facebook announcement to the effect that Izzy was going to be fine. Then she vowed that she would not look at that stupid page again. She hated all that rote sympathy. She hated that Izzy even knew these people who seemed to be only borderline literate. How had she come to know them? How was it possible that Izzy and Jessica, who attended one of the most expensive private schools in the country, would have come to socialise with low-life scum like Saul?

Saul had disappeared of course. He was long gone even as the girls were finding Izzy unconscious in her tent. Jessica claimed she hadn't seen him since they argued about taking the tablets. Annabel believed her.

Jessica had her own problems. She had to talk to the police. As did Gina and Chloe. Once, when Annabel went out into the hospital car park for a breath of fresh air – though that was hard to come by with the cluster of smokers around the door – she saw Gina's mother. She was there to pick up her visiting daughter. Though she said all the right things, Annabel couldn't fail to pick up on the hint of anger beneath the commiseration.

It was clear that Gina's mother considered that Izzy was somehow at fault and was responsible for Gina – sweet innocent Gina – having a brush with the drug-addled underworld.

After Gina had come out and her mother had ushered her quickly away, Annabel kicked a concrete bollard in frustration. The bollard won. Annabel had forgotten she was wearing open-toed shoes. It was just then that Jessica ran out with the news.

'Mrs Buchanan, you've got to come back inside. Izzy's waking up.'

Though her foot would later be covered in bruises, Annabel sprinted back to the ward.

Richard was there. He made space for Annabel at the bedside. Sarah was holding Izzy's hand. She let Annabel take over. Izzy's eyes were barely open but she was making a strange mewing sound.

'Izzy, Izzy, my baby girl.' Annabel stroked her daughter's forearm. 'It's all right. We're here. Mummy and Daddy and Granny Sarah. You're in hospital but you're going to be OK.'

Izzy said nothing. She burst into tears.

Chapter Eighteen

Izzy

Izzy was in a hundred kinds of pain. And she had no idea where she was. She'd gone to sleep in a tent in the middle of a field and had woken up in a nightmare. It was so bright in that room. And when gradually the things that surrounded her came into focus, she only became more scared. The machines. The constant beeping. Her father looking worried. Her grandmother looking distraught. And then her mother, hysterical and crying like somebody had died.

Izzy was in hospital. She had the feeling she had been there for a while.

'Am I OK?' she asked, when she finally worked out how to use her tongue again.

'Everything is going to be fine,' her father assured her, but she could tell from the sound of his voice that he wasn't sure.

'What happened to me?'

'We don't really know. We think you might have taken some bad drugs. Fake ecstasy. You might have had a reaction to one of the ingredients.'

A part of Izzy's brain still told her that she had to deny it. She would be in such deep shit if her parents found out she'd taken a pill. But she was already in hospital. By definition they already knew. Izzy turned her face away from her father in shame and focused on a drip that had been placed to the right of her bed. She followed the see-through tube down to the back of her hand. A swirl of Izzy's blood decorated the clear liquid that was being pumped into her. When she saw that, Izzy was suddenly very frightened and knew that the machines and liquid that surrounded her were keeping her alive.

'Mummy,' she whispered. 'Am I dying?'

'God, no,' said Annabel. 'Not on my watch. Never.'

Annabel pressed her lips to Izzy's forehead. Izzy could only cry.

Izzy spent the next few days in ICU while doctors monitored her progress and measured the damage caused. Unfortunately, she hadn't actually been through the worst by the time she got to hospital. Instead of getting better, her condition deteriorated. Izzy was retaining fluid. Her face and her joints began to look swollen. She couldn't seem to pee. Her kidneys were slowly closing down.

Richard and Annabel both held Izzy's hands when Dr Devon, the hospital's consultant nephrologist, arrived to deliver the bad news.

'Will my kidneys get better?' Izzy asked.

Dr Devon wouldn't be drawn but for now, she had no choice but to put Izzy on a regime of haemodialysis. Both Izzy and Annabel wept as a temporary catheter was duly fitted into Izzy's neck.

'You'll feel much more comfortable once the dialysis starts,' Dr Devon assured her.

Izzy didn't think she would ever feel comfortable again.

The days were full of tests and measurements and handfuls of medicine. Izzy was never alone. There was always someone wanting to take her blood pressure or her pulse. The ICU staff were uniformly lovely but still Annabel and Richard made sure that Izzy was never without a family member too. Together with Sarah, they formed a tag team so that the grey plastic visitor's chair by Izzy's bed was never empty. When she was awake, Izzy apologised to them all – her mother, her father and grandmother – a hundred times an hour.

'I thought it would be OK,' she said. 'I thought ecstasy was supposed to be safe. Saul told me I would be fine.'

Jessica's words kept coming back to haunt her: 'When you buy drugs you don't know what you're getting. You just don't. And that's why I won't touch anything like that.'

Why had Izzy been so stupid? Remembering that terrible moment, when she made the wrong decision and stayed with Saul rather than follow her school friend, Izzy wanted to weep. She had been such an idiot and now she was paying the price.

'You've got every right to be angry with me,' she told Annabel and Richard. 'I promised you I wouldn't take anything. I thought I could get away with it.'

Annabel smoothed Izzy's hair back from her forehead.

'Don't worry about that now,' she said. 'Just concentrate on getting better.'

Izzy went back to her silent prayers. If God would just let her get well enough not to have to stay on this dialysis machine, she would never disobey her parents, or anyone else who cared for her, ever again. But though Izzy prayed harder than she had ever done, even when she was a kid and she really believed it could make a difference, God didn't seem to be listening.

*　　*　　*

Of course, Annabel had googled 'kidney failure' and 'ecstasy' and 'MDMA' and 'benzylpiperazine (BZP)' the moment she got her hands on an iPad. Apparently, cases such as Izzy's were rare. Especially after just one dose, which Izzy swore was all she had ever taken. Kidney damage in the documented cases Annabel read about was usually cumulative, after a long history of drug abuse. Even then, it was almost always reversible. There was good reason for the Buchanans to believe that Izzy would make a full recovery. That was the normal prognosis. Izzy longed to be normal.

After a week in ICU, Izzy was moved to a renal ward. That felt like a big step towards her recovery. Dr Devon took over her care now. The nephrologist was kindly and unflappable. Her big smile made the Buchanans feel as though everything would turn out well, even as she was ordering another blood test or scan. With Dr Devon at the helm, everything was moving in the right direction, they were sure. Izzy would surely come off dialysis soon. They'd be able to bring her home.

'It's just a matter of rest and recovery, yes?' said Annabel, when Dr Devon did her rounds as Izzy entered her second week on the renal ward.

'We're doing our best to get her home as quickly as possible,' said Dr Devon. 'But it's not going to be anytime soon.'

Though Izzy was out of ICU, the haemodialysis machine was still doing the hard work.

At the end of her third week in hospital, Izzy's kidneys were still not showing any sign of getting better. They were operating at just a fraction of their normal function. Dr Devon still espoused a 'wait and see' approach, but gradually, it started to sink in that Izzy's was not a 'normal' case of acute kidney injury thanks to MDMA or BZP. Perhaps she had a congenital weakness or a prior infection had made her kidneys less able to cope. Perhaps there had been some additional toxin in the tablets that the initial tests had not picked up. Three weeks in hospital soon turned into a month. Five weeks. Six weeks. There was still no improvement. Dr Devon made the decision to move Izzy on to peritoneal dialysis.

'So she can do it at home,' Dr Devon explained when she met with Izzy's parents.

'Izzy's going to need to dialyse at home?' asked Richard.

'Of course.'

'For how long?'

'For as long as it takes,' said Dr Devon.

'What are you saying?' asked Annabel.

'Izzy's kidneys are not getting better. I'm going to advise that she's put on the transplant list.'

Chapter Nineteen

Annabel

Annabel was in shock. In less than six weeks her privileged, carefree life had completely fallen apart. She had gone from being a woman who considered the local supermarket running out of organic eggs to be a 'disaster' to being the mother of a child on the kidney transplant list. Annabel was dumbstruck as she and Richard left Dr Devon's office and returned to the ward after a long discussion about transplants and the possibility of a living or altruistic donation.

Still asleep for the moment, their daughter looked so perfect. The dialysis had gone some way to getting rid of the puffiness of retained fluid and Izzy's face was clean of the make-up she had taken to wearing whenever she wasn't at school. Without it, she looked her real age. Even younger. She was like a princess, just waiting to be woken from a spell, with a lifetime of magical adventures ahead of her. It just didn't seem possible that inside Izzy's young body, vital parts of her were actually grinding to a halt.

'What are we going to do?' Annabel whispered to Richard.

'We'll get tested to be donors of course. One of us is bound to be a match. We're both healthy and it's perfectly possible to live a normal life with one kidney, just like Dr Devon said. It's going to be fine.

Once she's got a new kidney she can come off that awful machine.'

Annabel nodded. And as Izzy stirred to wakefulness, she plastered on another smile.

The NHS could not move quickly enough for the Buchanans. Annabel and Richard decided they would pay whatever they could to speed the process along and just a few days after Dr Devon suggested living donation as a possibility, Annabel went to be tested. They had decided that she should be the first because Richard was the breadwinner . They needed him to be able to work, not least for the private medical cover that came with his job. Plus, Annabel felt so angry with herself for having ever let Izzy go to the festival in the first place, she needed to feel the prick of a needle as some sort of self-punishment.

She tapped her feet with impatience as the necessary paperwork was completed and a phlebotomist took a sample to compare against Izzy's blood. She was tired of waiting. She couldn't concentrate. Everything – all the paperwork, all the questions – was just keeping her from doing her duty as a mother.

'No history of high blood pressure?' the clinician asked.

'Of course not,' said Annabel. 'No.'

'Diabetes?'

Annabel shook her head.

Annabel had no reason whatsoever to believe that she would be refused. Her last well-woman check at the GP's had shown her to be in fine health. Her blood pressure was always right on target. Her cholesterol counts were good. She may be carrying a little more weight than she liked, but her cardio fitness was exemplary, thanks to years of hard work aimed at keeping her figure under control. She was sure that she would pass every test with flying colours and Izzy would have a new kidney within months.

Indeed, Annabel's blood test results were all good news – she was a perfect blood and tissue match for her child. An appointment was quickly made for the next step: an ultrasound scan to ascertain the size, structure and general fitness of Annabel's kidneys themselves. There was no need to hang around.

She told Izzy.

'You won't be on dialysis for a moment longer than you have to,' Annabel promised.

Izzy cried with relief.

On the day of the scan, Annabel drank the necessary liquid to enlarge her bladder and waited to be called in. The wait was terrible. She had never needed to pee so badly in her life. Not only that, she was anxious for more good news. She was almost certain she would get it. This scan was a technicality. Annabel was already planning ahead for the operation. Her mother Sarah would come and live with them while both Izzy and Annabel recovered.

When it was Annabel's turn, the radiographer smoothed the conducting gel on to her abdomen and applied the transducer. Annabel strained to watch the fuzzy images that appeared on the screen, though she wouldn't have know whether she was seeing her kidneys or her ovaries. It was all so much 'noise' to her amateur eyes. Still the radiographer seemed to be ranging over quite a wide distance, right down to her pelvic bone. Weren't the kidneys higher up than that?

'Is everything OK?' Annabel asked.

'Yes. I think so. We usually look a bit further down to see that the bladder and whole urinary tract are as they should be too.'

'But my kidneys? They're good, aren't they? That's what matters.'

'Your doctor will let you know,' the radiographer said. Like so many of the medics the Buchanans had encountered over the last seven weeks, she was infuriatingly inscrutable. But then she pressed down on Annabel's belly to get a better look at something and a frown crossed her face. Annabel saw the expression before the radiographer could hide it.

'What's the matter?'

'Are you sure you're not pregnant?'

'Why do you ask?'

'I think I'm seeing something.'

'No,' said Annabel. 'That's ridiculous.'

But Annabel's imagination started to roam. What if the weird way she'd been feeling lately was not due to the perimenopause, as she had self-diagnosed online? What if the way she had reacted to the smell of the wine the weekend of the festival was not because the wine was corked? When she was pregnant with Izzy, she hadn't noticed a thing for the first three months. No morning sickness. No peculiar cravings. She had just carried on as normal until Richard made a classically cack-handed comment about her looking a little bloated.

'Can you check?' Annabel asked. 'Can you look now?'

'I can't say for sure. That's not part of my remit, I'm afraid. Maybe you should take a test when you get home.'

Frustrated in her search for an instant answer, Annabel went via Boots on her way home from the clinic. She picked out the cheapest pregnancy test she could find.

Not that they were exactly cheap. Annabel had a sharp memory of an awful afternoon many years before, when she was just sixteen and convinced she was pregnant by her then boyfriend. The pregnancy test had taken a day's wages from her Saturday job, though the feeling of knowing that she wasn't up the duff just as she was about to sit her O levels was priceless.

Once home, she didn't even take her jacket off before she went to do the test. She peed on the stick, then closed the loo seat and sat back down on it to wait.

Two blue lines.

'What?' she said, to no one in particular.

Two blue lines.

She picked up the box and read the back: 'A positive result is indicated by two blue lines . . .'

It wasn't possible. Convinced that there must be some mistake, Annabel quickly did the other test in the box. She sat on the closed toilet seat again and watched as the first line appeared to show that the test was working. Then the second.

Two more blue lines.

'I can't be bloody pregnant!' Annabel cried out. 'I can't!'

Annabel didn't know whether to laugh or cry. It really couldn't be possible. Perhaps she should have bought a more expensive test. But on the other hand, why shouldn't it be right? When was the last time she'd had a period? Three months earlier at least. And the woman who did the scan had obviously seen something even if she wouldn't be drawn.

Meanwhile, Richard had texted, asking when she was going to come back to the hospital. She had promised she wouldn't be long. Richard needed to get to his desk. His colleagues at work were very understanding but there were questions that only he could answer and deals that would have to go ahead no matter how Izzy was doing.

'We have to talk before you head off,' Annabel told him. She had to share her news right away. The bad news.

They went to the coffee shop in the hospital lobby. The coffee was reasonable. The cakes were awful, but Annabel ordered one anyway. She felt like she had to have something or she might throw up. She supposed that was the baby making itself known. The baby! She still didn't quite believe it was possible.

Annabel bagged a table in the corner while Richard went to the counter. She watched him help a woman on crutches take her coffee to a table before he placed their order. Tears sprang to her eyes. He was such a good man it made her heart hurt. Such a good father. But what would he say about this? Now?

'Something's happened,' she said.

'Oh God. What?'

'No point beating about the bush. I'm pregnant.'

Richard gawped.

'How did that happen?'

Annabel glared at him.

'Fuck,' said Richard, lost for better words.

'I might be as much as three months gone,' said Annabel. 'I don't know. That holiday in Turkey . . . I'll have to go to the doctor tomorrow and find out and . . . get it sorted.'

'What do you mean, get it sorted?'

'Well, I can't give Izzy a kidney if I'm pregnant.'

'Annabel. What are you talking about?' He was raising his voice. In the coffee shop! Annabel shushed him.

'Izzy has to be our priority.'

'And she is . . . but . . . Fuck's sake, Annabel. We need a moment to think about this.'

'It wasn't planned. I haven't had time to consider the possibility of another child. If we act quickly—'

'We're not *acting quickly*. You're talking about a *baby*. We're going to sit down and discuss this reasonably and sensibly just as we would have done were Izzy not unwell.'

Annabel was shaking with the magnitude of the decision she felt loomed before her.

'Don't say anything about this to Izzy,' Annabel pleaded.

They went up to the ward. Izzy seemed a little brighter than she had been. She was pleased to get the cards that had been waiting for her at the Great House.

'Are you all right, Mum? You seem a bit weird. I mean, more than usual.'

Annabel forced a smile.

'What it stressful at the kidney place? Was your ultrasound OK?'

'Everything's fine, sweetheart. But if it's OK with you, I'm going to go back home with Dad. There are a few things we need to sort out.'

'That's all right. I'm tired anyway.'

Annabel kissed her only child on the forehead. Her only child until now.

Chapter Twenty

Annabel

Back at home, Richard put the kettle on.

'I feel like a proper drink but you can't and I'm not drinking alone,' he said.

'I thought you needed to do some work.'

'For God's sake, Annabel. Work can wait.'

They sat across from one another at the kitchen table. It was such a big house and yet, as in so many homes around the world, the kitchen table was where the truly important things happened. This same table had been in their old house – the first house they'd shared as husband and wife – when Annabel told Richard she was expecting Izzy. They'd celebrated that night. No question. Richard had done a circuit of the old kitchen beating his chest like a silverback.

This time he was more subdued.

'I thought you were, you know, taking care of things,' he said.

Talk of things such as the Pill had always made Richard squeamish.

'I came off the Pill a while ago. I wanted to see if I was menopausal.'

'What?'

'It's not impossible. I was feeling a bit weird. I thought I should probably check. But the doctor said she couldn't check while the hormones from the Pill were still in my body so—'

'Why didn't you tell me?'

'I didn't think there was a hope in hell I would actually get pregnant. Do you know how hard it's supposed to be for a woman my age to conceive? If you believe the *Daily Mail*, after twenty-three, you're just an old crone, whose eggs are slowly – or not so slowly – going off.'

'Well, yours are obviously still all right. As is my sperm.'

'Don't look so pleased with yourself,' said Annabel.

'But it's something to be pleased about, isn't it?'

'Is it?'

'Of course it is.'

'It's a disaster.'

'Annabel, please. Don't say that. We're married. We're financially stable. We live in this enormous house. We could have triplets and not even notice. So long as we got a nanny and put them in the west wing,' he joked.

'Richard, it's not that simple and you know it. We've already got a daughter and she's unwell. She needs a kidney. And if I have this baby, I can't give her one of mine. Not until the baby's born and that's half a bloody year away.'

'There's no need to panic. Izzy can still have one of mine.'

'You need to work.'

'Fuck work,' said Richard. 'They'll understand. I won't be out that long.'

'I can't have this baby,' Annabel insisted. 'What if there's some reason you can't donate?'

'There won't be.'

'But if you can't, we'll be stuffed. I've read about it, Richard. Pregnancy could change my immune system.

Even after I've had the baby, I might not be a match for Izzy any more.'

Richard raised his voice. 'You can't let that influence your decision about this child,' he said. 'What would you do if Izzy weren't in hospital? What if she were perfectly fine? What would you do then? Is this really about Izzy or is it that you don't think you can go through the baby years again? It's different now. You do know that, don't you? You could have all the help you wanted for a start.'

Annabel knew what Richard was getting at. Part of the reason Izzy was an only child was because those early years had been so tough. Richard was working all hours in his bid for partnership at the law firm. Annabel was often alone. And she doubted her ability. Though Richard didn't yet know it, Annabel had good reason to suspect that mothering might not come naturally.

'And I'll be here too. I can take that sabbatical I'm owed.'

'I thought you wanted to go to Australia and follow the cricket if you took a sabbatical at all.'

'Forget that. I can't think of anywhere I would rather be than at home with you and my children.'

Children. He'd said it. In his head, Richard's family had already grown.

'But what about Izzy? I'm letting her down.'

'You're not. I've got a feeling this is all going to work out.'

Richard got up and walked round to her side of the table so that he could put his arms around her. Annabel let her head rest against his chest.

'It will be all right,' Richard cooed.

Annabel so wanted to believe him.

* * *

The following week, Richard went to be tested for his suitability as a donor for their daughter. They had little doubt that Richard would be a blood and tissue match but all the same they decided to hold off for a while on telling Izzy about the developments regarding Annabel and the baby. Once Richard got the go-ahead, it would be so much easier. So far, apart from Richard, Annabel had only told her mother Sarah about the pregnancy. Sarah had, of course, been delighted to hear the news.

'Your luck is changing,' Sarah told Annabel. 'I just know there's going to be more good news to follow soon. Izzy will have that transplant before you know it. And she'll have a little brother or sister!'

Annabel hoped so. But the hours she spent sitting by Izzy's hospital bed and the effort involved in seeming cheerful whenever Izzy was awake; the pregnancy itself – it was all taking its toll. Annabel was far from blooming. Now all of a sudden she was sick too. Forget morning sickness. Annabel wanted to throw up all day long. She needed a miracle.

While Richard was at the clinic, Annabel went into the cathedral for the first time since Izzy's last junior school Christmas concert and lit three candles. One for Izzy, one for Richard and one for the tiny tadpole that flickered inside her. She had been to see her GP and a scan was arranged for the end of the month. A proper antenatal scan.

Annabel's phone rang while she was walking out of the cathedral. In the vast silence of the house of worship, the ringtone seemed especially loud. Annabel apologised to everyone she passed as she rushed into the car park to take the call. Several people frowned at the ringing but sod them. This was important.

It was Richard.

'I can't do it,' he said without preamble.

He sounded angry.

'I can't fucking do it.'

'What?'

Richard took a big gulping breath. Was he crying?

'I can't give Izzy one of my kidneys.'

Richard's high blood pressure had ruled him out. With his increased risk of a stroke or heart attack, the transplant operation would pose too great a challenge to Richard's own health.

'That can't be right,' said Annabel.

But it was.

Richard's condition was largely hereditary. His father had died of a heart attack before he was fifty years old. But that didn't stop Richard from being furious with himself for having failed to pass the criteria to be a donor for his daughter. When Annabel next saw him, in the car park of Izzy's hospital, Richard was in a terrible state.

'I've let her down,' he said. 'I've let our Izzy down.'

This time it was Annabel's turn to be strong.

Annabel got into Richard's car alongside him and gave him an awkward hug over the gearstick. She tried her best to comfort him. But Annabel was every bit as distraught as Richard was. The idea that Richard would give their daughter one of his kidneys had seemed so obvious. They shared genes. They shared a blood type. Annabel and Richard hadn't even thought that Richard's high blood pressure could stand in the way. Sure, Annabel had seen high blood pressure mentioned as a reason why people were turned down as altruistic donors but could it really prevent a father from helping his own child?

It seemed it could. And now they had to let Izzy know.

'Mum? What about you?' Izzy asked when they told her the verdict on Richard. 'You didn't tell me what the scan showed.'

They had to tell her about the baby now. Annabel took Izzy's hand. 'Sweetheart, I can't do it at the moment either.'

'Why not?'

'Because I'm pregnant.'

Izzy said she was happy. Of course she did. They'd brought her up to be thoughtful. But Annabel was sure she could see a sliver of fear in her daughter's eyes as the news sank in. She knew that Izzy had been convinced that one of her parents would be able to help her. Now that opportunity had fallen away. Or had been *stolen* away by the baby Annabel was carrying.

'Do you know what it is yet?' Izzy asked brightly.

'We've got a scan booked in,' said Annabel.

'I can't believe I'm going to have a little brother or sister. All those years I asked for one and it happens now.'

Why now? Why now when I need my mother most? That was the subtext.

'Whatever happens, you're still our number one priority, Izzy. This doesn't change that. We're going to make sure you get better,' Annabel insisted.

'I know,' said Izzy. She didn't sound convinced.

'There are other avenues for us to go down. Donors don't have to be an exact match these days. Remember what Dr Devon was telling us about plasma exchange?'

Dr Devon had explained all about 'plasmapheresis', a blood-separating process, which could enable a transplant patient to receive an unmatched kidney by removing those parts of the patient's blood that would otherwise cause a catastrophic immune reaction. It would mean spending yet more time hooked up to a machine but it could work.

'But she said that's not ideal,' Izzy reminded her mother. 'Not for someone as young as me. It's still better to have a tissue match. A relative. That's what she told us.'

'We'll find someone,' Annabel promised. Never had she and Richard, who were both only children, wished for siblings more. Meanwhile, Izzy was getting a sibling at the worst possible time.

That evening, back at the Great House, Annabel couldn't even bear to talk to Richard. She was afraid that if she opened her mouth, she would wish the baby away again.

Chapter Twenty-One

Annabel

At the end of the month Annabel had her appointment for a scan. Richard came with her. Sarah stayed with Izzy at the hospital.

Now it was Annabel's turn to be the centre of medical attention. When she and Richard arrived at the antenatal clinic, she was relieved to see that she didn't appear to be the oldest woman waiting to be seen. She had dreaded walking in there and looking for a seat among all the glowing twenty-somethings, who would make her feel like a freak.

When Annabel lay down on the table, she was briefly furious with herself for having forgotten that she'd need to expose her belly. She was wearing a dress. If she'd thought about it properly, she would have worn a separate top and skirt so that she didn't have to strip off altogether or flash her knickers.

The technician applied gel to Annabel's abdomen.

'This will be cold,' she said.

It always was.

It had been a long time since Annabel's first scan for Izzy but the memory of it came flooding back. Annabel had waited for that scan alone and she thought she would have to go through it alone too. Richard had called to say that he was really snowed under at work. Annabel had told him it didn't matter. She could go through it without him. But she had been disappointed. Especially since it seemed that every other woman in that waiting room had someone to hold her hand. She began to wish she'd taken her mother up on her offer but Sarah would have had to make a two-hour journey to be there.

On that day, seventeen years before, Richard came rushing in at the last moment. He arrived just as Izzy materialised on the screen. A strong heartbeat. She was on her way.

'There you go,' the technician smiled, now. 'That's lovely.'

Annabel and Richard stared at the screen that showed their new baby curled like a fern waiting for the summer.

'Everything is exactly as it should be.'

Izzy was still on dialysis when they got back to her hospital ward.

Annabel sat down on the chair next to her bed.

'How did it go? Is it twins?'

'It's not twins,' said Annabel.

'Can you tell what it is?'

'A baby?'

'I mean, what flavour, Mum? Boy or girl.'

'It's a bit early.' Annabel hesitated. She wasn't sure whether Izzy really wanted to talk about this or not. Was she just being polite? Making conversation? 'Do you want to see the pictures?' Annabel asked.

'Of course.'

Annabel fished them out of her bag and handed them over. Izzy turned the Polaroid-sized prints round and round as if trying to make head or tail of them.

'It just looks like static, I know. But the baby is in there. That darker patch there. That's its heart.'

'Wow.'

It was a genuine, kind 'wow'. Annabel was relieved.

'Everything is as it should be, apparently. They think I'm about three and a half months along, which means the baby should be with us in January.'

'That's great.'

Izzy was still holding one of the scan pictures and peering at it intently. At least, that's what Annabel thought at first. When she looked at her daughter again, she realised that Izzy was staring at the picture because she didn't want to look at her mum. She was trying not to cry.

'Oh Izzy! Sweetheart. What's the matter? Don't be sad!'

'I'm not sad, Mum. I promise. I'm really happy. I'm crying because I'm glad that you're having a baby. It will give you something to focus on, something to do when . . .'

When I'm gone. That was the end of the sentence. Izzy didn't say it. Annabel wished she hadn't heard it. Even if it was only in her head.

'There will be plenty for you to do too!' said Annabel, as brightly as she could manage. 'Don't think you're going to get out of changing nappies.'

Izzy forced a smile.

'I'd change nappies,' she said.

'Good. Hopefully your father will be persuaded this time round as well.'

'Didn't he change my nappies?' Izzy asked.

'If I shouted loud enough. He'd pretend he hadn't noticed it needed doing. You could be smelling like a sewer and he'd swear you were fresh as a daisy.'

'Mum, that's gross,' Izzy laughed.

The dark moment had passed just as the dialysis machine beeped to let them know that the cycle had finished. Annabel kept Izzy company while a nurse got her unhooked.

When they got back to the Great House, Annabel wanted to talk to Richard about her conversation with her daughter but at the same time, she didn't want to repeat it out loud at all. Izzy didn't think she was going to make it. How had she come to that conclusion? Had they not been positive enough in her presence? Was she really worried that when the baby came, they would forget all about her and start again with a new, perfect child? What on earth could Annabel do to convince her otherwise?

What on earth could she do, full stop?

In the darkness of the night, Annabel's mind turned the problem over and over, looking for a possible solution. She couldn't donate a kidney until the baby was born. And the baby was going to be born. That determined heartbeat seen on the scan had put paid to any thought of abortion. Meanwhile, Richard couldn't donate full stop. And Sarah, who had diabetes, was ruled out before she started, just like Richard. Who could they turn to instead?

Annabel made a mental list of the usual suspects. And then she made a list of the unusual ones. The ones who didn't have real names. At least, not to Annabel. Would she ever have the courage to ask them?

Chapter Twenty-Two

Annabel

When they next saw Dr Devon she commiserated with them over being unable to donate to Izzy themselves. Richard was still angry. Though it had been explained to him a hundred times, he still couldn't understand how it was possible that he couldn't give his daughter one of his organs.

'So that's it,' said Richard. 'We just have to wait for a donor to appear from nowhere? We have to wait for someone to die or for some stranger to decide on a whim to get tested and then we have to wait for them to be a match?'

'There could be someone testing on someone else's behalf right now,' said Dr Devon.

Dr Devon had explained the principle of paired donations, in which people who wanted to donate to loved ones but were not a good enough match were able to do a sort of swap with other people on the register.

'It happens more often than you think,' Dr Devon insisted.

'It can't happen quickly enough,' Richard sighed. 'Why do we have to wait for a match at all? Why can't we go down the plasmapheresis route?'

Dr Devon ran through the issues once more. Izzy was still very young and Dr Devon hoped to find her a kidney that would last for as long as possible. Maybe twenty or twenty-five years. There was no particular reason why Izzy wouldn't find an excellent match relatively quickly. That was better than rushing ahead with a 'good enough' match and subjecting Izzy to yet more procedures so that she wouldn't reject a kidney that probably wouldn't work out for as long anyway.

'There isn't quite the urgency you imagine,' Dr Devon said.

Richard was not in the least bit comforted by that. Like Annabel, as a result of his education and his wealth, he was used to being able to get what he wanted quickly. The Buchanans were ill equipped to understand why they couldn't just buy their way out of the situation.

Annabel couldn't bear it. Her wonderful husband laid so low. Her daughter on dialysis, with no hope of any improvement. And it was all her fault. If she weren't pregnant. If she hadn't let Izzy go to SummerBox. She had to do something to make it right. She took a deep breath.

'There is one other option,' she said.

Richard and Dr Devon both looked at her with interest.

'I may have some, er, some other relatives who might agree to be tested.'

'Then why the fuck haven't they been tested already?' Richard asked. 'Who are you thinking of, Annabel? Who? Your mum can't because of her diabetes. You haven't got any cousins. Who else is there?'

'Oh God.' Annabel buried her face in her hands and spoke the rest through her fingers. 'Richard, I can't believe I'm going to have to tell you this in a doctor's office.'

'I can step outside if you like,' said Dr Devon.

'No. No, it's fine,' said Annabel. If anything, she

thought, Dr Devon's presence would force Richard to react reasonably. Because she knew she should have told him earlier. He would have every right to go berserk. It beggared belief that she would have kept something so important secret from him for so long. She took her hands away from her face and tried to compose herself. 'Richard, the thing is, Mum – Sarah . . . Forget about the diabetes. She was never going to be a good match anyway because she and Dad are not my actual birth parents. They couldn't have children. I'm adopted.'

Richard just stared.

'I don't know why I didn't tell you before,' Annabel cried out.

'Oh, God. Annabel.'

Richard's face crumpled through confusion to compassion. And back to confusion.

'Why didn't you say?'

'I didn't want to. I didn't think I'd ever need to!'

'You *didn't want to*? What else have you kept from me?'

It was a reasonable question and she could only hope he believed her when she assured him that she had told him everything else. Everything. He was her best friend. There was nothing she hadn't shared with him. Nothing except the biggest thing of all.

'Please forgive me,' she begged him. 'Please.'

Placing a box of tissues in the middle of her desk, Dr Devon left the room as discreetly as she was able.

'I was just so ashamed about it!' Annabel wailed.

'But why, darling, why? It's nothing to be ashamed of. You were a tiny baby. I mean, you *were* a baby at the time, weren't you? How did it happen?'

'I was a baby,' Annabel confirmed. 'I was about six weeks old. I think my birth parents were teenagers. They couldn't cope. Mum and Dad had been trying for a baby for years with no success and when they finally decided to adopt, I came along just a couple of months later. Oh Richard. I'm so sorry. I didn't think it was relevant. Not any more. I didn't think it would ever be important. I promise I never set out to intentionally deceive you.'

Richard shook his head.

'But why? Why? I would have understood.'

'I know you would. But I just didn't want to have to explain the whole situation. It would have changed things.'

'How?'

'I didn't want you to look at Mum and Dad differently. I didn't want you to look at me differently. I didn't want you to think I was anyone other than Annabel Cartwright!'

'I'd never have guessed,' said Richard. 'You looked so much like your dad. The ears. The beard . . .'

Annabel swatted him. But that one flippant comment let her know that it was OK. All those years she had subconsciously worried that if he knew the truth, Richard would reject her. But now he knew, and here he was, still with her. Still joking. Still the love of her life. He pulled her towards him and rested his forehead on hers. They both started to cry uncontrollably now.

'Annabel, I don't care if you're the secret love child of Saddam Hussein and Cilla Black. You'll always be my darling and I love you. It's going to be all right.'

How many times had he had to say that since Izzy took that bloody ecstasy?

'But you have to get in touch with your biological family,' said Richard. 'We have to track them down.'

'I don't know how to do it,' said Annabel through her tears.

'We'll hire a detective if we have to.'

'They might not want to get involved if we do find them.'

'Maybe not. But Annabel, this is the best chance we have right now. In any case, they're not just your family. They're Izzy's family too. What right do you have to keep them from her?'

'I've got to talk to Mum about it.'

'Of course, but ultimately you have no choice. They might do it. They might donate. This is good news, my love. It's good news.'

He was right. Pandora's Box had to be opened for the tiny grain of hope that might be found inside it.

Sarah was still staying at the Great House, helping Annabel and Richard to keep on top of things while Izzy was in hospital. After they'd brought Dr Devon up to speed with this new development, they drove straight home to talk to her. Sarah Cartwright was a pragmatic woman. She wasn't given to jealousy or hysterics. She was kind and open-hearted and generous to a fault. She always put the happiness and well-being of others before her own. For all those qualities, Annabel had often wished that more than paperwork related them.

Of course Sarah was not going to say 'no' to Annabel tracking down her birth family, though they'd never really discussed the possibility while Annabel was living at home. They certainly hadn't discussed it since, apart from the day that Izzy was born, when Sarah commented privately as to how proud Annabel's birth mother would have been to see her beautiful granddaughter.

'I understand,' she said at once when Richard and Annabel explained the situation. 'There is absolutely no question that it is the right thing to do.'

'But what about your feelings, Mum?'

'The only feelings that matter right now are the love I have for you and Izzy. If your birth family can help Izzy recover then I shall owe them twice over.'

'Twice?'

'Yes. Because having you changed my life.'

Annabel started to cry again. Even though she felt as though she didn't have another tear in her body.

'I'm frightened,' she said to her mother.

Sarah enfolded Annabel in a hug. To Richard, it seemed that Annabel was expressing her fears about Izzy, but Annabel was sure Sarah knew what she really meant.

Though she hadn't told her husband, Annabel had never been indifferent to the fact that she was not her parents' natural child. The question of who she really was had haunted her ever since she first properly understood that there had been another mummy, before the one who read her bedtime stories and made her hot chocolate exactly the way she liked it.

For years she had told herself that she was not going to track down her birth family out of respect to the people who had raised her. It was easy to become a mother or father – all that took was an unprotected shag – but being Mum and Dad was another thing altogether. Sarah and Humfrey had raised Annabel with such kindness, care and love. That was what parenting was really about.

However, it wasn't only her parents that Annabel was trying to protect. She was trying to protect herself. When she was very small, she sometimes fantasised about being the secret daughter of a prince and a princess. As she got older, she of course realised that the story of her birth was unlikely to be quite such a fairy tale. Princes and princesses and other good, respectable people did not give their children up for adoption.

Annabel had been angry then. Who were the feckless people who couldn't cope with a single child? What kind of animals were they?

Having Izzy had not mellowed Annabel's feelings towards the woman who gave her up but intensified her fear of hearing the real story. Now that she had her own daughter to protect, she didn't want to uncover a past other than the one she had created for herself.

Annabel wanted to *be* the person she had *become*. She wanted her bloodline to stretch back across battle-fields. She wanted her private education and all the rest of the privileges she'd enjoyed to be her real birthright. She did not want to feel that she had come by her elegance, education and polish somehow fraudulently. She was Annabel Buchanan, née Annabel Cartwright, and she had never wanted to be anyone else. But she was also Izzy's mother and Izzy's health came before everything.

'I'll do it,' she told Richard that night. 'I'll get in touch with my birth mother.'

Richard wrapped his arms round her. Perhaps one day he would be angry that Annabel had kept such an enormous secret from him but for now it was clear that he was relieved to hear it. They had another chance.

Chapter Twenty-Three

Annabel

Annabel and Richard set to work on tracking down Annabel's birth family the very next day. However, because Annabel was born before 1975, it wasn't a simple matter of asking to see her original birth certificate and searching the electoral register for a match. It turned out that Annabel had to see a social worker first. Thankfully, she didn't have to wait long. As though some heavenly power was on the case with them, the children's services department at the County Council had an empty slot for a preliminary 'schedule two' appointment that very week.

Richard went with her, though Annabel protested that she didn't need him to be there. Not for the first half-hour-long meeting, at which they wouldn't show her anything anyway. They'd just discuss her motivation for finding out more and dish out some advice.

In the end, Annabel was very glad that Richard was there beside her after all. Though the social worker had no personal information to impart yet, towards the close of the session the conversation took an ugly turn. After discussing with Annabel and Richard the apparent urgency of their request, she brought up the elephant in the room.

'Your birth certificate will give you your mother's name, but it is quite possible, indeed probable, that there will be no name at all under "father". If your parents weren't married, your mother would not have been allowed to fill in your father's name unless he was present at the moment your birth was registered. And then there is the possibility that your mother did not actually know your father's name. It's possible that she was raped. Or that your father was someone she would never want to name. Like a relative.'

Annabel closed her eyes and pinched the bridge of her nose. Rape and incest. It was not what she wanted to hear. It was certainly a long way from the fairy tale her mother had used to explain the situation when she was very small. In that story, Annabel's mother and father had loved each other very much. They were just too young and poor to give her everything she needed and so they made the decision to give her to the Cartwrights for safe keeping because they wanted the best for her.

In the car on the way home, Annabel asked Richard what he thought they'd discover at the next meeting.

'I mean, it's far more likely that she did know who my father was, isn't it?' Annabel recounted the story her adoptive parents had told her when she got a little older. 'My mother was a teenager. She got pregnant by her boyfriend. They wanted to keep me but they were just too young.'

But suddenly the old story didn't seem quite as comforting as it had done through the years. Annabel's parents had never been very specific about the details of the situation that led to Annabel's adoption. Was that because the real story was so awful?

'What if I am the product of rape?' Annabel asked. 'My birth mother probably won't want to know me and we'll never track down the man who fathered me. Maybe he's even in prison!'

'Stay positive,' said Richard.

It was hard. How could Annabel stay positive when her daughter was so ill and their one chance to get her a transplant quickly might be languishing at Her Majesty's pleasure? Annabel's imagination was running riot. She desperately needed to know the truth.

Due to the circumstances of Annabel's wish to meet her birth family, the second appointment was rushed through. Though it was not strictly playing by the rules, Richard knew someone at the County Council who made sure that it happened. So just a fortnight after the lecture on the possibility of rape, incest and affairs, Annabel and Richard found themselves back in the same sparse meeting room with the same social worker to hear a 'birth summary' and look at the original paperwork. This time, the social worker carried with her a thick manila file. She put it down on the table in front of her. It was all Annabel could do not to snatch it up. She couldn't believe how much red tape had been involved in getting to know her own history.

Annabel held her birth certificate in her hands at last. Her original name was Daisy Benson Ross. Her mother's name was Jacqui.

As the social worker had warned her, there was no name in the space for 'father', but the rest of the file held good news. No rape and no incest. Annabel's birth parents had been going out for two years when her mother got pregnant. The rest of it was just as Sarah had told her. They were not together at the time of Annabel's birth. Her mother was too young and poor to cope with raising a baby on her own, but she wrote in a letter to the social worker who had handled that case back in the 1970s that she would always love the baby she had called Daisy Benson.

'Benson is a weird middle name,' said Annabel.

'That was your putative father's surname,' said the social worker.

Annabel held the birth certificate in her hands. Such an insignificant piece of paper and yet it was capable of changing everything.

There was no time to waste.

The social worker advised Annabel that the best way to proceed when you wanted to contact your birth parents was through an intermediary. As soon as she and Richard had bid her goodbye in the lobby of the council offices, Annabel was calling the first name on the list of intermediaries the social worker had given them. Two days later they had an address. Even better, there was a match on an adoption register. Annabel's birth mother had been looking for her. She'd been signed up to the register for more than twenty years.

'Then she'll definitely want to meet you,' said Richard.

'God, I hope so.'

A letter was drafted. Annabel read it and had it sent before she could change her mind.

'Have you done it?' Izzy asked that evening, when Annabel visited the hospital to wish her good night.

'Yes.' Annabel nodded. 'I have.'

'Did they send it first class?'

'Of course,' said Annabel.

'Then she should get it tomorrow, shouldn't she?'

'God willing.'

'And how long do you think it will take her to get back to us?'

'I don't know, sweetheart. But I shouldn't think it will be long, given that she's been looking for me all this time.'

'I don't understand why you didn't just email her.'

'Because I don't think this is something that should be done over email. A letter will get results just as quickly, I promise you. The intermediary has had lots of experience with this.'

'OK,' said Izzy. 'But if you don't hear from her in a week, you'll email then, right?'

'Of course I will.'

Annabel kissed Izzy on the top of her head. Izzy closed her eyes and smiled.

'I've got a good feeling about this,' Annabel said, as much to convince herself as Izzy.

Chapter Twenty-Four

Jacqui

For once, the Royal Mail lived up to their promise and Annabel's letter via the intermediary was delivered the very next day. What Annabel didn't know, however, was that Jacqui Benson was not at home in Coventry to receive the promptly delivered envelope. She was on holiday in Lanzarote, celebrating her sixtieth birthday with her husband, her father-in-law, her two other daughters and her grandchildren and would not be home for another six days.

The Bensons' family holiday was eventful to say the least. On the second evening, six members of the group were struck down by food poisoning, sparing only Chelsea, Jacqui's youngest daughter, and Jack, her six-year-old grandson. Once the food poisoning was out of the way, the week had progressed with family rows aplenty. Sophie, Jacqui's granddaughter, had even gone missing for a while.

The catalyst for that particular event would have interested Annabel. Jacqui had not told either Ronnie or Chelsea about the existence of their older sister or the adoption until that birthday celebration week. Chelsea's reaction had been muted but Ronnie had been furious. The big problem as far as Ronnie was concerned was that, like her mother, Ronnie had become accidentally pregnant as a teenager. Jacqui and her husband Dave had actively encouraged Ronnie to keep the baby, Sophie, and as a result Ronnie had abandoned her plans to go to university. Upon hearing for the first time that Jacqui had made a different choice some forty-three years earlier, Ronnie was convinced she had become a victim of Jacqui's guilty conscience. Jacqui had encouraged Ronnie to give up on her ambitions and follow through with her unexpected pregnancy in an attempt to set things straight.

While this argument raged, Sophie was eavesdropping in the hotel corridor. Upon hearing herself described as a mistake, Sophie had gone AWOL, heading into the arms of a local boy and a whole lot of trouble. The local boy, more accurately described as a man a good decade and a half Sophie's senior, got her drunk. She threw up all over him. Running from his anger, she headed down to the sea and, in her inebriated state, managed to walk off the end of a derelict pier. Thank goodness a fellow holidaymaker – a man called Adam, who had befriended Chelsea earlier in the week – saw Sophie fall into the water and went to rescue her. She sobered up pretty quickly once she'd been dragged out of the waves and the shock of almost drowning made her ready to forgive her mum.

Sitting on the aeroplane back to Birmingham Airport, Jacqui was just grateful that the two daughters she had raised were still speaking to her. She felt lighter, too, for having shared her secret. She was glad that she and Dave had explained the sadness that had bound them but, if she was honest, she didn't really think that anything would change. She didn't really believe that her long-lost daughter would ever come back into her life.

The baby that Jacqui had called Daisy would be more than forty years old. Forty years was a long time. Jacqui knew that Daisy could have had access to her birth records for more than twenty of those years. In the meantime, Jacqui had done everything she could, signing up to every post-adoption contact register she could find, because by law she was not even allowed to know the name Daisy had been given by her new family. She couldn't idly Google her or look up her address on the electoral roll. All Jacqui had been told all those years ago was that Daisy's adoptive parents were a happily married couple in their early thirties. He was in the army. She was going to be a stay-at-home mum. It would be the perfect situation.

Once Daisy's adoption was finalised, Jacqui had asked if her new family would send her photographs of Daisy in her new home. The social worker had promised to ask but the pictures never came. She didn't know whether she had the right to ask again. She decided that she probably didn't. The last thing she sent Daisy was a small box of gifts on her first Christmas. She never even knew if they arrived.

Jacqui moved to Essex and then Bristol and got herself a job as a secretary. She shared a flat with two other girls. They didn't know her from before and she didn't tell them why she never went back to Coventry. She lived in Bristol for almost ten years. On the way home from work she passed a playground. Sometimes, she would stand by the fence and watch the children playing there, looking for little girls of about Daisy's age. Would Daisy be walking? Would she be talking? Would she be that tall? Would she be wilful like that little girl who didn't want to get back into her pushchair? Would Jacqui ever see her baby girl again? Would she even recognise her if she did?

Not having Dave to talk to about it was the worst. But they had split up before Jacqui knew she was pregnant and somehow her parents had persuaded her that it was best Dave didn't know about the baby at all. For his sake, they said. He was just starting out as an apprentice. Being lumbered with a wife and a baby would really hold him back. Jacqui thought her parents were acting in her and Dave's best interests. As an adult, she realised they'd been afraid that Dave might try to stop the adoption. They'd never really liked him. They were hoping Jacqui could put her mistake behind her and start afresh once the baby was gone. As it happened, the adoption was so traumatic that Jacqui subsequently left home and never spoke to her parents again.

Even after she and Dave got back together, married, and went on to have Ronnie and Chelsea, Jacqui ticked off every year in terms of Daisy's age. On the anniversary of Daisy's birth, she would try to find a little time to be by herself and think about the girl Daisy might be now. That had become difficult when Ronnie and Chelsea arrived on the scene.

As Daisy's eighteenth birthday approached, Jacqui felt a swell of anticipation. At the age of eighteen, Daisy could have access to the records connected to her adoption. She could start the search. Jacqui even bought Daisy an eighteenth birthday present: a charm bracelet. She would buy identical bracelets for Ronnie and Chelsea when they reached the same landmark. But Daisy's eighteenth birthday came and went. She didn't get in contact. And the silver bracelet that Jacqui had chosen so carefully grew black with tarnish as it languished in a drawer while Daisy turned 21, 22, 25 . . . 30 . . .

Since then, Jacqui had tried not to hope so hard, but there were still the odd moments when she felt sure that a reunion was just a breath away. She read somewhere that adoptees were more likely to search out their birth parents when they themselves became parents. When might Daisy become a mother? In her early thirties? Late thirties? Aged forty? That wasn't so unusual these days. Jacqui imagined Daisy passing every milestone but still no letter came.

Dave was more stoical. Though Daisy was his daughter too, Jacqui knew he didn't have quite the same attachment to the baby she had given away. Dave had nothing to go on but his imagination as far as Daisy was concerned. Dave had not even known that Jacqui was pregnant, after all.

So Dave had not ever seen his first daughter. He hadn't held her in his arms and breathed in the warm yeasty smell of her new-born head. After the birth, Jacqui had spent six weeks in a mother and baby home, doing everything that new mothers do. Not breast-feeding, though. The nurses told her that it would only make things more difficult when Daisy was finally ready to be handed over. Jacqui should try not to get too attached.

But six weeks was a long time in the life of a baby. There were days during those weeks when Jacqui forgot that Daisy wasn't going to be staying with her. Those days, she felt happier than she ever had, looking down into Daisy's dark blue eyes and wondering whether they would soon start to go brown, like Dave's. Jacqui decided that she would make a good parent. She was always happy to go to Daisy the moment the bell rang and the unmarried mothers were allowed to go to the nursery. In between those times, Jacqui did her chores and comforted even younger, more fragile girls.

'This isn't the end,' she told one girl in particular. 'Perhaps we've got no choice but to give the babies up now, but I promise you it won't be the last time we see them. They will come to look for us. I know.'

Some of the other girls refused to hold their babies at all. They resigned themselves to the fact that the babies were going to be taken away and decided that refusing to get too attached was the only way to deal with the pain ahead. Those who could afford it paid for their children to be fostered as soon as possible. Jacqui had always thought differently. She would take whatever precious time she could. She loved Daisy so hard and so well because she wanted some memory of that time to imprint itself on the dear little child. She wanted Daisy to remember how well loved she was, as if that would bring her back sooner.

It hadn't worked. Not so far.

Jacqui didn't stay in touch with the other girls from the mother and baby home. It wasn't like boarding school. It wasn't even like borstal. It had been an experience utterly without levity and joy. None of the girls wanted to remember their time there. Even Jacqui tried to narrow down her memories of those six weeks to the sight of her baby's face. But Jacqui had seen, years later, a woman she thought she remembered, talking about her successful reunion in a newsletter from NORCAP, the society that helped bring families affected by adoption together. That gave her hope again. But then she read about reunions that didn't work. And even NORCAP didn't last, folding in 2013.

From hope to despair, from despair to hope. Jacqui was somewhere in the middle when she got home from celebrating her sixtieth in Lanzarote.

* * *

While Dave unloaded their luggage from the back of the car, Jacqui opened the front door. It didn't open smoothly. A small landslide of post had built up behind the door. Ordinarily, Ronnie would have been looking after the house, making sure no one knew they were away. Jacqui scooped up the post. Bills, bills. The bills kept coming, even on your sixtieth birthday. Fortunately, there were some cards too. Jacqui opened those as she pottered about the kitchen, waiting for the kettle to boil. She laughed at a rude card from one of her cousins. Way too rude to be put on display now that Jack seemed able to read just about everything.

Then she came to an envelope addressed in handwriting she didn't recognise. She tucked her thumb under the edge of the flap and eased it open. Inside was a single sheet of A4. She pulled it out. At the sight of the address at the top, Jacqui's heart almost stopped. It was from one of the adoption reunion registers they'd signed up to so long ago. Jacqui held the letter to her chest.

'Dave,' she called him into the kitchen. 'Dave, quick. I think it's happened.'

They sat opposite each other at the kitchen table, the letter between them in a circle of light. Jacqui couldn't look at it. Dave did the honours, though his hands were shaking as he picked it up and started to read.

'It's about Daisy,' he confirmed. He reached across the table to take his wife's hand. 'Our baby girl has decided she'd like to meet us.'

Jacqui almost didn't want to believe it. She had been disappointed so many times before.

'Read it out, Dave. I can't stand it!'

'Dear Jacqui Benson,' Dave began, 'I am writing to you on behalf of my client, Annabel B, who has reason to believe that she may be your daughter. She was born and named Daisy on the eleventh of September nineteen seventy-one—'

Jacqui snatched back the letter and waved it above her head.

'Our baby's coming back!'

Chapter Twenty-Five

Ronnie

Ronnie and her family had only just got into the house when Jacqui called. Her parents were on the same flight but Ronnie's family had had a slightly longer drive home, made longer still by a detour via McDonald's because Jack and Sophie were threatening meltdown if they didn't get fed soon and there would be nothing in the fridge back at the house. Seeing the name on her mobile screen, Ronnie almost let her mother go through to voicemail – she was knackered and all she wanted was to put the kettle on – but since they had just returned from a holiday at her mother's expense, Ronnie thought the least she could do was talk to her.

'Missing us already, Mum?' she asked.

'Oh Ronnie!'

Jacqui had been crying. Ronnie could tell at once.

'Can you come over, love? Something's happened.'

'What? What is it? Have you been burgled?'

'No. Not that sort of something.'

'Then what?'

'I want to tell you face to face, love.'

'I'll be right there,' said Ronnie.

Ronnie was true to her word. She was at her parents' house within half an hour, having left Mark, Sophie and Jack to do the holiday unpacking and put the first of many washes on.

When Ronnie arrived, her parents were both in the kitchen. They'd settled Granddad Bill into his favourite chair but everything else remained undone. Their suitcases were still by the front door. Jacqui was still wearing the mac she'd put on as they left the airport. It was almost ten degrees cooler in the Midlands than it had been when they left Lanzarote that morning.

Ronnie was relieved to see that neither of her parents was obviously ill and though she was red-eyed through crying, Jacqui was also slightly manic in a happy way. Suspiciously happy. She gave Ronnie an effusive hug.

'Come in, come in,' she said. 'Sit down.'

Dave put a mug of tea made exactly how Ronnie liked it on the table in front of her.

'What's going on?' Ronnie asked.

'You'll never guess!'

'I'm not even going to try,' Ronnie said.

Jacqui looked at Dave. He nodded to signal that she should carry on.

'Your big sister has written to me!'

'What?'

'Her name's not Daisy any more.'

Jacqui put the letter on the table.

'It's Annabel. Can you believe it? Very posh, eh? Look! Look at this.'

Now it was Ronnie's turn to cry. She wasn't sure why. The letter that her parents showed her wasn't exactly emotive. And it wasn't actually from this 'Annabel B' herself anyway but from an agency, which acted on behalf of adopted people seeking their birth families. It was very formal. A standard letter, Ronnie guessed. Someone had just filled in the personal details. The names, dates and addresses.

'So, are you going to say "yes"? Are you going to see her?' Ronnie asked.

'Of course we are!' Jacqui and Dave chimed.

'Are you excited, love?' Jacqui asked. 'You're going to get to meet your big sister at last.'

Ronnie nodded, though truth be told she wasn't yet sure what she felt.

'Well, this is a turn-up for the books,' she said.

Chapter Twenty-Six

Chelsea

The youngest of the Benson sisters, Chelsea, had to hear everything over the phone the following day as she was returning from the Canaries a day later than the rest of her family. Jacqui tried calling her while she was still on the island, but Chelsea didn't pick up, figuring that it would be cheaper to call when she got to Gatwick. Her mother or sister would text if there was a real emergency going on.

So Gatwick was where Chelsea heard the news. She was standing by the luggage carousel, waiting (and praying) for her bag to appear. She decided it would be a good time to call her parents. She soon wished she'd waited until she was safely at home.

It was impossible to give Jacqui's news the attention it deserved while simultaneously trying to pull luggage off the conveyor belt. In the end, Chelsea had to let her bag go round eight times while her mother talked and talked and talked. The letter from the intermediary was read out several times. It wasn't a long letter, thank goodness, or terribly personal, but still, Jacqui wanted Chelsea to give her view on it in as great a detail as Chelsea had once critiqued passages of Thomas Hardy for her English A level. There wasn't much to say but Chelsea agreed that it was 'strange' that the baby called Daisy she had never known was now a woman called Annabel that she didn't know either.

But Chelsea knew as well as Ronnie did that this was an important moment for the whole Benson family.

As soon as she got off the phone to her mother, Chelsea noticed she had missed three calls from her sister. She duly called Ronnie back. Ronnie, like their mother, *really* wanted to talk.

Chelsea stuck in her earpiece so that she could walk to the Gatwick Express platform and talk at the same time. It was awkward, trying to concentrate while negotiating her way out of the airport, but she couldn't just tell Ronnie she'd call her back later. Not when such a big thing was going on. Especially not when the sisters had so recently patched up their friendship after two years when they didn't speak to one another at all.

'Are you OK?' asked Chelsea. 'You don't seem very happy.'

'I'm not sure that I am.'

'But Mum's happy about it. And Dad.'

'They just can't believe she's got in touch. Mum's completely blind to the possibility that it could all go wrong when they actually meet her. What if she's not a nice person?'

'She's our flesh and blood. How could she not be nice?'

Ronnie snorted.

'You're just upset you're going to be moving down the pecking order. You won't be the eldest sister any more,' Chelsea teased. 'At least I'll always be the youngest.'

'Chelsea, I know you're trying to make light of it but it really isn't funny. You've got to come up here as soon as you can. This weekend. I want to tell Mum to take things slowly and I want you to be here to back me up.'

'Do you think she should take things slowly?'

'Yes, I do.'

'It's already been forty-odd years, Ron.'

'Then a couple more months won't matter. You've got to help me persuade her to give the consequences some more thought.'

'I'm sure it's going to be OK,' said Chelsea as she scanned the departures board for the next train to Victoria.

'I wish I could be so optimistic. I've got a really bad feeling about it. I want them to take their time.'

'Don't worry about it,' said Chelsea. 'There's a long way to go between getting the first letter and actually getting to meet her, I'm sure. Put it to the back of your mind. You've got a wedding to think about.'

'I have, haven't I,' said Ronnie. After sixteen years, Mark had proposed to Ronnie on the last day of their family holiday. Chelsea could tell that the change in subject pleased her sister. 'Are you going to be my bridesmaid?'

'I thought you'd never ask,' said Chelsea. 'But the answer's "no".'

'You cow. I'd let you choose your own dress. We can have a look online when you're up this weekend.'

'Who says I'm coming up this weekend? I didn't agree to that.'

'Chelsea, you've got to. I can't cope with Mum and Dad and all this Daisy stuff on my own. This is going to affect you as much as it affects me. You've got to get involved. Saturday. You can stay at my house.'

'Well . . .'

'Don't tell me you've got something more important on?'

As a matter of fact, there was something rather

important to Chelsea on the horizon. The real reason she wasn't terribly excited about having to spend the following weekend in Coventry was because she already had tentative plans for the Saturday night. Adam, the widowed father who had been something of a holiday fling for Chelsea, had asked if he could see her when they were back in London. Chelsea was very keen to see if the connection they'd made in Lanzarote would have survived the flight home.

But how could she tell that to Ronnie? How could she admit that she had any higher priority than finding out all about her new big sister?

There were other things that Chelsea had hoped to spend some time on too. She was keen to make an appointment to see her GP to talk about the possibility of getting some counselling. For years, Chelsea had been in denial about a serious problem. She was bulimic. She had long been too afraid to admit it, telling herself that because she didn't throw up *every* day and sometimes went months without making herself sick, the situation was under her control. But recently she had been purging again and, because they'd shared a room in Lanzarote, her lovely six-year-old nephew Jack had noticed and expressed his concern.

Chelsea didn't even try to explain but she promised Jack that she would see the doctor as soon as she got home. That was one promise she intended to keep. When she got back to her flat, she fired up her laptop before she unpacked, found the number for her local GP surgery and called.

As she finally set about unpacking her suitcase, Chelsea had the feeling that her life was about to change. She was ready to accept help with her eating disorder. She was soon to meet her oldest sister. And she had a date. That was most promising of all. Adam texted to say that he and his daughter were safely back at their house in south London.

With her unpacking finished, Chelsea made a cup of tea and sat down to call her mum again. She'd promised Ronnie some backup when it came to telling Jacqui to take her time. She could at least express her concerns over the phone.

'I've been thinking we should have a family conference before you respond to that letter, Mum.'

'Too late,' said Jacqui, full of excitement. 'We already have.'

Chapter Twenty-Seven

Annabel

In the kitchen of the Great House in Little Bissingden, Annabel Buchanan was sitting on a stool, looking out on to the rain-soaked lawn. In her hand she held the letter she had subconsciously been expecting her entire life. Now she had it, she didn't know what on earth she should do.

She folded it back into the envelope. Not knowing that the Bensons were on holiday when the intermediary's letter arrived, Annabel, Richard and Izzy had been on tenterhooks for a week. She would have to put her husband and daughter out of their misery and tell them the letter had come, but not yet. She needed to think about it alone for a moment. Because what was inside that envelope had already made just the tiniest tear in the fabric of who she was.

Dear Daisy, the letter began. Daisy! Even though she had let them know her name was Annabel. *I suppose I should call you Annabel* . . . Too right, Annabel thought.

It was frustrating and strangely belittling. It almost stopped her from being able to read on.

> *I can't tell you how pleased your dad and me were to get back from holiday and find your letter on the doormat. It was more than I ever could have*

wished for. It was the best birthday present ever. I just had my sixtieth birthday, you see. That was why we were in Lanzarote.

I have thought about you every single day since they took you from my arms. I have never stopped wondering what became of you. I know you must have been wondering what happened that I had to give you away – something for which I have never forgiven myself. It doesn't seem like much of an excuse now, but your dad and me were just teenagers and we were broken up when I found out I was pregnant. My parents told me that the best thing to do was have you adopted and without their support, I couldn't afford to give you a proper life on my own.

So I gave you up and my heart was broken. And then your dad, Dave, and me got back together ten years later. We got married and had two more little girls, Veronica (everyone calls her Ronnie) and Chelsea, your sisters. You've got a niece and a nephew. Sophie's fifteen and Jack is six. Your dad's dad Granddad Bill is still with us too. He's eighty-six this year and a right character. You're going to love him.

We can't wait to meet you and tell you more about your family. You can phone or email us any time you like and when you let us know where you live, we'll come and see you as soon as we can.

I promise you, Daisy / Annabel we have never stopped thinking about you. You were meant to come back to us!

All our love,
Jacqui and Dave Benson

The familiarity and the friendliness of the letter made Annabel slightly queasy. At least in the view of these people she had never met, Annabel Buchanan was Daisy Benson Ross once again.

She told Richard over supper.

'They've got back in touch,' she said. She didn't even need to say who 'they' were. 'They say they're willing to meet up. They're still together. Can you believe it? My mother and my father. They got married ten years after I was born.'

'Well, that's great. It means we don't have to go searching for two separate people.'

'I know. But it's weird, isn't it? It's like I was part of a trial run that didn't work out. They've got two more daughters now. Grandchildren as well.'

'Even better. One of them is bound to be a match. The more the merrier.'

'But what if they're awful?'

Richard told Annabel she should not worry about whether or not she liked the woman who had written that letter. All she had to worry about was whether there was someone in her family who would be a suitable donor for Izzy. And for that reason, she should get on with organising a first meeting without delay. Annabel agreed. Of course she did. But she still couldn't help feeling a twinge of relief when she called the number written in large childish letters and found her call put straight through to an answering machine, having hidden her own number first.

She didn't leave a message. That would have been too strange. Too ghostly, was the idea that came into her head. Annabel decided instead that she would make the necessary arrangements via text and email. People were never without Internet access these days. In all probability, Jacqui Benson would check her email before she checked the messages on her landline answering machine. That's certainly how it was in the Buchanans' house. No one ever called their landline any more except salespeople.

In a PS to her letter, Jacqui had also suggested that Annabel 'friend' her on Facebook.

> *You'll be able to see lots of pictures of the whole family on there. Your middle sister Ronnie is a Facebook nut and she's always tagging me and your dad. We can hardly sneeze without her posting the news in her status.*

Needless to say, Annabel was not a Facebook nut. She didn't think she had been on the site in the best part of a year. But this was the way people communicated with each other now. And perhaps seeing some pictures would help calm her fears about what they might be getting into.

'We've got to look on Facebook right now,' said Izzy when Annabel visited her in hospital the next morning.

Annabel sat on the edge of the bed while Izzy fired up her laptop. Facebook had once been one of Izzy's favourite sites. She and her friends did other things now but she still kept her old account. Annabel couldn't keep up with the new social media. Richard had once complained that for Izzy's generation, all life happened online. They attended parties only to have something to tweet about.

'Nobody tweets, Dad,' Izzy had told him. 'That's for old people.'

Richard had thought he was quite with it, signing up to Twitter so that he could follow the news as it happened.

Anyway, Izzy made Annabel turn away while she inputted her Facebook password and then made her promise not to turn back towards the screen until Izzy was certain there was nothing on there that would make Annabel freak out.

'You shouldn't have to worry about me being freaked out by anything you put on Facebook,' Annabel automatically started to reiterate the lecture she felt she trotted out ten times a month. If not ten times a week. 'You should make sure there is nothing on your profile at all that you would not be happy for a future employer to see.'

'Yeah, yeah . . .' Izzy made yapping mouths of her hands. 'It's all right, Mum. I've taken down the nude selfies.'

'Don't even joke about it,' Annabel warned her.

'It's all clear. OK. Remind me what we're looking for.'

'Jacqui Benson.'

'With a k?'

'With a "qu".'

'Fancy,' Izzy joked.

There were hundreds of people called Jacqui Benson. Putting in Coventry narrowed it down a little.

Annabel peered at the faces. 'Do any of these people look like me?'

'How about that one?'

Izzy pointed out a profile illustrated with a photograph of a female bodybuilder in one of those improbable poses.

'I don't think so,' said Annabel. 'Or if it is, I definitely haven't inherited those muscles.'

'This one?' Izzy pointed out a woman half her mother's age.

'Very funny.'

'We could be looking all day. What's her email address?'

Jacqui had included it in the letter of course. Izzy plugged it in to the search box.

'It's this one,' she said. The cursor hovered over a small photograph of a smiling woman holding a baby. The baby, who looked like a boy, was dressed in a tiny Coventry City FC shirt. Izzy clicked to enlarge the image. 'This is a picture of your mother.'

Annabel stared. It was incredible to think that she was seeing her birth mother for the first time on Facebook. And, if she was honest, it was an enormous anticlimax. Annabel had always secretly hoped there was a seriously juicy story behind her adoption. But the woman she was looking at now was just so very ordinary. She looked like any number of women you passed in the street every day. She was slightly overweight and dressed in a voluminous tunic top that did nothing to flatter her figure. Her hair was grey and cut too short for her face. Annabel winced at her unflattering make-up. She'd plucked her eyebrows much too thin at some point.

'She's got zero account security,' Izzy tutted, as she clicked her way into Jacqui's numerous photograph albums. 'Some people are just clueless. Anybody could be looking.'

Annabel wasn't sure she had very much security on her Facebook account either. She didn't really think about it from month to month. She'd only opened one because Izzy had wanted a Facebook account when she was just twelve and the ability of Annabel to monitor it was one of her conditions for allowing Izzy to break the Facebook age limit.

Izzy opened a file that said 'Grandpa Bill's 80th

birthday.' She enlarged the tiny thumbprints and started scrolling through them.

'Who are these people?' she asked out loud.

Her words were a direct echo of Annabel's own feelings.

Who were these people? The family that Annabel saw in those albums was definitely not the family of her dreams. That was for sure. They were the kind of family who came to look at the Great House when it was open to the public during the village fete. The men all wore football shirts. The women all so badly dressed and pictured drinking straight from bottles of Bacardi Breezer as they sat around on garden chairs indoors.

'Are you sure that's my grandma?' Izzy asked.

Annabel looked at another photo of Jacqui. In the picture, she was bending over a disposable barbecue, looking back towards the photographer with an expression of indignation as he focused on her backside in a pair of tight black leggings.

'Seriously. That can't be your mum,' said Izzy. 'Does that mean . . .? Have I got those genes too? There must have been a mistake.'

Annabel shook her head. She probably should have reprimanded her daughter for being so judgemental, but the truth was that Annabel was just as horrified at what she was seeing. The Bensons obviously lived a very different life from the one she was used to. They seemed to barbecue more often than they changed their clothes. Together with her daughter, she peered closely at every single one of the photos.

'That must be one of my sisters,' said Annabel. 'Your aunt.'

Annabel pointed at a woman who was oddly familiar

and not just because of any possible genetic resemblance. Maybe the Bensons *had* been to a Little Bissingden fete.

'I cannot be related to that!' said Izzy, as she recoiled from a photograph of her aunt giving the photographer the finger, her jaw set like a bulldog's. She could have illustrated a *Daily Mail* article on broken Britain. Just as Liz Hurley has a default pose for the paps – one hip angled forward to make her look slimmer – so Annabel's newly found sister seemed never to be photographed without one digit extended in anger.

'We've got nothing in common with them,' Izzy wailed.

'But we need them,' Annabel reminded her and instantly wished that she hadn't. Izzy's face crumpled. Up until then, she had seemed on good form. Just that morning, Dr Devon had suggested that Izzy might soon be able to leave the hospital and dialyse at home. They could start to get back to normal.

'I hate it,' Izzy sobbed. 'I hate it that we've got to know these people at all.'

Annabel held her daughter close and felt more than a little ashamed that she had raised her child to find the idea of ordinary so frightening.

'They could be lovely people,' she said soothingly. 'One of my new sisters has got a daughter your age. You might get on really well.'

'She'll be like those girls down the village,' Izzy countered, referring to the rough-looking bunch who hung around in front of the Spar shop. Jeering the smartly dressed girls coming home from the private school seemed to be the highlight of their day. One particularly awful evening, one of the rough kids had pulled Izzy's hair and challenged her to a fight.

'She won't be like that,' Annabel promised, wondering how she could possibly know. And there, in the next photograph, was the girl Annabel assumed must be her niece, dressed all in black and posing like her mother, giving the finger to the world.

Annabel felt like giving the world the finger too.

Chapter Twenty-Eight

Chelsea

With so much in turmoil, Chelsea found herself talking to her sister every day. Several times a day. On the Thursday after the Benson family got back from Lanzarote, while Chelsea was at work, Ronnie called from her own office, at a funeral director's, to tell Chelsea Annabel's full name, which she had just emailed to Jacqui.

'Annabel Buchanan. How posh is that? We need to check this woman out.'

'Our *sister* out. You mean you haven't already?'

Chelsea tapped Annabel's full name into Google.

'Bloody Internet's been down since we got back from holiday,' said Ronnie. 'And I can't get online at work. Looking at Facebook is disrespectful to the corpses. I need you to do it.'

'Well, I think I'm looking at her right now.'

'What's she like?'

'Brown hair. Shoulder length.'

'Is she thin?'

'Quite thin, yes.'

Ronnie sucked her teeth.

'There are a couple of pictures of her. In one of them she looks like she's opening a school fete or something.'

'What does she do?'

'Sits on a lot of committees by the look of things. Can't see any actual job so far.'

'A yummy mummy.'

'That's what I'm starting to think. But she looks friendly enough, Ronnie. That's got to be a good sign. She looks a bit like you.'

'Only thin.'

'She's not that much thinner than you. She might not be thinner at all. These pictures might have been taken years ago. Not that it matters.'

All the talk about weight was making Chelsea uncomfortable. It was hard not to join in but Chelsea's recovery relied on her breaking the habit. She couldn't let her first thoughts about her sister be weight related.

'I've got a bad feeling about this,' said Ronnie as she had been saying every day since the letter from the intermediary arrived.

'Don't keep saying that,' said Chelsea. 'I don't think there's any need. At least from these pictures, I'm pretty sure that she's not going to be coming to us for money. We could possibly tap *her* up for a bob or two, though.'

Ronnie attempted a laugh.

'Will you come up to Coventry as soon as you can? When can you come? How about Saturday morning?'

'Um, Saturday . . .'

'What's more important than coming up here on Saturday?'

'Well.' Chelsea took a deep breath. 'As a matter of fact, I've got a date.'

'Who with?' Ronnie asked.

'I wish you didn't sound so incredulous. With Adam. The guy from Lanzarote.'

Ronnie whooped.

'You go girl! That is amazing. You haven't had a date in what? Nearly a year? When did you break up with that Colin bloke? You're practically a virgin.'

'Thanks a bundle,' Chelsea sighed. 'As it happens, I've been on plenty of dates since I broke up with Colin. It's just that none of them were anywhere near as promising as this one. Look, I've got to go. I'm at work here.'

'Bring Adam with you on Saturday. He knows us. I'm sure his little girl would love to see Jack again.'

'And I'd quite like to see Adam on his own first,' said Chelsea. 'I'll come up to yours on Sunday, like I've been saying I would. Can you pick me up from the station?'

Ronnie agreed.

As promised, Chelsea caught the train up to Coventry first thing on Sunday morning, having stayed in London on Saturday night for her first proper date with Adam. The date had gone fantastically well. Adam left Lily, his daughter, with her paternal grandparents for the evening while he and Chelsea met for drinks and dinner in Soho. It was strange to be seeing each other in London, having begun their relationship in the Canaries. But Chelsea was not disappointed. Adam looked every bit as delicious in the context of the capital city and they were both grateful for a choice of proper wine, rather than the rotgut they'd had to drink at the Hotel Volcan.

Adam took Chelsea to Bocca di Lupo, an Italian restaurant tucked away behind Shaftesbury Avenue. Chelsea loved it. They laughed and talked all night long. There was never a pause in the conversation. On the contrary, they had so much to tell each other that they kept talking over themselves, so eager were they to share their stories.

'I can't believe we didn't meet years ago,' Adam concluded, when they worked out that they had been to several of the same gigs and frequented the same Shoreditch pubs back when Chelsea was first in London, working on a women's weekly magazine, and Adam was a young architect who had yet to meet his wife Claire, Lily's mother.

'Lily wanted you to have this,' Adam said, pulling out a piece of paper from his wallet.

Chelsea unfolded the piece of paper to reveal a rather good drawing of a flower.

'I suppose I should have bought you a rose myself,' said Adam. 'Maybe one of those guys will come in later on.'

'You mean a flower seller?' said Chelsea. 'Only twenty pounds a stem. I don't need one of those. This flower is much more rare and precious. And it will never wilt.'

Chelsea meant it. She was incredibly touched by Adam's daughter's gesture. The little girl hadn't exactly taken to Chelsea upon their first meeting. Things had only got worse when Adam and Chelsea tried to broker a friendship between Lily and Chelsea's nephew Jack. But this little drawing seemed like a good sign. And if Chelsea was going to fall for Adam, then she was well aware that he came as a package deal.

As the evening ended, with a mammoth snog at the tube station, Chelsea already knew that she would be seeing Adam again. She was so pleased by the prospect of another date that even the next day's train ride to Coventry – with the inevitable weekend delays – could not dampen her spirits.

Chapter Twenty-Nine

Chelsea

Despite the odds, Chelsea's train arrived in Coventry on time. Ronnie was waiting for her in the station car park. She wasn't on her own. She'd brought Jack along.

'He insisted,' Ronnie said.

'Auntie Chelsea, Auntie Chelsea. Sit in the back with me!'

Chelsea slid into the back of the car alongside Jack on his booster seat. Jack was overjoyed.

'I knew you would come and see me,' he said. 'This is brilliant. I can show you Minecraft.'

'Minecraft?' Chelsea asked.

'Don't get him started,' said Ronnie. 'Still, at least it makes a change from the bloody sonic screwdriver.'

There was no chance whatsoever that Ronnie and Chelsea would be able to talk properly on the drive back to Ronnie's house. Of course, Jack was convinced that Chelsea's visit was all about *their* newly minted friendship. When they got to Ronnie's he dragged Chelsea straight into the living room and treated her first to a slideshow of photographs from their recent holiday in Lanzarote. There were several that Chelsea would have preferred to delete.

'Ha ha! Look at that one,' Jack laughed at a photograph of Chelsea caught midway through a mouthful of pizza. 'You look like a hippopotamus.'

'I'm writing you out of my will,' said Chelsea.

After that, Chelsea simply had to be introduced to Minecraft, which seemed to be some kind of virtual Lego on the XBox. She watched and feigned interest while Jack attempted to build a Tardis. She nodded sagely as Jack explained the difference between 'creative' and 'survival' modes.

'And now you have to go to sleep,' he said. 'Before the creepers can get you.'

'I see,' said Chelsea. She had no idea what he was on about.

'Do you want to have a go?'

Jack passed Chelsea the controller and allowed her roughly twenty seconds to make the onscreen avatar move before he snatched it back.

'Like this,' he said, whizzing through the moves like the digital native he was.

'Bring back the sonic screwdriver,' Chelsea stage-whispered to Ronnie.

Jack heard.

'Do you want to play with the sonic screwdriver? I've still got it. I'll get it for you now.'

Over the top of Jack's head, Chelsea and Ronnie pulled faces straight out of Munch's *Scream*.

There was no peace until Jack had to go to a children's birthday party that had been in the diary for weeks. Mark took him there. Apparently, he protested loudly all the way. Parties were rubbish and he wanted to stay home with his auntie.

But at last Ronnie and Chelsea were able to sit down with Chelsea's iPad, connect to 4G and bring up the Googled photographs that Chelsea had looked at the week before. Ronnie's Internet service was still down and she was desperate to see what her sister already knew.

'Oh my God,' said Ronnie.

'What?'

'We've met her.'

'When?'

'She lives in a fucking mansion. We looked round it when we went to some fete at the beginning of May.'

'Seriously?'

'Seriously. Little Bissingden. It was a huge bloody manor house. Jack knocked over a suit of armour. I'll never forget her face when she came to see what he'd done.'

'Was she friendly?'

'What do you think? I mean, she asked if everyone was OK and all that but you could tell she was much more concerned about her precious antiques than my son.'

'Was Jack hurt?'

'No. But still . . .'

Chelsea nodded. This was already going badly. Ronnie had a tendency to have violent reactions to people and it was clear that she was having a very violent reaction to her newly discovered sister.

'She was a stuck-up cow. You've never seen anyone with her head so far up her own arse! I can't believe we're related to someone so horrible. I'm telling you, Chelsea, this is a disaster. What else can you find out?'

Chelsea was an expert at extracting information from the Internet, having honed her skills on keeping up with the comings and goings of a number of ex-boyfriends. It wasn't long before they had Annabel's address and a record of how much she had paid for her house.

'Oh. My. God,' said Ronnie when she saw the figure.

'Bloody hell,' Chelsea agreed.

'Where did she get that money?'

'She must have been adopted by millionaires. Or married it.'

Next Chelsea looked for references to Annabel's husband. His name was Richard. He'd studied at Cambridge. He'd been a high-flying lawyer. Currently he worked for a big investment bank.

'Can you find out what he earns?' Ronnie asked.

'I think it's safe to say "a lot",' Chelsea replied. 'They've got a flat in London as well as the stately home.'

'So we've established that she's not coming after us for money. Then what does she want?' Ronnie asked.

'Why does there have to be a motive? Perhaps she just wants to meet us,' said Chelsea. 'For the same reason that Mum and Dad want to meet her. The same reason I want to meet her! She's family.'

'No, she isn't,' said Ronnie firmly.

'Ronnie, we've all three of us got the same mum and dad.'

'Yeah. But why now? Why not years ago?'

'Maybe she didn't even know she was adopted until recently. Her parents might not have told her but perhaps they've died and she found a letter or something.'

Ronnie clicked back to the picture of Annabel at that fete. Annabel was standing on the steps to the Great House. The front steps. Not the steps to the scullery entrance where she had greeted the tour group.

In that picture, Annabel did look like them, like Ronnie *and* Chelsea. She had their mother's eyes and their father's nose. She had the same fine straight hair. There was no denying it.

'I don't want her in our lives,' said Ronnie.

'It's going to happen,' said Chelsea. 'We can't ask Mum and Dad not to see her. We don't have any right to do that.'

When Chelsea looked away from the screen and at her sister, she saw that Ronnie had tears in her eyes.

'I don't want anything to change,' Ronnie said. 'We don't need another sister. We're already a proper family as we are!'

Jacqui and Dave and Granddad Bill came over to Ronnie's house for tea that afternoon. Chelsea could see at once that the letter from the intermediary and the subsequent email exchanges had changed everything for their mother. Jacqui was elated in a strangely girlish way. She had the intermediary's letter and a printout of Annabel's emails in her handbag, safely protected by a clear plastic envelope. They were just pieces of paper but Jacqui carried them as though they were holy relics. In some ways, thought Chelsea, it was no wonder. As far as Chelsea knew, they were the only mementoes of her first daughter Jacqui actually had.

Jacqui smoothed the letter and emails out on the kitchen table so that Chelsea could read them, but not until she had made sure that the tabletop was absolutely clean. Jacqui did not want to expose these precious things to coffee spills and toast crumbs.

'She says she wants to see us as soon as possible,' Jacqui said proudly.

Indeed, why wait?

'You're pleased, aren't you, Chelsea?' Jacqui asked.

'Of course I am,' Chelsea said.

'I know you haven't had long to get used to the idea of having another sister.'

'But you've had a very long time to wonder what happened to your baby, Mum. The way I see it, the sooner you meet her, the better.'

'Annabel,' Jacqui murmured. 'I can't believe she's

called Annabel. I don't think I ever would have called her that.'

'Well, that's what she is called,' said Ronnie brusquely. 'She's not your Daisy now.'

Chelsea shot Ronnie a glance that said 'shut up'.

'Annabel,' said Jacqui again, as though she was trying the name on for size. 'I don't think I can get used to it. She's been Daisy in my head all these years. Daisy, Ronnie and Chelsea. My three girls.'

'This is getting weird,' said Ronnie. 'Knowing that while we've been completely in the dark, you've been thinking about another daughter all this time. It's like we've been living with a ghost that only you could see. Living a lie . . .'

Chelsea started to fear that Ronnie was about to reprise the argument they'd had in Lanzarote, when Jacqui first told them about the adoption and Ronnie went ballistic. Chelsea braced herself but fortunately, Jack interrupted them. He was back from the party. A fellow parent from school had dropped him off. As soon as he came into the kitchen, he jumped on to Chelsea's lap, knocking the wind right out of her.

'Jack!' said Ronnie. 'Be careful.'

'I'm getting a new auntie,' Jack told Chelsea then. 'Grandma lost her a hundred years ago.'

Jacqui winced.

'But she's found her now. Do you think she'll like cricket?'

Ronnie shrugged. 'I dunno.'

Chelsea said, 'I expect so. But she won't be as good at it as I am.'

'Hmmm. You're not actually very good at cricket, Auntie Chelsea. I only said it to be nice.'

'Check out the diplomat,' Chelsea laughed.

'Perhaps my new auntie's husband will be good at cricket instead.'

'Yeah,' said Ronnie. 'He probably played for England. Nothing less for The Lady of the Great House.'

Chapter Thirty

Annabel

At the Great House, Richard was finding it hard to concentrate on the cricket on the television. Izzy was out of hospital and back home with her portable dialysis machine but it still felt wrong to try to do any of the things he would ordinarily have done on a Sunday. Annabel was equally unable to relax. When she wasn't keeping Izzy company in the nest she had made for herself on the sofa or up in her bedroom, she was doing chores. She was always dusting or vacuuming or putting sheets through the washing machine despite the fact that she hadn't done her own dusting, washing or ironing for years. She just had to keep on the move.

And all the time she kept checking her phone. For news from the hospital about a possible donor. For news from the Bensons. When would they meet face to face?

A meeting was finally arranged by email. It would be the following Sunday. They couldn't meet her any sooner because of Dave's work shifts. Jacqui didn't want to go alone. They had to be there together. They hoped she understood.

'Why can't he just take a day off!' Annabel wailed in frustration.

'Perhaps he can't afford to,' Richard suggested.

'But . . . This is important, for heaven's sake.'

'We've got to approach this calmly,' said Richard. 'We are potentially going to ask them to make an enormous sacrifice. We can't try to rush them into it. We've got to make some kind of relationship first.'

Annabel knew Richard was right, but she didn't care. She was ready to call Jacqui and tell her that they would pay for Dave to take a day off. Time was of the essence.

Richard laid his hand on her arm.

'Izzy is OK. She's stable. We can wait a few more days to have this first meeting. We have to take this steadily or we could blow it.'

But each day was passing as slowly as a year for Annabel. She knew she wouldn't sleep. She had to do something. There was nothing worse for Annabel than the thought that she could do nothing to influence a situation. To be able to do nothing for Izzy was pure hell.

Meanwhile, the new baby was making itself felt. Now that she knew she was pregnant, Annabel wondered how she hadn't guessed before. The pregnancy was something else to worry about. Because Annabel was considered an older, if not flat-out *elderly*, mother, the list of tests the doctors had offered her seemed endless. There were, as the Mumsnet boards she browsed seemed to take some glee in reminding her, all manner of possible problems to consider. Down's was just the start of it.

What would Annabel do if they discovered that the baby had some kind of disability? Richard had always been firmly against abortion on such grounds, as had Annabel. But this time? When losing the baby could mean that Annabel would be free to be a donor again? Free to save her firstborn? Annabel hated herself for even considering that as a silver lining. Her desperation to help Izzy was sending her insane.

But as it happened, a second antenatal scan – done privately – was as reassuring as the first. The baby was developing exactly as it should be. Growing normally. Its tiny heart was strong and insistent. This baby was going to be born no matter what else was going on in the Buchanan family.

On the night after they had the second scan, Richard fell asleep with his hand on Annabel's baby bump. The weight of his arm kept Annabel awake though she didn't want to disturb him. The pressures upon them were weighing Richard down too. Sleep had been elusive for both of them. Instead Annabel lay and watched shadows dancing on the ceiling. What horrors were about to come dancing out of the past?

Chapter Thirty-One

Jacqui

Annabel was not the only one who couldn't sleep. Now that she had a date for the first meeting with her Daisy, Jacqui constantly felt as though she'd drunk too much coffee. Her stomach fluttered. She couldn't sleep. She couldn't eat. At work she simply went through the motions. At home she was distracted enough to burn three frozen pizzas in a row. In the end, Dave said, 'I'm taking you out,' and they went to Nando's. There, Jacqui could only pick at her chicken in pitta bread.

'I bring you out and you don't even eat anything!' Dave complained.

'I'm nervous about Sunday,' said Jacqui. 'Aren't you nervous?'

'What is there to be nervous about? We're only meeting our little girl.'

'But she's not a little girl any more is she? I've looked at her photos on Facebook. They look so posh! She was adopted by an army major, Dave. She's grown up in a different world.'

'I'm sure we'll still have plenty in common,' said Dave.

'Oh, I hope so. But I bet she's really grand. Her husband is related to Lord Somebody or other.'

'We're related to a genuine lord too,' Dave reminded her.

'Your great-grandmother having got pregnant by the

lord of the manor while she was in service does not count,' said Jacqui.

'She was acknowledged,' said Dave. 'The old bugger left her that cottage in his will.'

'That was to help her husband keep his mouth shut. The lord never actually admitted paternity.'

'Whatever. We all know it's in the Benson blood. You're not to worry about Sunday. If you talk in your telephone voice, everything will be dandy.'

'Don't tease me,' said Jacqui. 'I just want to make a good impression.'

'Of course we will,' said Dave. 'Blood is thicker than water.'

Chapter Thirty-Two

Annabel

Blood thicker than water? Annabel could not have agreed less. As the day of her first meeting with her birth parents approached, Annabel was also nervous. She too wanted to make a good impression but only because she did not want to have to spend time establishing any kind of proper relationship before she revealed the real reason she'd decided to get in touch. She wished she had been upfront from the start. Why had she and Richard decided that it would be a better idea to keep her motives hidden? If she'd asked outright in that first letter, they might have said 'no' right away and she wouldn't have had to meet them at all.

No. Annabel checked herself. That was not the right way to think. She needed them to say 'yes'. They had to say yes.

'They will say "yes",' Richard reassured her. 'How could they not want to help our little girl? She's their granddaughter.'

But human beings were strange creatures. While desperately searching the Internet for good news, Annabel had found plenty of bad news too. There were more than a couple of stories about families that had not pulled together when they needed to, about people who had refused to be tested or worse, tested as a match and then refused to get involved with a transplant. What if that was the kind of people they were dealing with?

Richard stroked Annabel's hair. 'If these people produced a baby who grew into a woman as wonderful as you, they really can't be all bad.'

Annabel thanked him for being so kind and so relentlessly positive, but of course Richard could never understand that in the heart of any adoptee, even as an adult, is the unshakeable conviction that they were given away because they were somehow 'wrong' and by extension, at least one of their parents must have been a 'wrong un' too. Why else would you end up in such a sordid situation? Giving away a child!

Annabel phoned Sarah, the only woman she would ever think of as 'Mum', for reassurance.

'Tell me what the social worker said again, when you came to fetch me from the adoption agency office.'

'It was a long time ago, darling,' Sarah reminded her. 'But we were definitely told that your mother was a nice young girl. She did well at school. She liked sport. And she came from a very good family.'

Annabel tried to be comforted but any family that allowed one of their kin to be given up to be raised by strangers could not be, by her definition, a 'good' family. Where had her maternal grandparents been when Jacqui was making her decision? Why hadn't they supported her?

No, Annabel was not looking forward to meeting her birth family at all. She was doing this for Izzy and only for Izzy. Unlike the woman who had given her away, Annabel was determined to be a proper mother. There was nothing she wouldn't do for her child.

Chapter Thirty-Three

Jacqui

On the morning of the meeting with her eldest daughter, Jacqui was surrounded by every other member of her family. Ronnie and Mark brought the children round after breakfast. Chelsea had come up from London again especially. The unspoken plan was that they would all hang around the house until Jacqui and Dave came back home. That way, they would all find out together and at once exactly what had gone on. More importantly, they would all be there for Jacqui if things did not go well.

'Of course it will go well,' said Chelsea. 'You've seen all those reunion shows, Mum. Everyone is always delighted.'

Chelsea had her fingers metaphorically crossed behind her back as she said this. Chelsea had always hated those reunion shows. Everyone looked so strained. She was certain that the minute the cameras were switched off the recriminations started. It was such a stressful thing to put oneself through. Why on earth would you think it was a good idea to do it in front of an entire TV-watching nation, while Davina McCall simpered in sympathy?

Ronnie helped Jacqui put the finishing touches to her hair.

'I swear you didn't put so much effort in for Jack's christening,' said Ronnie, only half joking.

'Don't start,' Chelsea mouthed at her sister across their mother's head.

'This is a big day for all of us,' said Jacqui. 'I know she said she only wanted to meet your father and me at first, but I'm sure she'll want to meet you all too, soon enough. She'll especially want to meet you.' Jacqui pinched her grandson Jack's cheeks.

'I've made this picture for my new auntie,' Jack said.

'Hmmm.'

The women all made approving noises. None of them could see what it was.

Jack looked at them expectantly.

'What do you think? Do you like it?'

'Well . . .' said Jacqui. 'Is it some kind of banana?'

'It's a sonic screwdriver, Grandma! A sonic screwdriver from *Doctor Who* made with Minecraft.'

'Ah yes. Obviously! I'm sure your new auntie will be delighted.'

'Tell her I'm looking forward to meeting her. And I can't believe I'm getting a cousin.'

Jack had no cousins. None of Mark's siblings had children and Chelsea was in no hurry. So the idea of an instant cousin was extremely appealing. Even if she was a girl. There was still a faint chance she would be a *Doctor Who* nut who knew how to bowl a cricket ball.

'Are you excited about getting a cousin, Sophie?' Chelsea asked her niece.

Sophie shrugged. After all, she had already met this new cousin and that was an encounter that still made her wince.

Having handed over the picture for Annabel, Jack skipped out to the patio where Granddad Bill was catching the last of the Indian-summer sunshine with his radio beside him. He was in his new wheelchair. Well, it wasn't exactly new. It was an old electric one that Dave had refurbished. Though Bill could still get around on sticks if he needed to, to go anywhere further than from his chair to the bathroom at any kind of speed he really needed wheels and pushing his old un-motorised wheelchair around had been playing havoc with Jacqui's shoulder. They hoped the motorised chair would make life easier. Providing Bill didn't steer himself into a ditch, that is.

'All right, Granddad Bill?' Jack squeaked.

'I'm in the sunshine, I've got the first match of the season on the radio and I just know you're coming to ask me if I want a cup of tea. I've won the bloody lottery,' said Bill.

'Don't say "bloody",' said Jack, as he moved the bricks that Dave had put in front of the wheelchair's back wheels to supplement the brakes because the patio was on a slight incline.

Jack was already au fait with the wheelchair's controls. With the bricks out of the way, he climbed on to Bill's lap and together they took a tour of the paved parts of the garden, with Jack steering. Bill, who was having one of his good days, told Jack he would have made a good tank commander.

'You're just like I was at your age,' he said. 'Young man, you could be a great soldier.'

'Granddad Bill,' said Jack. 'I'm going to be Doctor Who.'

Jacqui went upstairs to get changed.

'It's half past!' she yelled down the stairs a couple of minutes later. 'Why didn't anybody say? Dave, we need to get going.'

'It won't take us that long, Jacqui,' Dave yelled back at her.

'I don't care. I don't want to be late.'

'Do I look all right?' Dave asked Chelsea.

'You look magnificent,' said Chelsea, straightening his tie for him. 'I think you should wear a tie all the time.'

'No chance,' said Dave. 'After today, the only time you'll ever see me wear a tie again is at Ronnie's wedding. And yours.'

'Thanks, Dad.'

'How about me?' Jacqui asked.

She came downstairs slowly and carefully on her high heels. Chelsea wished she had made the time to come up to Coventry and help Jacqui find an outfit because the direction Ronnie had steered Jacqui in was all a bit 'mother of the bride'. In fact, Ronnie had been thinking 'mother of the bride' when she chose it, because she knew that Jacqui wouldn't have the budget for more than one new frock that autumn.

Jacqui was wearing a floral print dress with a peach jacket that picked out the colour of some of the flowers. She had matched it with peach-coloured handbag and shoes. Chelsea thought it was awful but it was undoubtedly expensive. Jacqui had seriously splashed out.

'You look beautiful, Mum,' said Chelsea.

'That means a lot,' she said. 'Coming from you. Because you know about fashion, love.'

'I do. And that outfit is "*le dernier cri*".'

Jacqui looked nonplussed.

'It's French. It means the very latest thing.'

'OK,' Jacqui nodded. 'Shall I put the hat on too?'

'I don't think you need the hat, Mum,' said Chelsea quickly. 'But you can definitely use it for Ronnie's wedding. You can wear the hat then.'

Chelsea straightened her mother's collar.

'Come on,' said Dave. 'You said we had to get going.'

'It's happening,' Jacqui sniffed. 'It's happening at last!'

'Don't cry,' Ronnie barked at her. 'You'll only make your make-up run.'

Ronnie, Mark, Chelsea and the children massed on the front step of the house to wave Jacqui and Dave off. Even Granddad Bill waved from the front-room window. Afterwards, the family went back inside and sat down round the kitchen table. Mark put the kettle on. Everyone was silent. Even Jack. It was as though they had just waved Dave and Jacqui off to some terrible fate. Finally, Sophie reached across the table and took both Ronnie and Chelsea's hands.

'It'll be all right,' she said.

Chapter Thirty-Four

Annabel

While Jacqui had gone to their rendezvous dressed for a Buckingham Palace garden party, Annabel was wearing jeans. Admittedly, they were designer jeans with a two hundred pound price tag, but they were jeans nonetheless. She teamed them with a striped T-shirt, a navy blue linen jacket and a pair of ballet flats. It was the kind of outfit she would have worn to meet her girlfriends for a weekend brunch at a gastropub. Richard was in his usual Sunday attire of a striped pink shirt and a pair of chinos.

Annabel had decided that anything else would be too much. Having seen the photographs of the Bensons on Facebook, she doubted they owned anything too dressy and Richard had suggested it would be a good idea to make them feel comfortable. They were meeting in a country house hotel, for sure, but it was not Relais et Châteaux. It was a three-star place that had been cut off from civilisation by a ring road at some point in the nineteen eighties. It wasn't a place Annabel would have chosen but that was OK, because neither was it a place that Annabel would ever have any inclination to go back to if she didn't have to. Annabel was still approaching this meeting like a blind date that was more likely to go wrong than right. In choosing the Ridgeview Hotel, Annabel was ensuring that if everything did go badly, she would not have to relive the moment every time she wanted to meet friends for a Sunday lunch.

Annabel's mother Sarah would be staying at the Great House with Izzy that day. When she turned up, Annabel hugged Sarah tightly and asked her again if she was sure she should be meeting the Bensons at all.

'Of course. I am quite clear on the matter. And your father would have been one hundred per cent behind this too,' Sarah assured her.

'I wish Dad were here,' said Annabel.

'He's always with us,' said Sarah, tapping first herself and then Annabel on the heart.

'What if Jacqui Benson wants me to call her Mum?' Annabel asked Richard as they turned into the driveway of the Ridgeview Hotel.

'Tell her you'd rather not. Look. Everything is going to be fine. I promise.'

Annabel's heart thudded in her chest. She wasn't ready for this at all and yet she couldn't put the moment off any longer. It wasn't about her. It was about Izzy. She needed to put Izzy at the front of her mind.

'Shall I be Davina?' joked Richard as he unclipped his seat belt.

Annabel managed a half-snuffle/half-laugh. 'I can't stand that woman. Always gurning her way through other people's lives.'

Richard laughed. He seemed glad that Annabel still felt able to snipe.

'How about that Scottish one?'

'Oh no. He's even worse.'

'Darling, I know we've been concentrating on Izzy, but I want you to know that I do realise what a big deal this is for you. I know you've had to do it sooner than you hoped for. Or rather, I know that you probably wouldn't have done this at all if it wasn't for wanting to help Izzy.'

'I just can't help thinking about Mum.'

'Sarah is totally for this. She's not in the least bit insecure in your love for her. And she loves you so absolutely that she would never stand in the way of your happiness. And Izzy's health is your happiness. If your mum were here with us in the car, she would be pushing you through that door, telling you to be brave and calm and bloody get a move on. Because she loves you and she loves Izzy.'

'You're right.'

Indeed, when Annabel checked her phone one last time, she found two text messages. One from Izzy, which contained only a smiley face and a kiss, and one from her mother that said, I'm thinking of you, darling. I love you very much.

'So, are you ready?' Richard asked.

Annabel nodded. She checked her eye make-up in the passenger vanity mirror one last time. Izzy had been absolutely right when she questioned the wisdom of wearing mascara. Annabel had been fighting back tears the whole journey and she already looked as though she had been awake for three months.

'Just a sec,' she said to Richard. Annabel got out her make-up remover pads and wiped the last of her eye make-up off.

Chapter Thirty-Five

Jacqui and Annabel

Jacqui and Dave had been sitting in the lobby lounge at the Ridgeview Hotel for forty minutes.

'I knew we'd end up getting here too early,' Dave complained.

'It's better than getting here late. I want this to be perfect.'

Jacqui was sitting with her back to the window. She hadn't always been sitting with her back to the window. She had previously been sitting so that she could look out on to the car park. But then, for superstitious reasons, she changed seats, as though not looking out to see if Annabel had arrived yet could somehow make her arrive more quickly. Of course, swapping seats did not actually stop Jacqui from turning round to check the car park once every thirty seconds. Likewise, she never put her phone down, in case Annabel called to say she was lost or late or, heaven forbid, not going to be coming after all. She was worse than Sophie waiting for that silly boyfriend of hers.

In the meantime, Jacqui refused all the young waitress's attempts to bring her something to eat or drink.

'We're expecting some people to join us,' said Dave.

'Some people!' Jacqui exclaimed. 'We're expecting our *daughter* and her husband.'

'That's nice,' said the waitress, naturally having no

idea whatsoever of the import of the occasion. 'I'll bring the menus back when they come then.'

'Yes, please. If you could,' said Jacqui.

'Telephone voice,' said Dave.

'Stop it.' Jacqui swatted him. 'I can't help it. I'm so nervous I'm practically wetting myself. I don't understand how you can sit there and not be nervous at all.'

Dave reached for Jacqui's hand. 'Believe me, I am bricking it. Right now, I'm just praying I don't fart through fear the moment they walk through the door.' He blew an extravagant raspberry. 'Can you imagine it?'

'I'm trying not to,' said Jacqui, but all the same a smile crept back on to her face. And then she started laughing. And it was while she was laughing that Annabel and Richard finally walked into the room.

'Oh.' Jacqui stopped giggling abruptly, as though a teacher had caught her. 'I'm sorry. We were just—'

'Laughing about how funny it would be if I farted just as you walked in,' said Dave.

'Dave!' Jacqui looked distraught. What a thing to say!

Annabel's smile was strained. Richard reached out his hand towards Dave to shake.

'I was just saying exactly the same thing,' said Richard.

'Well, this is off to a great start, isn't it?' said Annabel.

Jacqui, who had opened her arms for a hug, let them drop to her sides when she realised that the gesture would not be reciprocated. Annabel put out her hand and they shook on it instead. Jacqui tried not to let her disappointment show. Dave also shook his daughter's hand. It was as though they were meeting a local councillor to talk about a planning application. No one looking in on the scene would have guessed what was really going on.

Dave ushered Annabel to a seat on the sofa where he

had been sitting. She tucked herself right up against the arm, leaving as much space as possible between her and Jacqui at the other end.

'We thought we'd wait until you got here before we ordered,' Jacqui explained. 'They do a good cream tea here. The girls at work treated me for my sixtieth birthday.'

'You're never sixty?' said Richard.

'Oh, aren't you sweet,' said Jacqui. 'I'm afraid I am. Since your Annabel must be—'

'Forty-three,' said Annabel flatly.

'Yes. Forty-three. I knew that.'

'Yes. We knew that,' said Dave. 'But she doesn't look it, does she?'

'Youthful looks must run in the family,' said Richard.

Annabel rewarded him with another strained smile.

'So . . .' said Jacqui.

'So,' said Richard.

'Did you get here via the ring road?' Dave asked.

'I don't think there's any other way,' said Richard.

The conversation stalled. The four virtual strangers sat in silence for a while and all looked up gratefully when the ever-hopeful waitress reappeared with the menus she'd been trying to push all afternoon.

'Kitchen closes in ten minutes,' she said.

Chapter Thirty-Six

Jacqui and Annabel

Everyone ordered cream teas. It seemed like the only thing they could do, given how hard the waitress had been trying to get Jacqui and Dave to order something. The food, when it arrived, looked delicious and Richard and Dave dived on their scones straight away. Neither Annabel nor Jacqui touched anything, though both dutifully buttered their scones as though they might. Like mother, like daughter.

The conversation stuttered. There was so much to talk about, of course, and yet where to begin? It was all too serious, too huge. So, instead of diving straight into the deep water and talking about the circumstances of Annabel's birth, the newly reunited family talked about the traffic on the way to the hotel. They talked about how much time the Bensons had allocated to the journey that day because about three years ago, they had been invited to a wedding reception at this very same hotel, back when the Ridgeview had another owner and another name, and they'd arrived after everyone else was already seated. And the story about that wedding led to a brief discussion of the weather. The wedding had been rained on. In July! You could never rely on the British summer, could you? But wasn't the weather great this year? The *Express* said it was going to be a difficult winter though.

Richard observed that the *Express* always seemed to lead with a weather story. No matter what was going on in the rest of the world: war, famine, royal weddings, the *Express* always seemed to be warning of drought or floods or both. Not that Richard and Annabel really read the *Express*, he added as an afterthought. The Bensons claimed they didn't get it either. Dave said he was loyal to the *Sun*. Richard struggled not to look at his wife to see her reaction to that.

But it was so much easier to remain on the weather and the tabloids than talk about the other thing. The adoption.

They made small talk for the best part of an hour. The waitress came and took the plates away. She asked the two women if there was something wrong with the scones. Both were extravagant in their assurances that there was nothing wrong with the scones whatsoever. It was simply that they weren't hungry.

'All right,' said the girl, who would help herself once she was safely behind the swinging doors to the kitchen.

With the table cleared, Jacqui placed her handbag in the space and opened it to finally pull out an envelope of photographs.

'We thought you might like to see these,' she told Annabel. 'I know you've had a look at my Facebook page, but there isn't much old stuff on there. This will make it easier for me to explain what's gone on since you were born.'

Annabel shuffled forward to the edge of the sofa so that she could better see the photographs, which Jacqui now laid on the table one by one. There were pictures of a young woman in the sixties.

'That's me two years before you were born.'

Annabel tried not to see the resemblance between Jacqui and herself at the same age but it was undoubtedly there in the way Jacqui looked up through her fringe and in her shy smile.

'Lovely dress,' said Richard.

Next Jacqui laid down a picture of a young couple. He was in a badly fitting suit. She was in a blue dress with shoulder pads.

'That's me and your dad getting married.'

'My dad?'

'Dave. Sorry. That's me and Dave getting married. That was about ten years after you were born.'

'You really were apart for ten years?'

'Yes.'

Jacqui told the story at last.

'We were childhood sweethearts.' She looked at Dave as she said that and he reached across the table to take her hand. 'I went to the girls' school and Dave went to the boys'. At the end of the day, the boys used to walk to the bus station past our school and some of them would hang around and try to chat us up. Dave was shy but I liked the look of him. He had a haircut like David Cassidy. I thought he was a total dish.'

Jacqui looked at the wedding photograph. 'He'd lost a bit of his hair by then.'

Richard asked, 'Have you got any photos from when you first met?'

'No,' said Jacqui. 'No, I'm afraid I haven't. I did but . . . After what . . . after what happened, I just couldn't look at them. I didn't know if I'd ever see Dave again and it was just too painful to think about. I'm afraid I threw them all away.'

'It was for the best,' said Dave. 'I looked like a right plonker with that haircut.'

'You looked lovely,' said Jacqui firmly. 'And I fell in love with you right away.'

'Could have fooled me!' said Dave. 'She made me take her out four Saturdays in a row before she even let me have a peck on the cheek.'

'Annabel was the same,' said Richard.

'No I wasn't,' said Annabel.

Jacqui carried on with her story. 'So, we were fifteen when we first got together. It was all very innocent. Dave used to wait for me every afternoon after school and he'd walk me to the bus stop. I wasn't allowed out on school nights but I was allowed to see him on a Saturday. We'd go to the cinema and get our tea at the chip shop on the way home. Dave always walked me right back to my house if we were out after dark. He was always a proper gentleman.'

Annabel nodded. But her nod was not so much one of agreement as one that said 'go on'. All this reminiscing was taking up time they didn't have.

'Dave wasn't in Coventry when I found out I was pregnant. He was away doing an apprenticeship. We'd had a bit of a row before he went but I was sure that we would be back on again when he came home at Christmas. I told my mother about the baby first. She seemed to be all right about it and I thought that every-thing was going to be fine. But then she told my dad and suddenly everything was different. He wasn't happy in the least and after they'd talked about it, Mum said that when it came down to it they were both in agree-ment. There was no way I was blackening the family name with an illegitimate child.

'I said that Dave would marry me when I told him all about it but Mum told me I was dreaming if I thought Dave would be pleased. She said that he had abandoned me already, when he left Coventry to do that apprentice scheme. He was trying to better himself and he would probably want to get rid of the baby so he didn't get dragged back down. I don't know why I believed them.

'If I'd just been stronger,' Jacqui gave an anguished snort. 'If I'd just written like I wanted to, instead of listening to Mum and Dad. But they persuaded me they knew best and when Mum said that she'd heard a rumour that Dave had a new girlfriend, I didn't know what else to do.'

Jacqui could not keep from crying.

Dave searched in his pockets for a handkerchief but found none. Richard offered his own, which was perfectly clean and nicely pressed. It was one of the things Annabel loved about him. His habit of carrying a proper clean cotton hanky when everyone else went for Kleenex.

Jacqui blew her nose loudly.

'I never stopped thinking about you. You were in my mind every single day. There wasn't a single night went by when I didn't pray that you were safe and happy with your new family.'

'I had a very happy childhood,' Annabel interrupted.

'That's all I hoped for. That they were looking after you properly and giving you love.'

'I had all the love I needed,' Annabel confirmed.

'They were great,' said Richard. 'Annabel's parents. I mean, her adoptive parents.'

'You can just say "my parents",' Annabel corrected him. 'Dad died three years ago but Mum is still a huge part of my life. She's the centre of my family, in fact.'

'I'm so happy to hear that,' said Jacqui. 'So happy.' She let out another honking great sob. 'Oh, I'm sorry. I told myself I mustn't get all emotional.'

'But it's a very emotional time,' said Richard. 'It's OK, Jacqui. We understand, don't we, Annabel?'

Annabel just nodded.

'Oh, I'm such an embarrassment. People will be wondering what on earth is wrong with me.'

There was no one else in the room and the waitress had long since gone home, having placed the bill on the edge of the table.

'Do you want to carry on?' Richard asked. 'You don't have to.'

'Of course I do.' Jacqui pulled out the next photo. It was of herself and Dave and two little girls. 'Chelsea and Ronnie. Your sisters.'

A rare shot in which neither was giving the person behind the camera the finger, thought Annabel.

'And this is you,' said Jacqui. She placed a Polaroid photograph so old and faded it was almost blank on the table next to Annabel. 'This is the only picture I had of you. One of the nurses at the mother and baby home took it for me. You'd just had a bath. Look at that little tuft of hair.'

The photograph had obviously been taken out and looked at a thousand times. It was creased and dirty. One corner was all but ready to fall off.

Annabel picked the photo up and looked at it but it was Richard who said what she was thinking.

'Izzy had a tuft of hair just like that,' he said. 'It stuck up like the hair on one of those troll dolls. We could never get it to lie down flat.'

'Runs in the family,' said Dave.

Annabel felt tears pricking her eyes.

Chapter Thirty-Seven

Annabel

The only photographs Annabel had with her were on her iPhone and there was nothing on there that went anywhere near as far back as the photographs Jacqui had brought along. Annabel had felt uncomfortable with the idea of showing the Bensons photographs from her childhood with the Cartwrights. She wanted that piece of her to be private from them still, partly out of respect for Sarah and partly to protect herself. But Richard had insisted that they had to show Jacqui and Dave a photograph of Izzy at least and then they could tell the story of the recent weeks and, with luck, the Bensons would draw conclusions as to how they might help without Annabel and Richard having to be explicit. It was worth a try.

'I took this photograph of Izzy about two weeks ago,' said Annabel, handing her iPhone to Jacqui. Jacqui smiled broadly as she reached out for the phone. As soon as she saw the photograph, however, her expression changed, just as Annabel had known it would.

'She's . . .'

'She was in hospital, yes.'

'What happened?'

'She was taken ill at a festival. We think she must have eaten something poisonous.'

Richard half-frowned at Annabel as she trotted out

the lie, though it was probably a lie he would have told too.

'She had a violent reaction to it which caused her to have kidney failure.'

Jacqui put her hand across her mouth.

'She's at home now but she's still on dialysis. She'll have to do that every night until she gets a kidney transplant. We've got the equipment in the house.'

'Oh my goodness!'

'Her consultant is pleased with her progress and she's much better now she's at home but, of course, the sooner the transplant can happen the better.'

'Whatever must she have eaten?' Jacqui mused.

'The toxicology tests were inconclusive, but it doesn't matter,' said Richard. 'The outcome is what it is. It's just the most awful bad luck.'

'It's terrible,' said Jacqui. But she didn't make the next logical, to Annabel, step. And she wouldn't for the remaining time they were at the hotel that day. Eventually Annabel could bear it no longer. She said that they needed to leave. To get back home for Izzy.

'But we'll see you again?' Jacqui sounded desperate, like a teenage girl at the end of a date she'd had such high hopes for.

'Of course,' said Richard. 'Of course.'

While the question had yet to be asked . . .

Outside, Annabel sank into the car seat, thankful that the Bensons were parked on the other side of the hotel so there could be no protracted goodbyes.

'Thank God that's over,' she said.

Richard took her hand.

'They seemed like nice people,' he said. 'Decent, ordinary, kindly. I'm ninety-nine per cent sure they'll agree to help us. A hundred per cent, actually. We just have to find the right moment to ask.'

Annabel cried. 'Why didn't they just guess what we wanted?'

'I don't know. Perhaps it will cross their minds later. It was a weird moment for everyone. And not everyone knows that live donation is even possible.'

'Rubbish. Everyone knows you don't have to be dead to give a kidney. Why do I have to be related to the only pair of thickos in the world who don't?'

'Annabel, please. Try to be open-minded about them. I understand this isn't just about Izzy. You're bound to be feeling a bit shell-shocked.'

'This is daft. I'm a grown woman. Why did I feel like a little girl in there? Why did I feel so angry with them? I hated them. I wanted to pick up the teapot and pour it all over Jacqui's head. What was she wearing? She was dressed like she was going to a wedding, for heaven's sake. I don't want them to be part of my life.'

But they would have to be until they helped Izzy or until the Buchanans knew for sure that they couldn't.

Chapter Thirty-Eight

Jacqui

Jacqui and Dave drove back to Coventry in a state of some shock. When they got to the house, Jacqui told Dave she didn't think she was in a fit state to face her other daughters yet, so they sat in the car, until Jack pressed his face against the window and stared out at them. Once they'd been rumbled, they had to go in.

'What was she like?' everyone wanted to know.

'Does she play cricket?' asked Jack.

Jacqui ruffled Jack's hair. 'I didn't have a chance to ask, love.'

'Did she seem like one of us?' Sophie asked.

'She was very nice,' said Jacqui.

'They came in a Porsche,' said Dave.

'Bloody hell. Definitely not one of us, then,' said Ronnie.

'But she looked like you,' Jacqui told Ronnie then.

'Only thinner?'

'Not much. But she's got the same eyes. And when she smiles, she looks a bit like Chelsea. And when she frowns, you can see a bit of Granddad Bill.'

'Poor woman,' Chelsea laughed.

'Her voice is dead posh. She went to a private school. And then to Oxford.'

'I've been to Oxford,' said Jack, eager to join in.

'Not like your new auntie did,' said Ronnie.

'We went on the train,' Jack remembered. 'Did she go in a car?'

'Go and see if Granddad Bill wants a cup of tea,' Ronnie told her son. 'We need to talk seriously to Grandma and Gramps.'

The adult Bensons and Sophie gathered round the kitchen table, scene of so many big discussions, such as what Ronnie would do when she got pregnant.

'It was her house we went to in Little Bissingden that day, Ronnie. You were right.'

'Did she recognise you from there?'

'I don't think so.'

'Don't you think it's bizarre that we walked around their house and had no idea?'

'It's quite a coincidence,' said Chelsea. 'But I suppose it was the wrong context.'

'And Annabel was very busy that day. There were at least twenty other people with us,' Jacqui said in mitigation. 'Anyway, they haven't lived there long. They used to live in South Kensington.'

Chelsea and Ronnie already knew all this, of course, from their Google searches, but they pretended it was all new information.

'They still keep a flat in town for when Richard has to work late. They've got a dog called Leander. A black Labrador.'

'What about their daughter? She's the same age as Sophie,' Ronnie said.

'Just a little older,' said Jacqui. 'Dave, you tell them, will you? I don't think I can.'

Dave explained the full story, including Izzy's plight.

'Wow,' said Sophie, remembering the girl in the big house. The one who had been so full of herself? So privileged. 'She needs to have a kidney transplant.'

'She could be waiting a long time.'

'Just goes to show,' said Ronnie with an unfortunate hint of smugness in her voice. 'Money can't buy you happiness.'

'Don't,' said Chelsea. 'She's just a kid . . . Are you seeing them again, Mum? Will you get to meet Izzy?'

'I hope so,' said Jacqui. 'I just wish I thought Daisy liked us more.'

'It might be a good start to call her Annabel,' Ronnie observed.

Just then the kitchen door crashed open. It was Jack and Granddad Bill. In the electric wheelchair.

Jack was waving one arm ahead of him. 'Exterminate! Exterminate!' he said in his best Dalek voice.

'Mind the paintwork!' cried Jacqui as Jack steered Granddad Bill's chair into the doorframe. Jack jerked the chair forwards, crashing into a kitchen cabinet. Then backwards into a radiator. Then forwards again into Chelsea's chair. There was much shouting and Granddad Bill let out an enormous fart in the excitement. Jack jumped clear of Bill's lap and rolled on the floor.

'I need my gas mask!' he cried.

Granddad Bill had given Jack his old World War Two gas mask the previous Christmas. It was among Jack's favourite things.

'Stand up, young man,' Bill told him. 'This is nothing compared to the mustard gas they faced in the trenches.'

Jack stood up and staggered around the kitchen table, hamming it up for his audience. Granddad Bill forced out another fart for comedy's sake.

Sophie put her head in her hands.

'I can't wait until Annabel meets those two,' she said.

Chapter Thirty-Nine

Annabel

Unable to sleep again between her churning thoughts and the baby backflipping inside her, Annabel got out of bed and wandered down to the kitchen. There she looked through the album of photos her adoptive parents, her *real* parents – Sarah and Humfrey – had put together to mark the occasion of her fortieth birthday. Annabel had dug the album out that morning, while she was still wondering whether or not she should show it to Jacqui and Dave. She decided she was glad that she hadn't.

There were photographs in that album from every phase of Annabel's life. There were photographs from a holiday in Tuscany the year of Annabel's fortieth, on which Sarah and Humfrey had joined them. There were photos of Annabel with Izzy on her first day at secondary school. Izzy's first day at primary school. Coming out of the hospital with Izzy in a car seat, looking tired and slightly disoriented but very happy all the same. Then, going backwards, there were wedding photos. Annabel wearing that dress that had seemed so fashionable at the time but now looked incredibly dated with its voluminous skirt and huge leg-of-mutton sleeves. Ghost of Princess Diana.

Going further back still, there was Annabel getting engaged to Richard. Annabel graduating. Annabel matriculating. Annabel revising for her A levels in the garden at her parents' house. Picking up the Latin prize. A photograph from her fifteenth birthday. Her smile tight because she was wearing those train-track braces. Annabel's own first day at secondary school. Primary school. Her first steps.

On the very first page of the album, there was Sarah standing on the steps of the beautiful Victorian house Annabel had grown up in, cradling a tiny baby in a white blanket.

'That was the day we brought you home,' Sarah had told her. That was the beginning.

But now Annabel knew what had gone on before. All that sordid unhappiness. The mother and baby home and the secret teenage pregnancy. It felt like it had happened to someone else but at the same time, it was as though that knowledge had blown away the foundations of who she really was. How could those few short weeks with Jacqui suddenly seem to overshadow all those happy years with Sarah and Humfrey?

Annabel sank into the sofa with her head in her hands. It was awful and she felt so angry. The anger wouldn't abate no matter how hard she reasoned with herself.

She knew, logically, that all those years ago, when she was just a child herself, Jacqui had made a very brave and responsible decision with regard to Annabel's future. But Annabel couldn't make the thought stick. She couldn't find compassion for overeager Jacqui or hopeless Dave. They were so different from anyone she knew.

She was sinking back into the lowest place she had ever been, where she felt utterly unlovable. Exactly the kind of child that you would want to give away.

And yet she did still have to deal with these people.

She had to call them up and arrange to meet them again though she would rather have done anything else. And the baby that kicked and flickered inside her was their grandchild, no matter how she wished it wasn't the case.

In the end, Richard did the honours. He called Jacqui and Dave from work the next day and invited them to Sunday lunch at the Great House the following weekend. He asked them to pass on the invitation to Ronnie and Chelsea and whomever they wanted to bring along with them. He couldn't remember which of them had the partner and children and which of them lived in London and worked for a magazine.

Ronnie was delighted to accept the invitation. Chelsea agreed to come too. With Ronnie's partner and kids and Granddad Bill, Annabel would be cooking for eleven.

Cooking for eleven was no mean feat. Such an undertaking meant that Annabel would have to start preparations on Saturday morning. Especially since there wasn't a single member of the Benson family who didn't have some unusual dietary requirement. From Bill's false teeth to Ronnie's refusal to eat anything remotely resembling a green vegetable.

'Why don't you order in from Domino's and be done with it,' suggested Izzy.

'Because I want them to know that I have made an effort,' said Annabel, as she wrestled with an enormous turkey. When it came to feeding eleven, a turkey was the perfect option. Especially since Sophie would not eat red meat for ecological reasons and Bill's teeth couldn't cope with it.

As she slammed the oven door shut – the turkey only just fitted – Annabel wished once again that Sarah were by her side. Annabel was not entirely fluent in the art of cooking. For her, it was more like a science project than the art natural cooks believed it to be. When Annabel cooked, the kitchen counters were covered in timers, thermometers, calculators and scales. She had never quite picked up Sarah's ability to gently pierce a roasting bird with a skewer and recognise the moment when it was perfectly done. They'd invited Sarah to join them, of course, but she'd declined, claiming a prior engagement. Knowing her mother, Annabel suspected the truth was that she didn't really feel ready to meet the Bensons. Annabel could understand that. She wasn't sure that she was ready to see them again either.

Later that day, when Jacqui assured Annabel that she too had never been confident about roasting meat and always erred on the side of cremation, Annabel's heart would sag a little at yet another indicator of their consanguinity.

Richard did his best to help. He made a meringue. His speciality. Like most men Annabel had known, Richard's kitchen repertoire was limited but what he could make was flashy crowd-pleasers. He was in charge of alcohol too, his mantra being 'if in doubt, add wine'. Annabel wished she could add half a bottle of the stuff to herself, straight down the throat. But of course the baby prevented that. Annabel wondered how long it would be before Jacqui spotted that she was pregnant. They still hadn't told anyone other than Izzy, Sarah and Dr Devon.

At last, the moment came. The Bensons arrived.
    'They're here,' Izzy called down the stairs.
    'What? All of them?'
    'They've come in convoy.'
    Richard, Annabel, Izzy and Leander formed a

welcoming party. Leander was the most enthusiastic of the four.

With the three sisters all in one place for the first time, Jacqui could not resist getting out her phone to take a snap of them, on the front step of Annabel's manor house.

'I'll take one of you with the three of them if you like,' said Richard.

And then Jack wanted to be in the picture and before anyone could protest, it turned into a full family portrait there on the driveway, complete with Granddad Bill in his Coventry City FC shirt.

'A proper family portrait,' Jacqui sighed.

Chapter Forty

Annabel

Richard, thank goodness, was the consummate host. While Annabel seemed practically to have lost the ability to talk, Richard set about making introductions and ushering the Bensons into the house and handing out drinks to all and sundry. Once the gin and tonics were on the go, the awkwardness of the photograph on the doorstep began to fade away. There was easy conversation to be had on the subject of the Benson family's journey from Coventry.

'Roadworks. Should have come the other way,' said Dave.

And Chelsea's journey to Coventry from London.

'Replacement bus services. Always a nightmare at the weekend.'

And how strange it was that most of the Bensons had been to this house before, though they hadn't seen this room.

'Well, you know,' said Annabel, 'not everything is for the general public.'

Annabel thought she saw her new sisters share a look at that.

Annabel only realised how anxious she had been about meeting Ronnie and Chelsea for the first time ('Or for the second time,' as Ronnie reminded her) now that they were sitting in her living room. Ronnie was not as big as she had looked in most of the photos on Facebook and neither was she quite so hard-faced. She would look a good deal better if she simply sat up straight. Chelsea was different. She was dressed very stylishly, as befitted her magazine job, but she was delicate. She had more than a hint of vulnerability about her and seemed keen to be liked. Annabel thought she would probably have most in common with her. She was most at home in her surroundings.

In contrast, Ronnie's partner Mark seemed utterly discombobulated by the Great House and all but doffed his cap every time Richard asked him if he needed a top-up or some peanuts or anything else at all. His deference was almost painful. Richard kept having to tell him to sit down. There was absolutely no need for him to fetch a drink himself. Richard was their host.

Meanwhile Granddad Bill had captivated Leander, who rested his head on the old chap's lap as he sat in his electric wheelchair by the fireplace.

'Always keeps Trebor mints in his pocket,' said Dave when Annabel observed that Granddad Bill had made a canine friend. So much for Leander being a good judge of character. 'You all right there, Dad?'

'I've won the bloody lottery,' Bill said, raising his glass. He seemed to say that all the time.

Sophie, Annabel's new niece, was very different from Izzy's school friends at the same age. They were so much more confident around adults. While the likes of Jessica had no trouble whatsoever making conversation, Sophie sat and said nothing unless she was spoken to first. Her shyness was reflected in her posture. It was as though she was trying to sink into the sofa. She couldn't even look at Izzy.

Then there was Jack. Thank goodness. Whenever the

conversation seemed like it might be drifting back into silence, Jack could be relied upon to get things going again. He seemed to take an instant shine to Izzy, who recognised the significance of the tatty plastic wand Jack had brought with him.

'You know about sonic screwdrivers!' he trilled with delight.

'Who doesn't?' said Izzy, rolling her eyes. 'I've seen every episode of *Doctor Who* there is. Apart from the really old ones before Christopher Eccleston.'

Jack gazed at Izzy as though he was in love.

And of course he asked about the suit of armour he had almost knocked down the stairs. Annabel assured him that no harm was done.

'Then perhaps I could try it on?' he suggested shyly.

'Jack!' Ronnie hissed at him. 'No, you can't.'

'I think it's a bit delicate for that,' Annabel agreed.

'Then can I see the dungeon?' Jack negotiated. 'You said you had a dungeon,' he reminded her.

'Ah, the dungeon,' said Richard. 'Perhaps we should go there right away. Follow me.'

The 'dungeon' was now Richard's wine cellar. In fact, it had always been a cellar. No prisoner had ever been held there. Still, it was dark, damp and dusty enough to fuel any child's imagination.

While Jack was thus occupied, Jacqui and Ronnie apologised profusely for the day of the village fete. If only they had known who Annabel was back then. They would have paid more attention to her *very* interesting talk. How on earth did she keep a place like this going? Did she have many servants, asked Ronnie.

'Just cleaners,' said Annabel.

'How many?' Ronnie wanted to know.

'Two,' said Annabel.

'But you don't go to work?'

'Not at the moment,' said Annabel. 'No.'

Ronnie shared a look with Jacqui.

'But there is a lot of dusting,' Annabel said.

Annabel was grateful to be able to return to the kitchen when the timer on the Aga let her know the bird was done.

'Can I come and help you in there?' Jacqui asked.

'No,' said Annabel, with slightly more force than she intended to. 'I mean, no thank you, Jacqui. You're my guests. Please just make yourselves comfortable.'

'Hard to get comfortable when it's so obvious she's scared we'll mark the settee,' said Ronnie when Annabel wasn't quite out of earshot.

Chapter Forty-One

Annabel

Was the turkey done? Annabel had no idea, but she took it out of the oven anyway and left it on the side to rest. Richard would do the carving. If it still looked pink, they would simply put it back in the Aga.

Sarah had texted to see how Annabel was getting on.

Going OK so far, Annabel texted in response. No point worrying her mum with anything more detailed.

Lunch was laid out in the dining room that day. Annabel had rather hoped that the weather would be good enough to eat outside – the BBC had promised the Indian summer would continue for another few days – but the gods were not on her side and it had been grey and cold all morning. The dining room it would have to be, with a table protector beneath the crisp white tablecloth to protect the polished walnut.

There was soup to serve first. It was tomato soup. Not Annabel's first choice but Richard had told her it would be a crowd-pleaser. And what a crowd to please. Annabel had thought she was doing OK with her new sisters but Ronnie's comment as she left the living room had disabused her of that.

She poured the soup into the tureen and shouted, 'Lunch is served.'

The Bensons filed into the dining room and seemed to take an age to choose seats. For once, Annabel hadn't even thought about a table plan. She found herself between Dave and Granddad Bill.

'A rose between two thorns,' Dave said.

Fortunately, nobody had any objection to tomato soup. The fresh bread rolls too were accepted eagerly. Mark laughed as he took one.

'I thought you were going to make us eat oysters or some weird shit like that,' he said.

'Daddy!' Jack piped up. 'Don't say shit!'

'You shouldn't be saying it either,' said Ronnie, reaching out to tweak Jack's ear.

'Well, all I can say is, I'm bloody glad we're eating something I recognise,' said Mark.

'He said bloody!' Jack pointed out.

Mark pointed two fingers at his son as if to shoot him. Then he reached for his dessertspoon and began to eat.

Richard flashed a look at Annabel that told her not to point out Mark's mistake.

'All this cutlery,' Jacqui exclaimed. 'How many courses are we having?'

'Soup, turkey, cheese . . .'

'Leave room for my meringue,' said Richard.

'You made a meringue? Aren't you the perfect husband,' Jacqui said.

'Mark doesn't ever make anything but a mess when he's in the kitchen,' said Ronnie.

'That's not fair. I made you breakfast in bed the other day.'

'Only because you wanted to leave me with the kids while you spent the whole day fishing.'

'Ronnie,' said Jacqui. 'Annabel will think you're always bickering, you two. And you've only just got engaged.'

'After sixteen years!' Ronnie said to Annabel. 'Sixteen years I had to wait for him to make an honest woman of me.'

'You've always been honest,' said Mark. 'At least when it comes to my failings.'

There was a moment's silence while it seemed that Ronnie and Mark were considering having a full-on domestic. But Annabel need not have worried. It wouldn't stay quiet for long. While she was still racking her brain for something to say, Granddad Bill let out an enormous belch.

'Pardon me for being rude. It was not me, it was my food,' Granddad Bill said by way of an apology.

'Granddad Bill can burp to order,' Jack elaborated.

'I can indeed. It's my superpower, isn't it, Jack?'

'He does it to music. Show Auntie Annabel.' Jack clapped.

'Please, don't,' said Jacqui. 'Granddad . . .'

But it was too late. While Annabel could only sit and inwardly scream, Granddad Bill launched into a rendition of 'My Old Man's a Dustman' with a burp after every word. Jack was thrilled. He joined in with the words he knew.

'Bill,' said Jacqui. 'Please. We're at the dinner table.'

But Granddad Bill went for a second verse, while Jack got up from his chair on the other side of the table and did a little jig, pulling at imaginary braces and doffing an invisible cap. His Victorian urchin routine.

'Jack! Sit down!' said Ronnie.

Jack took no notice.

'Jack,' Chelsea tried. 'Mummy's asked you to sit down.'

'But we're nearly finished, Auntie Chelsea,' said Jack brightly. 'Just one more verse!'

'Bill,' Jacqui begged.

'*He wears cor blimey trousers . . .* burp . . .' Granddad Bill was not to be stopped. He was building to a grand finale.

Annabel closed her eyes in an attempt to lessen the horror like a child who imagines that because they can't see anybody, no one can see them either. Richard pressed his fist to his mouth as he tried not to burst out laughing. Izzy was wide-eyed with astonishment. And the awful thing was, it was rather impressive. Granddad Bill could hold a tune and the burps provided an oddly effective percussion. He was as good as anything they'd seen on *Britain's Got Talent*.

Eventually, the song ended and Richard and Izzy clapped politely.

'Well, that was . . .' Annabel gave a game shrug.

'I'm sorry,' said Jacqui.

'No, really. It was quite . . . something.'

But the trauma was not over.

Now Granddad Bill took Annabel's hand.

'I've won the bloody lottery,' he said. 'Having a grand-daughter as lovely as you.'

'Thank you, Bill,' said Annabel.

'So I'd like to sing you this song . . .'

'No!' said Jacqui, Ronnie and Chelsea at once.

The women were overruled.

Jack raised his arms like a conductor and counted Granddad Bill in.

'A-one, a-two, a-three!'

And Granddad Bill began.

'*Daisy . . .* burp . . . *Daisy . . .* burp . . . *Give me your answer do . . .*'

'For crying out loud, Granddad. Her name's not Daisy,' said Ronnie. 'Mum! Tell him to shut up. Shut up!'

'Granddad Bill,' Chelsea pleaded. 'Please. We've heard enough now.'

'Oh my God, oh my God, oh my God,' Sophie muttered.

Richard and Izzy both looked in panic at Annabel. She forced herself to smile.

'Well, isn't this great,' she said. 'What a lovely song. Thank you.'

'*I'm half crazy* . . . burp.'

Dave started to sing along. Until Jacqui pinched him.

'Bill, that's quite enough,' Jacqui said.

He wasn't stopping.

Time seemed to stand still in the dining room of the Great House. Jacqui covered her eyes. Chelsea and Ronnie slid a little lower in their seats. Annabel could hardly breathe.

Eventually, Bill ran out of steam. Or gas. Jack led the applause, leaping up from his seat to give a standing ovation, oblivious to the tension all around him.

'Sit down,' Ronnie hissed at him. This time, Jack did as he was told. He knew when he'd crossed the line.

'I am so embarrassed,' said Jacqui, on the verge of tears. 'I've never been so badly shown up. Bill, you have really excelled yourself this time.'

'It's OK,' said Annabel. 'Really. I enjoyed it.'

'No, you didn't. And it isn't OK. Bill, you need to apologise.'

'What for? I was singing a song about her loveliness.'

'Seriously,' said Richard. 'There's no need for anyone to be embarrassed or apologise. We feel thoroughly entertained. Don't we, Izzy?'

'Oh yeah,' said Izzy. 'I've never seen anything like it.'

'Granddad Bill can play the spoons as well,' Jack told her proudly. 'He learned in the war.'

Another ping from one of the timers in the kitchen gave Annabel an excuse to escape.

The rest of that lunch passed like a lifetime in purgatory.

Chapter Forty-Two

Sophie and Izzy

After lunch, Sophie was invited upstairs to Izzy's room. Jack wanted to come too but Richard persuaded him to join him for a walk around the gardens with Leander instead. Jack happily accepted a chance to throw a ball for the overgrown puppy.

'My room's this way,' said Izzy to her new cousin.

They carefully avoided the fact that Sophie already knew the way to Izzy's room because she had been inside it before. Sophie felt a little uncomfortable as she got to the landing where she and Izzy had last met. Would Izzy mention that meeting now? She didn't. It was as though she was pretending that they had never met before. Just as Annabel had pretended that she didn't really remember Jack's tussle with the suit of armour. And they all just carried on making small talk after Granddad Bill burped his way through 'Daisy, Daisy'. Stilted small talk, admittedly.

Perhaps that was the way posh people dealt with embarrassing situations. By pretending they had never happened. But Sophie sort of wished that Izzy would say something about the day of the village fete, so they could get it out there and clear it away.

Izzy opened the door. The room was much lighter than the landing and it took Sophie's eyes a little while to adjust to the difference. It was more cluttered than she remembered. The single designer dress still hung from the back of the door, but the armchair was piled high with clothes too: designer jeans and expensive branded T-shirts. Sophie caught sight of an Armani Jeans label. And there was Izzy's enviable array of gadgetry. The laptop, the iPad, the phone. The speakers. The flat-screen TV.

But there was something else. Sophie stared at it for a second before she realised what it was and quickly averted her eyes. It was definitely not the latest gadget from Apple.

'Oh yeah,' said Izzy. 'That's my dialysis machine. I bet you wish you had one of those.'

'How often do you . . .'

'Have to do it? Every night.'

'And where . . .' Sophie started to ask but chickened out.

'I've got a catheter fitted here.' Izzy pulled down the elasticated waist of her trousers to show Sophie the tube. 'I plug myself in around ten. The machine pumps fluid into my stomach and when it sucks it back out, it sucks out all the toxins my kidneys can't process with it. That's the technical description,' Izzy joked. 'It's called peritoneal dialysis. I'm mostly asleep while it's happening but if I wake up I watch *Game of Thrones* or something. Or go online.'

Sophie nodded.

'Or I do this . . . Look,' said Izzy, lifting up a book that had been resting on the windowsill. 'I want to show you something. Remember that graffiti that was supposedly done by the princes during the civil war? I'm adding some of my own. It's taking ages but God knows I have to spend a lot of time sitting up here now.'

Sophie traced the spiky 'I' and 'Z' with her fingers.

'Won't your mum go nuts if she finds out?'

'I shall tell her that in years to come, the people who own this house will show their visitors my scratches too. I'm just as much a prisoner as the princes were now.'

'Does it hurt?' Sophie asked. 'I mean, the dialysis.'

'Not really. You soon get used to it. And being able to do it at home is miles better than having to go into hospital three times a week. The thing that really pisses me off is that when I'm not hooked up I can't just have a drink of water when I feel like it. I'm only allowed five hundred mils a day. It sounds like a lot but it isn't. I used to get through two cans of Diet Coke and a litre and a half of Evian every day. The dehydration. It's making my skin look like shit. My lips are dry all the time. My idea of a serious treat these days is to be able to suck an ice cube.'

Sophie suddenly felt very self-conscious as she sipped from the glass of fizzy water she had carried upstairs.

'God, I wish I could just grab that drink out of your hand and knock it back in one,' said Izzy. 'Water, water everywhere . . .'

Sophie put the glass down on Izzy's desk. An exam paper lay among the clutter. Maths A level. According to Jacqui, Izzy was so bright that she had been going to take some of her A levels early. Before she got sick.

'Are you going to be able to go back to school this year?'

'That's the plan. They're sending me loads of stuff to do at home but it's difficult to concentrate, you know? I sit down and try to do some maths but all of a sudden my head is back at the festival and I'm thinking how it would be if I'd just said no.'

'So, you did take something? I thought that was probably what happened. Only your mum just said you were "taken ill". She said you might have eaten a poisonous mushroom.'

'Did she? That's funny. I'm in this desperate position and she still wants people to think we're the perfect family. I mean, Annabel Buchanan would never have a daughter stupid enough to take drugs, would she? I took an E. Actually, I took three . . .'

Sophie shrugged to convey that she was cool with that. She wasn't judgemental.

'Did you take them often?' she asked.

'It was my first time.'

'That's harsh,' said Sophie.

'Tell me about it.'

'First time . . .' Sophie shook her head. 'The very opposite of beginner's luck.'

'What about you? You're going to tell me that you take it all the time and you've never had anything bad happen.'

'I've never taken any drugs,' said Sophie. 'I've never had the money.'

Izzy smiled ruefully.

'And looking at the addicts around the bus station in town, I can't say it ever seemed all that glamorous. I suppose it depends on the circles you move in.'

'Like my friends.'

'Did they take it too?'

'Nope. I was the only one stupid enough.'

'I bet they were just too scared. You were daring. You had the guts.'

'You're very kind but I can't tell you how I wish I'd been more of a coward. You know, at first, right after it happened, the girls who were with me would all come round all the time, but now that school has started again, I don't really see any of them. They send me messages on Facebook but I don't really talk to them either. I don't think they know what to say any more. I think when they came to see me in hospital, they didn't imagine I would still be ill all these months later. Visiting your mate in intensive care is glamorous. Visiting her in her bedroom while she dialyses? Not so much. I know Jessica probably feels guilty because it was her boyfriend who gave me the pills. And Chloe's mother probably doesn't let her talk to me. She thinks I'm a bad influence. Not any more though, eh? Hey, kids! This is what happens when you take drugs. You get to spend half your time flushing your wee through a machine. I should be in one of those public service ads.'

Sophie didn't know what to say.

'Look,' said Izzy. 'I know you're probably not mentioning it because you're embarrassed but I do remember meeting you on the day of the fete. And I was a bitch to you and I'm sorry. I hope we can start again, seeing as how it turns out we're cousins.'

'Yeah,' said Sophie. 'Thanks. Why not?'

The girls tentatively bumped fists and went back downstairs.

'I'm sorry about Granddad Bill,' said Sophie just as they were about to go back into the dining room. 'He hasn't always been so embarrassing.'

'Don't worry about it,' said Izzy. 'After all, he's my great-granddad too now.'

Chapter Forty-Three

Annabel

The Bensons left shortly after five. Annabel had worried that they would linger on and she would have to find them something for dinner, but Chelsea had to catch a train back to London and Ronnie was dropping her off at the station. And Granddad Bill had to be taken back home to watch some football match on the telly. Thank goodness. The musical belching had been bad enough but the snoring when he fell asleep by the fire after lunch was truly spectacular. Like listening to planes taking off.

While Izzy went upstairs for a rest, Richard and Annabel started clearing up. After Annabel had expressed her utter horror at Granddad Bill's rendition of 'Daisy, Daisy' it was Ronnie who caught the next blast of Annabel's disappointment.

'How do you think it feels to know I'm related to that? She eats like she has never seen cutlery before.'

'I've seen far worse,' said Richard.

'At children's parties, perhaps.'

'Sweetheart, she's not that bad. I thought she was trying really hard to be friendly. She probably just feels a bit out of her depth here. Hell, *I* feel a bit out of my depth here sometimes. We do live in a bloody stately home.'

Annabel managed a smile.

'So cut her some slack. She seems like an intelligent woman who just didn't have the advantages we had. She probably went to some awful comprehensive with three thousand pupils. If she'd been at Benenden . . .'

'I can't imagine it.'

'I like her husband.'

'He's not her husband,' said Annabel.

'Oh.'

'You heard Jacqui. They got engaged this summer. Sixteen years and two kids after they met.'

'Well, at least they know they like each other,' said Richard, giving his wife a squeeze. 'Their daughter seems quite sweet under all the goth stuff and Jack . . . he's adorable.'

'They must have adopted him,' Annabel sniffed. 'I don't think I've ever had a worse day in my life. I have never felt so uncomfortable in my own home. I felt like I had to justify the way we live the whole time or play down how hard we worked to get here. You saw the way Ronnie looked at everything in the house. She looked at the stamp on the bottom of her coffee cup. I swear it! I felt like she was pricing everything.'

'Perhaps she's just interested in crockery.'

'I don't think she likes us.'

'Perhaps she's reflecting the way you feel right back at you. I think she's wary. That's all. You've got to remember that until you popped up, she was the older sister. She can't help but wonder where her place in the pecking order is now that you've come along.'

'I don't want to be in anyone's pecking order. Least of all hers. We've got nothing in common.'

Richard opened his mouth.

'Don't say it,' Annabel warned him.

Richard had already remarked on the fact that Annabel and Ronnie had the same chocolate brown eyes and their smiles were similar too, though Annabel had the advantage of expensive dentistry.

'This isn't like you, my love.' Richard put an arm round Annabel's shoulders. 'You're a snob, but you're not usually *this much* of a snob. You're a kind person. Why can't you be kind to them?'

'Because I'm afraid that I'm like them,' she said.

The following morning, Ronnie called from work to thank Annabel for hosting the Bensons that Sunday. They had enjoyed themselves enormously. Jack couldn't stop going on about having been allowed to go down into the 'dungeon'. And it was wonderful to meet Izzy. Jack and Sophie both adored Izzy. What a sweet, brave girl she was. It was such a shame she was unwell. It must be such a worry.

'So, I've got something important to ask you,' said Ronnie.

Annabel's heart fluttered. Was she going to ask how they could help Izzy?

No.

'Mark and me. We were wondering if you would like to come to our wedding.'

Annabel's heart sank.

'It's not going to be a posh affair,' said Ronnie. 'It's only in a register office and afterwards at the pub. And it isn't going to be a big party. No more than fifty. But Mum and Dad would like you to be there. Seeing as how it's the first big family event since . . . well, since we got the whole family together. It would mean a lot to Mum. And to me too, of course. It would mean a lot to me and Mark if you and your family could be at our wedding.'

'Thank you,' said Annabel.

'Is that a yes?'

Annabel felt cornered.

'I don't know. I mean, you haven't told us when it is yet.'

'We were talking about it at lunchtime yesterday, me and Richard. It's next weekend. On Saturday.'

Annabel looked out towards the garden as though she might find her response in the flowerbeds. Was it too late to make excuses? Ronnie had talked to Richard about it. What had Richard said? Had he inadvertently revealed that they weren't going to be doing anything the following Saturday and, in doing so, taken away Annabel's hope that she could decline?

'There will be other family there,' said Ronnie. 'Dad's cousins. People like that. You could get to know them.'

'We should get to know them,' said Richard later on. 'Any one of them could be the person we're looking for. In any case, we haven't asked the Bensons to be tested yet and that can only be easier once we've been to the wedding and they start to think of us as part of the gang.'

Annabel closed her eyes.

'And of course we'll take a great present,' said Richard.

'What? What will we take? Where do you think they've got their wedding list? Lidl?'

'Come on,' said Richard. 'All your friends go to Lidl.'

'Only when there's an offer on Bordeaux.'

'Sweetheart, please. It's all for the greater good. And it might be fun. God knows it's got to be better than some of the stuffy affairs we've been to in the past. A wedding reception in a pub. Beer and sausage rolls. What could be better?'

Just about anything could be better in Annabel's opinion, but she duly texted Ronnie to say that they would be delighted to be at her wedding.

Chapter Forty-Four

Chelsea

As soon as she got Annabel's acceptance by text, Ronnie called her younger sister, who was in the office finalising the articles that would be commissioned for *Society*'s January edition.

'I can't believe she's coming to my wedding,' said Ronnie, without even saying 'hello' first.

'It'll be nice,' said Chelsea. 'Mum will be pleased.'

'Yeah. But she's really going to show me up, isn't she? It's meant to be my day and she'll waft in wearing something far more expensive than my wedding dress.'

'Ronnie,' said Chelsea. 'You are going to look like a goddess. I'm going to see to that.'

'I'm going to look fat, is what I'm going to look like'

'Ronnie . . . stop it.'

'Why?' Ronnie asked.

Chelsea didn't tell her since her first counselling session, she had been trying to stop using the 'f' word.

'Just because it isn't helpful. You were really happy last week. You said the wedding was all going to plan.'

'Yeah. That was before Mum made me invite her.'

'By "her" you mean our sister?'

'Who else? What did you think of her, Chelsea? Really?'

'You know what I think. I told you on the drive to the station. I think she's a bit highly strung but she clearly made a huge effort when she had us all over and I'm sure she'll start to warm up eventually. And she seems interesting. Richard is a nice man too. Look how kind he was to Jack. I've never seen an adult fake being interested in *Doctor Who* for so long. There's no way Richard would have married Annabel if she was a total cow.'

'Some men like to be pushed around,' Ronnie observed. 'That much is true.'

'Anyway, I suppose if they do come, they'll have to buy us a wedding present. That could be worth a bit. I looked up both their cars online last night. If they sold the Cayenne and the Aston Martin, they could buy my house. Not that they'd want to. How can my Coventry semi ever compete with the Great House? It's Downton bloody Abbey. Still, I suppose you're more used to such luxurious surroundings.'

'Yep,' said Chelsea. 'It is pretty glamorous in Stockwell.'

'I mean at the magazine. You know what I mean.'

Chelsea knew that most people would consider her job glamorous, but there were moments lately when she wondered whether all magazines like *Society* did was make people miserable as they compared their ordinary lives with the lives of the rich and famous. It was so pervasive. Annabel had a daughter on dialysis, awaiting a kidney transplant, but Ronnie still envied Annabel the car in which she drove to the hospital appointments. What really mattered?

Chelsea had had that very conversation with Adam over the phone just the night before, when he was telling her about his wife Claire, who had died of an aneurysm before she made it to thirty-three, leaving him a widower with sole care of Lily, who was just a tiny baby at the time.

'No one knows how long they've got,' he said and he

was right. Why waste it being envious? The way Chelsea saw it, Ronnie should be enjoying the run-up to her wedding. She was marrying her childhood sweetheart, the father of her two *healthy* children. She wasn't in some kind of competition with Annabel but even if she was, it seemed like she was winning.

But there was no point telling people to count their blessings. If that worked, thought Chelsea, then the United Kingdom would not rank below El Salvador in the world happiness index.

So, Chelsea let Ronnie carry on making her verbal list of the things Annabel had that she would never be able to afford, while at the same time pointing out the failings they represented.

'That wine. Forty quid a bottle. Can't tell the difference between that and a bottle of Jacob's Creek. It's all about snobbery.'

Chelsea knew that deep down her sister was far better than this litany of envy. She was glad when Ronnie finally changed the subject.

'Have you asked Adam if he's going to come to the wedding yet? Have you told him he can bring Lily?'

'I'm going to ask him later,' Chelsea promised. 'Though it's early days, Ronnie. You know that. A family wedding might be a bit much.'

'We've known him longer than Annabel and she's coming,' Ronnie pointed out.

That evening, Chelsea had another date with Adam, but this time they would not be going out. Instead, Adam had invited Chelsea to his house in south London where he would cook dinner for Chelsea and six-year-old Lily.

Chelsea was slightly nervous about meeting Lily again. On the last day of their holiday in Lanzarote, Lily had been quite sweet, even holding Chelsea's hand at one point. But prior to that, she had been somewhat difficult. Chelsea might even have said 'spoilt'. All the same, Chelsea decided that the best way to deal with Lily was with a bribe. On her way to the tube station after leaving the magazine's central London office, Chelsea popped into Hamleys and came out with a Flitter Fairy doll. The girl on the counter assured her that Flitter Fairies were the way to any six-year-old girl's heart and with the plastic tat in hand, Chelsea felt a little more confident that the evening would go well.

It was Lily who opened the front door to Adam's house.

'What are you doing here?' she said. 'Daddy said I was going to have a *nice* surprise.'

The evening continued in much the same vein. Lily accepted the Flitter Fairy in much the same manner as the Queen might accept her hundredth bouquet on yet another official visit. She pulled it out of the bag and announced, 'I've already got this one.'

'But isn't it nice to have another? Say thank you,' said Adam.

'Thank you,' Lily sighed.

Chelsea tried not to let it faze her. Perhaps Lily was just hungry. But the little girl's mood and manners didn't seem to improve after supper, which was an incredibly bland pasta dish 'with no onions or garlic, because Lily doesn't like them'. Lily still left most of her plateful and insisted on going straight to pudding. Adam shrugged in an embarrassed sort of way as he cleared away the plates, leaving Chelsea and Lily to make small talk.

'Did you have a nice day at school?' Chelsea asked.

'No,' said Lily.

'Oh dear. Why's that?'

'Don't know,' was Lily's answer.

'Did you have to do a subject you don't enjoy? Did you have to do maths?' Chelsea persisted. 'I always hated maths.'

'Daddy!' Lily shouted out. 'Please may I leave the table?'

Adam came back into the kitchen balancing three bowls of ice cream.

'But you've got to eat your ice cream.'

'I'll eat it by the television,' Lily said.

Adam let her go and Chelsea was secretly glad. She couldn't imagine Jack ever getting away with such wilfulness but with Lily out of the way, at last Chelsea would get a kiss. Or so she hoped. As soon as Adam made his move, Lily reappeared.

'Put that lady down,' she said.

Chapter Forty-Five

Annabel

Annabel spent way too much time wondering what would be a suitable wedding present for Ronnie and Mark. Richard suggested John Lewis vouchers. Everybody secretly preferred a gift that allowed them to choose for themselves. But Annabel thought that was really bad form. It showed no effort.

She would at least go into Peter Jones and look for an actual 'thing'. Ronnie and Mark could always take it back and swap it for something they really wanted afterwards.

She changed her mind while she was having a coffee in Café Colbert in Sloane Square. Though Ronnie didn't know it yet, Annabel was going to be asking her for something worth much more than anything money could buy. A gift from Peter Jones wouldn't cut it. It needed to be more personal than that.

Having finished her coffee, Annabel headed in the direction of the Pimlico Road. She could pick something up at Daylesford for supper. It would also give her the opportunity to look in on the little art gallery where she and Richard had bought many of the paintings that hung in the Great House.

Nigel the gallery owner beamed when he saw Annabel come in.

'Annabel! How are you?'

They air-kissed.

'It's been a long time. I was hoping I would see you at my party in July.'

'July was a rather . . . busy month for us,' Annabel told him. Nigel's party was one of a hundred things that had slipped by while Izzy was in hospital. 'Did I forget to let you know we weren't coming?'

'Not a problem, my dear. I shall still invite you to the next one.'

'Of course he would,' Annabel could almost hear Richard say. 'We pay his mortgage.'

'Cup of tea?' Nigel offered.

Annabel shook her head.

'Glass of wine?'

Annabel was about to shake her head again but instead she said, 'Why not?'

Nigel always had very good wine and perhaps a little glass would help Annabel think creatively. And one, just one, wouldn't hurt the baby, would it?

'I'll leave you to look around while I get another bottle out of the fridge.'

There was an almost empty bottle on the counter. Having known Nigel for the past fifteen years, Annabel very much doubted that he'd had much help from customers in getting through it.

While Nigel was in the kitchen, Annabel wandered the walls, looking at the paintings. Some were familiar. There were a couple that Nigel just couldn't seem to shift, though he claimed it was because he didn't want to. He'd once told Annabel that he found homes for his paintings in the same way his sister, who ran a dog rescue centre in Dorset, found homes for her dogs. It wasn't simply a matter of handing them over to the first person who expressed an interest. You had to be sure they were a suitable match. Nigel couldn't do home visits, such as his sister insisted upon, but he said that over the years he had come to recognise the right buyers. The wrong ones always gave themselves away.

'They talk about how much they've made from the pictures they've bought in the past. But I'm not about money, Annabel. I don't care how much my paintings increase in value. I see myself as a conduit for art.'

It was just sales patter, of course, designed to make whoever was on the receiving end feel as though they were part of the inner circle and not just another punter. And when you were part of the inner circle, of course you didn't want to disappoint Nigel by leaving his shop empty-handed.

'Ah-ha,' said Nigel, returning to the room with a new bottle and another glass. 'I knew you would like that one.'

Annabel had actually been miles away. She wasn't really looking at the picture in front of her at all. But now that she focused on it, she saw that it was rather charming. It was a print. Victorian. The subject was a young girl. She was sitting on a window seat, half-turning to look out into the garden. She had a sampler on her lap. The needle was still in her hand as though she had just that second been distracted by something outside.

'Lovely little thing, isn't she?'

There was something almost familiar about the girl on the window seat. It took Annabel a second before she realised. The girl looked a bit like Sophie, her new niece. Underneath those dreadful clothes and the long black hair that hung like curtains, Sophie was terribly pretty.

'Oh, you're going to enjoy this one,' said Nigel.

'Actually, it's not for me,' said Annabel.

'Oh?'

Nigel waited to be told the story. It was a very generous gift.

'It's a wedding present,' Annabel explained. 'For my . . . for a family friend.'

'Lovely. I do love a wedding. Where are they having the party? Somewhere nice and flash, I hope.'

Prior to Izzy's illness, the old Annabel might have told Nigel the true story. He would have enjoyed hearing about the reception in the pub and they might have laughed about it together. But Annabel suddenly felt quite defensive. Defensive of Ronnie? She wasn't sure. But in any case, she told Nigel that the party was going to be in a country house hotel in the Midlands. She couldn't remember the name.

'Well, I'm sure they will be delighted to get this beautiful print. You know, if you hadn't come in today, I might have taken this lovely lady home myself.'

The drawing was the only kind of lady who would ever make it to 'confirmed bachelor' Nigel's home, that was for sure.

'But then you walked in. It's fate. She was meant for your friends.'

The glass of wine was forgotten but while Nigel wrapped the picture in its slightly too extravagant gold frame in bubble-wrap and brown paper, he brought Annabel up to speed with some of the local gossip. And he asked more questions about her.

'How's Izzy-Wizzy?'

'Well, she won't be called Izzy-Wizzy any more,' said Annabel. 'It's guaranteed to send her into a mood.'

'How old is she now?'

'Almost seventeen.'

'Crikey. How time flies. I remember when she was just

a little tot. You know, if she needs to get some work experience, I would be very happy to have her here for a week or two.'

Annabel held it together in the shop but she burst into tears on the corner of Pimlico Road and Lower Sloane Street. The thought of Izzy being well enough to do work experience in London seemed like such a distant dream.

Chapter Forty-Six

Ronnie and Chelsea

The day before the wedding, Chelsea travelled up to Coventry to support her sister. Though she and Mark had been together since they were teenagers and a piece of paper was hardly going to change very much, Ronnie was the archetypal bride. She was incredibly nervous and she wanted to do things properly. That meant that Mark stayed at home with the children, while Ronnie went back to Jacqui and Dave's house for the night before the wedding itself. She was superstitious and did not want to leave for the ceremony from the same place as her future husband.

Not that there was much room at Jacqui and Dave's. Since Chelsea and Ronnie had left home, much had changed at the Bensons' house. The former dining room had been converted into a bedsitter for Granddad Bill. Which meant that the dining-room table had been moved into the upstairs bedroom that Chelsea and Ronnie had shared as children. In fact, they'd shared the room until Ronnie got pregnant with Sophie, after which Chelsea had a brief stint sleeping on the sofa downstairs.

As a teenager, camping in the living room, Chelsea had been desperate to leave home and find a place of her own, but for one night, it was going to be fun to be back.

'When was the last time we shared a room?' Ronnie asked.

'I think it was when you were six months gone with Sophie. You started getting up and down to pee the whole time and I wasn't getting enough sleep. I had my GCSEs coming up.'

'I'm sorry,' said Ronnie. 'That must have been annoying.'

'I forgive you,' Chelsea said with a smile. 'I don't think I ever would have got more than a C in maths, no matter how much shut-eye I got.'

'You were always the brainy one.'

'Rubbish. You were brainy too.'

'Not brainy enough to take the Pill properly.'

'But you've got Sophie as a result.'

'Yeah,' said Ronnie. 'I didn't do too badly, did I?'

They were silent for a moment, then Ronnie said, 'I'm so nervous about tomorrow.'

'Why? It's not as though you've rushed into it. Sixteen years!'

'But everyone will be looking at me.'

'True. But you're going to give them something worth looking at. You're going to look amazing.'

'Do you think so?'

'I know so.'

'But what if she . . .' Ronnie didn't have to say the name. 'What if *she* turns up in something designer?'

'She probably will. It won't necessarily suit her. Whereas your wedding dress is you to a T.'

Chelsea had helped Ronnie to choose her wedding dress. Most of the work had been done online. Chelsea had ordered half a dozen dresses and had them sent straight to Ronnie's office at the funeral home in Coventry. Ronnie just had to choose. She'd tried them all on in the changing room where the pall-bearers kept their top hats and long coats, with some lilies pinched out of someone's floral tribute standing in for the bridal bouquet.

The one that she'd gone for in the end was from Monsoon. It was called 'Rosanna'. It had a high empire-line waist and fluttering twenties-style sleeves. The neckline was trimmed with diamanté. At almost three hundred pounds, it was way more than Ronnie had wanted to spend on a dress she would only wear once, but Chelsea had stumped up for it, in lieu of a wedding present. Mark and Ronnie had been together for so long, there wasn't anything they really needed for the house. But Ronnie needed to look her very best on her wedding day. And having something so beautiful would help her to feel special, as every bride should.

For 'something borrowed', Chelsea had come through again. She let Ronnie wear a treasured pair of strappy silver Louboutins, bought at a sample sale the previous year. Chelsea loved those shoes and had been saving them for a special occasion. She hadn't worn them at all except around the house. What better first outing could they have than to her big sister's wedding, on the feet of the bride? When Chelsea pulled them out of her suitcase, it was all Ronnie could do not to cry.

Meanwhile, 'something blue' would be a garter: an appalling tasteless scrap of elasticated ribbon that had been a gift from Ronnie's friends on her hen night. Fortunately that would be hidden by the dress. And for 'something old' Ronnie had a lace-edged handkerchief that once belonged to their grandmother, Jennifer, Granddad Bill's long-dead wife.

'If I could just lose fifteen pounds overnight,' Ronnie mused. 'Everything would be perfect.'

'Mark loves you the way you are. Being thin is not

the same as being fit or fanciable,' Chelsea said, a mantra from one of the books her new counsellor had suggested she read.

'Whatever,' said Ronnie.

'We ought to get some sleep,' said Chelsea. 'Big day tomorrow.'

'Yeah,' said Ronnie. 'I should have had that whisky Dad offered. That'd help me to drop off.'

'Just close your eyes and start counting backwards from a thousand.'

'Does that work for you?' Ronnie asked.

'No,' Chelsea admitted.

'Exactly . . . Thanks for being here,' said Ronnie. 'I can't tell you how much it means to me. I'm so glad we sorted things out in Lanzarote. I can't believe we went without talking for so long.'

'Me neither,' Chelsea admitted. 'Because it's a special relationship, isn't it? Being sisters? This is what Annabel missed out on.'

'Hmmm,' said Ronnie.

Chapter Forty-Seven

Ronnie

At ten o'clock the following morning, Mark dropped Sophie and Jack off at the house. Mark wasn't allowed in, of course. He would not see Ronnie until they got to the register office for the marriage ceremony.

Sophie had agreed to let Chelsea choose her a 'bridesmaid' dress. Chelsea had done both Ronnie and Sophie proud, choosing a dark blue dress that wasn't too far from Sophie's usual palette of black and dark burgundy. At the same time, it was similar in style to Ronnie's dress and they went very well together. It would ensure that they looked like an actual wedding party rather than a bunch of randoms.

At eleven o'clock, Ronnie's hairdresser made a home visit. Sophie allowed her to arrange her hair, which she usually wore loose and straight, in an elaborate up-do. Chelsea did their make-up. It was easy. Both Sophie and Ronnie had beautiful clear, smooth skin. It didn't seem to matter what they drank or ate or how late they stayed up talking.

Meanwhile, Jack was delighted with the little grey suit that his grandma had bought him in Marks and Spencer. He wore a navy blue waistcoat that coordinated with his sister's dress. Jack loved dressing up, especially if he could be convinced that he looked like a character from a film or TV show in whatever he was wearing.

That day, his grandfather Dave told him he looked like James Bond. Perfect. In fact, they would have a hard time persuading Jack to take the suit off later that night as a result.

Lunch was sandwiches. Jacqui wrapped a bin liner round Jack as a sort of mega-bib to keep the crumbs off his new outfit. Then she promptly went and spilled a blob of mayonnaise on her own skirt. Fortunately, the greasy mark it left was more or less hidden by the pleats.

At one o'clock, the Bensons gathered in the back garden at Dave and Jacqui's for a pre-wedding photograph. The sun was doing its best to shine but Dave waited for a small cloud to pass overhead so that the girls wouldn't have to squint.

'It's a shame that your sister isn't here,' said Jacqui.

'She is here,' said Ronnie. But Chelsea's anguished look reminded Ronnie exactly which sister Jacqui was really talking about.

'I expect they're going straight to the register office,' said Dave. 'It's closer to their house. They don't want to have to go all round the ring road.'

'We can get another picture with Daisy later,' Jacqui sighed.

'Annabel,' Ronnie reminded her. 'Annabel Buchanan is her name.'

At half one, Chelsea, Jacqui and Granddad Bill piled into a minibus with Sophie and Jack for the trip to the register office, leaving only Ronnie and Dave at the house.

Ronnie sat on the edge of a kitchen chair, trying not to crease her dress. Dave had a cigarette. Something he only ever did at Christmas or at moments of high stress. This was obviously not Christmas.

'I'm very proud of you, our Ronnie,' Dave suddenly announced.

'Are you, Dad?' Ronnie asked.

'Of course I am. You've always made me proud. Ever since you were a little girl. And now you're a mother, with two lovely children and you're going to make Mark the perfect wife. It makes my heart sing to look at you all dressed up to get married. I shall remember this day for the rest of my life.'

'Oh thank you, Dad,' said Ronnie. 'Thank you.'

For a moment, it was as though she was his only daughter and not the middle one of three.

At quarter to two, the bridal car arrived. Mark's boss Jim had kindly offered to be chauffeur for the day, driving Ronnie and Dave to the register office in the back of his white Mercedes. He had even gone so far as to get himself a peaked cap.

'Make the most of it,' Mark had told Ronnie, when Jim made the offer. 'That car was paid for by my hard work.'

Jim was very proud of his Mercedes. It represented everything he had worked for his whole life. Every Sunday morning, he could be found cleaning that car on the driveway of his house in Kenilworth. It was his religion. His pride and joy. He was satisfied that no one within twenty miles owned a better car. Until he got to the register office, that is.

There was an Aston Martin in the register office car park. An Aston Martin DB9 in timeless pewter grey.

Though the parking space right next to the Aston Martin was the closest one to the door, Jim chose to park his car another twenty feet away, meaning that Ronnie had to negotiate the gravel in her sister's Louboutins, which were beautiful but rather flimsy. Even with Dave's arm for support, Ronnie struggled to go more than three steps with any grace. Thank goodness nobody was watching.

'Whose do you think that car is?' Jim asked Dave.

Ronnie knew. But she pressed her lips together and said nothing.

Chapter Forty-Eight

Annabel

While Mark and Ronnie completed the short pre-wedding interview with the registrar, their guests continued to arrive.

Annabel and Richard had taken seats at the back of the room with Mark and Ronnie's friends and neighbours. Izzy wasn't with them. She had not been feeling too good that day, so she stayed at home with Sarah, who was visiting the Great House for the weekend. But when Jacqui arrived, she insisted that the Buchanans join the Benson family in the front two rows on the left (Mark's family were on the right). And she insisted so loudly that Annabel couldn't possibly refuse, though she had a strong idea that Ronnie would have been perfectly happy had the Buchanans stayed where they were.

Jacqui insisted on introducing Annabel to the rest of the clan.

Everyone seemed to be a cousin. Here was Bill's brother's youngest. Here was Bill's dead wife's sister's eldest son. That chap there was married to Dave's Auntie Linda. Annabel shook lots of hands and failed to remember half the names that went with them while Jacqui said over and over, 'This is our Daisy. Only she's called Annabel now. Annabel Buchanan.'

Annabel did her best to smile. After all, everyone was so friendly. Though they all asked the same questions.

How did Annabel find the Bensons? Had she always known she was adopted? Was it strange meeting her sisters after all this time?

'Did you change your name yourself?' someone wanted to know.

'No,' said Annabel. 'My parents chose it. Annabel was my paternal grandmother's name.'

'But your paternal grandmother was called Jennifer,' said the questioner.

'I mean my *adoptive* paternal grandmother,' said Annabel, hating that she had to explain. Hating that she had to use the word 'adoptive' when she talked about the first Annabel Cartwright. Her 'Grannie Annie'. It was as though it somehow invalidated the relationship that was far more real to her than any connection she had to 'Jennifer Benson', a woman she would never know now.

'Will you be going back to Daisy?' someone else asked her.

'No,' said Annabel. 'Of course I won't.'

'It's strange,' said the someone. 'I can't see you as a Daisy.'

'Funnily enough,' said Annabel; 'neither can I.'

She dare not look at Jacqui to see how that had played.

Annabel couldn't wait for the wedding to begin and be finished so that she could just go home.

Chapter Forty-Nine

Ronnie

Ronnie chose to process down the short aisle not to the 'Wedding March' but to the slightly gloomy 'Un-break My Heart' by Toni Braxton, which was the song to which she and Mark had their first kiss at a secondary school disco, almost seventeen years before.

Dave escorted Ronnie through the room to the registrar's desk. They had practised the walk in the kitchen back home. Step, pause. Step, pause. They had to take it slowly. Otherwise they'd have been right in front of the registrar before Toni had time to draw her first breath.

Mark looked nervous. He'd splashed out on a suit for the occasion but, unlike his son, didn't seem at all comfortable with being so dressed up. He had the top button of his shirt undone and his tie was already skew-whiff. Another of his colleagues from the kitchen-fitting firm – Paul – was best man. Paul had been at the same school as Mark and Ronnie. They couldn't wait to hear his best man's speech. Paul was known for his terrible sense of humour, which bordered on rude. He was the life and soul of every party they'd attended since they were teens.

But for now, Paul looked as nervous as Mark as he juggled the rings. He wasn't used to such responsibility.

'Tell him to stop it,' Ronnie hissed at her husband-to-be. 'He'll drop them.'

'See?' Mark said to the registrar. 'She's getting on at me already.'

'There's still time to say "no",' Ronnie reminded him. 'I might.'

'Love of my life,' said Mark. 'I'm not leaving this room until you are my missus.'

Even the registrar laughed.

'Are you ready?' she asked them.

The bride and groom nodded and the short ceremony began.

It wasn't complicated. There were no readings. Mark and Ronnie had chosen the most basic wording from the choices they were offered. Just the legal bits. They confirmed there was no reason why they might not marry each other and exchanged their promises without any drama or 'death do us part'. Mark put a ring on Ronnie's finger and she did the same for him, though he'd already explained that he would have to take it off for work. Health and safety.

The married couple looked down on their joined hands with the glittering gold bands. They shared a small, rather chaste kiss.

'Now, if the witnesses could please step forward to sign the register . . .' said the registrar.

Chelsea was signing for Ronnie. Mark's best man Paul was signing for him.

More music played while the paperwork was completed. This time it was LeAnn Rimes singing 'How Do I Live', another of the bride and groom's favourites, from the days when they were 'courting', before Sophie and Jack were born. And then they were finally married.

When the registrar told them that everything was done, Mark folded Ronnie into his arms and gave her a proper kiss. It was an emotional moment. Jack jumped up and down, clapping. He was touchingly pleased. Even Sophie allowed herself a grin at the sight of her parents making their family bond official. The guests broke into a round of applause.

'About bloody time!' shouted Granddad Bill.

Chapter Fifty

Annabel

The bride and groom led the way out of the room. Jacqui and Dave fell into step behind them along with Mark's parents, Eddy and Marie. Then came Chelsea with the children, Jack and Sophie. Then some more of Mark's relatives. One of Dave's cousins prodded the Buchanans into the procession next.

'You're family too,' he said helpfully.

The photographer – a friend of a friend – halted the whole party on the steps of the building so that he could take a group photograph. As the photographer arranged the tableau and Annabel tried to sink into the background she heard someone – another cousin – exclaim, 'Oh wow, an Aston Martin! Is that the wedding car?'

'No,' hissed Mark's boss Jim. 'The bride came in my Mercedes.'

'Oh,' said the cousin. 'That's a pity. That's a right proper car there.'

Annabel pinched the bridge of her nose and whispered to Richard, 'We've got to wait until everyone else has left the car park. We can't be seen getting into the Aston.'

Ronnie had printed out instructions on how to get from the register office to the pub for the reception, though in reality, apart from Chelsea's boyfriend, the Buchanans were the only people at the wedding who did not already know the King's Head. Going to the King's Head for the first time was a rite of passage for anyone who grew up in the Bensons' hometown. It was where Mark, Ronnie and Chelsea had all had their first (illegal) drinks, arming themselves with fake ID, though the landlord back then wasn't really a stickler when it came to drinking age. And neither, thankfully, were the local police, who had far better things to do than nick sixteen-year-olds for getting wasted on snakebite.

The King's Head was the kind of pub where you could order snakebite without blushing. It was not, however, the kind of pub where you could say Cabernet Sauvignon without raising eyebrows, as Richard discovered when he went up to the bar. The red wine on offer made vinegar seem a preferable tipple. Richard soon bowed to pressure from his new 'father-in-law' Dave and accepted a pint of lager instead.

Annabel was on water, of course, though she had possibly never wanted to get blasted more. What she would have given for a bottle of champagne. Or even a bottle of cider. When Dave asked why Annabel wasn't drinking she said it was because she would be driving back.

'Fair enough,' said Dave. 'If I had an Aston, I wouldn't let anyone else drive it if they'd had a drink this year.'

Richard went to the buffet and filled two plates with food.

'Is it all brown?' Annabel asked.

'Be nice,' Richard reminded her. 'The cake looks good.'

The Buchanans' gift to the newlyweds was placed on a table by the cake with all the others. The 'cake' was in fact a tower of cupcakes. They were iced in the colours of Coventry City FC. Jacqui and Ronnie had made them.

At the appointed time, the newlyweds stepped up to the cake table and made a big show of cutting a very small cupcake in half with a ceremonial sword that had hung above the bar in the King's Head for years (except for one memorable night, when Jason Collerick – Harrison's uncle – fetched it down and threatened to cut off his own brother's head after a fierce argument over who should buy the next round). Anyway, that afternoon the sword was used for much more peaceable purposes. The newlyweds posed for photographs and then Jack and Sophie helped to hand the cupcakes round. Annabel took one for Izzy at Jack's insistence.

'They're going to open the wedding presents next,' said Jack. He was very excited. 'I can't wait to see what they've got.'

Annabel agreed. Though for different reasons.

'They're opening the presents now?' she mouthed at her husband when Jack and Sophie had moved on to the next table. 'In front of everybody?'

It wasn't what happened at any of the weddings Annabel and Richard had attended. Richard shrugged.

'Well, I suppose at least we'll get to see what Ronnie really thinks of our gift.'

As the wedding guests ate their cupcakes and wandered to the bar for top-ups, Mark and Ronnie set upon the gift table. They enthused over tea towels and an apron that was printed with a naked lady's torso. They went into ecstasies over a coffee machine. They were effusively grateful for a beer-making kit.

'Though this present isn't really for the bride,' Ronnie complained.

'What are you talking about?' asked Mark. 'You drink way more beer than I do.'

Finally, Ronnie picked up the Buchanans' gift. Annabel squirmed just a little. Though she had pretended otherwise, she had actually put a great deal of thought into the gift she'd chosen for her newly found sister and right at that moment she felt as she had done at school, when the English teacher picked up her homework book with the intention of reading an extract aloud to the rest of the class. The awful possibility that no one else would think the work was any good left Annabel paralysed with fear. Ronnie read the label.

'To Ronnie and Mark, with best wishes for a wonderful future together as Mr and Mrs Edwards, from Annabel, Richard and Izzy Buchanan.' Ronnie smiled at Annabel. It seemed as though the entire room turned to see who Annabel was, though Annabel doubted there was anyone who didn't know. Jacqui had already made sure of that. 'We're going to be Benson-Edwards, actually,' said Ronnie. 'So we can be all posh like you.'

'It'll take more than a name change!' shouted the best man.

Ronnie went as if to shake the present.

'Only joking,' she said. 'I ought to be careful. I bet this is something good.'

Ronnie began to pull away the sticky tape. It was fairly easy to get into the package. Annabel prided herself on being especially good at gift-wrapping. She'd once even taken a day-long course in wrapping, back when she was heavily pregnant with Izzy.

'Oooh,' said Ronnie, as she revealed the first corner of the drawing's gilded frame.

The guests all seemed to strain towards her to find out what was so good.

'Oh, that's lovely,' said Mark. 'Thank you. We really appreciate that.'

Mark seemed genuinely pleased with the gift. Annabel felt her shoulders sag in relief.

Ronnie turned the frame round so that the guests could see the print inside. Annabel was struck once again by how special that little picture was. She almost wished she'd kept it for herself. But she was sure that Ronnie was as delighted by it as she had been when she spotted it in the window of the shop in Pimlico. It was such a delicate rendering of a young girl. She hoped that Ronnie too might be struck by the resemblance to Sophie. Annabel was going to point it out but then Ronnie said:

'This is really great. Thanks very much. We'll be able to put one of our wedding photos in this.'

And Annabel realised with horror that Ronnie didn't even realise that the picture was the gift. She thought the Buchanans had given her a frame!

Richard coughed. Annabel was about to say something. That beautiful print. That carefully chosen picture. It was worth five hundred pounds! And Ronnie thought it was just some random image to be replaced by a wedding picture. But Richard had reached over and was squeezing her thigh, quite tightly. Annabel glanced at him.

'Don't,' he mouthed.

So all Annabel said was, 'I'm so glad you like it.'

And she had to leave it at that.

'Now for the entertainment,' Mark announced. 'Ronnie, you know you are the love of my life. From the moment I first saw you smoking behind the bike sheds at school—'

'I never smoked!' Ronnie insisted.

Laughter from the guests who had known Mark and Ronnie for years suggested otherwise.

'All right. Let's rephrase that. From the moment I first

saw you doing your homework in the library, I dreamed that one day you would be my wife. That day has finally come and because I'm a man of few words—'

'Whatever, Dad,' said Sophie.

'Because I'm a man of few words, I'm going to celebrate our love with a song. Jack? Bill? Are we ready?'

Granddad Bill and Jack sailed into the middle of the room on Bill's wheelchair. Jack was carrying a CD player. He jumped off Bill's lap and placed it on the cake table.

'Tonight, ladies and gentlemen,' said Mark, 'we are the "Two and a Half Tenors".'

Jack, Bill and Mark took a quick bow.

'A-one, a-two, a-three . . .' Jack counted. Then he skipped to the CD player and pressed 'play'.

'Well,' said Richard, when the entertainment was finished. 'You've never lived until you've heard 'Nessun Dorma' played on spoons . . .'

A little later, Jacqui came over to join them.

'What was your wedding like?' Jacqui asked.

'It seems like such a long time ago,' said Annabel. 'But it was wonderful.'

What would her wedding have been like if she had grown up with the Bensons? Would Granddad Bill have serenaded her with burps in front of Richard's extremely grand relations?

'We had a marquee in the garden,' she continued. 'I had three bridesmaids. One was Kate, my best friend from college. The other two were distant cousins of Richard. They were only little girls. Seven and nine. They wore floral dresses to match my bouquet, which was made of peonies. I've always loved peonies.'

'Oooh, lovely. I've always like peonies too. Isn't that funny?'

Jacqui seemed keen on pointing out the likes she and Annabel had in common.

'Mum made my dress,' Annabel continued.

'Did she?'

'She's a very talented seamstress. She was always making clothes for me and my dolls. I still have the dress tucked away in a cupboard. I'll never get into it again but I thought that perhaps Izzy might like it.'

'I'd love to meet her,' said Jacqui. 'Sarah. Your mum.'

Annabel paused. She didn't know what to say to that.

'I mean, I'd like to have the chance to thank her for looking after you. If I had known what a lovely family you'd gone to, I'd have been a lot happier all these years.'

Annabel had a flash of sympathy for Jacqui then.

'Yes. Well, you certainly couldn't have chosen a better set of parents. I have been very well loved. I never wanted for anything and I can honestly say that, on top of being a great mother, Mum is one of my very best friends. I've been blessed.'

Jacqui blinked as though trying to stave off some tears. Without thinking, Annabel reached out and squeezed her hand. So far, since that first meeting at the Ridgeview, she had avoided any physical contact with any of the Bensons as far as she was able. With Jack it was impossible – he was always launching himself at her for a hug – but with the adults, Annabel had largely succeeded in keeping her distance.

But now, just for a second, Annabel could actually feel something of Jacqui's pain, rather than the anger and disappointment that had characterised her feelings for her birth mother thus far. That it should have happened then, at Ronnie's wedding, over a plate of sausage rolls, was odd, but it was definitely there. Annabel knew what Jacqui meant. How awful must it have been? Annabel could not imagine entrusting Izzy to a stranger. Knowing that Sarah was with Izzy while she and Richard were at the wedding was a huge comfort, even now that Izzy was almost seventeen.

'I don't blame you,' said Annabel. 'For what happened. You did your best for me and, as it turned out, I couldn't have had a better upbringing and a happier childhood. I'm grateful to you for that.'

Jacqui nodded and they might have gone deeper still but they were soon interrupted.

What seemed like hundreds of people dropped by the table in the next hour, all hoping for an introduction. Jacqui had not been shy about telling people how Annabel had suddenly come back into her life. Annabel heard plenty of bitching about her maternal grandparents, who would have had to eat their words if they'd seen how little Daisy had turned out. Private school! Oxford!

Annabel was tempted to point out that if she had stayed with Jacqui and Dave, both of those would almost certainly have been out of the question. Eventually, she knew she had to get out of there, before she did say something upsetting. This was not the right moment for it.

'We'd love to stay longer but we've got to get back home for Izzy,' she told Jacqui.

No one could argue with that.

'Should we say goodbye to Ronnie and Mark?' Richard asked.

Of course they should say goodbye to the bride and groom but Annabel wasn't sure she wanted to. It would mean inserting themselves into another group of strangers – possibly more relatives. Annabel was feeling tired thanks to the baby and the effort of making so much small talk for so long. It was bad manners not to say goodbye but . . .

'They're busy,' said Annabel. 'They won't notice us slipping off.'

However as they started to make their way towards the door, Ronnie did spot them and she shouted right across the room.

'Wait!' she said.

Annabel froze. There was nothing worse than being caught in an act of rudeness. She turned to the bride with a smile.

'You can't go yet.'

'Izzy—' Annabel began.

'I know. But I've got something to give you first. Where is it, Mark? Quick.'

Mark went over to the bar. The landlord handed him an envelope, which Mark passed to Ronnie so that she could give it to Annabel.

'We had a collection. Every time someone went up to the bar, we asked them to stick a quid in the jar. Not to pay for their drinks, because obviously we're covering that this afternoon, but to give to you. So you can give it to the Kidney Foundation.'

Ronnie gave Annabel the envelope.

'There's about five hundred quid in there,' said Mark.

'Most of it's ours,' shouted the wife of the best man.

Jacqui joined them in the centre of the room now.

'Everyone was really sad to hear about Izzy,' she said. 'Everyone wants to help in whatever way they can. You can give it to someone at the hospital, can't you? They'll know the right person to pass it on to.'

'And there's going to be more,' said Ronnie. 'We got given two coffee machines so we've asked for one of them to go back to the shop so that you can have the money instead. Same with the pressure cooker. I'm never going to use that. Even if I am a married woman now.'

'Better hope it wasn't stolen,' said someone nearby.

'Thank you,' said Annabel. 'This is really . . . it's really something.'

Ronnie opened her arms to give Annabel a hug. Annabel let herself be embraced. She was glad of it, in fact, because her eyes were filling up. She felt a hundred emotions all at the same time and one of them was guilt. The generosity of the wedding guests she had not wanted to spend time with was real and overwhelming. These were good people.

'This is really very kind of you, Ronnie. And Mark,' said Richard. 'We'll make sure it goes to the right place.'

'We've got to go now,' said Annabel. 'Can't leave Izzy too long.'

'Of course. We'll see you soon though,' said Jacqui. 'Won't we?'

Annabel assured her they would.

Chapter Fifty-One

Chelsea

The Buchanans may have left by eight o'clock but the party went on until much later. Chelsea had brought her new boyfriend, Adam, to the wedding. She'd been hesitant about asking him – after all, they had only been dating for six weeks – but he seemed delighted when she finally plucked up the courage. He said it would be an honour. And it wasn't as though he didn't already know Chelsea's family, having met them all in Lanzarote in August. Even if she had yet to be persuaded about Chelsea, Adam's daughter Lily was certainly keen to see her holiday friend Jack once more.

Lily had been charging around with Jack for much of the day. It was hard to believe that they had once been sworn enemies. Meeting in Lanzarote, they had immediately gone head to head over playground equipment and ice creams. Now it seemed they were the very best of friends. At one point, they both disappeared, causing a brief panic, until they were found beneath the cake table, sharing the last of the cupcakes between them.

But at ten o'clock in the evening, it was as though the children's batteries had run out. Soon Lily was snoozing in her father's arms.

'I suppose I ought to put her to bed,' said Adam.

Adam and Lily were staying at a nearby Holiday Inn.

Chelsea would not be staying with them. She was billeted at her sister's house that night, to keep an eye on Sophie and Jack while the newlyweds spent their first night together at a hotel.

'Did you have a nice time?' she asked him, wishing even as she said it that she hadn't asked such a lame question.

'It's been great. Lily has really enjoyed herself.'

'What about you?'

'I've enjoyed myself too,' said Adam, kissing the tip of his finger before touching it to the end of Chelsea's nose.

'It wasn't too . . .?'

'It wasn't too anything. It was a lovely day and I've had a lovely time.'

'You're next,' said Mark, sidling up to their table and pointing at Adam.

Chelsea shrivelled inside. But when she dared to look at Adam again he was smiling at her, with a hint of laughter in his eyes.

'Help me take Lily out to the car,' he said.

They settled Lily into her child seat and strapped her in without her making so much as a murmur. Then Adam took Chelsea into his arms and kissed her and she was flooded with warmth and happiness.

Chelsea could not have been more content right in that moment. She floated back into the pub and sat down on a banquette next to Jack and Granddad Bill, who were both past their best and needed to go to bed as much as Lily had. Jack pulled his feet up on to the banquette and lay down with his head in Chelsea's lap. She played with his soft fair hair. They'd become so close on their holiday in Lanzarote that Chelsea couldn't remember why she'd ever thought spending time with children was a bore.

Ronnie joined them.

'Have you had a good day?' asked Chelsea.

'I've had the best day ever.' Ronnie stretched out her hand so that Chelsea could admire the golden band that now adorned her ring finger. 'I can't quite believe it. I'm Mrs Benson-Edwards.'

'Very posh.'

'At least I've got the same name as my kids now. I didn't think it would ever happen.'

'It was always going to happen,' said Chelsea. 'Mark has adored you from day one. Just like he said.'

'He has, hasn't he? I can't believe I ever thought he might be having an affair with Cathy from Next Door.'

'It did seem unlikely.'

The sisters looked towards the bar, where Cathy from Next Door was challenging the barman to an arm-wrestling match. He sensibly declined. She would have beaten him quite easily.

'Do you feel different?' Chelsea asked.

'A bit. It might just be the Spanx. I can't wait to get them off.'

'Oh the glamour.'

'It'll be you next.'

'Don't you start. Mark's already put his foot in it. He came right out with it in front of Adam!'

'But why shouldn't it be? He's clearly besotted.'

'Who?'

'Adam!'

'Oh . . .' Chelsea looked away as though she could hardly bear to hear it. At the same time, she wanted to hear it again and again.

'He is.'

'Maybe. But it's only been a few weeks.'

'Mark says he knew the day he first met me.'

'But he waited sixteen years . . .' Chelsea reminded her.

'Different circumstances. You're both grown-ups. You've got your own places. There's no reason why you shouldn't be together.'

'I'd like that very much,' Chelsea admitted.

But though she was delighted by the thought of a lifetime with such a wonderful man as Adam, Chelsea knew that there were obstacles to be overcome before she could really think about a future. For a start, it wasn't just a matter of beguiling Adam. Lily had to be won over as well. That day, Lily had barely acknowledged Chelsea, preferring to race around with Jack. Whenever they were alone together at Adam's house, Lily was as monosyllabic as any grumpy teenager.

Plus, six weeks after their return from Lanzarote, Chelsea was still only taking the very first steps along the road to recovery from the bulimia that had blighted most of her adult life. If she and Adam were to get really serious, she would have to tell him what was going on.

How would he take it? Would he understand? Would he think it was too much to deal with so early in their time together? It was not so long ago that he lost his wife, the woman he had pledged to love for the rest of his life. He had been candid about the difficulties of coping alone with Lily and had explained to Chelsea that he hadn't become involved with anyone since his wife's death because he was concentrating so hard on getting himself and Lily through their grief, he could only short-change a new girlfriend. He wouldn't have been able to offer her the support she deserved.

Would Adam think that Chelsea needed too much from him?

In Chelsea's lap, Jack stirred and half-opened his eyes.

'Are you looking after us tonight, Auntie Chelsea?'

Chelsea felt such a huge rush of affection for her nephew that it almost caused her pain.

Love, real love, is an enormous responsibility.

Chapter Fifty-Two

Annabel

Back at the Great House, Richard went straight upstairs
to see Izzy. Annabel remained in the kitchen. She opened
the envelope that Ronnie had given her. Mark had esti-
mated five hundred but there was almost six hundred
pounds in crisp notes. It was an unbearably kind gesture.

Still, Annabel wished she had taken the opportunity
to tell the assembled guests that there was one way they
could help which would be altogether more important
to the Buchanans. Who knew how many people in that
room might have been a match? Everyone they'd met
that night seemed to be related to Jacqui or Dave in
some way or another. By extrapolation, they were related
to Annabel and Izzy too.

Annabel was frustrated that nobody had asked her
about the possibility. Surely they must have been online
and seen something about live donation? Were they really
so naive that it had never crossed their minds? Or, more
likely, had they already thought about it and ruled it
out?

When she came downstairs from where she had been
sitting with Izzy, Sarah looked at the money spread out
on the table and sighed.

'Richard told me about the collection. If only money
was all it took, eh?'

Annabel nodded. 'But it was a lovely thought. I think

it was a good thing that we went today. I think we can ask them next time we see them.'

'When will that be?'

'I don't suppose it will be too long.' Annabel paused. 'Mum, Jacqui asked about you. She said that she would like to meet you.'

Sarah listened quietly while Annabel told her about the conversation she and Jacqui had at the reception.

'I don't think I can meet her,' Sarah concluded. 'Not yet. If you think this is confusing for you, it's just as difficult for me. While I wouldn't know Jacqui if I bumped into her on the street, I can still tell myself I'm your only mum.'

'But you *are* my only mum. That will never change,' Annabel promised her. 'I swear it.'

The following day, Jacqui called Annabel as soon as was decent to thank her for coming along to the wedding.

'It meant a lot to our Ronnie,' she said. 'She was so glad to see you and as for that beautiful frame you bought them! Oh, it's really lovely.'

The frame. Annabel bit her lip.

'But when are we going to see you again?'

'As soon as possible,' said Annabel.

'Really?' Jacqui sounded surprised but delighted. 'That's wonderful. Ronnie's going away for a couple of days for her honeymoon but she wants to have a lunch at her house when they get back, to thank us for organising the wedding. You should come too.'

Annabel agreed.

'Next Sunday?'

'It's in the diary.'

This time they would ask the big question.

Chapter Fifty-Three

Ronnie

As soon as she and Mark got back from their honey-moon, which was two nights at Mallory Court, a smart hotel near Leamington Spa, Ronnie started preparing for that Sunday lunch with the Buchanans.

Mark, Sophie and Jack were all walking on eggshells from Tuesday night onwards. The fridge was full but there was nothing for Ronnie's husband or children to eat. Every time one of them ventured into the kitchen for so much as a glass of water, Ronnie would fly in there after them, screeching, 'You're not to touch anything in the fridge. It's for Sunday!'

'Anyone would think the bloody Queen was coming,' said Mark. 'It's only your sister. You wouldn't make this much effort for Chelsea.'

'I would,' Ronnie insisted. 'I would do exactly the same.'

'But you never have,' Mark pointed out. 'Look, can't I just have some of these sausages? I'll go out and replace them before Sunday comes.'

'No. They're for the devils on horseback,' said Ronnie.

'Who has devils on horseback except at Christmas?'

'We do.'

'Right.'

Mark contented himself with a bowl of cornflakes.

It wasn't just the food that was off-limits until the

weekend. On Thursday evening, Ronnie washed every glass in the house and spent an age polishing them. Once the glasses were sparkling like they were on display in the crystal department at Harrods, they were put back in the cupboard and Ronnie marked the cupboard door with a Post-it: *Do not use*. The family was reduced to using a variety of battered plastic cups. This upset Jack in particular. He was horrified to be presented with his Bob the Builder sippy cup again.

'I'm not a baby,' he protested.

But Ronnie was not to be persuaded that a visit from the Buchanans did not warrant going to such extremes.

'You've seen her house, Mark. She lives in a mansion. She has two cleaners. Two! I've *worked* as a cleaner. I don't want her coming round here thinking we live in a pigsty.'

And so the whole house was vacuumed twice on Saturday and when Jack dropped a piece of toast on the kitchen floor on Sunday morning, causing Ronnie to shriek like a banshee, the row that ensued between Mark and Ronnie was almost grounds for divorce just a week into their marriage.

'I don't want the Buchanans to come,' said Jack, as he ran upstairs for cover. 'They're ruining my life.'

'See?' said Mark. 'See what you're doing? Your son is crying because of this. Do you think Annabel Buchanan would be impressed by that?'

'All I ask is that you all pull together to make the house look nice when they come.'

'We've been living in terror all week. Jack dropped a piece of toast. You bawled at him like he did it deliberately. He's a kid. He's always dropping stuff.'

'He should be more careful.'

'You should take a look at yourself. You're tying

yourself up in knots for that woman. She's your sister, Ronnie. Your *sister*. If she can't take us as we are, then fuck her.'

'Will you mind your language?'

'What? In case Lady Buchanan hears? Ronnie, just because she grew up with the aristocracy, doesn't mean you're suddenly all posh too.'

Ronnie wouldn't address another word to her new husband until the Buchanans pulled into the drive.

As Annabel knocked on the door, Ronnie was just arranging a wedding photograph, in the frame that Annabel had given them as a wedding present on a console table in the hall.

Chapter Fifty-Four

Sophie

Ronnie was not the only one who had been working hard to make a good impression on the Buchanans. While Ronnie locked herself into the kitchen and cursed her devils on horseback, Sophie was trying to transform her room. She could never make it as big as Izzy's, but she could make it just as interesting.

She spent the first week's wages from her new Saturday job in a bakery on a couple of sarongs. She attached them to the wall with drawing pins, covering up the Flower Fairy wallpaper that Mark had been promising to change for years. She arranged her most treasured possessions on the shelf. She hung her second-hand Beats headphones from her desk lamp and then took them down and put them up again, aiming for a more casual arrangement, as though she had just tossed them to one side when she got home. No big deal.

Then she opened the window, even though it was raining outside. Sophie had a dread fear that Izzy would think her bedroom smelly. Sophie's friends had never commented but whenever she walked into the room after being away for a while – such as when they got back from Lanzarote – Sophie's nose picked up the faintest whiff of mould when she opened the door. She didn't want Izzy to notice that.

When she had finished, Sophie stood in her doorway

and imagined she was seeing her room for the very first time. It wasn't perfect. It could never be perfect with the Flower Fairy wallpaper. But Sophie was pleased that it looked like the room of someone quite sophisticated. Someone a little bit different. Someone who would impress Isabella Buchanan.

Jack too wanted to impress Izzy in particular and as soon as the Buchanans walked through the door, Jack was right there, grabbing Izzy by the hand, eager to show her the cardboard pyramid he had been making for a school project. Sophie rolled her eyes at her little brother's enthusiasm, but Izzy said she would be delighted to see Jack's masterpiece. And she did seem interested. She even watched a couple of Minecraft videos with him. It seemed like ages before Sophie could spirit Izzy off to her room, without Jack in tow.

'He's such a pain sometimes,' said Sophie.

'I'd love to have a little brother,' said Izzy. She waited a beat. 'I could use him for his kidneys.'

'You're nasty,' said Sophie, with a laugh.

'I'm only joking. He's sweet, your brother. He cracks me up.'

'You should try living with him *all* the time.'

'I like what you've done with your room,' said Izzy. 'I got some silk scarves like that when we went to the Maldives, but Mum won't let me put them up. I'm not allowed to mark the wallpaper.'

'This wallpaper can only be improved by a few marks,' said Sophie.

'*True dat*,' said Izzy.

They laughed. And Sophie was relieved to realise that it was a real laugh and not a cruel one. Izzy was laughing with her and not at her.

'Isn't it funny, me ending up in your room like this, after I was so vile to you back in May,' said Izzy.

'That was understandable. I think I'd have been the same if I'd found a stranger in my room. Especially if I had so much nice stuff.'

'No. I was rude. And it is just stuff,' said Izzy. 'I'm starting to understand that now. All those times my mum said that you haven't got anything if you haven't got your health . . .'

'Do all mums say that?' Sophie asked. 'Because mine says it too.'

'Maybe it's because they're related. It's true though isn't it?'

Sophie nodded.

'I'd give everything I own to have my kidneys working again. Everything.'

Both girls were silent for a moment.

Izzy fingered a little china dish that Sophie had brought back from Lanzarote. 'This is pretty,' she said.

'You can have it,' said Sophie quickly.

'That wasn't why I said it.'

'I know. But you can have it. Think of it as me making up for all those years I missed your birthday. Cuz.'

'Cuz!' Izzy laughed. 'Isn't that just weird? There's me kicking you out of my bedroom and less than six months later I'm in yours. Because we're related.'

'Yep. And because we're friends,' Sophie dared.

'Definitely,' Izzy agreed. 'Mum didn't want to meet you lot, you know. She was really strange about it. She said it was disloyal to Grandma Sarah and Granddad Humfrey, though Grandma's totally fine with it and Granddad died a few years ago.'

'I can understand that. They did bring her up.'

'Yeah.'

'I used to wish I was adopted,' said Sophie. 'So I could know for sure I wouldn't turn out like my mum or dad.'

Izzy laughed. 'I feel *exactly* the same.'

'But your parents are really cool. And they're rich.'

'Yeah, well that brings its own issues. At least your parents let you be yourself. You don't have to be constantly thinking about what the neighbours will say.'

'Are you kidding? If you'd seen the way my mum has been this week. She cleaned the house on Monday and we haven't been allowed to touch anything since then. It's all because she wants to make an impression on your mum. You would think the Queen was coming to stay.'

'Funnily enough,' said Izzy, 'that is what we call her. The Queen. Or HRH.'

As the girls were laughing about their mothers, they heard the tap of something hitting the window. They both peered out to see what was going on. Harrison Collerick was on the pavement below, straddling his BMX. He had tossed a little piece of gravel at the glass to see if he could get Sophie's attention.

'Who's that?' Izzy asked.

'Oh God,' said Sophie. 'That's my ex-boyfriend.'

Sophie and Harrison had called time on their 'relationship' just that week. In truth it was over the moment Sophie heard he got off with Skyler on the school trip to Berlin, but when school started again, Harrison had somehow wheedled his way back into Sophie's affections. Until she heard that he'd been telling the other guys at school that he'd taken her virginity. He hadn't. Sophie's virginity was still very much there to be taken. By the right man.

Sophie dumped Harrison for being so unchivalrous but she had been wondering since whether she'd done the right thing. Even a hopeless boyfriend was surely better than none at all.

'You went out with him?' asked Izzy. 'He looks about twelve.'

'I'm afraid so,' said Sophie.

'Swipe left!' said Izzy, referencing Tinder. 'Seriously, Sophie. You can do so much better.'

Izzy's disapproval was all it took for Harrison Collerick to fall from his pedestal once and for all. The poor boy could only gaze up at the window in vain as the two girls collapsed on to Sophie's bed with the giggles.

'Swipe left!' Sophie echoed with glee. 'You are so right!'

'Ladies and gentlemen,' came the sound of Jack's high-pitched voice from downstairs. 'Dinner is served!'

'I think he means lunch,' said Sophie, blushing at her brother's gauche mistake. Sophie had been reading up about etiquette online.

'All the same to me,' Izzy assured her.

Chapter Fifty-Five

The grown-ups

After lunch – it did not escape Ronnie's notice that Annabel hardly touched a thing – Annabel suggested that perhaps Sophie might like to show Izzy the neighbourhood. And perhaps they could take Jack and Leander with them? Leander had been waiting patiently in the Buchanans' Porsche. He'd been brought along precisely with the purpose of currying favour with the Benson children. The girls groaned but Jack was over the moon at the prospect of walking the dog. Leander too was delighted and wagged his tail so hard as he was let out of the car that he almost managed to knock Jack over.

Sophie protested but only half-heartedly. She had the sense that Izzy's mother wanted them out of the way for some important reason. So she told Ronnie that she would take Izzy, Jack and the dog over to the rec. But that she would not be doing any pooper-scooping.

'I will!' said Jack, full of enthusiasm.

Izzy and Sophie pulled disgusted faces at one another. Jack clearly had no real idea what pooper-scooping involved. But if he was happy to do it . . . There were few other perks to having a little brother in tow.

The dog-walking team departed, watched from Sophie's bedroom window by Fishy the furious cat, leaving only the adults round the table and Granddad

Bill dozing in his chair in front of the television. Everyone was relieved that he'd made it through lunch without resorting to burping out a popular song.

While Jacqui and Mark cleared the table, Ronnie made coffee using the most expensive ground coffee Sainsbury's had to offer in the machine she had received as a wedding present. Mark had complained bitterly when she refused to let him try even the smallest cup until the Buchanans had been. Soon he would complain bitterly that it hadn't been worth the wait. It wasn't anywhere near as good as the instant they used to drink. But Richard and Annabel seemed to like it. And they both dipped into the box of After Eights that had been in the cupboard since Christmas. Thank goodness Richard only came out with one empty paper sachet before he found one that still had a chocolate inside.

'Everybody does it,' he assured Ronnie when she started to apologise.

'I know it was you, Mark,' Ronnie glared. 'How many times have I told you not to put the empties back—'

'Ronnie and Mark,' Richard interrupted. 'We just want to thank you for having us here to lunch today. We've been overwhelmed by how keen you've all been to welcome us into your family.'

'Well, you *are* family,' said Jacqui at once.

'Thank you, Jacqui,' said Richard. Annabel lifted the corners of her mouth in a smile that seemed to agree. 'It means more to us than you can possibly imagine.'

Jacqui beamed.

'We've told you about Izzy and what happened at the festival,' Richard continued. 'I know she probably seems relatively well to you at the moment but it's hard to describe just how different she is from the daughter we knew this time last year. The dialysis has been really tough on her. She's got next to no energy and the whole thing has really taken its toll on her moods. She can't go to school and she misses her friends. It's been lovely to see how quickly she's clicked with Sophie.'

'Sophie's a good girl,' Jacqui said.

'She certainly is. She's so bright and full of life. She's got a great future ahead of her. I've got no doubt about that. She could get into any university she wanted to and take the world by storm.'

Ronnie nodded. 'I'm sure she will.'

'The world is Sophie's oyster. And that's what we wanted for Izzy. That was what we all expected for her until the festival happened. Now everything's changed and we have had to start living from day to day, week to week. Izzy's condition is not going to improve. The consultant has been quite clear on that. In fact, it is likely to deteriorate. With the sort of energy levels Izzy has right now, there's no way she can finish her A levels, let alone think about going to university. And dialysis brings its own issues. The side effects are not insignificant. Her life is on hold.'

Jacqui blinked away a tear.

'The only chance she has of living the life that she wished for . . . The sort of life that she and Sophie both deserve . . .' Richard paused. 'Is if she gets a transplant.'

'She's on the list, isn't she?' said Ronnie.

'Of course,' said Annabel. 'But the average waiting time on the transplant list is two years. If you're waiting for a transplant from a stranger, that is.'

Annabel let her last sentence hang in the air for a moment to give the Bensons a chance to fill in the gaps before she had to make her request explicit. No one said anything. Annabel looked down at the table.

'Look,' said Richard. 'There's no easy way to say this. We've come here today to ask you an enormous favour. Izzy has much more chance of getting the transplant she needs if it comes from a live donor. And she has much more chance of that live donor being a good match if they're a member of her family. And that now includes you.'

Richard waved his hand to indicate everyone present at the table.

'Of course, Annabel and I tested as potential donors right away. As did Annabel's mother. But unfortunately, none of us is able to give Izzy a kidney right now.'

'But if you and Annabel aren't matches, then how can we be?' Ronnie asked.

Annabel interrupted. 'What Richard says doesn't entirely explain what's been going on. Richard can't donate because of his high blood pressure. The operation and its aftermath are too big a risk to his health. And I might well be a good match but I can't donate for the foreseeable future.'

'Why not?' asked Ronnie.

'Because I'm pregnant.'

'You're never . . .' said Ronnie. 'But you're . . .'

'Forty-three, I know.'

'Oh!' Jacqui couldn't hide her delight. She clapped her hands together.

'The baby is due in January, by which time Izzy will have been on dialysis for seven months. Every month that passes she gets a little less resilient. A little more ill.'

'A baby!' Jacqui was still stuck on that point.

'So we'd like you to think about testing for us. We need you to,' Annabel added. 'We know it's a lot to ask . . . After all, until a couple of months ago, we were complete strangers. But now, as you said, dear Jacqui, we're family. And we're hoping that counts for a lot.'

Just then Sophie and Izzy came back with the dog. Jack, who had clung on to Leander's lead all the way round the block, was red-faced with exertion. Despite attending several expensive dog-training courses, Leander had yet to learn to walk to heel. The adults fell silent as the children came back into the house with Leander at the fore. Jack filled the void with excited chatter, of course. He wanted everyone to know that Leander actually sat to command. *His* command. He tried to make Leander do it again, to no avail.

'I don't think Leander should be in the house, Jack,' said Richard. 'What about your cat?'

Leander's ears pricked up at the word 'cat'. He rarely seemed to understand 'sit', 'heel' or 'stay' but 'cat' was a word he always responded to. And unfortunately, Fishy chose that very moment to venture down from Sophie's bedroom and poke her delicate nose round the dining-room door.

Jack had no hope of holding on to Leander. Richard and Annabel's yelled commands were in vain. Leander was off like a rocket after Fishy, who fled upstairs faster than anyone had ever seen her move in her entire pampered life. While the humans were still gathering themselves in the dining room, they heard the chaos whirl around upstairs as Leander chased Fishy from room to room, barking like a hound straight from hell.

By the time Richard got upstairs and was able to grab hold of Leander's lead, Fishy was clinging to the top of the curtains in Ronnie and Mark's bedroom. This was a room Ronnie had hoped the Buchanans would never see, with its half-stripped wallpaper (Mark had started decorating two years before but didn't get any further than taking the paper off one wall). The bed was piled high with the crap that usually lived in the hallway. The clothes Ronnie had discarded the previous night – including her saggy old bra – were still draped across the dressing table. And now Fishy was shitting all over the Laura Ashley curtains, which had been an extravagance even in the sale.

'I'm so, so sorry,' said Richard, taking Leander firmly by the collar and yanking him out of the room. 'Of course, we'll do whatever needs to be done to sort out the damage.'

Meanwhile, the curtain pole finally gave in beneath Fishy's weight.

After that excitement, Annabel announced that it was probably time for the Buchanans to be heading home. Nobody, not even Jack, protested.

'Did you ask them?' asked Izzy as soon as they were out of sight of Ronnie and Mark's house.

'We did,' said Annabel.

'And how did they react?'

'I think they probably need a bit of time to take it all in.'

'They reacted badly,' Izzy translated.

'No,' said Richard cautiously. 'I wouldn't say that. It's just like your mother said. They're going to need a bit of time to take on board what we've actually asked them. It's not a small thing, Izzy.'

'I know.'

Back at Ronnie's house, the Benson family were indeed struggling to take Annabel and Richard's request on board. Jacqui and Dave helped Ronnie and Mark put the wrecked bedroom straight, then they all settled down in the living room to go over the lunch's events. Mark broke out his special supply of Spitfire to lubricate the debate. Granddad Bill accepted one gratefully.

'I've won the bloody lottery,' he said as he raised the bottle in a toast.

'I wish you bloody had,' said Ronnie.

'Don't say bloody!' Jack chimed.

'It's a bloody sort of day.'

Jack hopped around the room, mouth open, looking scandalised at all the language. Meanwhile, Fishy curled up on Ronnie's lap and allowed herself to be consoled.

'Poor thing. It's a wonder she didn't have a heart attack. And my lovely curtains,' Ronnie muttered.

'Richard and Annabel have said they'll replace them,' Jacqui pointed out.

'They would say that, wouldn't they? They want one of us to give them a kidney!'

Jacqui looked in Jack's direction. This was not a conversation for little ears. Not yet.

'Jack,' said Ronnie. 'Go and play Minecraft.'

'You said I couldn't play it today,' he replied.

Jack had spent so long playing the game the previous day, his eyes had started to look like Minecraft blocks.

'I've changed my mind,' said Ronnie. 'You can play it in our room.'

'I've won the bloody lottery!' said Jack.

He rushed to carry the Xbox up to his parents' bedroom before Ronnie had time to clip him round the ear.

With Jack otherwise occupied, the debate continued. Sophie was considered old enough to be included.

'Are you going to do it, Mum?' Ronnie asked Jacqui. 'Are you going to be tested?'

Jacqui nodded. 'Of course I am. We both are, aren't we, Dave?'

Dave's eyes widened as he took another gulp from his bottle of beer.

'Dave,' said Jacqui. 'Izzy is our granddaughter. We'd do the same if Sophie had eaten something that made her ill.'

Knowing the truth about how Izzy had come to damage her kidneys, Sophie looked down at her hands to hide the look in her eyes. 'Thanks, Gran,' she said. 'I know you would.'

By the time Dave had finished his beer, Jacqui had persuaded him that they should both be tested right away. Jacqui called Annabel on her mobile and spoke to her before the Buchanans were even home.

'Thank you, thank you,' said Annabel. 'It's so good of you. But you've got to want to do it. I really don't want you to put yourselves out.'

'We wouldn't be putting ourselves out, love. We'd do anything for our Izzy.'

The word 'our' made Annabel wince. How quickly Jacqui had appropriated Izzy as her granddaughter. It made Annabel feel fiercely protective of her mum, who had been a real grandmother, turning up to stay for a month when Izzy was a newborn, making sure that Annabel was able to keep an even keel during those awful early weeks when Izzy would neither sleep nor feed when Annabel wanted her to. Annabel knew she would have gone stark staring mad without Sarah. But it was because Jacqui claimed Izzy as one of her own that she was willing to be tested for her. Annabel had to be grateful for that.

'Can you put Izzy on the phone?' Jacqui asked.

'She's asleep in the back of the car,' Annabel lied.

'Well, tell her that her Grandma Jacqui sends her love. And her Grandpa Dave too. We hope we'll see you all very soon. You, Richard, Izzy and the Bump! I can't believe you're having a baby!'

'Me neither,' Annabel said.

Chapter Fifty-Six

Chelsea

Chelsea wasn't at Sunday lunch at Ronnie's house so she wasn't there when Richard and Annabel asked for help. She got the news via Ronnie, who had called her younger sister as soon as their parents had left to go home. Ronnie was full of excitement and not a little outrage. Not least because of her wrecked curtains.

'But we should have guessed! No wonder she wanted to get to know us. I knew they had an ulterior motive. Didn't I tell you?'

It was painful for Chelsea to recall how excited her mother in particular had been that Annabel seemed so keen to be part of the family when it should have been obvious that Annabel's decision to embrace her new family so quickly was motivated by something other than a desire to connect with her roots.

'Spare parts is what they want us for. That's the beginning and the end of it,' Ronnie ranted.

'Ronnie,' said Chelsea. 'Their daughter is ill. Cut the Buchanans some slack.'

'You should have seen the way Annabel looked at her dinner, Chelsea. She hardly ate a thing. I slaved over that roast from eight o'clock this morning.'

'Perhaps she was nervous about what she had to say.'

'Or perhaps it was because . . . you'll never guess?'

'What?'

'She's only having a baby! At her age! That's why she can't give Izzy a kidney herself. Mum is over the moon of course. That's far bigger news to her than the fact that Annabel wants our organs. She's getting another new grandchild. She's like the cat that got the cream.'

Chelsea could imagine how that had played with Ronnie. She was grateful when she was able to cut short the conversation because Adam was at the door.

Adam had swung by, with Lily, to have tea at Chelsea's flat. Lily had been to a birthday party nearby that lunchtime. It was the perfect opportunity for another casual get-together. No pressure. Though of course Chelsea had spent at least five hours cleaning her place from top to bottom. And hiding her self-help books.

When she opened the door, Lily was standing in front of Adam. She was wearing the beautiful dress she had worn on the flight to Lanzarote, when Chelsea first encountered Lily's wilful streak. Her expression was the same as it had been that day as well.

'I would have preferred to go straight home,' she said.

'Yes, well,' said Adam. 'It's not all about what you want, Lily Roberts.'

Lily rewarded him with a glare. She stepped into Chelsea's hallway.

'It's quite small,' she said. 'And it smells.'

Chelsea was mortified.

'Lily,' said Adam. 'Don't be rude. It's a lovely flat,' he added. 'And look at this beautiful vase. Just right for these flowers.'

He flourished the bouquet he had been hiding behind his back. Gorgeous pink roses with heads the size of artichokes.

'Oh, they're lovely!' said Chelsea.

'Careful of the thorns,' said Lily. 'You might prick your finger and die!'

Chelsea shuddered.

'Too many fairy stories,' said Adam.

Chelsea wasn't in the least bit surprised that Lily didn't want any of the food she'd prepared for that evening, resorting instead to snacking on a packet of Mini Cheddars that Adam found at the bottom of his man-bag. Adam went into raptures over the delicate sandwiches to make up for his daughter's disapproval. That went some way to making Chelsea feel better, but she was extremely glad when Lily asked if she could watch television and Adam replied that it was up to Chelsea, as their host.

'Of course you may,' said Chelsea, mightily relieved to be out of the glare of Lily's disdain for just a little while.

With Lily safely occupied by the television in the other room, Chelsea told Adam about the surprise at her sister's Sunday lunch.

'She needs a kidney transplant. It's either one of us or waiting for someone suitable to die.'

Adam paused with his glass halfway to his mouth. It was just for a moment, but Chelsea noticed and realised almost instantaneously what she had said to make him lose track of what he was doing.

'Oh God,' she said. 'I'm sorry. I mean, I shouldn't have said that.'

'Why not? It's the truth.'

'But . . .'

'I'm really glad that my wife was on the donor register,' Adam said steadily. 'The thought that some good might have come of her death is a comfort to me, as I'm sure it will be to Lily later on, when she's old enough to understand what happened.'

Chelsea still felt awful. She continued to apologise.

'I wasn't thinking. I just said what came into my head . . .'

But Adam put the glass down and came round the table to stand beside her. He wrapped his arms round her shoulders and rested his chin on the top of her head. Then he kissed her crown.

'It sounds like your new sister is bringing you all sorts of things to think about,' he said. 'It can't be easy.'

'I know, but . . . I should have thought before I started talking . . .'

Adam kissed her again. 'I never want you to think that you can't say whatever you want in front of me. If you feel you have to censor yourself, what kind of future can we have together?'

At the word 'future', Chelsea felt her heart contract. She turned her face up towards him so that he could kiss her on the mouth. A future with Adam sounded like the most wonderful thing in the world.

How had she got so lucky? And was it possible that she could hang on to this wonderful man? They stayed like that for a while. Her sitting on the kitchen chair and him with his arms round her and his mouth pressed to her hair.

I love you. Chelsea's heart beat the words in silence. She couldn't wait for the moment when she would be able to say it out loud.

However, Chelsea's moment of bliss was interrupted when Lily came back into the kitchen. Under her disapproving gaze, the adults sprang apart. But Chelsea's disappointment turned to confused surprise when, rather than grabbing hold of Adam to reclaim him as her own, Lily insisted on climbing into Chelsea's lap.

'I think I will have a sandwich after all,' she said. 'Thank you, Chelsea.'

Adam and Chelsea smiled at one another over Lily's head.

Chapter Fifty-Seven

Ronnie

Ronnie had called Chelsea hoping her sister would be as outraged as she was by Annabel and Richard's request but Chelsea's response had been muted. It was clear she empathised with Annabel. So Ronnie called again the following morning, hoping that, having had time to think about it, Chelsea might be ready to bitch. She wasn't.

'Put yourself in her shoes,' Chelsea said. 'What would you do?'

Ronnie knew that she would have done the same. And of course she would have wanted Annabel's help. Of course she would have tracked Annabel down and asked for it. She probably wouldn't have waited so long after their first meeting to reveal her true intentions either.

'If you asked me to get tested for Sophie, I would be down at the hospital in a heartbeat,' said Chelsea. 'And I'm going to do the same for Annabel. If she needs me to.'

Shamed by Chelsea's open-hearted attitude and by how quickly her mother and father had agreed to be tested, Ronnie told Mark that they should get tested too. Then she finally texted Annabel her 'yes'.

Annabel called back right away. 'Thank you, Ronnie. I knew you would come through.'

* * *

The thing is, it was easy enough to agree to be tested as a match. Annabel moved quickly to get everyone an appointment at the private clinic and the family travelled there en masse (with the exception of Granddad Bill and Jack who remained at home for the day with Jacqui and Dave's neighbour). Sophie wasn't tested, as she was still too young, but she was keen to come along because Annabel, Richard and Izzy were going to meet them all for lunch afterwards. Sophie and Izzy had been talking to each other online. Their friendship was growing by the day.

And lunch was going to be the Buchanans' treat.

'The very least we could do,' Richard said.

Yes, on the morning of the tests, Ronnie felt good and brave and strong. She had never been a fan of needles – she'd always sent Mark to take the children for their vaccinations – but that day she had mustered her courage and stared ahead, full of stoicism, as the nurse at the clinic took what felt like a pint from her arm. It was for a good cause. It was for her *family*.

The momentary pain was more than outweighed by the pride Ronnie felt as she regarded the little plaster on her arm from which the sample had been taken. It made Ronnie feel selfless. A proper decent person. It made her feel a little closer to being Annabel's equal. Annabel's obvious gratitude was tremendously sweet for her sister. That was something money couldn't buy.

Lunch was at a country house hotel, altogether smarter than the Ridgeview where Jacqui, Dave and Annabel had their first meeting. The car park was full of fancy cars and, apart from Dave and Mark, all the men were wearing jackets. That might have been a problem were it not for the fact that Richard and Annabel were obviously regulars. The maître d' was all over them, taking coats and pulling out chairs and treating them all like royalty.

Once everyone was seated round a large round table, Richard suggested that they order a bottle of champagne as an aperitif to reward everyone for having given blood.

'As I understand it,' he said, 'champagne will help replace that lost blood more quickly than ordinary wine.'

'Do you mind if I have a beer?' asked Dave.

Mark, who had tested despite not being Izzy's blood relation, had the waiter line up two beers at once.

'They seemed to take an awful lot of blood out of my arm,' he explained.

Yes, it was very easy to agree to be tested for a match. It was nothing. A pinprick and less than a minute's discomfort in return for a lavish free lunch and Annabel's gushing gratitude was an absolute bargain. Though she didn't say it out loud, Ronnie couldn't see how it was possible any of the Bensons would be a match for Izzy in any case. If Richard had been ruled out because of something as common as high blood pressure, why should a grandparent or an aunt on her mother's side work instead?

Ronnie enjoyed the free lunch, drank enough champagne to fell a Shire horse and forgot all about the blood test. Until, four days later, she got the call from Dr Devon.

'Good news! You're a great match for Isabella,' said the consultant.

'What does that mean?' Ronnie asked.

'It means that if you decided to go ahead and become a donor, there is a good chance that Izzy would thrive with your kidney. Isn't it fantastic?'

Ronnie could only gasp in disbelief.

Chapter Fifty-Eight

Annabel

When she heard the news from Dr Devon (Ronnie had asked the consultant to make the call), Annabel danced around the kitchen, forgetting in an instant that she was dog-tired and aching on a daily basis as she entered her third trimester. Suddenly it was all worth it. Suddenly the agony of facing up to her past had come good in the most miraculous way. Ronnie was a match. Ronnie! Of all people. The Benson family member with whom Annabel felt she had the least in common turned out to be the one who could make Izzy well again. Annabel was ecstatic. With her mobile phone still in her hand, she whooped and punched the air.

But Richard was less excited.

'Hold on,' he said.

'What do you mean, "hold on"? Ronnie is a match. Izzy is going to get a new kidney. Thank God.'

'*If* Ronnie agrees to a transplant.'

'Of course she will. This is fantastic. It could happen within a couple of months. Dr Devon foresees no compatibility issues. There's no need for plasmapheresis. Assuming that everything goes well when Ronnie sees the psychologist, Izzy could be on the road to recovery by the New Year.'

'Annabel, we've got to give Ronnie time to think about it. I think it's quite possible that this news has come as a shock to her and to Mark.'

'How can they be shocked? They agreed to be tested. They knew this was the possible outcome. The best one. The one everybody wanted.'

'I don't know. There's a huge way to go from a blood test to letting someone have one of your organs. They said "yes" to being tested so quickly. They can't have really thought about it that hard. And perhaps they were assuming it would be Jacqui or Dave who came up trumps.'

'But it isn't.' Jacqui and Dave had both been ruled out for their high blood pressure. Just like Richard. Mark wasn't a close enough match. 'It's Ronnie. We have to see them all again as soon as possible. We need to do everything we can to make this happen and soon.'

'Perhaps we should give them a little while to digest the news first?' Richard suggested.

'Richard, we're talking about our daughter's health! When can we see them?'

Izzy's birthday was coming up. It was the perfect opportunity to bring the two families together again without it seeming forced. Except that of course the whole thing would be planned with great precision. It wasn't Izzy's eighteenth – that was still a year away – but it could still be very special. Impressive.

The Twilight, one of Izzy's favourite bands, were going to be playing at the O2. Ordinarily, Izzy would have been glued to her laptop the moment the tickets went on sale, desperate for a chance to breathe the same air as her heroes. This time she hadn't bothered. It hadn't seemed worth it. Not when she was so ill. But the news that Ronnie was a match had given everyone a new burst of energy and now Izzy *did* want to see her heroes. Alas, the tickets were all sold out.

'Leave it with me,' said Richard.

There was nothing that couldn't be solved with cold hard cash. Two days later, Richard announced that he had secured the use of a corporate box at the stadium, which meant that Izzy could take as many friends as she wanted. So long as Sophie Benson-Edwards was top of the list.

Chapter Fifty-Nine

Jacqui

Jacqui was as delighted as Annabel to discover that Ronnie was a match. When Ronnie told her, over coffee in Jacqui's kitchen, Jacqui hugged her middle daughter so hard, she almost squeezed the life out of her.

'You'll make us all so proud,' said Jacqui. 'You are going to do it, aren't you?'

Ronnie nodded. Jacqui didn't notice if it lacked enthusiasm and as soon as Ronnie left to go home and make tea for the children, Jacqui called Annabel and told her that Ronnie was 'raring to go'.

Perhaps Annabel had only reconnected with her birth family because she was looking for a donor for Izzy, but Jacqui was sure that the dynamics were shifting. Annabel seemed to want to be a proper part of the family at last. Jacqui was starting to feel as though they really knew each other now. She was no longer hesitant about calling up to see how Izzy was getting on. Annabel always seemed pleased to speak to her on the phone. And she always asked how *everybody* was getting on. Annabel even asked after Granddad Bill. Not that there was ever very much to report where he was concerned. He lived in his chair with the TV tuned permanently to Sky Sports, occasionally taking a trip as far as the corner shop in his wheelchair if Jack was visiting and wanted to go along for the ride.

As the autumn marched on, Jacqui began to wonder whether it would be premature to invite the Buchanans to spend Christmas at her and Dave's house. They could just about do it, if they moved Granddad Bill's bed out of the dining room for the day and brought the table back downstairs. That could easily seat eight adults. The children could sit at the kitchen table. Jack would love that. But then Jacqui considered that Annabel had probably already made Christmas plans. With Sarah, her adoptive mum.

Most evenings, after putting Granddad Bill to bed, Jacqui went online. She'd always been a big fan of Facebook. It was a great way of keeping up with Ronnie's children during the week. She loved to see pictures of Sophie and Jack. But now she had Annabel and Izzy to check in on as well. She had scrolled through Annabel's photographs a hundred times, so that she almost felt as though she had been there when Izzy picked up the Latin prize at school or at Annabel's fortieth birthday party, which had been themed around black and red. Annabel looked so beautiful in the dress she'd had made especially for the occasion. She had such elegance and style. Jacqui wasn't sure where she'd got that from. Was it down to Sarah? Or, as Jacqui preferred to think, perhaps Dave's insistence that his great-grandmother had fallen pregnant by a lord was the truth after all.

Now that she and Annabel had been reunited, Jacqui looked at two other sorts of sites too. She looked at a forum for people who were awaiting kidney transplants, searching for good news about live donations. She was heartened to see so many success stories. And then she looked at an adoption reunion forum.

Jacqui had lurked on the adoption forum for quite some time but it was only when Annabel came back into her life that she finally felt able to stop lurking and say something herself. She felt it was her duty to give hope to the other women – and some men – on the site, who had been waiting years for contact. There were so many sad stories. So much pain. They had to know their dreams might still come true.

Eventually Jacqui drifted into a couple of discussions about ongoing relationships between adult adoptees and their birth families. She read that the initial reunion was the easy part. Finding a way forward was harder. It was difficult to work out what the relationship should be. It couldn't be the usual dynamic of parent and child when the 'child' had never been around that parent. In fact most reunions eventually broke down.

'You have to remember,' someone wrote, 'that your child has had parents for the whole of the time you've been apart. Those people adopted your child for *life*. They're not going to disappear and your child won't want them to either. They are every bit as much your child's real family as you think you are. You must respect that. You can't try to force a closer relationship than your adult son or daughter wants.'

Patience was the key, according to those who had been through it and succeeded in forming a close bond. So Jacqui continued to sit on the urge to ask Annabel for Christmas. Though she did take a tape measure to the dining room and look online for a bigger table. Perhaps she could invite Sarah too.

Chapter Sixty

Sophie

With the concert tickets secured, the Buchanans set about organising Izzy's birthday celebrations in earnest. Because the O2 was such a faff to get to and from, they decided in the end that they would stay overnight in the flat Richard used during the week for work. Sophie could join them there. A London sleepover.

Sophie was over the moon at Izzy's invitation. At fifteen years old, she had never been to London before. The thought of going to the capital city, of spending the day seeing the sights (or, more accurately, hitting the shops) and an evening at the O2 watching her new favourite band, The Twilight, was more than she could possibly have hoped for. And Izzy's parents were paying for everything.

'We're going to be in a box at the O2,' Izzy explained. 'One of Dad's clients got the tickets. We might even be able to go backstage. Dad's working on it.'

It just got better and better.

Sophie shared her excitement with Izzy online.

'I can't believe you invited me.'

'Why wouldn't I?' Izzy asked. 'You're my friend.'

With the knowledge that she was going to London to take part in such an exclusive event, Sophie walked a little taller at school. She no longer cared about Harrison and Skyler and their small-town ambitions. The gossip they indulged in seemed pathetic. Sophie was on a different trajectory now.

The only problem was what to wear.

Sophie took as many hours at the bakery as she could outside school but she was on the minimum wage and unless she found a black market for damaged buns, she could think of no other way to increase her income in time to smarten up her look ready to meet Izzy's other friends, the ones who had been at the festival where Izzy took the pills. That was something Sophie's parents still didn't know about – the real reason for Izzy's kidney failure. The secret knowledge had brought Izzy and Sophie even closer. Sophie had promised never to tell.

When it came to impressing those private-school girls, however, it was Auntie Chelsea who came to the rescue. It was part of the plan that Chelsea would meet up with Sophie and the Buchanans while they were all in London. Chelsea promised Sophie that she could have her birthday present early if she liked. Maybe they should have a quick look in the gigantic Topshop at Oxford Circus for a start?

Sophie was delighted. London, a gig at the O2 and shopping. As far as she was concerned, Annabel's reconnection with the Benson family was the best thing that had happened to them in a long time.

Chapter Sixty-One

Chelsea

The Buchanans picked Sophie up in Coventry and drove down to London in the Porsche, leaving Leander back at Great House with Sarah. They dropped the car off outside Richard's Fulham pied-à-terre and caught a taxi into town where they met Chelsea at Bond Street. They would go to a restaurant nearby before hitting the shops for a while. Sophie had been excited enough by the thought of Topshop. The thought of going to Selfridges was enough to blow her mind. It was a teenage girl's equivalent of Disneyland.

Meanwhile, Chelsea welcomed the opportunity to spend time with Annabel without having Ronnie there as well. Chelsea had wondered what it would have been like had the three women grown up together. Ronnie and Chelsea had been close as children. Would she have been close to Annabel too? From what little she knew of her long-lost sister, Chelsea was beginning to think they had quite a bit in common. While Ronnie was hot-headed and quick to take offence, Chelsea was better able to sit on her feelings. She sensed that Annabel was the same. More measured. Perhaps more anxious too, though maybe that was just because of the current circumstances. Who wouldn't be anxious when their child was so unwell?

As it turned out, Chelsea and Annabel did have plenty

in common and without Ronnie and Jacqui to monop-
olise the conversation, they were soon chatting like old
friends. Away from Ronnie in particular, Annabel seemed
much more relaxed and open.

Chelsea thought that perhaps she had some understanding of how Annabel must feel when talking to
their middle sister. Chelsea herself often toned down
tales of her own life for fear of being called hoity-toity
or a snob. Though Ronnie was kind at heart and would
give you the shirt off her back if you needed it – as
demonstrated in her decision to give Izzy a kidney –
she could get quite nasty if she thought she was
somehow being left behind by the conversation or
patronised. But Chelsea and Annabel had none of
those worries when they talked to each other. They
could talk about London to their hearts' content
without fear of leaving anyone out or appearing to be
too exclusive. They could talk about restaurants and
shops they both liked visiting. Chelsea could talk about
her work. Annabel even seemed slightly in awe of
Chelsea's job at the magazine.

'It's five per cent glamour and ninety-five per cent
spellcheck,' Chelsea assured her.

'I wish I'd done something creative,' Annabel admitted.
'I worked in the City until we had Izzy. I didn't really
like my job but I do sometimes miss the buzz of an
office. I was thinking about setting up my own business,'
she added. 'Before Izzy and . . . this.' She indicated her
bump, which could no longer be mistaken for the results
of a weekend of overindulgence.

'What sort of business?' Chelsea asked.

'Events. We've got some outhouses at the Great
House. I thought we might do weddings. Something
like that.'

'Perhaps you still will. The baby won't always be a baby and Izzy will soon be leaving home.'

Annabel smiled. 'She will, won't she? Once she's had the transplant and gone back to school. In two years she could be at university just as we always hoped.' Annabel exhaled deeply. 'Oh, Chelsea. I can't tell you what your sister is going to do for us. What a difference it will make. I thank God a thousand times a day that we met you all.' She reached over and squeezed Chelsea's hand. 'We were totally without hope. Everything was looking so desperate. Now we can start looking forward to the future again. *Our* sister is an amazing woman.'

'She is. I know she can sometimes come across as a bit hard before you get to know her, but she is the softest person you could ever hope to meet under all that. And she's so generous.'

They raised a toast to Ronnie. Chelsea with white wine. Annabel with sparkling water.

When lunch came to an end, Sophie and Izzy announced that they wanted to hit Selfridges. Because Izzy still got tired so easily, Richard volunteered to go with them to make sure they didn't come to any harm. He promised that he would lurk behind the rails so that no one had to know he was with the girls at all.

'Dad, that's even worse,' said Izzy. 'You can't *lurk* in the women's fashion department. Someone will call the police.'

Sophie, fortunately, was not as embarrassed by the thought of being seen with Izzy's father as she was about being seen with her own. Richard was so worldly and cool.

'Are you kidding?' Izzy rolled her eyes when Sophie suggested as much to her. 'Dad's a dork.'

*　　*　　*

Annabel and Chelsea stayed behind in the restaurant. Chelsea had done Selfridges a thousand times and Annabel was only too happy to stay put, cradling her bump while the baby inside turned somersaults as was its new habit after every meal. It got very excited after eating.

Now that they were alone together, the conversation could go a little deeper. Emboldened by the wine Richard had pressed on her over lunch, Chelsea asked a question to which she'd been longing to know the answer. She knew that Jacqui, Dave and Ronnie all wanted to know the answer as well.

'Why didn't you look for us before?' Chelsea asked. 'Why did it take Izzy getting ill to make you find us?'

Slightly taken aback by Chelsea's directness, Annabel put down her teacup and looked into space for a moment, as though hoping someone would prompt her with what she should say next.

'You don't have to talk about it if you don't want to,' Chelsea back-pedalled.

Annabel shook her head. 'No. It's fine. I can understand why you're asking.'

They waited while a waitress cleared away their plates.

'Well,' Annabel began when they were alone again. 'For a start, I didn't know there were so many of you. I had no idea that Jacqui and Dave would have married and that I would have two full siblings. Had I known that, then I might have looked sooner, but . . .'

Chelsea leaned forward to hear.

'Maybe that's not the truth.'

Annabel sat back in her chair and continued to speak without looking at her new sister, as though making eye contact would render her unable to speak again.

'It was a strange feeling, you know, finding out that

Jacqui and Dave got back together and went on to have more kids. In some ways it made things worse. It made me feel as though I'd been a trial run that didn't work out. It added what I can only describe as another layer of rejection, to find out that they'd raised two daughters after giving me away.'

'Dad didn't know about the adoption,' Chelsea reminded her. 'And Mum wouldn't have given you away if she could possibly have looked after you on her own.'

'I know,' said Annabel. 'I know. And I understand. But what you have to remember is that growing up, all I heard was that I was the child of teenage parents who gave me up. That wasn't a lot to go on. And my imagination filled in the rest in a variety of dark and unhappy ways. Mum and Dad claimed, and now I've seen the files, I believe, that they weren't given much information. But I decided that there were things they did know and were keeping from me because they were too awful. I'd have a flash of irrational anger – just hormones probably – and wonder if it was because my father was really a violent psychopath. Or maybe I'd been taken away from my mother because she was mad and one day I would end up like that too.'

Chelsea shook her head. 'That's crazy.'

'I'm serious. When you've never met your biological family, these worries seem very real.'

'How could you ever have thought you might have a psychopath for a parent?'

'You haven't seen me with PMT,' Annabel said with a smile.

'So, wouldn't delving into your past sooner have set your mind at rest?' Chelsea asked.

'Perhaps. But I couldn't take the risk that one of my fears would be confirmed instead. It seemed safer not to know. And I had happier fantasies too. Like my parents were Charlotte Rampling and Bryan Ferry. Or Mick Jagger and Princess Anne.'

Chelsea laughed.

Annabel looked down. She picked at a hangnail and made her next pronouncement very quietly. 'And I wanted to punish them.'

'Punish them? Who?'

'Jacqui and Dave. Jacqui especially. I know that must sound awful to you but she gave me away, Chelsea. *Gave. Me. Away.* I can't explain how profound an effect that's had on my entire life.'

Much as she wanted to defend the only mother she had known, Chelsea let Annabel carry on.

'I know, rationally, that Jacqui did what she did with the very best intentions. But when you're a six-year-old child and your school friends are calling you a bastard and telling you your beloved mum and dad aren't your "real parents" and someone's going to come and take you away to a children's home, it's frightening. And later you start to believe that you must have been given up because of something you did. And it doesn't matter how often someone tells you that's ridiculous. You were just a few weeks old. What could you possibly have done? That feeling of being bad or somehow lacking is so strong and so deep.'

Chelsea nodded.

'I blamed Jacqui for that. And I wanted her to know some of my pain. Even though, objectively, I had the best childhood I could have hoped for and I would not have changed a thing. I'm glad I was adopted but there were still moments . . .' Annabel sighed. 'I was terrified of being taken away from Mum and Dad and as a result I built up a kind of armour that affected all my relationships. I was a prickly child and a nightmare teenager.

283

All because I wanted to be safe and thought that keeping everyone at arm's length was the best way to protect myself from being abandoned again. I always felt like I needed to hold something of myself back. I didn't even tell Richard I was adopted until Izzy got ill and I had to.'

'Oh Annabel,' Chelsea whispered. 'I didn't know.'

'He's taken it very well, thank goodness.'

'It must have been hard to have to tell him under such circumstances.'

'It was . . . When I became an adult, I read a lot about adoption and how having children of their own can mellow an adoptee's feelings towards their birth family but that didn't happen for me. The moment they put Izzy in my arms, I knew that the only way I could ever be parted from that baby was if someone shot me in the head first. That only made me angrier still towards Jacqui. What kind of unnatural woman was she to not feel the strength of maternal love I did? So, even when Mum – I mean, Sarah – suggested to me that Jacqui might like to know how I'd turned out because surely she must have spent all those years wondering what became of me and maybe I should put her out of her misery, I continued to hold out. I didn't want Jacqui to share my happiness. I didn't want her to turn up and try to be Izzy's grandma when Mum was the one who had been there all those years. After all, Mum was the one who had rocked me to sleep when I was a baby and dried my tears and kissed me better. Not Jacqui.'

Chelsea felt tears spring to her eyes.

'You might think I'm a bitch,' said Annabel. 'I know Ronnie did. Probably still does! But more than anything, my decision not to track you down was mostly about self-preservation. I didn't want Jacqui to have the opportunity to reject me all over again.'

Annabel closed her eyes and smiled sadly, holding in the emotion. Chelsea dabbed a napkin at the corner of her own eyes. She wished that Ronnie might have heard Annabel's speech. It was hard for Chelsea to imagine Jacqui, her 'Mum', as the awful rejecting monster of Annabel's nightmares but what Annabel had said did make a lot of sense. Chelsea suddenly saw her big sister as the small child she had been, struggling to understand her painful backstory.

Annabel opened her eyes again and smiled more widely. A happy smile. After a fashion.

'But now we're here and you're not anywhere near as bad as I imagined.'

She gave Chelsea a playful punch in the arm.

'And neither's Ronnie. She's one of the kindest, loveliest women I've ever met.'

'She is,' Chelsea agreed.

'I wish I'd met you both years ago.'

It almost sounded true.

After that, Chelsea suddenly felt that she could tell Annabel her own truth. Since Ronnie had been found to be a match for Izzy and the transplant was going ahead, what Chelsea had to say didn't matter anywhere near as much as it might otherwise have done. And Chelsea wanted to say it. She didn't want Annabel to have the wrong idea about what had actually happened since she made her request.

'I have a confession to make,' said Chelsea. 'Since we're sisters now and sisters aren't supposed to keep secrets from one another.'

'Go on.' Annabel looked bemused.

'Annabel, I didn't ever get tested to see if I was a match for Izzy. I know I said I was going to and I did go to see my GP to get things started. But you see, the thing is, I've been facing a few problems of my own. And when I talked to my GP and afterwards to my counsellor, they thought that perhaps I shouldn't put myself through it. Not right now at least.'

'What do you mean?'

'I'm being treated for bulimia.'

Annabel opened her mouth as if to say something but thought better of it. Chelsea carried on.

'I'm sure that had Ronnie not tested as a match, I would have found the guts to do it but I'm not certain that Izzy would want one of my kidneys anyway. I must have given them a bashing over the years.'

Chelsea chuntered on to cover the silence that she started to take for disapproval.

'Anyway, I'm sorry and it goes without saying that if it doesn't work out with Ronnie, I'll do everything I can. It's just that at the moment—'

'It's OK,' said Annabel at last. 'I understand. When did . . . when did you start?'

'Sixth form. At least that's when I started to be more careful about what I ate. But I didn't start throwing up until I was at university. I don't think I would have guessed it was a possible strategy but there was another girl on my corridor in the halls of residence who told me that was what she did when she'd eaten too much.'

Annabel nodded.

'I've never enjoyed doing it,' Chelsea continued. 'I'm always disgusted in myself. I'm disgusted with the puking and I'm disgusted with the lack of willpower I sometimes have around food.'

'I know how that feels.'

'It's all about control, isn't it? I was so unhappy and I felt like I would never be as good as Ronnie or the other girls at school or university. But I could be the thinnest. Now I know I've got to kick it. I can't be like this for the rest of my life. I shared a room with Jack in Lanzarote and he noticed I was always throwing up. You can't imagine how bad that felt. The thought of letting him down is one of the things that is going to get me through this.'

'Jack's a thoughtful child.'

'Funny how it sometimes takes a child to point out the obvious. He told me I had to see a doctor, though I hope he didn't know that I was making *myself* be sick.'

'You'll be able to talk to him about it when he's older.' Annabel squeezed Chelsea's hand. 'But I'm glad you told me now. Anytime you need to talk, please know that you can call me, won't you?'

Chelsea felt sure Annabel meant it.

'And this is just between us.' Annabel confirmed what Chelsea dare not ask. 'I understand why you perhaps don't want to tell Ronnie.'

At that moment, Sophie and Izzy returned to the restaurant with Richard in tow.

'There is *nothing* in Selfridges. Nothing,' Izzy announced.

'Did you go round the whole shop?' asked Annabel.

'Felt like it,' Richard confirmed.

Shortly after the girls' and Richard's return, Chelsea left them to do her own thing. She had a date with Adam that evening. His parents were kindly babysitting Lily again. If Chelsea was honest, she was nervous. Though she and Adam had been seeing each other for a couple of months now, they hadn't ever spent the whole night together. Lily's presence had been a very effective form of contraception.

But that night Lily would not be there. She would be staying with her grandparents at their house and Adam and Chelsea would be at his place alone. They had until teatime on Sunday.

After leaving Annabel and the others, Chelsea caught a bus to Knightsbridge and Harvey Nichols. There she treated herself to a new set of La Perla underwear. Well, it was not so much a frivolity as necessary armament. Though he had seen her in her bikini on holiday, Adam had not seen Chelsea anywhere near naked since. She wanted that night to be special. Her stomach churned and gurgled with anticipation and by the time she arrived at Adam's house at seven thirty, she was just about ready to faint with excitement.

Adam cooked. While he chopped onions and crushed garlic, ingredients forbidden when Lily was in the house – 'You have to have some too or you won't be able to kiss me' – Chelsea told him about the conversation with Annabel. Not the gory detail of it. Certainly not the stuff about her bulimia or her not having been tested. Just that they had finally had a chance to talk one-to-one and get to know each other a little better. It simply hadn't been possible before. Jacqui monopolised Annabel whenever she was around.

'And I think we understand each other,' Chelsea said. 'I think the whole posh thing is a bit of an act. It's a way of keeping people at arm's length.'

'Good,' said Adam. He took a spoonful of sauce from the pan and asked Chelsea to taste it.

'Delicious.'

'Like you,' he said, kissing her long and hard.

Later that night, they made love for the first time.

'You are beautiful,' said Adam. 'Every bit of you. Inside and out.'

In the darkness, Chelsea snuggled into Adam's side and allowed herself to believe it.

Chapter Sixty-Two

Izzy

Nothing was going to prevent Izzy from enjoying her birthday weekend in London to the full. The dialysis machine may have had to go with her, but she was determined that while she wasn't actually hooked up to it, she would pretend that the whole past four months had never happened and she was as happy and healthy as she had been when she turned sixteen twelve months earlier. Fingers crossed, in another twelve months she would be happy and healthy again.

Izzy could tell that Sophie was nervous about meeting Izzy's old school friends. Sophie had admitted as much while they were walking around Selfridges, trying and failing to find something new to wear.

Sophie had brought a huge suitcase with her to London, which basically contained every single thing she owned. She had packed for all eventualities. She had her jeans. She had her trackie bottoms. She even had the dress she'd worn to her mum and dad's wedding. None of it was quite right and Izzy could tell that Sophie had set all her hopes on finding something to buy with the money Chelsea had given her at lunch. When they came out of Selfridges empty-handed, Izzy felt slightly guilty. She knew that they hadn't been able to shop anywhere near as long as Sophie would have liked to because she, Izzy, got exhausted so quickly these days.

They didn't even get to the massive Topshop at Oxford Circus. Sophie's insistence that having something special to wear didn't matter made Izzy feel even worse. To a point. What Sophie didn't know was that Izzy had a fallback plan.

When they got to Richard's flat, Izzy took Sophie into the guest bedroom and pulled something out of her own bag.

'I think you should try this. I brought it along with you in mind.'

It was the All Saints dress that had caught Sophie's eye when she saw it hanging on the back of the wardrobe door in Izzy's room way back in May. The dress she could never have afforded for herself.

'It's clean,' said Izzy. 'I've never worn it.'

'Then don't you want to wear it first?' Sophie asked.

'No. I think you should wear it. I know it's going to suit you better than me anyway.'

'Are you serious?'

'Yes. I don't know why I bought it. Black doesn't suit me but on you it looks great.'

'If you're sure . . .'

'Sophie,' said Izzy. 'Don't be so wet. I told you I brought it here especially for you. Just try the dress on, will you? If you don't like it, you can go in your jeans.'

Sophie went into the bathroom and changed out of her tatty clothes and into the dress. When she came back out to see what she thought, Izzy was delighted. She had been right that the dress would be perfect for her cousin. It was transforming. Sophie definitely had no need to worry whether she could hold her own against Jessica now. She grinned from ear to ear. Izzy was surprised at how much Sophie's happiness improved her own mood. She had started to feel a little jaded after lunch and Selfridges but Sophie's excitement lifted her up again. And she was so glad she could give Sophie that dress that she almost forgot the reason she would never wear it wasn't the colour at all. It was because dialysis seemed to leave her permanently bloated. She'd put on six pounds since she started. That was another thing Izzy wished she'd known before she took those stupid pills.

With their outfits finally sorted, there was just time for the girls to do their hair and make-up before they set off to the O2. The rest of Izzy's friends would meet them there.

Soon Jessica, Chloe and Gina were talking to Sophie as though they'd known her for ever. Sophie got bonus points when she explained that her Auntie Chelsea – now Izzy's aunt too – worked on *Society* magazine and met celebs all the time. She held everyone rapt with the story of how Chelsea had met Eugenia Lapkiss, the actress of the moment, who turned out to be so thick that she quoted Homer Simpson and attributed what he said to Socrates.

The band were great. They were far better live than Izzy had expected. And the girls had such a spectacular view. They leaned over the balcony at the front of the box and screamed along.

From time to time, Izzy retreated back into the hospitality room that was attached to the box to sit on one of the sofas and regain some energy, but for once she didn't feel as though she would rather be in bed. She felt almost herself again.

They stayed until the band had played their encores and then, the best part of all, they got to go backstage. Izzy was aware that her status, as someone waiting for a kidney transplant, had almost certainly earned them this privilege but – fuck it – if anything good could come out of what she was going through then she was going to make the most of it. The girls took a thousand pictures of their idols from up close.

'And I will never wash my hand again,' said Jessica, after the lead singer signed the back of her hand with a biro.

Jessica, Chloe and Gina went back home to the Midlands that night but Sophie and the Buchanans only had to go as far as Fulham.

Izzy and Sophie shared the guest bedroom. Annabel had suggested that perhaps Sophie might prefer to sleep on the sofa bed in the living room, since Izzy was going to have to dialyse overnight and the noise of the machine could keep Sophie awake. But Sophie and Izzy did not want to be parted.

'And the noise won't bother me,' said Sophie. 'I can hear my dad snoring through the wall at home. If you can sleep through that, you can sleep through anything.'

'If you're sure,' said Annabel.

'Mum,' said Izzy. 'She's said she's OK with it.'

There were two single beds in the spare room. The dialysis machine was set up between them. Sophie politely busied herself with a pile of old copies of *Elle* while Annabel donned a mask and helped Izzy sterilise the equipment and set up the bags of dialysis fluid Izzy would use that night. Sophie looked at the wall while Izzy plugged a tube into the catheter that protruded from her stomach. The machine was started.

'You can look at me again now,' said Izzy, who had, of course, noticed Sophie's painful efforts to give her some privacy.

'Good night, girls,' said Annabel.

She kissed both Izzy and Sophie on the foreheads then left them alone at last.

Annabel need not have worried about the noise the dialysis machine made. It was far quieter than Sophie had expected. Just a faint humming, like the sound of distant traffic.

All the same, Sophie and Izzy did not fall asleep right away. They were still way too wired from their night at the O2.

'This has been my best birthday ever,' said Izzy. 'I don't think I could have imagined anything better.'

'Me either,' said Sophie. 'I am going to remember this day for the rest of my life. I can't believe I got to meet The Twilight. Skyler will be sick when she finds out. And Harrison.'

'Swipe left,' Izzy reminded her. 'You don't even need to care about what those two think. You know,' she continued, 'the concert was brilliant, but the best part of all was having you here with me. We're properly friends now, aren't we? You've forgiven me for being a bitch when we first met?'

'If you've forgiven me for getting hard in return.'

'Yeah. You were scary.'

'Got to be scary when you come from the rough part of town like I do,' Sophie opined.

'Yeah. It's *so* rough where you are,' Izzy mocked. 'Even the toddlers carry knuckledusters.'

'Not much to look forward to except fighting, having four babies and getting fat.'

'Oh bullshit.'

'Seriously, though, my town is like some sinkhole that sucks you in. I don't know anyone who's escaped it.'

'What do you mean? Your Auntie Chelsea did.'

'She's an exception.'

'You could be an exception too.'

'Yeah,' said Sophie. 'I don't think so.'

'Why not? You should go to university, Sophie. You don't have to leave school and go straight into a job. Think about it.'

'I've thought about it already. I can't afford the tuition fees.'

'You don't have to be able to. You can get a loan and you don't have to start paying it back until you're earning seventeen grand.'

'How am ever I going to earn seventeen grand?'

'That's a starting salary!' said Izzy.

'For the kind of jobs people like you get, perhaps.'

'People like me?'

'Posh people.'

'I'm not posh.'

'You've got fish knives.'

'Exactly. Really posh people would never have fish knives.'

'Now I'm just confused,' Sophie said.

'But what do you mean "people like me"? Come on. Fill me in. What makes me any different from you?'

'A private education, of course. And knowing all the right things to say. And which fork to use at the dinner table.'

'I forgot your family eats with their fingers,' Izzy joked. 'Look, don't be so pessimistic about your chances, Soph. Think about what you want to be and go for it. Don't limit yourself because, trust me, plenty of other people will try to do that. Or you could make one stupid mistake, like I did, and see all your options disappear in a heartbeat. Right now, you could be anywhere, doing anything. So, while you've got the advantage, take it, for fuck's sake.'

Chrissie Manby

Sophie opened her mouth to say something.

'And don't give me that stuff about not being clever enough. There's no one in my class at school who *isn't* planning on going to uni and I know for a fact that hardly any of them are more intelligent than you are. It's just a different kind of school. Where I go, they assume you'll make it.'

'Where I go, making it is getting a job in a call centre.'

'You're better than that. Raise your expectations.'

'Easy for you to say.'

'Easy for you to *do*. Sophie, seriously. What right do you have not to make the most of your talents and every advantage you've got when there are people like me who can't get out there because we have to spend every night hooked to a dialysis machine. It makes me so angry when you talk yourself down.'

'I didn't grow up like you did. I didn't get your education. I didn't even know that half the jobs you talk about, and the places you've been to, existed.'

'Well, you do now. And you know which fork to use,' Izzy added.

'Now I feel like you're patronising me.'

'I don't mean to.'

'You're only a year older than me.'

'And I've seen my life flash before my eyes,' Izzy reminded her. 'I want the best for you, Sophie, because I think you're one of the nicest people I've ever met.'

'Really?' said Sophie. 'I feel the same about you.'

'Then I hope you'll let me keep on nagging you. Dream big. Like I'm still trying to.'

Izzy was glad that the lights were out so Sophie couldn't see her cry.

Chapter Sixty-Three

Annabel

The following evening, having dropped Richard and Izzy off at the Great House on the way, Annabel drove Sophie back home to Coventry. When she got there, she went up to the front door, expecting, if she was honest, to be invited in. After all, she had spent the entire weekend looking after Ronnie's daughter. A cup of tea wouldn't be too much to ask in return, would it? Except that Annabel didn't want a cup of tea. She wanted a firmer promise of something much more important.

'Did you have a good time?' Ronnie asked her daughter.

'The best,' Sophie confirmed.

Jack, who had just been put to bed, had heard his sister's return and was now standing at the top of the stairs.

'We got you a present, Jack!' Sophie went on inside. Jack careened down the stairs to meet her. She and Izzy had bought Jack a Doctor Who baseball cap from a stall on Oxford Street. It had a cheesy glow-in-the-dark Tardis decal on the front. He would love it.

'Thank you for taking Sophie along,' said Ronnie.

'Oh, it was our pleasure,' said Annabel. 'Sophie is such a lovely girl and she really brings out the best in Izzy. It's almost as though they're sisters.'

Ronnie agreed. 'Sophie always wanted a sister. When

she came to see Jack in the hospital the day he was born, she asked if we could swap him for the little girl in the next cot. I sometimes wish I had!'

The real sisters laughed at the thought. They both knew Ronnie adored her son and Annabel couldn't help but be charmed by him too.

'He's such a poppet,' Annabel said. 'Seeing him always brightens up my day.' But still Ronnie wasn't inviting Annabel in. She kept her standing on the doorstep until, at last, Annabel admitted to herself that she wasn't going to get a cup of tea, or a chance to discuss what she *really* wanted to talk about. Not that night.

'Well, I suppose I'd better get back home,' she said. 'It's been a busy couple of days. But perhaps you and I should go out together on our own one evening soon. So that we can have a proper talk about . . .'

Annabel let Ronnie complete the sentence in her head.

'Sure,' said Ronnie. 'That'd be nice.'

'I'll text you with some dates,' said Annabel.

She stepped forward to give Ronnie a hug. Ronnie hesitated for a moment before returning the embrace somewhat perfunctorily. Annabel squeezed tighter to see if perhaps she could squash some sign of affection from her. She couldn't. She gave up.

'See you soon,' said Annabel. Walking back to the car, she tried to push away the uncomfortable notion that something wasn't quite right.

Chapter Sixty-Four

Ronnie

What Annabel didn't know was that Ronnie had been giving the whole issue of the transplant some very serious consideration that weekend and the conclusions she had drawn were not good news for Izzy.

'Oh God. I can't stand it,' Ronnie wailed to Mark when they were alone in the lounge after Jack and Sophie had gone to bed. 'She wants to go out, just me and her, to talk. You know what she wants to talk about.'

'Well, she'll have to wait until we've finished talking about it between ourselves,' said Mark.

Truth be told, since they got the news that Ronnie was a match, the atmosphere in Mark and Ronnie's house had been somewhat tense. Ronnie had been shocked by the news. There was no other way to put it. She'd simply never really considered that it could be her. She tried to be happy that she'd been discovered to be a match; that she could help a poorly child. She read everything she could lay her hands on about what it meant, looking for reassurance. And Jacqui had been *so* pleased. Ronnie couldn't remember when she'd last felt quite so loved, appreciated and looked up to by the rest of her family. The donation would make her a heroine to her parents, her new sister, her niece . . .

But it wasn't that simple. Inside, Ronnie was not sure she wanted to be a donor at all, which was why, though she put up a good argument in favour of donating, she was secretly glad that Mark was suddenly quite strongly against the idea. He'd been investigating the process too and was not in the least bit comforted by what he had found online either.

'It's a proper, major operation, Ronnie. We're not just talking about an afternoon in hospital. You could be in there for weeks. And we've got our own kids to think of,' said Mark.

'And that's why I should do it,' said Ronnie. 'Because if the situation was reversed and we were the ones who needed help, I'd bloody well hope she would do the same for us.'

'But what if you get ill from the operation? What if one day Sophie needs a kidney? Or Jack? And I can't give them one of mine like Richard can't give one to his daughter? Or what if we lose you altogether during the op? It's possible.'

Yes, Mark was giving Ronnie all the excuses she needed to tell Annabel that she could not go under the knife. But when it came down to it, Ronnie was going to have to be the one who looked Annabel in the eye and actually say it wasn't going to happen. That was why Ronnie hadn't invited Annabel in that evening. That was why seeing how happy Sophie had been to spend time with the Buchanan family was so difficult, because there was no way that Sophie would be invited to spend time with them again. Not after Ronnie dropped her bombshell.

Ronnie felt absolutely physically sick at the prospect. She understood Annabel only too well. What fellow mother wouldn't? What decent human being wouldn't?

Annabel texted with potential dates for their 'girls' night' the very next morning. And when Ronnie didn't respond at once, Annabel texted to make sure you got my text. And then she called and left a message.

'I'm not sure my texts are getting through,' she said. 'Would you call me to let me know which of the following dates might work for you . . .'

Ronnie was frozen. She couldn't possibly call Annabel back. She didn't know what to say. But while she was holding off on making that call, she found it impossible to settle. Eventually, she texted Annabel back to suggest the very latest of the dates Annabel had offered her. Anything to buy some time. Ronnie would pluck up the courage to tell her before Annabel took her out on the worst possible girls' night Ronnie could imagine. She would. She had to.

Chapter Sixty-Five

Ronnie

Alas, Ronnie didn't pluck up the courage to tell Annabel she didn't want to go through with the kidney donation and the date of their 'girls' night' soon came round. When Ronnie woke up in the morning, she felt physically sick but she knew, alas, that it wasn't from some sort of virus that could have given her a reason to cancel the night out. Ronnie was sick from worry and that was a nausea that wasn't going to go away until she addressed what it was that was on her mind.

This was to be the first time Ronnie and Annabel had spent time alone. Annabel had chosen a lovely little restaurant in Warwick. It was somewhere that Ronnie had seen reviewed in the local paper, run by a young chef who had trained under Gordon Ramsay. Ronnie had fantasised that one day she and Mark might go there for a romantic evening. There was a moment when she'd thought that perhaps they could even have their wedding reception there. But it was so expensive. They could only afford the King's Head. And now Annabel was taking her to this fancy place. Ronnie's fantasy of dinner for two with the man she loved was over. She had to tell Annabel she wasn't going to do the transplant and the ensuing row would ensure that Ronnie never wanted to go anywhere near that restaurant ever again.

'Maybe she'll be OK about it,' said Mark. 'She'll

understand what a big deal it is. She's probably expecting it, after the way you were with her the other night. Just make sure you get something to eat before you do the deed.'

'Mark,' Ronnie sighed. She was so sick with the anticipation of what she had to do that she was pretty sure she wouldn't be able to eat so much as a bread roll.

Annabel was bang on time. When Ronnie went out to the car, she saw her neighbours' curtains twitching. It wasn't often you saw a Porsche on their street. The two little boys who lived three doors down actually came outside to have a look. Seeing them, Jack insisted that he too be allowed out to look at the car, even though he was already in his pyjamas, and had of course seen it before.

'Let him put his coat on and come out for a minute,' said Annabel. She played along, letting each of the boys take a turn behind the steering wheel.

'This is my auntie,' said Jack proudly. 'And my uncle has got a James Bond car. A Martin Aston.'

'An Aston Martin,' Ronnie corrected him. 'Come on, you. Time for bed.'

Annabel helped Jack down from the driver's seat and gave him an effusive hug. He squealed with delight when she tickled him.

Once Jack had kissed his mother good night, Mark took him inside. Sophie waved from the window. Annabel got back into the car. Ronnie settled into the passenger seat.

'Are you warm enough?' asked Annabel. 'I can put the seat heater on if you like.'

'That'd be nice,' said Ronnie. It was a bit chilly.

Before long, however, Ronnie could feel the heat

seeping through the seat of her jeans and it wasn't much longer after that before she started to feel *too* warm. She didn't want to say anything, however, because she didn't want to put Annabel to any trouble. Even if that trouble was only flicking a switch. Ronnie tucked her hands beneath her bottom in an attempt to stop herself from getting any hotter.

'Are you sure you're comfortable?' Annabel asked when they stopped at a traffic light.

'Oh yes,' said Ronnie. 'Who couldn't be comfy in this car?'

The staff at the restaurant seemed to know Annabel well. They assured her that they'd reserved her 'favourite' table. It was the perfect spot, in a corner right by the fireplace. Very romantic if you were there for that sort of thing. Very private if you needed to have a serious discussion. The flickering light from the fire was incredibly flattering too. But also very hot. It wasn't long before Ronnie was sweating like a pig, as Mark would have said. She downed a gin and tonic and sucked on the ice cubes. Annabel seemed completely unflustered. But then she wasn't having to deal with guilt as well as the heat. She wasn't the one who was going to have to be a complete bitch that night.

As Annabel sipped her mineral water and Ronnie raced through her gin, they looked at the menu. Mark had told Ronnie that, given what she had to say, she should probably offer to pay for her share of the meal, if not for the whole thing. For that reason, Ronnie swooned when she saw the prices. The cost of a starter was more than she would have paid to feed the whole family at their local pub.

And Annabel wasn't stinting on her choices. She chose

salmon to start with and a sirloin steak to follow. Apparently, lately she had been craving red meat. Ronnie, already imagining her credit card being refused at the end of the evening, chose a pea soup followed by the vegetarian option – some pasta – that was cheaper than everything else on the menu but still cost a whopping twelve pounds. For pasta! The raw ingredients could not have cost more than a quid.

Then there was the wine. Annabel said she was only going to have half a tiny glass to be sociable, seeing as she was pregnant *and* driving, but that perhaps they should order a bottle because there was no need for Ronnie to hold back. But Ronnie did want to hold back because there wasn't a bottle on the menu that cost less than thirty-five quid. Adding up the things they'd ordered so far in her head, Ronnie saw her family having to eat baked beans on Christmas Day. So Ronnie suggested that they both just have one glass.

Annabel ordered two glasses of Cabernet Sauvignon at fifteen pounds apiece.

'Might as well have a couple of really nice glasses if we're not having a whole bottle,' she said.

The food arrived. It was delicious, but Ronnie could only think of the money as she spooned the pea soup into her mouth. Pea soup shouldn't cost so much. Not even if the peas were picked by virgins under a crescent moon.

'Isn't this lovely?' said Annabel. 'Just the two of us having a chance to get to know each other properly.'

'Yes,' said Ronnie.

'Richard and I come here quite a bit,' said Annabel. 'It's the perfect place for a casual dinner.'

'Casual?'

'Yes.'

Ronnie thought it was the perfect place to come if you'd won the Premium Bonds.

'Could we have another bottle of water?' Annabel asked a passing waitress.

The water was a fiver a bottle!

'Tap's fine,' Ronnie said.

Chapter Sixty-Six

Annabel

The restaurant was lovely, the food was delicious but the conversation was difficult and Ronnie was soon grateful for the bottle of wine she couldn't afford (Annabel had ordered the whole bottle in the end). While Annabel sipped at just that half a glass, mindful of the baby on board, Ronnie powered on through the rest, hoping that she would find the point at which it made her brave enough to say what she needed to before it made her incoherent. But then Annabel started to open up.

'Richard and I got married really young,' she said. 'We met at university and it was love at first sight. For me, anyway. I had to work on him a bit.'

'He really adores you,' Ronnie observed.

'We were the first of our friends to tie the knot and the first to have a child. Once we were married, Richard was desperate to start a family. I took a bit of convincing. I didn't think I'd be very good at it.'

'Well, I got pregnant by accident,' said Ronnie, failing to pick up on why Annabel might have worried about her parenting skills. 'I definitely wasn't trying. I was going to do my A levels and go to university. But one unlucky shag . . .'

'Or one very lucky one,' Annabel observed.

'Yeah,' said Ronnie. 'I can see it like that now. Sophie

can be a right pain in the proverbial but I wouldn't be without her.'

'I know. The teenage years are tough – it was like Izzy became a different person the day she turned fourteen – but she is so precious to us. I don't know what I would have done if we'd lost her back in the summer. I don't think I could have carried on.'

'It must have been horrible,' Ronnie agreed.

'When she was first in intensive care it was as though I had stopped breathing. I couldn't think of anything except how we were going to save her. I couldn't eat. I couldn't drink. I was like a zombie. When she opened her eyes and looked at me, it was just like it was all those years ago when I'd just given birth and the midwife handed her to me. Such a rush of relief and love. I felt I had been given a second chance.'

All the while that Annabel was telling her how much Izzy meant to them, Ronnie was feeling worse and worse. And then Annabel said, 'Sometimes, it's the very darkest times and the worst possible circumstances imaginable which change life for the better. I mean, we're sitting here now. You and me. Sisters who might never have known one another. And because of your generosity, my daughter – your niece – will have a shot at an ordinary life. She won't have to spend those years when she should be out there enjoying herself with friends, getting her degree, perhaps meeting a husband . . . hooked up to a dialysis machine in her bedroom.'

Annabel reached across the table and grabbed Ronnie's hand.

'Ronnie, I can't tell you how much what you are doing means to me. You could not have given me a greater gift if you had given me your own child. You're giving me back my daughter. And you're able to do it because you're my sister. I think I finally understand the saying that blood is thicker than water.'

Ronnie nodded.

Annabel's eyes started to swim with tears and Ronnie understood that there was no way on earth she was going to be able to break the news to Annabel that night. Ronnie took the opportunity to wrestle her hand free of Annabel's grip on the pretence of looking for a paper hanky.

'Here,' she said, handing a tissue to Annabel. 'You're making your mascara run.'

'Oh, I don't care,' said Annabel. 'I'm not unhappy. These are happy tears.'

That made it even worse for poor Ronnie.

'But I need to tell you something,' said Annabel. 'Because I think it's only fair that you know everything about the situation before we go any further.'

Ronnie leaned forward. Was Annabel about to give her an 'out'?

'When you talk to the specialist Dr Devon, she will probably tell you that Izzy's kidneys were damaged because she took ecstasy. Now, we don't know that for certain and, given the circumstances, we haven't pressed Izzy on it too much. We're furious at the very thought of it of course. We always told her to stay away from drugs and we didn't think she ever mixed with the kind of people who supplied them. But teenagers do make mistakes and I wouldn't want you to hear that out of the blue and draw all the wrong conclusions. Izzy is certainly not a drug addict.'

'Of course not,' said Ronnie.

'So, I don't want you to think that she is. It's very important. She deserves this second chance you're giving her. She really does.'

Annabel nodded along with her assertion and Ronnie found herself nodding too.

'Of course she does,' said Ronnie.

'She won't waste it.'

'I know.'

Ronnie's 'out' all but disappeared. If she told Annabel she wasn't going to do the transplant now, it would seem as though it was because of the ecstasy and Ronnie would look an even bigger bitch than she was already going to. All she could do was sit and smile as Annabel once again told her what a difference her generosity would make to the Buchanans' lives.

When they got back to Ronnie's house, Ronnie couldn't wait to unclip her seat belt and get out of the car. But Annabel wasn't finished with her. She got out too and practically ran round the car, despite her ungainly size, and insisted on giving Ronnie a huge hug. She squeezed so hard that Ronnie actually felt slightly winded.

'You are the most wonderful sister a woman could ever hope to have,' Annabel told her. 'I mean it. Not just because of the kidney thing. Because you're a really good person. You're kind and straightforward and down to earth. I really wish I'd got to know you sooner, Ronnie. As it is, I know that we are going to be great friends for the rest of our lives.'

'Yeah,' said Ronnie. 'You're a great sister too.'

'We're family, aren't we?' said Annabel.

'We are.'

Ronnie patted Annabel on the back to signal that it was time to let go now.

Annabel watched until Ronnie was safely in the house, then she drove home, singing along to the Christmas songs on the radio. Richard was waiting up for her when she got in.

'That went really well,' she said. 'We talked about so many things. I just know she's going to help us. I'm going to ask someone from the hospital to call her in the morning and answer any questions she's got about the process.'

'That's great,' said Richard.

He poured himself another glass of wine from the bottle he had opened earlier that evening. He found Annabel some elderflower cordial.

'Here's to my lovely sister.'

They toasted Ronnie in her absence.

'Who would have believed it?'

Chapter Sixty-Seven

Ronnie

The atmosphere in Ronnie's house was less festive. Ronnie didn't wait for her husband to fetch her a drink. She helped herself to his newly opened bottle of beer and downed it in one.

'Did you tell her?' Mark asked.

'What do you think? You saw the way she hugged me when I got out of the car.'

'You didn't tell her!'

'I couldn't. I was going to. I swear I was all ready to come out with it the minute we finished our dinner but then she launched into this speech about how much it means to her that I would give up my kidney for Izzy and how she now truly understands what it means to be a sister and what people are really on about when they say blood is thicker than water.'

Mark pinched the bridge of his nose.

'So she still thinks you're going to do it.'

'She says she's going to arrange for me to see the transplant surgeon this week! They're going to pay for it all to be done privately and she's going to make sure I see the best psychologist and have the best surgeon and the best aftercare. Then she said that when I'm feeling up to it again, she and Richard would like to pay for us to have a holiday – all of us. You, me and the children – at this resort they've been to in the Caribbean. All-inclusive.

Seven stars! It's where all the celebs go and they're paying for the lot. Mum and Dad too. She's got it all planned out.'

'Ronnie, you've got to tell her.'

'Don't you think I know that?' Ronnie wailed. 'But do you know what it's going to do to her? She thinks I'm her last chance. She thinks her daughter is going to die without my kidney. Can you imagine if it was the other way round and our Sophie needed her? I'd be desperate for her to help us. She's going to be devastated when we say no.'

'Sooner the better.'

'I know! But you've got to come with me, Mark. I'm not telling her on my own. I can't. I need some backup. If you say all the things that you've said to me over this last week, all those reasons why you don't think I should, then perhaps she'll take it more calmly. It won't look like I'm just too scared. If it's both of us and both of them too, Richard will keep a lid on it. He always seems pretty reasonable.'

Mark agreed. 'We'll have to invite them round.'

'No. I don't think I can stand it, having them here. Shouldn't we meet them somewhere neutral?'

'What about the Ridgeview?'

'Yes. The Ridgeview will have to do. I'll arrange it with Annabel tomorrow.'

As it was, Ronnie didn't have to wait to make the phone call. Annabel called her first thing the following day to ask when might be a good time for them all to go to see Dr Devon and the transplant surgeon.

'This week's bad,' said Ronnie. 'One of the girls at work is having a hysterectomy. I've got to do her shifts. But I was wondering if we could have Sunday lunch somewhere together.'

'Yes!' Annabel leapt at the chance.

'The Ridgeview?' Ronnie suggested. 'Where you first met Mum and Dad?'

'No. Not the Ridgeview. Come here.'

'To yours?'

'Why not? It'll just be a casual lunch. Between sisters. No bother at all.'

Nothing was too much bother for Annabel now.

Chapter Sixty-Eight

Annabel

Of course it wouldn't be casual in the least. This was no ordinary catch-up between siblings. As soon as she had Ronnie's acceptance, Annabel went into overdrive. She called the organic butcher and ordered a fabulous joint, big enough for Ronnie, Mark, their kids and Jacqui, Dave and Granddad Bill if they wanted to come too. She could even ask if Chelsea wanted to come up from London and stay overnight. Annabel was feeling extremely warm towards the whole Benson clan.

But Ronnie texted her that afternoon to say that it would just be her and Mark. Jack had a birthday party to go to on Sunday afternoon and Sophie had very generously offered to take him there. It was only a short walk from their house.

'Oh,' said Annabel. 'Izzy will be disappointed.'

So, it was just lunch for five. The Buchanans, Mark and Ronnie. Never mind. Leander would be more than happy to help polish off the surplus meat. And it would definitely be easier to talk transplant logistics if Jack wasn't around. Jack was an adorable child, but he required a lot of attention. If they didn't have to worry about whether he was breaking some Buchanan family heirloom, then Mark and Ronnie would be much more relaxed and

Chrissie Manby

able to concentrate on more important matters. On the only thing that mattered: Izzy's transplant.

Though the numbers had dwindled, Annabel still bought a big chocolate gateau for pudding. She'd noticed that Ronnie had a sweet tooth. She asked Richard to bring up something really special from the cellar. They would pull out all the stops.

On the day, Mark and Ronnie arrived a little early. They had brought a bottle of wine of their own. Annabel subtly spirited it away into the kitchen. She might be able to use it for cooking.

Richard played host again, settling the Benson-Edwards in front of the fire. It was a cold day outside and there was nothing nicer than sitting by a real log fire with a glass of champagne and some smoked salmon canapés while you waited for lunch. If you were feeling nice and relaxed, perhaps.

Izzy came downstairs a little later. She made small talk with her aunt and uncle about schoolwork and the upcoming festive season.

Annabel noticed that Izzy looked far younger than her years that day in the black velvet dress that she had bought her a year earlier in Peter Jones. Having been lukewarm about it at the time the dress was new, for some reason, Izzy had decided that it was the perfect thing to wear all the time that winter. Annabel suspected she had been somewhat influenced by Sophie's gothic look. Or perhaps it was simply that it was loose around the waist, which was more comfortable with the catheter. Annabel shook that thought off. Still, if it made Izzy look a little vulnerable, that wasn't such a bad thing. Not today. They needed to get the transplant possibilities nailed down.

* * *

316

Annabel had chosen the lunch menu specifically to appeal to Ronnie, so she was disappointed when her sister all but turned her nose up at everything she was offered. Ronnie even put her hand over the mouth of her wine glass when Richard offered her a top-up.

'Not today, thanks, Richard. I've got to keep a clear head.'

'But Mark's driving, isn't he?' asked Annabel.

'Yes, but you know what it's like. You can't process booze like you used to when you get to our age. I don't want to be feeling bad when I go into work tomorrow. I've got an early start.'

'Then how about some more beef? You'll have some more of that?'

'Actually, I won't.'

Annabel tilted her head questioningly.

'Oh, it isn't that I don't like it. It's really lovely and you've cooked it just right.'

Annabel considered the beef practically cremated but she knew that Ronnie liked it well done.

'I just don't feel all that hungry right now.'

'You don't think you're coming down with that winter vomiting bug, do you?' Annabel asked.

That would be awkward. If Ronnie was ill, they would have to ask her to leave. They couldn't risk Izzy coming down with anything, least of all the norovirus. But Ronnie said, 'It's nothing physical. I've just got something on my mind.'

'Then perhaps we'll have some pudding later. Perhaps you'd like to go and sit by the fire again for a bit?'

Ronnie looked at Mark in a way that immediately set alarm bells ringing in Annabel's head. Ronnie opened her mouth as if to say something but then she looked back at Annabel and smiled.

'I'm OK here.'

'Does anyone mind if I go back upstairs?' Izzy asked. 'I'm feeling a bit tired.'

None of the adults present objected. In fact, they positively encouraged her to go and lie down for as long as she wanted. While Izzy made her excuses, Annabel could feel her throat tightening. Something was going on and she had a feeling that she wasn't going to like whatever it was when she finally found out.

With Izzy safely out of the way, the four adults made awkward small talk for a little longer.

'Can't believe it's Christmas in four weeks,' said Mark.

'I know,' said Richard. 'It creeps up on you. Seems like we've only just taken the decorations down.'

'Ronnie.' Annabel could stand it no longer. 'Is everything all right?'

Ronnie opened and closed her mouth a few times, like a goldfish that had leapt out of the tank and found itself on the carpet.

'Mark,' she said. 'You tell them.'

Mark suddenly looked equally distressed.

'What is it?' Annabel tried to keep her own panic out of her voice. 'Tell us what?'

'Look,' Mark said. 'I don't know how to say this. You've been so generous to us today with this lovely lunch. It isn't really what we wanted. We wanted to take you out somewhere because we've got to tell you—'

'What?' asked Annabel. Her focus was all on Ronnie but it was Mark who kept talking. Ronnie just stared at her plate.

'We've been talking. Me and Ronnie. We've looked at all the information and we've been giving it some serious thought and we've decided that we can't go through with it.'

'With what?' Annabel asked, as if she didn't already know.

'With the transplant. We're sorry but it's too big a risk. We've got our own children to think about. We can't risk them losing their mum.'

'Are you serious?' asked Annabel.

'Annabel,' Richard laid a calming hand on her arm. 'Let Mark finish talking.'

'Ronnie, well, she's been in good health all her life and she's never had any kind of operation and we're worried that she might have some kind of reaction to the anaesthetic. We just don't know. And then there's the practical aspect of it. Jack's only young. He needs to be picked up from school and—'

'The school run? This is about the school run? Can't Jacqui do that?'

'Well, I suppose she could but—'

Ronnie found her voice. 'I just don't want to do it, Annabel. I'm scared. I'm sorry. I've been trying to tell you for weeks. I tried to tell you at the restaurant the other night but you were so happy and I couldn't do it to you then. I know I should have done but . . .'

Ronnie's eyes were swimming with tears.

'Oh, Annabel. I feel like a total cow. I've been really struggling with this, I promise you. I know that if I was in your position, I'd want to punch me in the face right now. Believe me, I know how you must be feeling.'

No you don't, thought Annabel. *You don't have any idea how murderous I am.*

Ronnie looked at her beseechingly.

'It's OK,' said Richard. 'It's fine. We understand. We've been asking a great deal of you and you have every right to consider it from your point of view, looking at the impact on your family. Isn't that right, Annabel?'

Just at that moment, a timer in the kitchen pinged to let Annabel know that the French bread she had been heating up for the cheese course was ready. She was out of the dining room like a greyhound from a trap. Richard followed her, catching the kitchen door before she had time to slam it. He closed it quietly. Annabel crashed around the kitchen. She got the bread out of the oven and dropped it on to the work surface without any concern for the heat of the baking tray.

'Well, this is a disaster,' she all but shouted. 'How can she turn up here and tell me that she's not going to do it now?'

'Come on. We always knew this might happen,' Richard reminded her. 'The transplant wouldn't be without risk for Ronnie and she's got her own children to think about.'

'The risk is tiny!' Annabel protested. 'While our daughter is so ill.'

'We have to let it go.'

'We can't let it go. Richard, she's a match. A proper match. Our little girl wouldn't have to have dialysis any more. Go back in there and persuade her.'

Richard took Annabel by the shoulders and forced her to look at him. 'But their fears are legitimate. Ronnie is right to wonder how it would affect her own health and she would have to take time off work. She wouldn't be able to look after Sophie and Jack.'

'Sophie doesn't need looking after. She's nearly an adult. And surely Mark can look after his own son for a few days. Ronnie wouldn't have to be in hospital for long. A week, max.'

'Look. We can't keep pushing it. Let's forget it for now.

We'll keep in touch and maybe at some point in the future she'll change her mind.'

'For God's sake, Richard. You're being ridiculous. The longer Izzy stays on dialysis, the less chance she has of a successful transplant. You can't do it. I don't know whether this pregnancy will have ruled me out too. We have to persuade Ronnie to give her a kidney now.'

'Darling, we can't keep pushing. And in my opinion, the more we push, the less likely it is to happen. Perhaps in time they'll change their minds but we don't want to scare them away.'

'Bollocks, Richard. You know what this is really about? It's about money. Ronnie isn't scared about the transplant. She's wondering how much it's worth. I've known that about her from the first time we met, when she came round here and looked the place over like she was an insurance salesman. It's obvious. They're waiting for us to make them an offer. I thought the all-expenses-paid holiday might be enough but clearly I was wrong. She's waiting for us to write a cheque. See how quickly she changes her mind then.'

'I don't know . . .' said Richard cautiously.

'We've got to do it. How much can we offer them? How big do you think their mortgage is? Offer them a hundred grand. We can do that. Two hundred. I'll sell the bloody car.'

'Annabel, you need to calm down.' He manoeuvred her and her bump towards a chair. 'You're going to go into labour if you keep this up. Sit down. We're not going to offer them any money. You saw how upset Ronnie was in there. Offering cash isn't going to change that. We need to respect their decision—'

'Respect their decision! Richard, you're so naive! These people are not like us. I may be related to her by blood but we come from different planets. I just want to get the transplant over with and get them out of my life. If a quarter of a million is what it takes, then I think it's well worth it.'

Chapter Sixty-Nine

Ronnie and Annabel

Ronnie was standing in the doorway. She had a plate in each hand.

'You really didn't have to do that,' said Annabel, standing up and bustling over to whisk the dirty plates away.

'I'm glad I did,' said Ronnie. 'Gave me a chance to find out what you really think about us all, didn't it?'

'Oh God.'

Ronnie savoured the look on Annabel's face, knowing she was wondering how long Ronnie had been listening. She would be horrified to know that Ronnie had pretty much heard it all, having followed Richard to the kitchen when Annabel first fled. When Ronnie got up from the table, she was ready and willing to try to calm Annabel down. Now she felt very differently. She was furious.

Annabel looked to Richard for support. Richard put his arm round his wife's shoulders in solidarity.

'Well?' said Ronnie.

'Ronnie, we're sorry,' said Richard. 'It's been a stressful few months and we were so hopeful when you tested as a match. Annabel has been under an enormous amount of strain. I'm sure you can understand.'

Ronnie remained in the doorway.

'I should probably apologise,' said Annabel.

'Probably? That's an understatement. You're lucky I didn't just throw those plates in your face.'

'Now, Ronnie,' said Richard. 'There's no need for that.'

'You're all right, Richard. I'm not quite the savage pikey your wife seems to think I am. Money, Annabel? You really believe that this is all about money and I'm holding out on the transplant until you pay me to go under the knife? You think I want to *sell* you my kidney?'

'We don't believe that,' said Richard. 'Annabel was just shocked by your announcement. Stress makes people say things they don't—'

Annabel interrupted him. 'You don't think I wouldn't have given everything I had to buy my daughter a kidney if money was all it would take? You think I wanted to get involved with you and your family, Ronnie? I didn't. I did it for my daughter's sake. I hoped that you would have compassion for her. And that is what I am asking you for now. Don't think of this as helping me. Only think of it as helping Izzy. She's seventeen. She's never harmed anyone. She doesn't deserve to be facing death before she's even finished school.'

'And my son and daughter don't deserve to be left motherless.'

'They wouldn't be left motherless! You're being dramatic.'

'Even a one per cent chance of me dying on the operating table is too much of a risk for me. Jack is six. He needs me every bit as much as Izzy needs you. And he definitely needs me more than he needs your money. That doesn't seem to be something you appreciate. You think of me like I'm some woman in the third world, who needs to sell my organs to save my kids from the slums. So, Jack might lose his mum but bountiful Auntie

Annabel would pay for him to have a nanny and a private education, eh? You probably think he'd be better off with none of my horrible influence anyway. He'd have a chance to be all nice and upper-class like you are. That's got to be better than being one of the common people like me, eating the wrong food with the wrong cutlery and living in the wrong part of town, getting fat and being feckless. It's a wonder I haven't lost my kids to social services already, eh? I probably leave them home alone while I go down the pub and get wasted, right? Well, guess what, Lady Muck, it's not *my* daughter that ended up taking drugs.'

'Ronnie!' Richard exclaimed.

'But that's what happened, isn't it? All your money and all your class and your daughter still ended up fucking up her kidneys on ecstasy. She's no better than the kids on our estate,' Ronnie crowed.

'All teenagers make mistakes. I would have thought you of all people would understand that. But I don't know why I ever expected you to be kind about it,' Annabel spat at her. 'Looking at you now makes me glad I was adopted. You're nasty and envious. Always have been I've no doubt.'

Ronnie just shook her head.

'We don't need you and we don't need your money,' she said. 'I'll send back that crappy frame you bought us for our wedding and all. You weren't too flash with the cash when you bought *that*, were you?'

'And you were too thick to know it contained a valuable print, you stupid cow. I clearly dodged a bullet, not growing up with a bunch of ill-educated idiots like you. I can't believe I'm related to such chavs.'

'I can't believe it myself. You can rest assured, Annabel, I'm just as surprised that my long-lost sister has turned out to be a bitch as you are surprised that I'm a chav. Mark,' Ronnie shouted back towards the dining room. 'We're going home now. Tell Izzy that we all hope she gets a kidney soon,' was Ronnie's parting shot.

Chapter Seventy

Annabel

Annabel spent the rest of the day after the Sunday lunch debacle battling a tremendous migraine. She hadn't suffered such a bastard of a headache in years. She knew what had caused it. Her neck had gone into spasm while she and Ronnie argued in the kitchen and it hadn't loosened up since.

Annabel's response to the whole disaster was a split one. On the one hand, she was mortified that Ronnie had heard her bitching and, as a result, had flat out refused to help. On the other hand, she could not help but feel relief that it was over. Over at last. She never had to see the Bensons again. She could go back to being herself without the constant reminders of where she was really from. But she understood that mortification should be the winning emotion here.

Ronnie was still Izzy's best hope and for that reason alone, Annabel knew she was going to have to apologise. She was going to have to apologise and apologise and apologise until Ronnie felt appeased and looked at the Buchanan family's dilemma in a more reasonable light.

'Tomorrow,' said Annabel to herself. 'I'll do it tomorrow. That will give her more chance to calm down.' Everything would look better after a good night's sleep. Annabel popped three painkillers and lay down on the sofa with a chilled face mask over her eyes while the baby inside her flipped and rolled as though it was as anxious as she was. Tomorrow she would be ready to face Ronnie again. How bad could it be? The most awful things had already been said out loud. The situation couldn't possibly get any worse.

Chapter Seventy-One

Jacqui

Jacqui, of course, knew that Ronnie was going to have lunch with Annabel and she called by that evening to see how it had gone. She still jealously sought out every bit of information about the daughter she hadn't raised and she couldn't concentrate on anything else until she got a report from Ronnie. She wanted to know how Izzy was and how Annabel was coping as she rolled into the eighth month of her pregnancy. Jacqui had already started planning for the new baby. It was such a thrill to think that she would know this new grandchild for the whole of its life, just as she had known Sophie and Jack since the days they were born.

But Ronnie had no time for small talk about Annabel's pregnancy or how Izzy was coping with her schoolwork. She just wanted to offload the horror of the row in the kitchen of the Great House.

It all came as a complete surprise to Jacqui. She'd assumed, just as Annabel had, that the transplant would go ahead. Why wouldn't it? And Ronnie and Mark had not told her otherwise, because they did not want Jacqui or Dave – but Jacqui in particular – to try to have any influence over what they decided to do. So, when Ronnie explained exactly why she and Annabel had fallen out, Jacqui was shocked.

'But why, love? Why? Why wouldn't you give Izzy a kidney?'

'I'm not going to do it because I've got children of my own to think about. That's the bottom line, Mum. Izzy is ill but she's not dying. She's on dialysis. People stay on dialysis for years. She's only been on it a few months. But what if I have the operation to give her my kidney and it all starts to go wrong for me? I've never had a general anaesthetic. I don't know how I might react. What if I die on the operating table?'

'You wouldn't die. It's perfectly safe.'

'It's not a hundred per cent safe.'

'But it's ninety-odd—' Jacqui began.

'I might be that one in a hundred, Mum. I might never come round. And then Sophie and Jack would be without a mum. Or is that OK by you? You're probably thinking that if I did die on the operating table, Izzy could have both my kidneys.'

'Ronnie, I would never—'

'And that would be just fine, wouldn't it? Sophie and Jack would be orphans but wonderful Izzy would be perfect again and that's all that matters to you now. Annabel's daughter is more important than both my children. Ever since Annabel came back into our lives, you haven't given the rest of us a second thought. Except in how we might be able to help your precious number one daughter out by giving her our vital organs. It's like you only had us to ensure that when the time came, Annabel could just harvest the bits she needs from us. It's like that bloody film with Keira Knightley.'

'Ronnie, you don't know what you're saying. Your father and I were the first to be tested. If either one of us could have given Izzy a kidney, we would have been straight into hospital. The last thing we wanted is for the rest of you to have to step in. If we could have done it—'

'But you can't. And it seems Chelsea can't either. So she's off scot-free. And all the pressure is on me. You're making me feel like I'm killing that girl by not doing this. I'm not killing her. I just don't want to die myself!'

Jacqui went to hold Ronnie's hand but Ronnie snatched her hand away.

'You've made it perfectly clear who your favourite is. Why don't you go and console her? If she'll still let you in the house now she knows she can get nothing from us. The chavs she never wanted to meet in the first place. Because that's what she called us, you know.'

'Ronnie, love . . .'

Jacqui tried to take Ronnie's hand again but Ronnie shook her off with shocking force.

'Go, Mum. Go. I don't want to talk about this any more.'

Jacqui left her daughter's house but she didn't get into her car right away. Instead she stood on the pavement, wondering what to do next. Should she insist that Ronnie let her back in so they could talk about the situation some more? Or should she call Annabel? Ronnie wasn't telling the truth when she said that Annabel had called them chavs. Was she?

Chapter Seventy-Two

Chelsea

Ronnie's decision set off a proper chain reaction. When she eventually gave up on being allowed back into Ronnie's house and went to her car in tears, Jacqui called Annabel. Annabel would not come to the phone. Richard said she was asleep. Jacqui had to hope that was true though of course she suspected otherwise. Then she phoned Chelsea. Until Jacqui called her, Chelsea was oblivious to Ronnie's decision not to do the transplant.

'She really isn't going to do it?'

'She says she's too worried about what it might mean for Sophie and Jack.'

'Ah. Well, she's got a point, Mum.'

'And I understand that. But now she says she thinks I love Annabel more than the pair of you,' Jacqui sobbed. 'She kicked me out of her house. Jack was watching from the top of the stairs when she did it. He looked so upset. Oh, Chelsea. It's all gone horribly wrong. Can't you ring her up and tell her that I love you all equally? I always have. You know that, don't you? I just want you all to be happy and well. Can't you persuade Ronnie to think again? She'll listen to you. You'd have done it, wouldn't you, if you'd been a match for Izzy?'

Jacqui didn't know that Chelsea hadn't tested and neither did she know the reason why. But Annabel did. While Jacqui replayed the terrible row she'd had with her middle daughter, all Chelsea could think was that the next phone call she got would almost certainly be from Annabel and Richard. She would have to be tested now. She had promised that she would do whatever she could to help Izzy if Ronnie hadn't been able to come through. But Chelsea had been thinking in terms of the transplant not working, of Izzy's body rejecting Ronnie's kidney. She hadn't thought for a moment that Ronnie would actually decide not to go ahead with the transplant at all. She started to feel dizzy with the consequences. She wanted her mum to get off the phone so she could sit down and take a deep breath.

'We all would have done it,' Jacqui continued. 'I know you would.'

'I don't know, Mum,' Chelsea said. 'It's impossible to say. I didn't have to make the decision. If I had my own kids . . . Look, perhaps you should give both Ronnie and Annabel some space. Until it all blows over.'

'I don't know if this will ever blow over. I've never seen Ronnie so upset and I'm sure Annabel's avoiding my calls.'

Jacqui continued to talk about the situation for a whole hour and wanted to keep talking after that but Chelsea was expected at Adam's house for supper. She desperately wanted to be there already. While her mother talked and cried and cried again on the landline, Chelsea's mobile was vibrating with so many messages that it was practically shaking itself off the kitchen table. With her mother still in full flow, Chelsea picked up her mobile and scrolled through the messages. Predictably, there were plenty of texts from Ronnie, all telling her to call as soon as she could. And there was one from Annabel too, asking the same. The only message Chelsea was glad to see was the one from

Adam, which said that he was looking forward to seeing her later.

'Mum,' Chelsea broke into Jacqui's stream-of-consciousness-style speech. 'Mum, I've got to go. Adam's expecting me.'

'Oh,' said Jacqui. 'Then I should shut up and let you go. But you'll call Ronnie, won't you, love? You'll tell her that I love you all exactly the same. Every one of you.'

'Of course, Mum. I will.'

While Chelsea dressed to go to Adam's house, another five messages accumulated on her phone. Three from Ronnie, one from Annabel and one from Jacqui, seeking more reassurances that Chelsea would mediate between her and her middle daughter. Chelsea deleted all five messages. She was not going to try to deal with this now. She couldn't. Her mum's distress had been very upsetting but the thought of having to come clean to Jacqui and Ronnie about how her bulimia kept her from offering her own kidney was even worse. Chelsea needed to see Adam and have him wrap his arms around her and make everything feel OK.

It was five to eight by the time she arrived at Adam's place. Lily was still up, but only just. She was wearing her pyjamas.

'She insisted on staying up until you arrived,' said Adam.

'I want you to read my bedtime story,' she told Chelsea, pointing at her with a star-shaped plastic wand.

'Do you mind?' Adam asked.

'Of course not,' said Chelsea, feeling guilty that she had hoped Lily would be in bed already. She followed Lily up the stairs.

Lily's bedroom was a Disney princess's dream. All decked out in pink and glitter. Adam had constructed a small canopy for the bed, which was draped in delicate tulle and spangled with glow-in-the-dark stars. Lily sat beneath it, surrounded by an enormous number of teddy bears and dolls.

Still using her wand, she pointed Chelsea in the direction of the bookshelf.

'Do you have a favourite?' Chelsea asked.

Lily did. It was an old Ladybird classic edition of *The Princess and the Pea*, a story that Chelsea herself had loved as a child.

With Lily settled down on her pillows with her fluffy entourage, Chelsea opened the book. She knew the Ladybird edition well but what she saw inside the covers still gave her something of an uncomfortable surprise. On the first page, in girlish handwriting, someone had claimed ownership of the book.

Claire.

Chelsea recognised the name of Lily's mother at once. It made her catch her breath. She was in Lily's bedroom, in the house that Claire had lived in but still, somehow, she'd been more or less able to put the thought of Claire to the back of her mind until she saw her name written in that book.

'Hurry up,' said Lily. 'Start reading.'

Chelsea forced herself to start and Lily was soon entranced by the tale she'd already heard a hundred times. She made sure Chelsea showed her all of the pictures from the moment the princess arrived at the castle, dressed in rags and drenched from the rain, to her triumphant walk up the aisle to claim her prince.

'And they all lived happily ever after . . .' Chelsea ended the tale, closing the book with a snap, before she could read what was written on the endpaper in the same writing as Claire's name. It was probably only Claire's childhood address but Chelsea couldn't bear to see it: the writing of a small girl who thought she had it all to come.

'Thank you,' said Lily.

'It was my pleasure,' Chelsea said. 'Now it's time for you to go to sleep.'

Lily was strangely compliant that night. She told Chelsea which of her dolls and bears were to be taken off the bed and put on the dresser first. Chelsea arranged them as instructed in order of size from Small Rabbit to Big Ted.

'Now you have to give me a kiss,' Lily said.

Chelsea kissed Lily on the forehead. She couldn't resist brushing the blonde hair off Lily's face too. Lily smiled.

'Now it's time for you to close your eyes,' said Chelsea firmly. She made for the bedroom door, leaving it open so that light from the landing would keep Lily's bedroom from being too dark.

'Chelsea?' Lily called before she reached the stairs.

'Yes,' Chelsea responded.

'You will come back again, won't you?'

'Of course I will, Lily.'

'Good.'

Lily nodded. She closed her eyes.

Chelsea felt a catch in the back of her throat. Looking at Lily's little blonde head on the pillow then, she was overwhelmed by a sudden flood of affection for the tiny girl. Just as she was continually surprised by how much she had come to feel for her nephew. Turning from Lily's open bedroom door, Chelsea paused on the landing and had to press her fingers to the sides of her nose to stop herself from crying because suddenly she knew what Lily had really meant by her question.

'You will come back again, won't you?'

It wasn't as simple as wanting to know when Chelsea would next be round. Lily was asking Chelsea whether she could trust her? Whether she was around for the long haul? Whether it was safe for Lily to let her guard down and start investing in Chelsea? Start loving her even?

In the context of her relationship with Lily, the conversation she'd had with Annabel in the restaurant near Selfridges started to make more sense. Annabel claimed she had developed a prickly exterior because she felt she'd been rejected as a baby and subconsciously feared it could happen again. Was that why Lily had been so difficult? Because she too felt abandoned by the mother everyone assumed she couldn't remember? Of course, Adam and Lily's grandparents had told Lily about her great loss. Had Lily been trying to protect herself from future pain?

The responsibility made Chelsea feel giddy.

Down in the kitchen, Adam was putting the finishing touches to their supper.

'Did she give you much trouble?' he asked.

'None at all,' Chelsea confirmed.

'Good,' said Adam.

He dished up. They ate. Chelsea was surprised to find that she felt a churning sensation throughout the meal. She knew what it meant. She wanted to leave the table and go straight to the bathroom and throw up. But she couldn't do that. She pressed her fingers to her temples.

'Are you all right?' Adam asked.

'Sort of,' said Chelsea. 'No. Not really.'

She had to tell him. She had to tell him about Ronnie refusing to go ahead with the transplant and how she'd fallen out with Jacqui as a result and then she had to tell him exactly what the consequences were for her. How Annabel had already called her, doubtless anxious to get Chelsea tested as a match as soon as possible. And then she would have to admit to Adam that she hadn't already tested because of the bulimia. But Chelsea was sure it was still too soon to tell him. It would frighten him off. He would reject her. She wasn't strong enough.

'Want to tell me about it?' Adam asked.

'I can't.'

'Come on.'

'No, really.'

'Claire,' said Adam then. 'Please tell me what's wrong.'

He didn't even know he'd said it. The wrong name. The name of his dead wife.

Chelsea looked up at him. Her eyes were swimming.

'You just called me her name,' she said. 'You just called me Claire.'

'Did I? Oh God. Chelsea, I'm sorry.'

'There's no need to apologise, Adam. But it shows me where your head is. Where your heart is. And I can't compete.'

'Chelsea.' Adam made a grab for her hand. 'It was just a slip of the tongue. I don't know why Claire's name popped out then. I wasn't thinking about her. I was entirely focused on you.'

Chelsea shook her head.

'How can I prove it to you?' Adam asked.

'You can't,' said Chelsea.

338

'So you'll have to take my word for it. Come on. Tell me what was bothering you before.'

'I can't do this,' said Chelsea. 'I just can't. I shouldn't be here, getting closer to you and getting more involved with Lily when I'm never going to live up to your dead wife. She'll always be at the front of your mind.'

'Don't say that. You're being ridiculous,' said Adam. 'You're overreacting in a big way.'

'Don't tell me I'm overreacting,' said Chelsea. 'I'm trying to protect my heart.'

'Fine,' said Adam. 'Though I still don't get what you're trying to protect it from. So, I called you Claire. She and I were together for eight years and there's been no one since. It would be bloody strange if I never thought about her and never said her name *entirely by accident*. What is strange is how you're reacting to it. I don't know what to do about that.'

The sudden harshness of Adam's tone surprised Chelsea.

'It seems a bit immature to me,' he added.

'Immature? In that case I'd definitely better go,' she said.

Chelsea got up and headed for the door.

'Oh, please!' Adam sighed. 'How has this become an argument? This is just crazy.'

'To you, perhaps. But right now I think I should be on my own.'

'Fine,' said Adam, throwing his hands up. 'Fine. I don't know what to say to you. I'm sorry. You go.'

As soon as she was at the tube station, Chelsea started to regret her decision. If Adam was confused, he wasn't the only one. She wasn't sure where the argument had come from either. It must have been because she was

339

scared. But before Chelsea could get back to Adam's house, he had already sent her a text.

Maybe you're right. Maybe it is too early for me to be in a relationship and I certainly don't want to have you get more involved in Lily's life if you're not sticking around. I'm sorry, Chelsea. You're a great girl and I wish things could have ended differently. Take care of yourself, love Adam.

Chelsea was so shocked she could hardly breathe. She'd accidentally called Adam's bluff and he'd dumped her.

At home, an hour later, Chelsea was still poleaxed by what she had done. She went straight to her kitchen and opened the fridge. There was hardly anything in there, but what there was, she ate without thinking. A whole block of cheese. A four-pack of yogurts. Eight slices of Parma ham. Then she worked her way through a packet of Ryvita, eating mechanically, crying all the while. When she was done, she went to the bathroom and got rid of the lot of it.

It didn't work. She didn't feel any better. The following day she was going to have to talk to Annabel and tell her that she was too scared to be tested as a donor match. And then she would have to face Ronnie's anger and Jacqui's disapproval. And Dave's. And Richard's. And Sophie's. And Izzy's. And Jack would find out too. That she was too weak and pathetic to help her niece and she was scared of the responsibility of Lily and as a result she'd lost the man she loved.

Chapter Seventy-Three

Jacqui

Christmas looked set to be miserable. Jacqui was desperately upset at the way things had gone between Ronnie and Annabel. She didn't know where to put herself. Ronnie wasn't speaking to her at all now. She had banned Jacqui and Dave from the house. Annabel had called and was civil, but that was it. All the warmth that had been building between them was gone. Maybe Ronnie was right and Annabel really only had ever seen the Bensons as spare parts. If that was the case, Jacqui should probably back off for good. But there was another part of her that couldn't bear the idea of letting her eldest daughter go again. If they had all just had more time together, without the spectre of Izzy's illness, she was sure they could have established a proper relationship.

When it came down to it, Jacqui was willing to forgive Annabel everything. What mother wouldn't be stretched to her very limit by the horrors she was experiencing with her daughter so ill? That was enough to make anyone irrational, or curt, or desperate enough to insult her own sister by waving a chequebook at her as though money was the only consideration. But she could see Ronnie's side of the argument too. Ronnie could be abrupt and rude and quick to judge but there was no doubt that she loved her own children. Of course she placed their welfare above Izzy's. Jacqui had been foolish to try to intervene on Annabel and Izzy's behalf. Challenging Ronnie on a decision she had made for the good of her children was like getting between a bear and her cubs.

Both Ronnie and Annabel had very legitimate reasons to be unhappy with each other and Jacqui was caught in the middle. How could she bring them closer together?

Three weeks before Christmas, as was their habit, Jacqui and Dave put up their Christmas decorations. It was something Jacqui always looked forward to. She had especially loved putting the decorations up when Chelsea and Ronnie were small and for the past few years, now that Jack was old enough to appreciate Christmas and still young enough to be enchanted, she invited him to help. But not this year. While Ronnie wasn't speaking to her, Jacqui could not see her beloved grandson. Sophie, who had her own phone, had texted Jacqui to say that she was sorry about the row, but Sophie would not visit on her own. Jacqui understood that. She didn't want Sophie to be on the wrong side of her mother too.

So Jacqui and Dave decorated the house alone. Even Granddad Bill stayed in his room, snoozing through an ice hockey game on Sky Sports. When Jacqui turned on the Christmas tree lights, she almost burst into tears at the sight. She didn't know why she was bothering. She didn't feel very Christmassy. It was just a waste of electricity. Dave gave her a hug.

'We'll all be speaking again by Christmas,' he said. 'Ronnie wouldn't keep Sophie and Jack from us on the day.'

Jacqui was no longer so sure.

Having put on the gas fire – it was turning out to be a horrible winter – she stood up and looked at the photographs on the mantelpiece. The old photos of Chelsea and Ronnie as children were still there, as were the school photos of Sophie and Jack. But the ranks had been swelled that year and there was a new favourite.

Jacqui picked up the photograph taken on the front steps at the Great House the first time they had Sunday lunch with the Buchanans. There she was, dressed in her Sunday best, with all three of her daughters. Annabel wasn't looking at the camera. Her attention was elsewhere, probably on that dog of hers, which had tried to mate with Granddad Bill's wheelchair. Chelsea had her eyes half closed and Ronnie was actually scowling. But it was a picture of all of them. Her girls. If only she could get them all in the same place again.

Jacqui wrote to Annabel and got a Christmas card in return. She wrote to Ronnie too but her letter went unanswered. She spoke to Chelsea on the phone a couple of times but her youngest seemed distracted and couldn't wait to get off the call. Chelsea wouldn't say what she was doing for the holidays but she told Jacqui not to count on her being in Coventry. Jacqui's dream of having her whole family around her that Christmas seemed more distant than ever. There was only one Christmas in Jacqui's memory that had ever been so bad. That was the Christmas she spent alone in a bedsit in Essex, just seventeen years old, estranged from her parents and broken up from Dave, while Daisy spent her first 25 December as Annabel Buchanan.

Jacqui cried for the girl she had been and the baby she had given away. Then she cried for the women they had become.

Chapter Seventy-Four

Ronnie

Meanwhile, Annabel wrote to Ronnie, tucking a letter inside a Christmas card.

When she saw the envelope on the kitchen table and recognised the handwriting from the note Annabel had attached to their wedding gift, Ronnie's first instinct was to rip the letter up and throw it away without reading it. But of course she did read it. She wanted to see how far that snooty cow would go.

Dear Ronnie,

I don't suppose for one moment that you're ready to forgive me and I can perfectly understand why. Since you left our house on that Sunday afternoon, I have thought of little but how badly I have behaved towards you and your family. Though I have been under enormous stress since Izzy fell ill after taking a tablet of ecstasy, I said things to you that were unforgivable under any circumstances.

You have been nothing but kind to us since the day we first met. I shall never forget your thoughtful gesture at your wedding, asking your guests to chip in for kidney charities. Then, when we asked you to make the ultimate gesture for Izzy, you did not hesitate to be tested. Mark too.

*We should have given you more time to help you
make a more informed decision about what
you might be getting into. In fact, Richard was
always far more cautious. He wanted to give you
more time. I feel I have only myself to blame for
putting you under pressure.*

*You were right to make the decision you did
for your children. I, of all people, should know
that. We are both of us mothers, who care deeply
for our babies and would do anything to keep
them safe. I hope that will help you to understand
my bad behaviour. But whatever you think of me,
please don't take it out on Jacqui. She loves you
as dearly as I love Izzy and you love Sophie and
Jack.*

With love and best wishes,
Annabel

It was a nice letter but it wasn't enough. If Annabel had
opened a vein for Ronnie it wouldn't have been enough
right then. Ronnie was still furious.

Mark picked up the letter.

'It must have taken a lot for her to write that,' he
tried.

'What? She did that in fifteen minutes max. Forget it.
Just like I'm trying to forget her. I don't think of her as
my sister,' said Ronnie. 'I never did. I didn't know her.
We didn't grow up together. And if she hadn't wanted
to track us down to act as some kind of organ donors,
we would never even have met. We might be related by
birth, but we've got nothing in common and I don't see
why we have to be in each other's lives at all.'

'You've got to feel sorry for her . . .' said Mark.

'Why? Why should I?'

'Izzy . . .'

'Izzy got ill in the first place because they let her go to a festival and take drugs. They got their just deserts.'

'For heaven's sake, Ronnie. What parent hasn't taken their eye off the ball for a little while? Izzy's seventeen. Look what happened in Lanzarote with Sophie! What if Adam hadn't been there that day and he hadn't pulled her out of the water, would that have been our fault?'

'I do think of that as my fault,' said Ronnie. 'As it happens.'

'Well, I don't,' said Mark. 'Kids grow up and they live their own lives. You can't keep an eye on them twenty-four seven. What happened to the Buchanans could have happened to us. It could have happened to anyone we know.'

But Mark's words were falling on deaf ears. Ronnie just wasn't ready to hear them.

Chapter Seventy-Five

Sophie

While their parents were estranged and looked set to remain so, Izzy and Sophie were still very much in contact. They spoke on Skype pretty much every day and Izzy had sent Sophie a pair of jeans for her birthday. When Ronnie saw them, she told Sophie she should send them back.

'We don't want anything from them.'

Sophie had refused, risking her mother's wrath. She didn't see why she should stop talking to Izzy just because her mother had fallen out with Annabel. If anything, Sophie had taken the Buchanans' side in the row. She could see why Annabel might have gone nuts when Ronnie said she didn't want to do the transplant. Ronnie had promised to help them. Izzy was taking it remarkably well.

'I'll get a kidney from somewhere,' Izzy said. 'Even if I have to wait for my new brother or sister to grow up so I can have one of theirs.'

'That's not funny,' Sophie told her.

'Gallows humour,' said Izzy.

That evening, over Skype, Izzy was helping Sophie with a GCSE history assignment. But the conversation strayed off the Great War reparations that ultimately led to World War Two on to the cold war that had engulfed their families.

'It's miserable here,' said Izzy.

347

'Same here,' Sophie admitted.

'I wish there was some way for us to get our parents to talk to each other again. I don't mind about the transplant. I really don't. I wouldn't want to give my kidney to someone I hardly know either.'

'But we do know you. You're family.'

'I do feel like you and me are part of the same family,' said Izzy.

Sitting at her computer in Coventry, Sophie blushed with pride.

'Yeah. Cousins for ever,' Sophie said. 'No matter what the grown-ups are doing, we'll always be friends. What are you doing for Christmas?'

'We'll be here. We were supposed to go skiing this year but with my kidneys and Mum's bump, there's no chance. So Gran will come over and it will be just the four of us and Leander. Mum's not even doing her usual Christmas cocktail party. Though I can't pretend I'll miss that. How about you?'

'Normally we'd be at Grandma and Granddad's but since Mum's not talking to Grandma, that's the end of that. It's Jack I feel sorry for. He doesn't really understand why Grandma isn't coming round any more. They don't want to tell him about the transplant thing. Don't want to scare him. He really worries about you being ill though. He did a talk about you at school.'

'Wow. I wish I'd seen that.'

'You'd have liked the pictures he drew. You looked like a cross between Peppa Pig and Miss Hooley off *Balamory*.'

'Accurate then.'

'He says he wants to do a sponsored walk for you.'

'That is so sweet. I hope that this little brother or sister I'm getting in the new year will be half as lovely.'

'How are you doing? You said you were having some more tests this week. Some check-up?'

'It went OK. As well as can be expected.'

'Are you sure?'

'Actually, it was shit. Apparently, I'm getting worse.'

'You're kidding.'

'Nope.'

Izzy outlined the issues that had shown up during the latest round of tests.

'Do you feel OK?' Sophie asked.

'I just feel tired. It pisses me off that it's Christmas and there are loads of parties I would normally have gone to with my mates and instead I'm just stuck here at home, sat in front of the TV with Mum and Dad, who are treating me really weirdly since the last hospital visit. They're constantly watching me, like they think I haven't got much longer. It's spooky.'

'But it's not that bad, is it? I mean, you haven't been told you've only got a few months to live or something like that? You would tell me.'

'I'll make it through Christmas,' Izzy said dramatically. 'And apparently they always do loads of transplants around New Year. People have more accidents when they've been out drinking.'

'Grim.'

'I know. Fuck, Sophie. If I had known this time last year how my life would pan out, I would have done things so differently. You've got to promise me that you won't waste a single day. I want you to live your life to its absolute fullest. Don't waste time. Get the grades. Get out of the Midlands. See the world! I want you to send me postcards from the four corners of the earth while I'm stuck here on this bloody machine.'

'You won't be stuck on it for ever. We'll go travelling together,' said Sophie.

'Don't wait for me. Don't wait for anyone.'

'What? Not even Harrison Collerick?'

'Swipe left!' Izzy laughed.

Once she had finished her Skype conversation with Izzy, Sophie remained at her desk, looking at the screen of her laptop as if for inspiration. Though they'd had a laugh talking about Sophie's terrible taste in blokes and subsequently concocting a strategy to make sure she got to snog someone worth bothering about under the mistletoe, Sophie knew that the joking was all bravado. She could tell that Izzy was afraid.

Before she met Izzy, Sophie hadn't given much thought to mortality. Death was something that happened to old people, though Granddad Bill just seemed to go on and on. He would almost certainly make it to a hundred so long as he kept on belching his way through the songbook. Sophie would certainly miss Granddad Bill's wind version of 'Silent Night' if her mum didn't make it up with Jacqui before Christmas Day. But talking to Izzy had made Sophie thoughtful. Her 'seize the day' speech was meant to be uplifting but to Sophie it felt sad. Too much like a farewell.

The following evening, Sophie had volunteered to babysit Jack while Mark and Ronnie went to Ronnie's office Christmas party. They were expecting a good evening. Apparently no one parties quite like undertakers. They're all about seizing the day.

Sophie had hoped that Jack would be sufficiently occupied by Minecraft that she wouldn't really have to do much at all but he wandered into her bedroom while she was Skyping Izzy again. He wanted to talk to her too.

'Hey, Jack,' said Izzy. 'How's my favourite cousin?'

'I thought I was your favourite,' Sophie laughed.

'How could I resist lovely Jack with his chubby cheeks?'

Jack beamed at the camera on Sophie's computer so that his chubby cheeks filled the whole of Izzy's screen.

'What have you been up to?' Izzy asked.

Jack launched into a very long-winded description of his recent adventures in Minecraft. Neither Izzy nor Sophie could follow it but they let Jack carry on.

'Am I going to see you at Christmas?' Jack asked.

Izzy shook her head.

'I don't think so.'

'Why not?' Jack asked.

'It's to do with our mums,' Izzy told him. 'They're not friends any more.'

'But what did they argue about?'

'Grown-up things,' Izzy said.

But Sophie, full of teenage righteousness, no longer saw why Jack needed to be kept in the dark.

'Our mum was going to give Izzy one of her kidneys,' she said plainly. 'So that she wouldn't be on dialysis any more.'

Izzy shook her head. 'Don't,' she mouthed.

Jack looked to his sister for more information.

'But Mum didn't want to do it because she's scared. And Auntie Annabel was angry because it really needs to be someone in the family who gives Izzy a kidney otherwise it won't work. And she's worried that Izzy won't get the kidney she needs and she'll get much more ill as a result.'

Jack frowned.

'It's all right, Jack. There's no need to look worried,' said Izzy. 'I'm OK. I'll find a new kidney somewhere.'

'But someone from the family has to give it to you,' Jack recapped. He still looked worried.

'Well, that's sort of the ideal. But it's not the only way. Sophie, what have you started? Let's talk about something else. Let's talk about *Doctor Who*! Are you looking forward to the Christmas special, Jack?'

Fortunately, Jack was instantly distracted from the confusing business of Izzy's kidneys. There was nothing better than talking about *Doctor Who*. The cousins speculated as to what treats the Christmas episode might hold, then Jack went off to find his sonic screwdriver so that he could act out part of the trailer for Izzy.

While Jack was gone, Izzy said, 'You shouldn't have told him that stuff about the kidney transplant, Soph.'

'Isn't it better that he knows the truth?'

'Yeah, but he's not old enough to understand it.'

'He'll have forgotten by tomorrow.'

'I hope so. I don't want to give him nightmares.'

'I'd do it, you know,' said Sophie then.

'What?'

'Give you one of my kidneys. We're cousins. It would be a good match.'

'You're too young.'

'I'm not. There's no minimum age for donors in the UK except in Scotland. And I'll be sixteen soon anyway. If anyone tried to stop me, it wouldn't stand up in court.'

'Sophie, you can't. But thank you.'

'If nothing else comes up, I'm serious.'

'You're nuts.'

Jack bounced back in with his sonic screwdriver.

'Ladies and gentlemen, boys and girls, tonight I'm going to be Doctor Who.'

Chapter Seventy-Six

Chelsea

Because Ronnie wasn't talking to Jacqui, she needed to have someone else to offload on. Mark was no good. He'd never understand the office politics or the personal slights that occupied his wife's psyche. Chelsea would have to do instead. But Chelsea wasn't being terribly good as a stand-in.

When she saw Ronnie's number on the screen of her phone, Chelsea didn't pick up the first time. Or the second. Or the third.

Ronnie texted.

Are you still in bed? Call me.

Chelsea called back. She knew she sounded as though she had flu. But Ronnie didn't bother to ask if that was the case. She launched straight into a rant about Annabel, reading out the letter she'd sent in a wheedling, nasty voice.

'I don't want to hear it,' said Chelsea. 'I've had enough of all this.'

Ronnie was taken aback.

'Oh. All right. In that case . . . Jack wants to know if you're going to be here on Christmas Eve.'

Chelsea took a deep breath.

'I'm not.'

'You're not going to Mum and Dad's on Christmas Day then?'

'No.'

'Are you going to be at Adam's?'

'I'm not. We've split up.'

'What? Chelsea! Why didn't you tell me? What did you do?'

'I didn't tell you because you haven't drawn breath long enough for me to tell you anything the last twenty times you've called. And I didn't do anything either. I just decided he's not ready for a relationship. We both decided. It's too soon after his wife and he's too fragile.'

'Bullshit,' said Ronnie.

That was not what Chelsea wanted to hear.

'You've got to come here for Christmas,' said Ronnie. 'You can't be on your own at Christmas.'

'I can. It's just a day,' said Chelsea.

She hung up.

It was just a day. Twenty-four hours. No longer than any other day in the calendar. Chelsea could get through it on her own. She couldn't face the alternative, which was a day at Ronnie's, listening to her middle sister rant about her big sister. Or at her mum and dad's, listening to Jacqui lament the state of her relationships with Ronnie *and* Annabel. Neither could she face the idea of having to be cheerful for Jack's sake when she felt as though all she wanted to do was go out into the garden and howl.

She had heard nothing from Adam since she left his house, except for that awful text. She'd replied, of course, saying she'd been stupid and asking if they could talk about it but he hadn't responded. That he hadn't done so persuaded Chelsea that she had been right after all. He wasn't over Claire. She couldn't compare.

Chelsea made an appointment with her counsellor to

talk things through and try to stop her inner voice from persuading her that stuffing her face then throwing it all up would be a good way to deal with how she was feeling.

'Christmas can make everything seem so much harder,' the counsellor acknowledged. 'We act as though this one day a year needs to be perfect. Everyone must be happy. Everyone must be on their best behaviour. Everyone needs to spend Christmas in the bosom of a loving family. But it is just a day. Just twenty-four hours.'

Chelsea decided she would arm herself to get through the holiday. She ordered a box set of *Breaking Bad*. She would be catching up two years later than her friends at work who had raved about it. She hoped it would still be able to grab her attention the way it had grabbed theirs.

Distraction was what she needed.

Chelsea went to the office party and did her best not to drink too much booze. She stayed off the canapés, which meant that whether or not to purge became a moot point. She seemed to be doing OK. But when the office closed for the Christmas break and Chelsea found herself wandering home alone through crowds of happy people preparing for the biggest party of the year, she struggled to keep her focus. She wondered what Adam was doing. She was desperate to hear from him. Just one word. She had sent him a Christmas card, spending hours crafting the message inside it to make it seem as though she was doing fine and was only writing to him as a friend. But of course writing that casual message didn't mean she felt at all casual about him and every hour that went by without a text or a call took her just a little deeper into her sadness.

'Cheer up, love. It's Christmas!' said the down-and-out who lived in the bus shelter next to the tube station.

Chelsea duly gave him a smile. There were people worse off than her, she told herself. There were people who would be spending Christmas on a park bench with nothing but a bottle of cider to keep them warm. And it was just twenty-four hours. Just a day! Like any other day. Chelsea would get through it on her own.

Oh, how had that Christmas which once looked so promising turned out to be such a disaster?

Chapter Seventy-Seven

Annabel

Standing at the kitchen counter, Annabel looked out into the garden. It was hard to believe how much life had changed in the space of a year. If only she had known, that previous Christmas, exactly how different her world would be. To think she had thought last year's Christmas a near failure. She'd been such a perfectionist. Around the world, wars raged and children died of starvation and Annabel had thrown an enormous fit because the local organic supermarket couldn't fulfil her order for an organic turkey and she had to make a special trip to London to find one instead. She'd let so many silly little things get the better of her back then. She cringed as she remembered being beastly to the village girls who served canapés at her annual cocktail party.

Now she would give anything to be so spoilt again. Now she knew for certain what was really important in life and it wasn't the embarrassment of the woman from next door seeing you'd got your devils on horseback out of a packet from M&S.

Annabel found herself praying for a proper Christmas miracle. For so many years, she had looked upon Christmas as a time to stuff one's face and accumulate more material luxuries. That year's Christmas list had only one item upon it and it definitely wasn't something that money could buy. She cringed as she remembered the moment when Ronnie overheard her telling Richard they needed to offer her money and all the horror that ensued. They'd heard nothing from her since. No response to the heartfelt letter Annabel had sent in a Christmas card.

Richard said they just had to forget that Ronnie had ever tested as a good match for Izzy. If Annabel carried on acting as though she could still somehow change Ronnie's mind, she would only drive herself crazy. There were other possibilities. Richard was trying to get his blood pressure under control, though they didn't know if that would make a difference. They'd sent out a note with all their Christmas cards, reminding their friends of Izzy's plight in the hope that someone might be moved to help. And of course the transplant team were on the case. Any day now, they might get the call telling them that someone they'd never met had tested as Izzy's match. And there was always a chance that once the baby was born and thriving, Annabel could donate herself.

For now, Izzy was upstairs getting ready to start dialysing for the night. She'd had visitors that afternoon. The girls from school. It broke Annabel's heart that when Jessica, Gina and Chloe left to go and meet the rest of their friends at a party, Izzy had to go upstairs and plug herself into that awful machine. To think that a year ago, they had worried that Izzy would go out drinking with her friends and end up in a ditch. Now, far from downing shots, she could only suck ice cubes.

Richard had gone upstairs to sit with her. They were watching some cheesy film. They spent a lot of time in Izzy's room these days. Richard had moved one of his favourite chairs in there. Sometimes, all three of them watched TV in Izzy's bedroom. That was one outcome that Annabel would never have predicted. Her daughter's illness had somehow brought their little family closer together. They certainly spent more time with each other than before.

But how much time did they have? Ultimately? If Izzy didn't get a transplant?

Chapter Seventy-Eight

Jack

Jack was fed up. He wanted to see Grandma and Granddad and Granddad Bill but his mum told him that he wasn't allowed.

'Why not?' he asked.

'Because I said so,' said Ronnie. 'Because Grandma's not been very nice to me,' she added when he continued to whine.

'Is it because of Auntie Annabel?' Jack asked.

'Who said anything about Auntie Annabel?'

Jack kept his lips sealed.

'Did Sophie say something?'

Jack shook his head.

'Whatever your sister's said you mustn't take any notice of her. We're not talking to Annabel either because of grown-up stuff. You don't need to know any more.'

'I know what grown-up stuff is,' said Jack daringly.

'What has Sophie been saying to you? I'll teach her to gossip.'

Fortunately Sophie was not at home to get into trouble. The school holidays had started and Sophie had gone into town with some friends. Mark was working round the clock to finish off someone's kitchen before Christmas started. Jack had no choice but to go to the shops with his mother. It was his least favourite thing, now that he was no longer allowed to sit in the trolley or even to hang off the front of it while his mother pushed it round.

'You're too heavy,' she said. 'You'll make it tip over.'

So Jack had to walk around the supermarket next to Ronnie, keeping his hands to himself and staying out of the way of other determined lady shoppers who drove their trolleys like chariots in the Colosseum. It seemed to take so long. Ronnie could never make her mind up about which jam to choose, or which cereal was better.

'The chocolate ones,' Jack told her every time.

And every time Ronnie picked the cereal that tasted like dog biscuits instead.

Jack had asked for a dog for Christmas. He wanted one like Leander. He reminded his mother as they stopped in the pet food aisle and loaded up with cat food.

'No way,' said Ronnie. 'Not while Fishy's alive.'

'Then can I go and see Leander at his house?' Jack asked.

'No!' Ronnie snapped. 'I've told you. Those people are not our friends.'

'Why not?'

Jack was fishing for more information. He knew that it was to do with Izzy, just as Sophie had told him. The previous evening, he'd heard part of an argument between Ronnie and Sophie. Sophie said that Izzy was going to *die* if no one would give her a kidney. But when Jack asked Ronnie if it was true – was Izzy really dying? – she scolded him for eavesdropping and told him Izzy would be fine.

Now Ronnie was at the butcher's counter, asking about the chances of getting a turkey so late in the day.

'You've had it, love,' said the butcher. 'You should have ordered one weeks ago.'

'Well,' said Ronnie. 'My mum usually gets the turkey but this year . . .' She tailed off. 'How about a really big chicken? It's only got to do four.'

'Let's see what we've got, shall we?'

Ronnie followed the butcher to the other end of his counter. Jack stayed next to the trolley, keeping guard of the bounty Ronnie had already gathered. 'Do not let it out of your sight,' she'd told him. She'd already come close to fighting for the last bag of frozen roast potatoes.

'Jack!'

Jack looked up at the sound of his name. His grandma was at the top of the cereal aisle. She was pushing her own overflowing trolley. Granddad Bill was beside her in his electric chair, with a basket in his lap that was empty but for four bottles of Spitfire.

'I know that young man!' said Granddad Bill.

Jack didn't wait for permission to leave his post. He ran straight into his grandmother's arms.

'Oh, Jack. Am I glad to see you!' she said, smothering him with kisses.

'I've missed you, Grandma.'

'I know,' said Jacqui. 'And I've missed you too.'

'Why won't you come round any more?' he asked.

'Oh,' said Jacqui. 'It's complicated. It's a grown-up thing.'

Jack was getting tired of all this 'grown-up' stuff.

'Give your Granddad Bill a kiss. Quickly before your mum starts to wonder where you are.'

'How are you, Granddad Bill?' Jack asked.

'Now I've seen you, I've won the bloody lottery,' he said.

'He really has and all,' said Jacqui. 'Thirty pounds last week. He says he wants to give ten to you, ten to Sophie and ten to Izzy. For Christmas.'

Jacqui looked suddenly sad.

'Sophie said Izzy's dying,' said Jack.

'Oh.' Jacqui put her hand to her throat. 'You mustn't say that. Izzy isn't dying, dear. But she is very poorly, yes. She needs a new kidney.'

'I've been thinking about that. Fishy's food has got kidney in it,' Jack said.

Jacqui stroked Jack's cheek.

'It doesn't work like that, dear. She needs a whole one.'

Just then, having settled on two medium-sized chickens in lieu of a turkey, Ronnie noticed that Jack wasn't by her side.

'Jack!' Her voice was an alarm.

'I'm here,' he said. 'With Grandma. And Granddad Bill.'

'By the sugar!' Jacqui added.

Ronnie was ready to be angry when she appeared at the top of the aisle.

'I told you to stay by the trolley,' she said to Jack.

'Ronnie, love,' said Jacqui, opening her arms. 'It's not his fault. I called him over. He was being ever so good.'

'Was he?'

'He was. You're looking well, sweetheart.'

'Yeah,' said Ronnie. 'I'm fine. You?'

'Well, I'm OK but your dad has had a bit of a cold.'

'I'm sorry to hear that.'

'It's been hard on him,' said Jacqui. 'Not seeing you all.'

'That's not my fault,' said Ronnie. 'You know what happened.'

'Oh, Ronnie. Can't we talk about this?' Jacqui pleaded.

'Not in the middle of the bloody supermarket, we can't!'

'Then let's go and have a cup of tea. Jack can keep Granddad Bill amused.'

'I've got to finish my shopping,' said Ronnie. 'I've got a lot to do before Christmas Day.'

'Please, love. I've been praying that I'd find a way to talk to you. You've not answered any of my calls or texts. It's been horrible, not knowing how you're getting on. Just a quick cuppa?'

Jack looked up at his mum with big round eyes, willing her to agree.

Ronnie nodded.

'All right then,' she said. 'I'll just put this lot in the back of the car.'

Ronnie paid and loaded her shopping into the boot of her Fiesta. Jacqui did the same. Her car was parked just a few spaces away. They left Granddad Bill and Jack holding a place in the supermarket's cafeteria. Jack was pleased to be able to have a ride in Granddad Bill's wheelchair after so many weeks of estrangement.

'You're getting good at this,' said Granddad Bill, as Jack steered them through a narrow gap between tables.

Jacqui and Ronnie returned from the car park and joined the self-service queue to get three teas, an orange juice and a cake for Jack. Meanwhile, Jack tried to talk to his great-grandfather about Izzy.

'I think she's dying,' he said. 'It's making me worried. She needs a kidney.'

'Kidney!' said Granddad Bill. 'I could do with some of that myself. Haven't had kidneys in years. Let's go and see if we can't get some.'

'Get some where?' Jack asked.

'They'll have them on the meat counter. Come on,

Jack. Steer us back into the shop. You've made me want some kidneys now.'

'Granddad Bill, can I get one too?'

'If you like, son,' said Granddad Bill. 'Come on. Let's hurry along.'

The queue at the cafeteria checkout seemed endless. Someone at the front had dropped a tray loaded with a teapot and four cups and most of the staff were busy cleaning up the broken crockery. Jacqui and Ronnie were absorbed in watching the whole palaver. They didn't notice a small boy and his great-grandfather setting off for the meat counter and thence to the high road in an electric wheelchair capable of eleven point six miles an hour.

By the time Ronnie and Jacqui had paid for their refreshments and were looking around the vast cafeteria for Jack, Bill and their table, Jack and Bill were well on their way. They left the supermarket with no problem whatsoever. No one thought to stop them. People smiled as Jack and Bill sailed by.

'Isn't that sweet,' they said. 'He's giving his grandson a ride.'

They didn't know that Jack was only six and that Granddad Bill's dementia meant Jack was most definitely the one in charge.

Chapter Seventy-Nine

Ronnie

Ronnie sank down on to a hard plastic chair just inside the entrance to the supermarket. The moment she realised that Jack and Bill were not in the cafeteria, she dumped her tray full of teacups on the nearest table and raced to the supermarket's door with Jacqui close behind her.

'They won't have gone far,' said Jacqui. 'They can't. Jack's only six and Bill's in his wheelchair.'

'Who says they're together?' said Ronnie. 'Jack! Jack! Where have they gone?'

'Jack wouldn't leave Granddad Bill,' said Jacqui. 'We told him not to. And who's going to take both of them at once?'

'Where are they? Where are they? Has anybody seen my son?' Ronnie shouted. 'He's about this tall. He's got blond hair. He's wearing a blue Puffa jacket and a Doctor Who baseball cap.'

'And he's with an old man in a wheelchair,' said Jacqui. 'His great-granddad. He's wearing a Coventry City scarf, a brown overcoat and a pair of carpet slippers.'

'What's going on?' a security guard asked them.

'I can't find my son,' said Ronnie. 'I left him with his great-granddad.'

'His great-granddad's disappeared too,' Jacqui said.

'Then they're probably somewhere in the shop,' said

the security guard. 'Having a look at the toys, I'll bet. He's probably getting his old grandpa to buy him something or other for Christmas. They'll be all right.'

'You don't understand,' said Ronnie. 'My grandfather has dementia. He shouldn't be in charge of a child.'

'But you left them alone together?' the security guard pointed out.

'Only for a minute,' said Jacqui. 'We hardly let them out of our sight. We were paying for our tea.'

'I should never have left them together,' said Ronnie. 'We shouldn't have taken our eyes off them for a second.'

'I'm sure they won't have come to any harm,' said the guard. 'We'll find them.'

The guard took Ronnie and Jacqui to the toy aisle. As they moved, he radioed his colleagues.

'Anyone seen an old man in a wheelchair with a six-year-old boy in tow?'

The supermarket was full of old men in wheelchairs that morning. Having drawn a blank in the toy aisle, Ronnie and Jacqui and the security guard raced from one end of the enormous shop to the other to ID potential Granddad Bills. Likewise, there seemed to be hundreds of small boys in Doctor Who hats. As they responded to one false alarm after another, Ronnie and Jacqui grew more and more anxious.

'They must have left the shop,' said the guard after they'd been up and down every aisle several times.

'Why didn't somebody stop them?'

Ronnie ran out on to the street but the pavements were thronged with Christmas shoppers, who blocked her view as they meandered from shop window to shop window, oblivious to the crisis unfolding in their midst.

'They'll be OK,' Jacqui insisted. 'They'll be together and who would want to steal Granddad Bill?'

'Oh Mum.' Ronnie clung to her mother. 'I can't stand it.' Jacqui helped her back to the plastic chair just inside the supermarket's doors. Ronnie's legs gave way beneath her. 'This is a nightmare. I just want my baby back. Where have they taken my baby?'

'There's no "they",' Jacqui said forcefully. 'No one's taken Jack anywhere. He'll be with Granddad Bill. They've just wandered off. They won't have gone far.'

By now the supermarket security team had alerted the police. A community officer was there within minutes, taking details to be circulated to her colleagues. Ronnie showed the community officer her most recent photograph of her son. Jack had taken a selfie using her phone just that morning. Ronnie could hardly bear to look at his grinning face. Where was he? Who was he with?

'We'll find them both,' the community officer promised. 'We'll have everyone looking for them and they'll be back before you know it.'

Jacqui phoned Mark and Dave and texted Sophie. She texted Chelsea too, though Chelsea was too far away to help down in London. Feeling somewhat furtive, Jacqui also composed a text to Annabel. She didn't have time to send it. They were interrupted by the security guard they had first approached when they'd realised Jack and Bill were gone.

'The CCTV shows your son and his great-granddad leaving the store about half an hour ago,' he said. 'Your boy is steering the wheelchair.'

Chapter Eighty

Jack and Bill

Outside on the high street, Jack increased the wheel-chair's speed to eight and a half miles an hour. The passers-by who had smiled to see the young boy and old man having such fun together were a little more concerned now they had to jump out of the way. Jack was taking no prisoners as he steered a route right down the middle of the pavement.

'Those things are too fast!' someone commented.

'Hooligans!' shouted a mother as she snatched her toddler out of the wheelchair's path.

'We're on a mission,' said Granddad Bill to a pair of old ladies who were blocking the pavement ahead of them. 'Get out of the bloody way.'

'Don't say bloody!' Jack yelled.

Jack pushed forward on the wheelchair's speed control and it quickly reached its maximum. At eleven point six miles an hour in just under ninety seconds, they sailed across a pedestrian crossing on a red light, narrowly missing being squashed by a bus.

'Steady on, boy,' said Bill.

'We're in a hurry,' Jack reminded him as they bumped down another kerb at such speed that they were almost tipped out into the gutter.

'Where are we going again, lad?'

Jack wasn't sure. He'd assumed Granddad Bill was navigating.

But what Jack didn't understand was that Granddad Bill was in one of those episodes where the years had dropped away and he couldn't remember that he had a son, let alone three granddaughters and three great-grandkids. That afternoon, Bill was a lad again and this trip with Jack was just a great adventure between two friends. He thought Jack was an old pal from school.

'Let's sing!' Bill said. 'That'll make these slowcoaches get out of the way.'

Bill began to sing 'It's a Long Way to Tipperary'.

When Jack took up the words – he knew most of his great-grandfather's repertoire – Bill concentrated on his usual, windy percussion.

The singing and belching certainly made the Christmas shoppers notice Jack and Bill, but they still didn't question what the pair were up to, or where they were heading.

'We're not going fast enough,' Jack complained, even as the electric wheelchair was breaking new records. 'We need to get on a bus. Which bus is it, Granddad Bill?'

'We'll have to ask a policeman,' Bill said.

'There's one,' said Jack. The uniformed woman was actually a traffic warden, but when Jack told her where they were headed, she happily told him he was looking for the 172.

'There's the 172!' Jack trilled, spotting the bus coming down the street. 'There's the bus stop. We can get on it. Quick.'

Pushing the wheelchair to warp speed, Jack steered towards the queue. Again, no one seemed at all bothered by the sight of a six-year-old driving his great-grandfather's chair. They just tried to make sure they didn't get run over.

'You having a nice day out, are you?' an elderly lady asked.

'We've got a kidney,' Jack explained.

'Oooh, kidneys,' said the elderly lady. 'I love a bit of kidney, me. Youth of today turn their noses up at offal though, don't they?' She addressed this last comment to Bill. 'You want to share yours with me?' she asked with a flirtatious wink.

Jack was horrified. 'You can't have it. We need it.'

He clutched the supermarket carrier bag close.

'If you were the only girl in the world . . . burp . . .' Granddad Bill sang to his new admirer. She blushed and fluttered her eyelashes as though she were just a girl once more.

'Granddad Bill,' said Jack impatiently. 'Stop singing. We're getting on.'

The bus driver lowered the disabled access ramp and Jack steered the wheelchair forward. He found it tricky to get the chair properly lined up but he and Bill were soon assisted by a couple of young men in the queue. The proximity of Christmas was making everyone feel happy and helpful. Still no one asked whether Jack and Bill should be heading out of town on their own.

'Will you let us know when we get there?' Jack asked them.

They assured him that they would.

Chapter Eighty-One

Ronnie

Meanwhile, Ronnie and Jacqui were pounding the streets near the supermarket with a team of security guards, police officers and well-wishers keen to help. But they had sorely underestimated how far and fast an electric wheelchair could travel in half an hour and nobody had even considered for a moment that Jack and Bill might be on a bus. They kept their search to the immediate surrounding area of the supermarket and of course they found no clues. No one had seen them. Everyone was too focused on finishing their Christmas shopping to notice even such a peculiar pair. Plus, the boy was with his great-grandfather. Where was the need to panic?

If only they knew. Ronnie was in pieces. This was worse, far worse, than when Sophie had gone AWOL in Lanzarote back in the summer. Jack was so young and Bill was so daft. Who knew what kind of trouble they might get into? Might already be in! Together with Jacqui, Ronnie made a list of all the places Jack might have wanted Bill to take him. Someone called ahead to the toyshop and the pet shop, warning them to be on the lookout. Someone else was checking the park. The staff at the children's library were alerted. And then they made a list of all the pubs in the city where Bill had ever had so much as half a pint. It was a long list.

'We'll contact them all,' said the community officer. 'Don't you worry.'

How could Ronnie and Jacqui not worry?

It was starting to get dark. While Jacqui and Ronnie continued to scour the city centre on foot, as they waited for Dave and Mark to join them, social media swung into action. Chelsea, who had called Jacqui as soon as she got her text, immediately put a plea for help on Twitter. The local radio station put out an alert to its listeners and featured a picture of Jack on their Twitter feed too. Sophie, who had been hanging out in the town centre with her friends, came to find her mother and grandmother. Sophie also tweeted and Facebooked. Her friends, who all knew and loved her little brother, spread the message. Izzy saw Sophie's plea for help. She sent her a message at once.

OMG. Stay calm. They won't have gone far. I'll tell Mum and Dad.

Annabel covered her mouth with her hands as Izzy told her the news.

'Poor Ronnie,' she said. 'Tell her if there's anything we can do to help.'

'Tell her I can be there in forty-five minutes,' said Richard. 'If she needs an extra pair of eyes and ears.'

The fact that Ronnie had stormed from their house spewing curses was soon forgotten.

Izzy called and spoke to Sophie.

'They were last seen taking Granddad Bill's wheelchair out of the supermarket,' Sophie explained. 'The police have been informed. They're sending Jack's picture to all the border agencies. Oh, Izzy. What if somebody's kidnapped my brother? I can't stand the thought of it.'

'Then don't think it, Soph. Jack is going to be fine. Seriously, who in their right minds would want to kidnap

Jack and Granddad Bill? After two minutes of listening to Jack talk about Minecraft and Granddad Bill doing his burping songs, they'd bring them both straight back.'

Sophie tried to laugh but she couldn't.

'I hope you're right,' she said.

'I wish I could come and help,' said Izzy. 'I love your little brother. We all do. Dad wants to know if he should drive over and help.'

Sophie asked her mother.

'No,' said Ronnie. 'We don't need their help.'

Sophie protested.

'There are plenty of people looking already,' Ronnie said.

Sophie didn't push it. She passed the message on to Izzy but without mentioning how angry her mother had seemed. An hour had already passed since Jack and Bill were last sighted. Mark had arrived. He hugged Sophie and consoled his wife. Dave appeared minutes later. He had a photograph of Granddad Bill, though it was a decade out of date.

Then, suddenly, a breakthrough.

'There's been a sighting,' someone shouted. 'They were seen heading towards the bus station about half an hour ago.'

Chapter Eighty-Two

Jack

'Oi! Laurel and Hardy!' shouted the bus driver. 'Shall I let you two off here?'

'Yes, please,' Jack called back up the bus.

The wheelchair ramp was lowered. Jack and Granddad Bill had no trouble getting off. They'd been entertaining their fellow passengers all the way with a Christmas singalong (it was amazing how many of the passengers were able, like Granddad Bill, to burp 'Away in a Manger') and everyone who was able to leapt up from their seats to help them. None of them quite understood where the odd pair were going but they wished them well. And the old lady who had asked Bill to share his dinner with her even pressed a fiver into Jack's hand.

'You buy yourself something for Christmas, you lovely young man.'

'I'll give it to the Kidney Foundation,' Jack said.

All the grandmothers on the bus sighed.

With Jack, Granddad Bill and the wheelchair safely deposited, the bus travelled on towards Warwick, with everyone on board feeling slightly warmer for their encounter with the strange pair in the electric wheelchair. It would not be until the bus got to Warwick that one of the lads who had helped get the wheelchair on board would idly check his Facebook page on his mobile and realise he'd been travelling with two fugitives.

It was properly dark by now and the pavements out here in the little country village were rather narrow, so Jack and Bill had to stick to the road. Fortunately, there wasn't any traffic that evening. And Dave had fitted Bill's chair with headlights. Jack soon worked out how to turn them on.

'I remember a town like this in Normandy,' Granddad Bill told his great-grandson. 'It was all quiet, just like it is here. The Nazis had all fled ahead of us but they left their supplies and their wine behind. We drank champagne like it was water. It was like winning the bloody lottery.'

'Don't say bloody,' said Jack reflexively. 'Granddad Bill, is their house up here?'

'I don't know, lad. You're the navigator.'

'I'm the pilot,' Jack said.

But Jack was feeling a little less sure of himself now. It was cold and the trees that had looked so pretty back in the early summer loomed over them like long-fingered monsters. Something stirred in the undergrowth. It was probably just a fox but the noise it made had Jack clinging to the arms of the chair in panic.

'Granddad Bill! What was that?'

'Just a Nazi deserter,' said Granddad Bill. He was somewhere else now. In some other time. He started singing one of his favourite songs. '*Hitler has only got one ball . . .*'

This time Jack didn't join in. He was too worried. The wheelchair trundled on. But it was going less fast over the rough country road than it had done on the smooth pavements in town. Jack suddenly felt a wash of fear. Not just of the dark woods to either side of them but of his mother too. She would be wondering where he had got to by now. He should have told her where they were going. She might have driven them if he'd explained what he was thinking. Ronnie was always telling him that he should never go off on his own. Jack was going to be in big trouble when they got back home. Far worse trouble than he had been in only the day before, when he spilled hot chocolate all over the front of his anorak.

'Granddad Bill,' Jack said. 'We need to phone Mummy.'

But neither of them had a phone.

And then the wheelchair's battery ran flat. And the thick white clouds that had hung over the Midlands all day finally began to snow.

Chapter Eighty-Three

Ronnie and Annabel

Ronnie listened intently as the woman who had spotted Jack and Bill en route to the bus station relayed the details of the sighting.

'They looked like they were having a gay old time,' the woman said. 'And they must have been going at twenty miles an hour. People were having to jump off the pavement so they didn't get run over.'

It was a comfort to Ronnie and Jacqui to hear that Jack and Bill were still together. What was less comforting was how much the search had suddenly widened. The police now concentrated their efforts on the bus station. They quizzed everyone in the bus queues as to whether they'd seen Jack and Bill boarding. Of course, the problem with that was that the people in the bus queues had not been there half an hour before. They hadn't seen anything to help work out where the missing pair were going.

And Ronnie was beginning to appreciate that an hour was a very long time indeed when you were worrying about your lost child.

At the Great House, the Buchanans had just finished supper. Not that anyone was particularly hungry with the thought that Jack and Granddad Bill were missing foremost in everyone's minds. Richard ignored his doctor's advice and finished off half a bottle of wine, hoping it would quell his anxiety though he pretended it was no big deal.

'They'll show up,' he said. 'They'll be in a pub somewhere.'

Izzy excused herself as quickly as she could to go upstairs and check the progress of the search online.

Meanwhile, Annabel texted Jacqui, offering her moral support. She wanted to text Ronnie too but wasn't sure that it would be welcome. She'd guessed that Ronnie had vetoed Richard joining the search.

'I suppose I should take Leander out,' said Richard once the table was cleared and the dishwasher loaded.

Leander was less than enthusiastic. Richard had to prod him towards the back door. Perhaps it was just the cold but even Leander seemed somehow anxious that night.

'We should send you out to look for them, eh?' Richard suggested to the dog as they stepped out into the bitter December night. 'See what you can do with that superior sniffing power of yours.'

Leander stood his ground on the garden path and refused to follow Richard towards the road.

Richard looked up at the sky and saw the winter's first flurry of snow. He was sorely tempted to abandon the walk himself. But he knew that Annabel would disapprove. It was always easy to find an excuse not to exercise and both he and Leander definitely needed it.

'Come on,' said Richard, actually getting behind Leander and pushing him with his knee. 'This is for your own good, fatso. You don't think I want to be out here tonight either? Once around the village and we'll be back by the fire before you know it.'

They headed out of the gate towards the church. Alas,

the village pub had long since closed and been converted into someone's holiday home. Richard kept his hands tucked into his armpits to keep them warm as he walked. Even though he was wearing gloves, the tips of his fingers were numb within moments. It was no kind of night to be out.

Chapter Eighty-Four

Jack

Granddad Bill had fallen asleep with his head lolled to one side and his mouth wide open. Jack couldn't wake him up. Bill didn't even wake himself up when he let out one of his enormous snores.

The wheelchair would not move. The battery was completely dead. Jack had jumped off his great-grandfather's lap and tried to push the chair from behind, but he could not move the chair and its heavy load even an inch. The wheels were in a rut and it was snowing quite hard by now. Jack didn't have any gloves to put on. His mother hadn't bought him a replacement pair since he left the last lot behind at school at the end of term.

'Granddad Bill, wake up!' Jack pleaded.

Bill sank deeper into his doze.

Jack was properly scared now but he knew that he had to do something. He should walk to the nearest house and knock on the door. But Ronnie had told him not to knock on strangers' doors. She'd told him that if he was ever lost or in trouble, he should find a policeman. There was no sign of a policeman right then.

They must be close, though. Jack was sure they had asked the bus driver for the right village. If he walked just a little way he might come across the house. Jack set out to the north, but he was only ten steps away from his sleeping great-grandfather when a barn owl swooped low overhead and had Jack running right back to the wheelchair and cowering behind it. How long until morning came?

Chapter Eighty-Five

Leander

Ordinarily, there was nothing Leander the Labrador liked more than going for a walk but on a night like this not even the fresh scent of fox on the wind was enough to make up for having to leave the fireside. Leander dragged his paws, letting Richard set the painfully slow pace. The dog would walk no further than he had to. The moment Richard turned for home, Leander would use all the energy he was conserving to race back ahead of him and bag the best seat in the house even though, technically speaking, he wasn't supposed to sit on the furniture.

'Come on, boy,' Richard called encouragingly. 'Come on. Let's pick the pace up. I know it was you who stole the mince pies off the counter. You're going to have to do a lot of running to burn those calories off.'

Leander only took in his master's tone, which was jovial. No need to take any notice of the words.

Still muttering encouragement, Richard made it to the war memorial in the centre of the village and waited for Leander there. The simple stone cross already had a covering of snow. Richard brushed flakes from the names of the fallen while he gave Leander a chance to catch up.

'This is as far as we go,' he said when Leander got there. 'Too bloody cold to be out any longer. I'll race you back to the fireplace.'

And Leander would have beat him to it, had he not caught another scent – even more interesting than fresh fox – as they passed Green Lane. It was the smell of meat. The smell of offal, specifically, that sent him into paroxysms of delight whenever Annabel brought some home from Waitrose.

'What's the matter, boy?' Richard asked, noticing that Leander's attention had been caught by something down the dark road that led to nowhere in particular. 'Come on. Let's go home.'

But Leander was off the lead. Richard didn't have a hope of catching him before he set off in this new direction, taking him further from the house and the comforts of the hearth. As the scent of offal grew stronger in his nostrils, Leander picked up the pace. He could smell something else now too. Leander knew this scent and he knew it belonged to someone he was fond of. Had he been able to describe it in human terms, he would have said there was a tang of hair oil, old-fashioned shaving cream and underneath it all, the smell of Trebor mints. And what was that? The smell of baby shampoo, a dash of Savlon and hot chocolate spilled down the front of an anorak?

Leander raced out of sight.

'Leander!' Richard shouted. 'Leander! Come back, you bloody idiot hound!'

Richard was furious at the idea of having to find his Labrador in the woods on a night like this.

Jack Benson-Edwards was delighted to be found.

Chapter Eighty-Six

Annabel

While Richard and Izzy attended to Granddad Bill and Jack in front of the fire, plying them with beer and hot chocolate respectively, Annabel picked up the phone and called Ronnie.

'What do you want?' Ronnie asked, brusquely. 'I need to keep this line open for calls from the police.'

'No need. Your son is here,' said Annabel. 'And Granddad Bill too.'

'Oh, thank God. What are they doing with you?'

'Richard found them in a lane on the other side of the village when he was walking the dog. They're pretty cold but they're both in one piece. Apparently they wanted to see Izzy. They came on the bus. I'm going to drive them both back to you.'

'We'll come and fetch them,' said Ronnie.

'No, I'll bring them,' said Annabel. 'It will be quicker and it's really no trouble. The wheelchair may have to come separately though. Your house or Jacqui's?'

'Mine,' said Ronnie. 'But wouldn't it be better for Richard to come? You're having a baby in a month.'

'I am,' said Annabel. 'But Richard's had most of a bottle of wine. He'll stay with Izzy. I'm fine to drive.'

At last Ronnie managed, 'Thank you.'

* * *

Forty-five minutes later, Annabel pulled the car up outside Ronnie's house. Bill and Jack were both strapped into the back. It was the first time Annabel had seen the Benson-Edwards family's legendary Christmas display. Mark had outlined every contour of the house in fairy lights. It must have cost a fortune to have them on even for an hour a day.

Still, the neighbour's house had even more lights and a huge inflatable Santa tethered to the chimney. It was a windy night and the blown-up Santa looked in serious danger of lift off.

'People drive from all over the world to see what Dad and Mick next door have done,' Jack said proudly.

When Richard first found Jack and Bill, shivering in the Green Lane, Jack had been hysterical with worry. Annabel had assured him that she would talk to Ronnie and make sure he didn't get into trouble. After all, he and Granddad Bill had only come to Little Bissingden because they wanted to help Izzy. With Auntie Annabel on his side, Jack had soon calmed down and now he was just excited to be able to show her the Christmas decorations. Annabel told him that she had never seen anything like it. Which was true.

Of course Ronnie had been listening out for the arrival of Annabel's car. As Annabel heaved herself out of the driver's seat and went round to open the car door for Jack, Ronnie came out, followed by Jacqui, Dave, Mark and Sophie. And a pair of community police officers who were there to make sure the day's excitement reached its proper conclusion.

Ronnie swept Jack into her arms and hugged him tightly.

'You silly, silly boy,' she said. 'The whole of the police force has been looking for you. What did you think you were doing?'

'Granddad Bill bought me a kidney in the supermarket so I was taking it to Izzy,' Jack explained.

The collected adults gave a gasp of horror.

'It's all right,' said Annabel. 'It's the thought that counts.'

'Izzy can't have it so Leander did,' Jack continued. 'It helped Leander find us. When we were lost in the woods.'

'They got the wheelchair stuck in a lane,' said Annabel. 'Leander sniffed them out. Good job Richard was walking him. It was getting pretty cold.'

Granddad Bill was safely back in his old wheelchair. The one without a battery. Jacqui wrapped a duvet round him.

'Are you all right, Bill?' Jacqui asked. 'Warm enough?'

'Aye,' he said. 'I've won the bloody lottery.'

'I'd better get back,' said Annabel. 'The snow is starting to settle. Have a lovely Christmas, won't you?' She gave Jacqui a kiss on the cheek and reached out to squeeze Sophie's hand.

'Aren't you going to come in and see our tree?' Jack asked.

Annabel looked to Ronnie.

'I'm not sure . . .' she began.

Suddenly everyone was looking to Ronnie for an answer. Jacqui, Dave, Mark, Sophie, Granddad Bill, Jack and the community police officers.

'You've probably got to get back to Izzy,' said Ronnie. 'Have a good Christmas.'

'And you.'

Annabel turned to head back to her car. As she did so, she exhaled painfully.

'Are you all right?' Jacqui asked, rushing to her eldest daughter's side.

Annabel winced.

'The baby has been lying on a nerve. Sometimes it gets me. Do you mind if I sit down for a minute?'

With Jacqui's help, Annabel lowered herself on to Ronnie's doorstep. Jacqui glared at Ronnie. Then everyone was glaring at Ronnie.

'Oh for goodness' sake. You can't sit on the step,' said Ronnie. 'It's freezing. Come inside.'

'I don't want to be any trouble,' said Annabel.

'Just come in,' said Ronnie.

'Before the neighbours see!' Sophie chimed.

'Shut up, you,' said Ronnie.

It was already too late for that. The neighbours, who'd all been aware that Jack and Bill had been missing, had been watching everything from behind their curtains. Ronnie offered Annabel her hand and pulled her back to her feet.

'How long have you got to go now?' Jacqui asked as she and Ronnie helped Annabel inside.

'Another month. I don't know how I'm going to stand it. I don't remember getting anywhere near this big with Izzy.'

'I was as big as a house both times,' said Ronnie. 'Second time I stayed that way too.'

Annabel opened her mouth to protest automatically.

'If men had to get pregnant, the human race would die out in a single generation,' Ronnie continued. 'Come on. Come through into the living room. Do you want a mince pie?'

'You know what,' said Annabel. 'That would be lovely.'

Chapter Eighty-Seven

Ronnie and Annabel

Jack led the way into the living room. The Christmas tree, which had been dark while Jack and his great-granddad were missing, blazed into life when Jack flicked the switch at the skirting board.

Annabel was settled on to the sofa with a cushion at the small of her back. The community police officers took their leave (and a couple of mince pies). Dave and Jacqui loaded Granddad Bill into the car and drove him back to their house. It was well past Bill's bedtime. Annabel promised she would text Jacqui to say that she'd made it back to Little Bissingden safely when she drove home later on. Meanwhile, Mark put the kettle on. Sophie helped him lay out some more mince pies on a tray. Jack gave Annabel the rundown on all the baubles on the Benson-Edwards' tree.

'This one is from when I was born,' he said, showing her a blue bauble marked 'Baby's first Christmas'. Sophie had the same bauble in pink.

Ronnie sat at the other end of the sofa, picking at a hangnail. Though Annabel was back in her home, the frost between them had yet to entirely be thawed.

'Jack,' said Ronnie suddenly. 'Why don't you go upstairs and find that picture of Father Christmas you did last week?'

It was an excuse for the two sisters to be alone.

'I'm sorry for what Jack did,' Ronnie began. 'Turning up with a kidney like that. Izzy must have been upset.'

'Actually,' said Annabel. 'I think she was quite touched. Your son is a very special young man. He wanted to help. It's not his fault he didn't understand quite how. He's thoughtful.'

'I don't know where he gets that from,' said Ronnie.

'He gets it from the same place Sophie does. You and Mark. You know, Sophie told Izzy that she'd give her a kidney if she could. We won't let her of course. She's much too young.'

'When did she say that?'

'A week or so ago. Izzy and Sophie talk on Skype all the time.'

Ronnie had no idea.

'Look, Ronnie, I want to apologise for what happened in November. I was stupid and arrogant. I could only see the situation with the transplant from our point of view. I didn't think about how it might affect your children. And the money thing. I'm so embarrassed about that day. What I said to you and about you was vile. But I was desperate. I still am desperate if I'm honest.'

'Don't worry about it,' said Ronnie. 'About the money thing. I think I seized on it because I was scared. And I wanted to make it your fault I wasn't going to go ahead. I'm still scared.'

'It's all right. We'll find another way. After the baby is born, I'll be tested again myself. Even if the pregnancy has changed my HLA profile, I'm sure we can still go ahead. They can transplant unmatched kidneys much more easily now. Izzy will be fine.'

Annabel winced again.

'It's really giving you trouble tonight,' Ronnie observed. 'The baby.'

'Obviously takes after its father.'

'You still don't know what it is then?'

Annabel shook her head. She was in too much pain to talk. She blew out her cheeks as though she had been winded by a punch to the stomach from an invisible assailant. And then her waters broke, all over Ronnie's sofa.

'Shit,' said Ronnie.

'Oh Ronnie! I'm so sorry,' said Annabel. 'I'll pay for the cleaning but right now I should just go home.'

'You can't go home. We need to get you to hospital. You're having a flipping baby.'

'No, I'm not. It's too early,' said Annabel. 'The baby can't be coming now. After my waters broke with Izzy, I had two days.'

'I don't care. I can't let you go anywhere on your own in this state,' said Ronnie. 'What's Richard's number? I deleted it off my phone.'

Annabel puffed the number out.

'Which hospital are you supposed to go to?'

Annabel told her.

'That's too far away. You're going to have to go to the one where I had my two. Will that be OK?'

'I'll go anywhere,' said Annabel.

She tried to get up but she was thrown back on to the sofa by another contraction.

'This doesn't feel right,' she said. 'It all feels much quicker. Is it meant to be happening like this?'

'I can't remember. I had so much gas and air I didn't come down for a week after Jack. Mark! Mark! Phone an ambulance.'

'Wouldn't it be quicker for one of you to drive me?'

'We've both had too much to drink. After you called to say you found Jack, we both had a couple to calm ourselves down. Mark! Mark!'

Sophie appeared at the sitting-room door. 'The ambulance is coming. Dad says he's staying in the kitchen in case he faints.'

Jack peeped from behind Sophie's legs.

'What's wrong with Auntie Annabel?'

Annabel grasped Ronnie's hand.

'You're breaking my fingers,' Ronnie complained.

'I need an epidural,' said Annabel. 'I've got to have one.'

'No chance of that here,' said Ronnie.

'Shall I get my sonic screwdriver?' asked Jack.

Chapter Eighty-Eight

Humfrey

Baby Humfrey Buchanan was born in the front room of Ronnie and Mark's house. He shot out with such speed that Ronnie almost dropped him. She ended up on her backside beneath the Christmas tree with Humfrey in her lap.

Sophie described instructions for dealing with the placenta and umbilical cord from a video on YouTube. Fortunately, the paramedics arrived before anything actually needed to be done. Richard arrived shortly afterwards with Izzy.

Jack was beside himself.

'I asked for a boy cousin and Father Christmas sent me one. Early!' he announced to Richard.

'It's a boy?'

'It most certainly is,' said Mark.

'Oh wow,' said Izzy. 'I've got a brother.'

'Welcome to my world,' said Sophie.

Chapter Eighty-Nine

Annabel, Jacqui and Sarah

The paramedics took Annabel and Humfrey directly from Ronnie's house to the hospital. The following day, Annabel and the new baby had plenty of visitors, starting with Sarah, who had set out from home at six in the morning. Sarah was delighted to meet her grandson. She was over the moon to hear that he was to be named after her late husband, Annabel's dad.

Ronnie and Mark came a little later with Sophie and Jack. Jack brought a drawing. It looked rather bloody. Annabel assumed that it was something to do with Doctor Who.

'No,' said Jack. 'It's you having the baby in our living room.'

She promised she would have it framed.

Jacqui and Dave came in the afternoon. Jacqui was carrying an enormous pink teddy bear.

'I was sure he was going to be a girl.'

Annabel accepted the bear gratefully.

'He's already got one pink bear,' she said. 'Well, grey. But it used to be pink.'

Jacqui peered into the cot. Suddenly she straightened up again. She gasped as though she'd seen something rather shocking.

'What is it?' Annabel straightened up in bed. 'Is everything all right with the baby?'

'Yes,' said Jacqui. She reached into the cot and pulled out the bear that Richard had tucked in there earlier that morning. 'Where did you get this?'

'Oh, it's mine. Looks a bit shabby now but it was mine when I was a baby. Then Izzy had it. It's the family bear. At this time of the year it's normally on top of the Christmas tree instead of a fairy.'

'But I gave it to you,' said Jacqui.

'You did?'

'I sent it for your first Christmas.'

'I thought it was from one of my godparents.'

'No,' said Jacqui. 'It was from me. And you kept it all this time?'

'It was my favourite. I loved it to bits.'

'Did you give it a name?'

'I called it Jane.'

'I can't believe they gave it to you. I told myself they wouldn't.'

While Jacqui was marvelling at the scruffy stuffed toy that had stayed by Annabel's side during all those years when Jacqui didn't know what had become of the baby she called Daisy, Sarah returned, bringing Izzy.

The two most significant women in Annabel's life met for the first time over their shared grandson's crib.

'I know who you are,' said Sarah to Jacqui. 'You've got my daughter's eyes.'

Without stopping to think about it, the two women embraced.

'Thank you,' said Jacqui. 'Thank you for loving my baby.'

'Thank you,' said Sarah. 'For giving me the chance.'

Chapter Ninety

Annabel and Humfrey remained in hospital for two nights, coming out on Christmas Eve. The weather had turned. It was cold and crisp. Humfrey was wrapped up in two blankets: one from Sarah and one from Jacqui.

Izzy and Richard had done their best to finish setting up the nursery but Humfrey had taken everyone by surprise. The pram that Annabel had so carefully researched and ordered had yet to arrive. Richard had to make an emergency dash to the shops for Babygros and Pampers.

Ronnie dropped round with a pram that had belonged to Jack. She had presents for the new baby too.

'But you just gave us a whole load of gifts at the hospital,' said Annabel.

'Those were for his birthday. These are for Christmas. The poor little thing is going to miss out his whole life because people will lump his Christmas and birthday presents in together but he's always going to get separate pressies from me and his Uncle Mark.'

Annabel put the gifts under the tree.

'What are you doing tomorrow?' Ronnie asked. 'I mean, are you still doing Christmas this year?'

'I suppose so. Though it won't be like normal. I'd forgotten what hard work new babies are.'

'I'm sure the last thing you feel like doing is making the dinner. You can come to my place if you like?'

Annabel hesitated.

'I know it's not what you're used to . . .' Ronnie started.

'No, it's not that. But . . .' Annabel imagined Richard's reaction. And then she knew that he wouldn't be horrified by the offer at all. He would be pleased. He would say 'yes', Annabel knew it.

'Mum and Dad are coming to mine. And Granddad Bill of course,' Ronnie continued. 'And Chelsea, with a bit of luck.'

Annabel totted up the numbers in her head. She added in Sarah.

'My mum is coming here.'

'She can come to ours too. If she doesn't mind, that is. Twelve,' Ronnie said. 'I can do that with my eyes closed.'

'Really? Without a caterer?'

'I'll have my sisters there to help me, won't I? Bring your turkey over. Mum's got devils on horseback from Sainsbury's. I've got enough veg to feed an army. Do you usually have a Christmas pudding? None of my lot like Christmas pudding except for Granddad Bill so we only get a small one just for him.'

'Richard loves it. He buys one from Fortnum's every year.'

'Then bring that too. Mum will have done a Christmas cake. She's pretty good at it.'

'I remember your wedding cake,' said Annabel. 'Or cakes.'

Indeed, though they had looked awful, with their purple and orange icing, they had tasted delicious.

'Crackers,' said Ronnie then.

'It is a bit. I mean, lunch for twelve.'

'No. I'm talking about Christmas crackers. Have you got any?'

'We've got something better,' said Annabel. 'We've got a table bomb. Mum always gets one. Dad started the tradition when Izzy was about six.'

'I'm not going to ask what that is but I know that Jack will love it.'

And so, everything was set. The Buchanans would be having Christmas with the Benson-Edwards. It was a wonderful solution all round. Annabel wouldn't have to worry about anything but the baby. Mark rubbed his hands in glee at the thought of Richard's likely contribution to the booze.

'Are you sure this is OK, Mum?' Annabel asked Sarah, when she arrived at the Great House that evening.

'It will be lovely,' she said.

'And you don't mind sharing the day with Jacqui?'

'No,' said Sarah. 'After all, I've had you to myself for forty-three years.'

'Then it's sorted.'

Baby Humfrey gurgled with what seemed like approval. Of course it was probably wind.

Chapter Ninety-One

Chelsea

It was five o'clock in the afternoon on Christmas Eve.

Chelsea had been asleep for a couple of hours. Her sleep patterns were completely shot. Since breaking up with Adam, she had been unable to sleep most nights but during the afternoons she could barely stay awake.

'Chelsea! Chelsea! Open the flippin' door.'

Chelsea stirred. She had been in such a deep sleep it took her a while to wake up and stagger to the door. She wasn't expecting anyone so she was surprised and cautiously delighted to find Adam on the doorstep, with Lily.

'We've come to deliver your Christmas present,' Lily said. 'Daddy said that Father Christmas couldn't do it because you haven't got a chimney.'

'He's right,' said Chelsea. 'I don't have a chimney here.'

'Are you going to invite us in?' Adam asked.

Chelsea glanced back into the flat behind her. She knew it was in a right state. If Adam came in, he would see the pizza box on the coffee table and the pile of dirty laundry on the kitchen floor. But he had already seen her straight from bed, having slept in the clothes she had been wearing the day before. And she had a cold. She'd been battling it for three days. She was entitled to be looking pretty bloody ropey.

Lily looked up at her expectantly. She looked like the perfect Christmas angel in her red coat trimmed with fake fur.

'Don't you want to see what we've got you?' Lily asked.

'Come in,' said Chelsea.

Fortunately Chelsea had bought Christmas presents for Lily before the break-up and the shop had wrapped them, so they were ready to go. Somehow, Lily managed to persuade Adam that he should let her open one of them early. She chose the largest, which was a Barbie doll dressed as a 1950s starlet. It was probably a little sophisticated for Lily, but Chelsea had fallen in love with the doll the moment she saw it. It was the doll she'd always dreamed of as a child.

Lily was enchanted too. She had her father release Barbie from the box immediately – no mean feat, the doll had been packaged to survive being dropped from the top of the Shard, while tied to an elephant – and settled down at the coffee table to play.

Meanwhile, Adam followed Chelsea into the kitchen. She made them both a coffee. Black. She had no milk. She did have Bailey's, however. She offered Adam a shot of that instead.

'Thanks,' he said. 'But no.'

Chelsea poured herself one. Then she poured it straight down the sink. The last thing she needed was for Adam to think she was a lush on top of everything else.

'I'm sorry,' she said. 'That this place is such a state. I've had a crazy few days.'

'We saw the news about Jack and Bill online. It must have been a scary time.'

'I'll say,' said Chelsea. 'You must think my sister is always mislaying her children.'

'It could happen to any of us. The other day, I almost lost Lily in Hamleys. She was going up the escalator, hanging on to the back of some other dad's jeans. I guess she does mostly see me from the waist down, being so short.'

Chelsea laughed.

'I've missed you,' said Adam then.

'I've missed you too.'

'I've been thinking a lot about what you said that night at my house. You were right to be upset that I called you by Claire's name.'

'It was bound to happen at some point,' said Chelsea. 'I should be used to it. When I was growing up, it seemed like each time she called me, Mum would go through the whole family's names, including the cat's, before she settled on mine.'

'This is different though. And you were right to ask whether I was ready for a relationship. Not just to protect yourself either. There is Lily to think of too. Any relationship we entered into would be a case of three hearts. It's important to be careful.'

Chelsea clutched her coffee mug tightly.

'But not too careful, because that's a sure way to miss out on all the good things in life.'

'Adam,' Chelsea interrupted at last. 'What are you saying?'

'I'm saying that perhaps we should try again? Slowly? Carefully? But with open hearts?'

To Chelsea's ears, it was as good as a marriage proposal. She put her mug down and wrapped her arms round Adam, pressing her head against his chest.

'That's a yes,' she told him.

'Are you kissing?' asked Lily from the doorway, with her head delicately turned away to spare herself from the sight.

'Just hugging,' said Chelsea. 'Want to join us?'

Lily inserted herself into the middle of what was now a group hug.

'We're going to Mum and Dad's for supper,' said Adam. 'Do you want to come too?'

'You're asking me to come to your parents' house?' said Chelsea. 'On Christmas Eve?'

'You're going to have to meet them at some point,' said Adam.

'In that case,' said Chelsea. 'It's another yes.'

Lily helped Chelsea choose her outfit for Christmas Eve at her grandparents' house.

'Granny will like that one,' she said, pulling out the red velvet dress that Chelsea hadn't ever actually worn. It was one of those dresses that seemed like the perfect thing for Christmas but, whenever she put it on, Chelsea felt as though she was an extra in some cheesy film. She wasn't sure she could pull it off. But now Lily was insisting it was the very thing.

'OK,' said Chelsea. She put it on and Lily helped her accessorise it with a glittering crystal necklace, which was Adam's Christmas present to her.

'You can open it early,' he'd said.

'You look like a Christmas princess,' Lily said approvingly.

That was good enough for Chelsea. Adam also seemed to agree.

'I love it. Mary Christmas.'

Chelsea frowned. 'It's too much.'

'No!' Adam insisted. 'In any case, you don't have time

to change. Come on. My mother will have food on the table at seven o'clock sharp. If we're not there on time there will be trouble.'

Getting into the back of Adam's car alongside Lily, at last Chelsea felt ready for Christmas to start.

Chapter Ninety-Two

The Benson-Edwards

Christmas morning at the Bensons-Edwards' house began early.

Jack was up at half past five. Sophie got up, reluctantly, at seven, as her parents told her that Jack wasn't allowed to open his presents until she got up. It would have been cruel to insist on staying in bed any longer and, though she would never admit it, Sophie was just as keen to see Jack's excitement as her parents were. She'd bought him a whole cast of miniature *Doctor Who* characters. She knew that he'd be thrilled.

Sophie was delighted with her own gift from her parents. It wasn't a new iPhone but it was a perfectly refurbished one. She threw her arms round her father's neck.

'I know it's not new,' he began.

'It's perfect, Dad. Thank you.'

Mark had another iPhone for Ronnie. 'Now you can do FaceTime with your mum,' he told his daughter.

Sophie and Ronnie both looked horrified at the thought.

There were more gifts when the Buchanans arrived. Of course, they weren't specially chosen – the invitation for the family to spend Christmas Day at Ronnie's house had come too late for that – but Annabel's emergency present drawer came into its own. And there were plenty of things in there that anyone would have been happy to receive. In any case, Jack was more excited about giving Leander a Christmas present than getting one in return. He'd bought a packet of Trebor mints for the dog, using the last of his pocket money. Richard had to intervene before Leander scarfed the lot. Fishy wisely stayed out of the way in Ronnie's bedroom, with the door firmly closed.

Annabel found a quiet spot for baby Humfrey in his Moses basket in the corner of the dining room, though someone or other visited him every two minutes. Izzy and Sophie couldn't resist looking in on him. Jack showed Humfrey every one of the ten *Doctor Who* miniatures he'd received, waving them in front of the poor baby's unfocused eyes while giving him the low-down on the character's special powers.

Chelsea arrived at midday. In the depths of her misery, she'd been expecting to miss Christmas altogether but now that she and Adam were back together, she couldn't wait to celebrate. After a very lovely supper with Adam's parents, Chelsea had spent the night at Adam's house. He'd let her borrow his car for the drive up to Coventry on the condition that she would hurry back to spend Boxing Day with him and Lily.

'Auntie Chelsea!' Jack in particular was over the moon to see her. He made her open the gift he'd bought for her from the second-hand stall at his school's Christmas fete.

'Oh,' she said. 'A sonic screwdriver! At last I've got my very own.'

'I knew you'd like it,' said Jack.

Ronnie and Chelsea cooked the lunch together. Annabel offered encouragement from a kitchen stool as she fed Humfrey. Everyone else was banned from the kitchen.

Mark and Richard were in charge of the booze. Richard had raided his cellar and brought enough alcohol to kill a horse. They started by giving everyone (except the children) a glass of champagne. Granddad Bill announced that it was the best champagne he'd had since he was in France after the war. Then he sang a version of 'Non, Je Ne Regrette Rien' that Edith Piaf could only have imagined.

Sophie and Izzy found it in their hearts to entertain Jack. Izzy brought out a strange sort of skittles game she'd inherited from her mother and they played it for ages, letting Jack win. When he wasn't being fed, Humfrey slept through most of the day, even when Leander, racing through the dining room after a Trebor mint thrown by Jack, managed to tip the Moses basket over.

The lunch was perfect. It wasn't quite what Annabel would have produced, left to her own devices, but she had to admit that the frozen Aunt Bessie's Yorkshire puddings were a revelation. As were the oven-ready roast potatoes.

'Life's too short to peel a potato,' said Ronnie.

Annabel had to agree.

'I will never peel a potato again.'

Chapter Ninety-Three

Jacqui and Sarah

'I'm sorry it isn't much,' said Jacqui. 'But I wanted to get you some sort of gift.'

Sarah held the scented candle in her lap. As she looked at Jacqui, her eyes filled with tears.

'Jacqui,' she said. 'You already gave me the best gift a woman could ever hope for.'

Jacqui waited for her to continue.

'You gave me our daughter. I have thought about you so often since we got the letter saying that an adoption match had been found. All the way through Annabel's life, whenever she reached those milestones that every mother longs for, I thought about you and what you were missing out on. I knew that you weren't a silly woman. You were a wonderful woman and a strong one to have made the decision to give your little Daisy up.'

Jacqui started to hear the name she had given Annabel from Sarah's lips.

'I knew you hadn't done it lightly and that your gift to me was also a responsibility.'

'You certainly lived up to it,' said Jacqui. 'I couldn't have wished for Daisy to find a better home.'

'I never thought this would happen. Sharing Christmas like this, with you. But I'm glad it has.'

Sarah reached for Jacqui's hand and squeezed it.

'This is what Christmas is all about, isn't it? Being

together as a family. Everyone from the old to the very new.'

Jacqui nodded. They both looked towards Humfrey, who was momentarily awake and being shown the baubles on the Christmas tree by Annabel.

'I always worried what it would be like if Annabel decided to search for you. I told myself that I didn't mind but in reality, I knew I would probably take it as an insult. A slight on the way I had raised her. I think she knew that and out of loyalty to me and her dad she sat on any urge she had to know more. Izzy's illness changed everything. Of course, I couldn't object to Annabel tracking you down when it might save Izzy's life, but I was still very afraid. I couldn't bear the thought of losing her to you.'

'You haven't,' said Jacqui. 'And you never will. I might have given birth to her, Sarah, but I'll never be her mum. That title will always and only belong to you.'

Sarah nodded.

Right then, Annabel's voice called out.

'Mum! Could you hold on to Humfrey for a minute while I pop to the bathroom, please?'

Jacqui and Sarah looked at each other. They both knew exactly who Annabel was calling for. Sarah got up and went to take care of her grandson.

Chapter Ninety-Four

Ronnie

Ronnie was quiet after the Buchanans went home. They were all quiet. Jack was exhausted. He'd had so many grown-ups to entertain that day. He'd been so spoiled too. Sophie was pensive. She had her headphones in her ears as she looked out of the window. Mark was sparko in his armchair. Richard had been more than generous with his wine cellar. Even Fishy, who was finally able to come back downstairs now that Leander was gone, was asleep on top of the radiator.

Ronnie pottered around the house, beginning the clean-up operation. She filled two recycling bags with Christmas paper. She wrapped what little remained of the turkey and two chickens in silver foil. She lined up empty wine bottles by the back door. Sophie put Jack to bed, reading him a 'story' from that year's Minecraft annual, and then turned in herself. Mark was snoring. Ronnie rearranged the Christmas cards on the mantelpiece. She found one that had been drawn by Jack. It wasn't exactly a Christmas card, it was one of his many lists of demands to Father Christmas, folded in half so that it could stand up alongside the Christmas wishes from their family and friends.

Ronnie read Jack's Christmas list. Most of its contents were familiar. A dog. A 'real' motorbike. The latest version of Minecraft.

'Kidnee for Izzi' was the very last item.

Ronnie shook her head sadly.

By the time she went to bed, Ronnie had decided that the following morning, she would go back to Annabel's house alone and talk to her about the transplant. There was no way she was going to let Sophie do it. But Ronnie had to. Izzy was her niece. She was proper family.

Chapter Ninety-Five

Annabel

Whenever they'd spoken to someone who had been through a transplant, it seemed that the phone call always came in the middle of the night. This time was no exception. Christmas Day ticked into Boxing Day. It was quarter to one. Annabel and Richard were still awake. Annabel was in the bathroom, taking off her make-up and running through that day's events. Christmas lunch with the Bensons at the last minute. What fun it had been. They'd all had such a good time. Even Humfrey.

Then the phone rang. The landline. It was so rare that the landline rang anymore that Annabel was immediately alarmed.

'Will you get that?' Annabel called out to her husband, but Richard was changing Humfrey, who had just woken up again.

'Got my hands full,' he called.

The phone continued to ring. Annabel abandoned her toilette and picked up the handset in the bedroom before the answering machine could kick in.

'Hello,' she said.

'Is that Annabel? It's Dawn,' said the caller. 'From the hospital. We need you to bring Isabella in as soon as you can.'

Annabel drew breath. 'Is it . . .?' she whispered.

'Yes,' said Dawn. 'It is. For a possible transplant. We think we've got a match.'

Sarah volunteered to look after Humfrey. Annabel woke Izzy and helped her to gather the things she would need for a hospital stay. Richard got the car out of the garage and sat in the driveway, warming up the engine and working out the fastest possible route to the hospital on his satnav.

Everyone was excited and terrified all at the same time.

'Do you think it will happen tonight?' Izzy asked.

'If it's a match,' said Annabel. 'As soon as they're able.'

Izzy grabbed her mother for a hug.

'I'm frightened,' she said.

'It's going to be OK,' Annabel promised. 'You're going to be in safe hands. But we've got to get going.'

'I've just got to kiss Humfrey,' Izzy said.

Annabel sat in the back of the car with Izzy for the drive to the hospital. She hugged her daughter the whole way and could hardly bear to let go of her when the transplant team took her off to begin their preparations.

In the waiting room, Annabel and Richard sat side by side, holding hands but not speaking. Annabel's thoughts ranged far and wide. She could see Izzy as a tiny baby. A toddler. Eight years old and winning her first trophy at Pony Club. Now there was a very real possibility she would see her well into the future too. Perhaps even having her own baby and beginning the cycle again.

At the same time, for another family, a family she didn't know, a story was coming to a close. They were saying goodbye to their loved one for ever. There would be no happy ending for them.

Annabel went into the chapel and offered a prayer for the family whose brave decision had given her daughter a second chance. She didn't know anything about them. She only knew that the donor was a man in his thirties. Annabel prayed that he wasn't a father.

Annabel kept praying until Izzy sat up in bed the following afternoon, post operation, and asked for a turkey sandwich.

Chapter Ninety-Six

Annabel

So after all that, it turned out that the Bensons were not the key to Izzy's recovery. In the end it was a stranger, dying in a road accident, who gave them the ultimate gift.

The next few weeks passed in a blur. Annabel had never been so busy in her life. Between Humfrey and Izzy, she was always engaged in something to do with one of the children. Izzy had to stay in hospital for a couple of weeks. Humfrey became a popular visitor. Every time Annabel brought him in, she had to take him on a tour of the wards so that he could be cuddled and kissed by all the staff and patients.

Now that Izzy had her kidney transplant, Annabel felt as though she too had been given a new lease of life. There was suddenly so much to look forward to. Izzy and Humfrey both seemed to be growing and changing day by day. To see Izzy's return to form was every bit as exciting as watching Humfrey get bigger and stronger.

On the day that Izzy came home, which happened to be St Valentine's Day, Annabel threw a small party for her elder child. Sarah was there, of course. Izzy's old friends from school were there too. As was Sophie, her new best friend. And Jack and Ronnie and all the Bensons. It was a family affair.

Granddad Bill, Mark and Jack reprised their 'Two and a Half Tenors' act to celebrate Izzy's recovery. There was a cake, like a birthday cake, to mark the start of Izzy's new life. Towards the end of the party, Richard proposed a toast, to the anonymous young man who had given the whole family so much and enabled them to look forward to a great year full of health and happiness and, God willing, at the end of it, another proper family Christmas.

Epilogue

On the other side of the country, Jane Thynne was raising a toast of her own, to the man she would have married that Valentine's Day – her fiancé Greg, who died in the early hours of Christmas Day. She would miss him for ever.

For the past seven weeks, she had existed in some kind of fog, almost unable to admit to herself that he had gone. Alone in the house they had decorated together, she took out a box of keepsakes from beneath the bed they had once shared. The box contained everything, from the very first postcard he sent her. He'd gone to Ibiza, on a lads' holiday, the week after they met. Jane had expected him to meet someone else on that trip and forget all about her, but he had texted twenty times a day, sent her a postcard and brought home the shell bracelet that she now put on again, remembering how he had given it to her on their first proper date.

She re-read everything. The Valentine's cards. The birthday cards. The Christmas card 'For my fiancée' of which she had been so proud. There were silly notes and notes that said nothing more (or less) than 'I love you'. There was one letter that she hadn't opened. He'd written it when he was about to go on a tour of Afghanistan. To be opened in the event of his death. She had wanted to throw it away when he came back from the tour in one piece. She wanted to rip it into tiny pieces and burn it on the fire on Christmas Eve, right after he told her that he was going to leave the army and train to be a plumber. But then he went and got himself killed. Not in some foreign field but on the high street not three minutes from where they lived. Driving home from the pub just after midnight. A drunk driver T-boned him at the junction.

He was so close to home.

Of course, he was on the donor register. They'd had that conversation many times. You had to have that conversation when your loved one was in the army. And in his death, he'd changed the lives of so many. His retinas. His liver. His heart. His kidneys.

Jane opened the last letter from her one true love.

Cheer up, babe, was how it began. *You're reading this because I'm gone, but the truth is, I'll be with you for ever . . .*

Jane smiled and cried all at once.

ACKNOWLEDGEMENTS

This is my thirtieth novel (counting those written under my various pseudonyms) and I don't mind telling you that at times it was hell-on-a-stick to write! For their help in getting me to 'the end' once more, I would very much like to thank the following people:

Dr Chris Browne, Dr Anna Trigell, Dr Conor Byrne, Professor Tariq Massoud and Roy J Thomas and Melanie Wager of the Kidney Wales Foundation for their thoughts and advice on the kidney transplant storyline and related medical issues. Any mistakes herein are absolutely mine.

Francesca Best, Sharan Matharu and the gang at Hodder for their magic in taking my Word doc and making it into the book you now hold in your hands.

My agents Antony Harwood and James Macdonald Lockhart for their continued hard work on my behalf.

My co-conspirators at the Notting Hill Press: Matt Dunn, Michele Gorman, Rosie Blake, Sue Welfare, Victoria Connelly, Belinda Jones, Talli Roland, Ruth Saberton and Nick Spalding, for the tweeting, the Facebooking, the mind-boggling factoid threads and for reminding me how lucky I am to live a writer's life.

Victoria Routledge for being the very best kind of friend, always ready with jokes, sympathy and wonderfully accurate advice. Even if I never take it.

My dear Mark, for being understanding when the muse is in the building (mostly moaning, crying and making a mess) and for making the very best tea. Still.

Finally, I would like to thank – again and again and a thousand times over – Ann and Don Manby, my mum and dad, who changed my life for the better when they adopted me back in 1971. All adoption stories begin in sadness. I wish they could all have such a happy ending as mine. Together with my sister Kate, Mum and Dad became my very own proper family and I love them with all my heart.

To find out more about how you can help kidney patients, visit: www.kidneywales.com.

If you enjoyed *A Proper Family Christmas*, catch up with the first hilarious instalment following the lives of the Benson family and their friends:

A PROPER FAMILY HOLIDAY

Chrissie Manby

Could you survive a week-long holiday with your entire family? Newly single magazine journalist Chelsea Benson can't think of anything worse.

Your grubby small nephew torpedoing any chance of romance with the dishy guy you met on the plane . . .

Your eighty-five-year-old granddad chatting up ladies at the hotel bar . . .

Getting nothing but sarcastic comments from your older sister, who's always been the family favourite . . .

And all this is before your parents drop their bombshell.

Is a week enough time for the Bensons to put their differences aside and have some fun? Or is this their last ever proper family holiday?

Out now in paperback and ebook.

Now read on for a taster . . .

HODDER

Prologue

Of the many family photographs that graced the shelves in Jacqui Benson's living room, there were three of which she was particularly fond. The first, taken in the mid nineteen-eighties, was a photograph of an apple-cheeked baby girl, her younger daughter Chelsea, smiling in toothless delight as her grandfather Bill held her for her first paddle in the shallows of the sea. Chelsea's big sister Ronnie, just two, stood alongside, gripping their father Dave's hand for balance. Ronnie's smile was big and proud as she waved a plastic spade at her mother behind the camera. That photograph was taken at Littlehampton, on a rare bright day in a fortnight of rain. They were staying in a borrowed caravan that smelled of Benson and Hedges and wet dog, but didn't they have a great time?

The second photograph had been taken four years later. Same resort. Different caravan. Chelsea was five by now and Ronnie was six and a half. This time, neither sister needed an adult for support as they dashed in and out of the sea. Together with Granddad Bill, they had built a sandcastle and were filling the moat bucket by bucket. It was a thankless task; they spent the entire afternoon going backwards and forwards, spilling more than they managed to tip into the channel and finding it soaked away altogether before they got back with another load. In the photograph, the sun was shining, though Jacqui remembered it as another wet fortnight.

Stormy even. Wasn't that the holiday where the caravan's awning blew away in the middle of the night? All the same, they had a laugh.

The third photograph was taken in the late nineteen-nineties. Littlehampton again. Granddad Bill liked the old-fashioned seaside town so much he'd bought a static van on a proper full service campsite when he retired. It was a great idea – free holidays for all the family when money was especially tight. In this photograph, the girls were on the beach once more but they were too old for paddling and sandcastles now. They'd spent the morning – a brief respite of sunshine in a fortnight of near monsoon conditions – stretched out on their beach-towels, listening to music, playing it super-cool whenever a good-looking boy walked by and dissolving into giggles once he was past them. They sat up for the photograph, taken by their father. Ronnie had slung her arm round her sister Chelsea's shoulders. Chelsea's expression, eyes rolling even as she tried not to laugh, suggested their dad had just told one of his 'jokes'. This photograph was especially precious to Jacqui. It was the last photograph she had of her daughters together, great friends as well as sisters, enjoying each other's company on a family holiday.

Sixteen years later, Jacqui had decided that it was time to recreate that togetherness again. Only this time with more reliable weather.

Chapter One

Chelsea

Saturday morning, five thirty-seven. The alarm clock on Chelsea Benson's bedside table had been going off for five whole minutes. Chelsea remained in a deep slumber, flat on her back, legs and arms spread wide like a starfish, and snoring so hard that her breath actually stirred the panels of the Japanese paper lampshade hanging above her bed.

Six twenty-three. The alarm had been sounding for fifty-one minutes. Chelsea snored on. She was finally woken by the sound of hammering on the front door of her flat and staggered to answer it, still half asleep. Her next-door neighbour, Pete, stood on the doorstep, in his pyjamas.

'You're in. I told myself she can't be in. I told myself it would stop automatically. Or the batteries would run out. Or . . . or . . .'

With a good portion of her brain still stuck in the Land of Nod, Chelsea looked at Pete in confusion.

'Your alarm clock!' Pete spluttered. 'I can hear it through the walls.'

'Be-be-beep, be-be-beep, be-be-beep . . .' The little clock had not given up.

As if hearing the alarm for the very first time, Chelsea turned back towards her bedroom.

'No!' She was suddenly very wide-awake indeed. 'What time is it?'

'It's twenty-five past six on a Saturday morning!'

'Sorry, Pete. I'll make it up to you, I swear.'

She closed the door as quickly as she could without causing offence, then raced for her bedroom, turning off the alarm clock with a slam to its button while simultaneously working out her next move. Her brand-new wheelie case, still empty and bearing its shop tags, was on the floor by the wardrobe. The pile of holiday ironing she had meant to tackle the previous night was still resolutely wrinkled. No time to fix that. Her passport was . . . Where on earth was her passport?

Now Chelsea's mobile phone was vibrating on the dressing table.

I hope U R on yr way 2 Gatwick.

It was a message from her sister, Ronnie, who, together with her partner, Mark, and their two children, Jack and Sophie, was already well on her way from her home in Coventry to Birmingham Airport. There was no time to respond.

Chelsea chewed on her electric toothbrush as she threw clothes in the general direction of the suitcase. She hopped into the dress she'd been wearing the previous evening and dragged a wide-toothed comb through her wavy brown hair. The undeniably gorgeous dress at least made her look a little more put-together, and looking more put-together always made her *feel* more put-together, which was useful. Despite the hurry, Chelsea paused for a moment and looked more carefully at the clothes she was planning to pack. Her favourite Chloé tunic? Check. Hepburn-style capris by Michael Kors? Check. Three new designer kaftans that were very Talitha Getty circa 1965? Check. Chelsea wasn't sure it was the perfect holiday capsule wardrobe, but it was certainly getting there.

'Passport?' Chelsea muttered.

She spotted her passport on the table by the front door with her keys. Of course. She'd put it there so she wouldn't forget it. Six forty-five. She could still do this. She could still be on time and looking pretty stylish too, she thought, as she glanced in the mirror. The beautiful dress was made perfect for travelling with ballet flats and a fitted denim jacket. She stuck her bug-eyed Oliver Peoples sunglasses in her hair and gave herself a quick pout. Yes. Looking all right, considering.

It was only as she got to the tube station at Stockwell that Chelsea realised her passport was still in the very place she had put it to make certain it was not left behind.

'Aaaaaaagh!'

Seven fifteen. Chelsea was back at the tube station with her passport.

'There are slight delays on the Victoria line . . .'

Eight thirty-five. Chelsea stumbled off the train at Gatwick Airport. Her new wheelie case was more unwieldy than the average shopping trolley. It had gone totally rogue. Which terminal? North or south? She didn't have a clue.

We're checking in now, said her sister's latest text message. Are you even at your airport?

Chelsea found her airline. North Terminal. She made a run for it.

The girl on the check-in desk agreed it seemed cruel that she could not allow Chelsea to board her scheduled flight even though the delayed nine o'clock to Lanzarote would be on the stand for at least another forty minutes as it waited for a take-off slot.

'But I can put you on a flight for tomorrow,' the girl

suggested. 'I'm amazed there's space, to be honest. It is the school holidays.'

'Of course,' Chelsea sighed. Everybody was going away. The airport was absolutely heaving with new wheelie cases and their amateur drivers. Chelsea especially hated those stupid bloody Trunkis. Even as she stood at the check-in desk, a four-year-old boy was ramming a green one designed to look like a frog into the backs of her ankles.

'Is tomorrow the best you can do?' Chelsea asked the check-in girl again.

'Unless you want to swim there,' the girl joked. 'Sorry. There are no more flights today.'

Had she any choice in the matter, at this point Chelsea would have given up on the whole idea of a week away, cut her losses and headed home. Unfortunately, she didn't have any choice in the matter at all. 'Stick me on tomorrow's flight,' she said.

The girl put out her hand expectantly. 'I'll need your credit card. Your old ticket isn't exchangeable.'

'You're kidding me?'

'Oh.' Having done some more tapping on her keyboard, the girl winced as though feeling the pain of what she was to say next. 'I'm afraid you'll have to buy a different flight home as well. Because the return portion of this ticket is dependent on your having flown out there today.'

'That can't be right.'

'It's in the conditions of your fare. The only available return flight is next Sunday, so a day later. The total cost is three hundred and sixty-five pounds forty. Unless you also want to check in some luggage? That's another twenty-five pounds per item.'

'For heaven's sake,' Chelsea cried. She gave her credit

card to the girl on the check-in desk, then turned and glared at the child with the ankle-bashing Trunki. He glared right back at her and gave her one more bash on the heels for luck.

It wasn't as though Chelsea wanted to go to Lanzarote anyway. Lanza-*grotty*, as the girls in her office all called it, had never featured high on Chelsea's list of places to see before she died. Chelsea was sure she knew everything there was to know about the tiny island. It was a volcanic dust bowl with nothing but slate-grey beaches. It was overrun with Brits. Every once passably beautiful bay or romantic cove now sported a burger bar and an Irish pub with an enormous flat-screen TV showing non-stop Sky Sports. The airlines that flew to Arrecife Airport said it all, as far as Chelsea was concerned. British Airways didn't go there. Serena, Chelsea's colleague at *Society*, the monthly fashion and gossip magazine where Chelsea was assistant features editor, said one should never fly to an airport that isn't served by British Airways. With the exception of Mustique.

Chelsea hadn't even told Serena she was going to Lanzarote. She just said 'Spain' and let Serena and the other uber-posh girls in the *Society* office imagine a carefully refurbished *finca* in an orange grove just outside Cadiz. Serena would have recoiled in horror at the very idea of the Hotel Volcan in Playa Brava, with its sports bar, mini-golf and 'Kidz Klub'. Its functional bedrooms with their wipe-clean walls would never feature in a coffee-table book by Mr and Mrs Smith, that's for sure. The moment Chelsea clicked on the hotel website and looked at a depressing shot of an en-suite bathroom, she fancied she could actually smell the tiny bars of cheap white soap and feel the scratchy pink toilet paper that must not, under any circumstances, be flushed down the loo. Nothing turned Chelsea's stomach faster than the thought of a holiday resort without adequate plumbing. But what could Chelsea have said when her mother, Jacqui, called so full of excitement to confirm that the Lanzarote trip was on?

'We're going to the Hotel Volcan. They can put us all on the same floor with disabled access,' said Jacqui.

Same floor and disabled access. Such considerations were extremely important when your party included, at one end of the scale, an adventurous six-year-old and, at the other end, an eighty-five-year-old who was about as steady on his feet as a newborn wildebeest suckled on Guinness. Five rooms had to be booked in all, for this was to be a 'proper family holiday' involving the entire Benson clan – six adults and two children. No one was to be left out. No matter how much they might wish to be.

This proper family holiday was Jacqui Benson's idea of the perfect way to celebrate her upcoming sixtieth birthday. It was Chelsea's idea of pure hell.

Chapter Two

Ronnie

Ronnie Benson, Chelsea's big sister, was altogether more excited by the idea of a week in Playa Brava. After the year she'd had, she needed a week in the sun.

When Ronnie asked her mother what she would like as a gift for her milestone birthday, she had expected Jacqui to suggest her daughters chip in for a new watch or some more charms for her Pandora bracelet. Never in a million years did Ronnie think her mother might suggest a family gathering, much less a week-long family gathering in *Lanzarote*.

'You want to go *abroad*?'

'Your father and I have been planning this trip for years,' Jacqui told her.

'You never said.' After a second of delighted astonishment, Ronnie's thoughts immediately turned towards cost.

'We wanted it to be a surprise,' said Jacqui. 'And I know it sounds over the top, but you're not to worry – your dad and me are paying for everything. We just want you all to be there – you and Mark and the children. I can think of no better birthday gift than to have all my family around me. Especially . . .'

They were standing in the kitchen. Jacqui nodded through the open sitting-room door towards her father-in-law, Bill, Ronnie's beloved granddad, who was asleep in his special chair. At eighty-five, having had just about every internal organ in his body replaced with a plastic valve, Bill was constantly threatening to shuffle off this mortal coil.

'He's always said he'd like to go to Lanzarote,' said Jacqui.

'Mum, are you sure?' Ronnie asked.

'Oh yes. He's always going on about it.'

'I mean, are you sure you and Dad want to pay for us all? We'd love to go, we really would, but it's going to be expensive. You're talking at least four rooms. More if Chelsea's coming.'

'Of course your sister's coming.'

'Really?' Ronnie fought the urge to voice her scepticism. Chelsea on a package trip to Lanzarote seemed as likely as the Duchess of Cambridge rocking up at Nando's.

'Really.'

'It'll cost a fortune. Mark and me will at least chip in for our lot.'

Even as Ronnie said it, she wondered how on earth she and Mark could afford even four easyJet flights to the island. Their finances were more overstretched than Donatella Versace's facelift. Mark worked as a kitchen fitter. It wasn't a badly paid job, but once the recession hit, his hours had been cut from full time to just three days a week. Ronnie had picked up the slack with a part-time admin job at a funeral director's (the credit crunch could not stop people dying), but still they had had to cut back. A holiday had not been on the agenda for that financial year, not when there were school uniforms to buy. A washing machine on its last legs. Gas bills. Council tax. A car that needed servicing . . . Every time Ronnie thought she had the family finances under control, they were beset by some new disaster. To Ronnie's shame, she'd even considered having Fishy, the family cat, put down rather than pay for an expensive operation to fix her leg when the poor thing got run over. Things were that bad. (In the end, she'd stuck the op on her credit card). A holiday in Lanzarote was exactly what Ronnie needed and precisely what she couldn't afford.

'I know you've had a tough couple of years and that's why we're paying for you,' her mother insisted. 'I just want you all to be there.'

'But—'

'No buts, Veronica Benson. This is important to me. The money's already in the bank and I want to take you all away. If I don't spend it on this holiday, I'll only spend it in Per Una.'

'All right, Mum. Anything but more tat from Per Una.'

How could Ronnie refuse?

When he heard the news, Mark also expressed concern, but underneath his polite protestations that Ronnie's parents were being too generous as usual, he seemed delighted, as did the children. A free holiday was not to be sniffed at – especially a holiday in the sun – and, unusually, Mark actually enjoyed hanging out with his almost in-laws. Sophie, who was fifteen and a half, tried to play it cool, of course, but Ronnie knew her daughter was secretly pleased and relieved to be able to tell the girls at school she would be going on a proper foreign holiday that summer after all. Meanwhile, Jack, aged six, was still at an age when the idea of a family gathering appealed to him enormously. Ronnie was sure Jack would have been equally thrilled to spend a week in a Travelodge near Wolverhampton so long as he had his family around him. His grandparents doted on him, but it was the thought of a week with Auntie Chelsea that seemed to tickle Jack most of all.

'Auntie Chelsea!' he squealed. 'Is she really coming? *Really* really? She can play cricket with me,' he added, remembering the last time he had seen his aunt, almost two years earlier, at a family barbecue. Chelsea had thrown a few balls for Jack that afternoon, in between turning her nose up at Mark's burgers and moaning to Ronnie about how hard she found her job at that posh magazine. She'd really hardly paid Jack any attention at all, but for some reason she'd left an indelible impression.

'I can't wait to see her,' said Jack.

'If she can be bothered to come,' Ronnie muttered to Mark. 'I can't imagine Miss Hoity-Toity is terribly excited by the idea of a package holiday in the Canaries. What will she say to the people at *Society*? I suppose she could always write a *hilarious* article about slumming it with the working classes.'

Mark just nodded. He knew better than to disagree with Ronnie where Chelsea was concerned.

From time to time you hear people refer to their siblings as their 'best friends'. Well, Ronnie and Chelsea definitely didn't have that sort of relationship. They hadn't spoken in nearly two years.

It hadn't always been like that. Born just eighteen months apart, the Benson sisters had once been inseparable. Ronnie had doted on her sweet younger sister Chelsea and Chelsea had considered big sister Ronnie the ultimate heroine and role model. As teenagers, in their shared bedroom in the terraced house where they grew up, they had talked late into the night about their plans to escape their boring hometown and make their way together in London. They'd go to university, become successful businesswomen and travel the world first class. Chelsea was going to work in fashion. Ronnie was going to have her own recruitment company by the time she was twenty-five. The sisters were each other's cheerleaders. No way were they going to get stuck like their parents had.

Those ambitions were nipped in the bud when Ronnie turned seventeen and discovered she was pregnant.

It was a disaster. Just days earlier, Ronnie and her form teacher had been talking about university applications. Her teacher had suggested a string of top colleges. 'The sky's the limit for you, Ronnie Benson,' were her encouraging words.

It certainly hadn't been part of the plan to become a teenage mother.

Jacqui and Dave were strangely unfazed by the news of their elder daughter's unplanned pregnancy. Ronnie had expected them to be furious. She had expected recriminations and talk of having let them down. Let herself down. In the end, there was nothing of the sort.

'We'll get through it,' said her dad as he squeezed her in a bear hug. Jacqui agreed.

'We're right behind you, love,' she said. 'Every step of the way.'

Likewise, Ronnie's teachers were sympathetic and did all they could to help her continue with her A-level courses, but Ronnie found her pregnancy surprisingly difficult and postponed her exams, with the intention of going back to a sixth-form college after the baby was born. However, when Sophie arrived, Ronnie was hit with a malaise she now knew to be postnatal depression.

By the time Ronnie had enough energy even to brush her hair in the mornings again, her brightest contemporaries were already on their way to university. Although she had actually only missed out on a year, Ronnie felt she would never be able to catch up and so she didn't bother.

Fifteen years later, Ronnie told herself that everything had turned out for the best. For a start, despite everyone's predictions to the contrary, Mark had stood by her. They'd been together since they were both fourteen. Mark had already left school and was working as an apprentice at a joinery company when Ronnie told him she was pregnant. He vowed right away he would provide for Ronnie and his child, and he had definitely made good on that promise.

Mark moved in with Ronnie and her parents as soon as the baby was born. When Sophie was two, the little family was able to move out of Ronnie's parents' house and into a rented place of their own. With overtime and a bit of work on the side at weekends, Mark earned enough for Ronnie to stay at home until Sophie could go to school. When Sophie was nine, Ronnie considered finishing her A-levels at an adult-education college, but then she fell pregnant with Jack and the cycle started all over again. Including the postnatal depression.

But this makes it all worth it, thought Ronnie, at such moments as when she watched twelve-year-old Sophie, tall as a giraffe, make her precocious debut as goal defence in the school netball team. And what high-flying job could have been more satisfying than seeing four-year-old Jack play a sheep in his first school nativity play? These were the consolations for having so spectacularly short-circuited her plans for world domination with an unprotected shag. Ronnie might not be living in a posh house or driving a fancy car like some of her old friends from school, but she had been able to see her children grow up, while her contemporaries were so scared of stepping off the career ladder they put their carefully planned babies into childcare at six months old. You never got those early years back. If you missed the first word, the first steps, that was it. Those were the things that magazine writer Chelsea didn't understand when she talked about how bored she would be if she were a stay-at-home mum.

'I don't know how you can stand not using your brain,' Chelsea had said the last time she and Ronnie were together. It was at that barbecue to celebrate their grandfather Bill's eighty-third birthday (Bill was celebrated every year now, just in case). That was the comment that sparked the discussion that became a full-blown row that ended with Chelsea accusing Ronnie of having become a mummy martyr and Ronnie accusing Chelsea of having turned into a self-obsessed snob, and subsequently led to the sisters' two-year-long estrangement.

'*Not using my brain!*'

Mark had become used to hearing Ronnie exclaim those four words at random moments during their week. It was usually when she had finished overseeing Sophie's maths homework or had finally deciphered an incomprehensible instruction in a letter sent home from Jack's school. Ronnie would then segue into a rant about how Chelsea had no idea how taxing family life could be. Ensuring that two children and one other adult were fed, dressed, happy and healthy, all on the kind of budget that would have been tight enough for a singleton? That was no mean feat. And now Ronnie was working part time as well. She never had a minute to herself. From time to time, she really did feel as though she was running an army battalion. Chelsea did not have a clue what a mother's life was like.

Perhaps that's why she didn't see the need to apologise for her remarks, Mark occasionally dared to suggest. Only when Chelsea had a family of her own – assuming she could ever hang on to a man for long enough – would she realise the gravity of the insults she'd delivered over a chargrilled sausage in a bun.

'I don't care. I won't ever forgive her,' Ronnie claimed.

Jacqui's birthday wish was to change all that. Ronnie had to promise their mother she would put her anger to one side for just this week. For what might be their last 'proper family holiday'.

'The best birthday present you could ever give me is for you girls to be friends again, like you used to be.'

As though to emphasise her point, Jacqui looked towards that ancient photo of the sisters building a sandcastle on Littlehampton beach.

'All right,' said Ronnie. 'But Chelsea has to make an effort too.'

'I'm sure she will,' said Jacqui.

If only Ronnie could believe that. As it was, about a month before the trip, when Ronnie picked up the phone to offer the olive branch so that their first face-to-face meeting would not be too strange, Chelsea acted as though those two years of radio silence hadn't even happened. She just went straight into a story about some fancy cocktail party she had attended for work. As Chelsea twittered on about the guest list, Ronnie was mortified to realise that while she had been nursing the mother of all grudges, Chelsea had carried on regardless, not questioning her sister's absence because her swanky London life and career were just *so* fulfilling. She simply hadn't noticed she and Ronnie were not on speaking terms.

Reading Chelsea's text from Gatwick, as she stood in the check-in queue in Birmingham, Ronnie fumed. She was certain that her snooty sister had missed her flight deliberately. Next thing, Chelsea would claim she couldn't get another flight. Ronnie would have put money on Chelsea not coming to Lanzarote at all.

WHAT I DID ON MY HOLIDAYS

Chrissie Manby

Sophie Sturgeon can't wait for her annual summer holiday. Not only will it be a week away from work, it will be a chance to reconnect with her boyfriend Callum.

So this upcoming trip to Majorca is a big deal. Sophie's spent a lot of time getting ready. She's bought a new wardrobe. She's been waxed to within an inch of her life. She's determined she and Callum will have the best time ever.

Then Callum dumps her, the night before they're due to leave. In a show of bravery and independence, Sophie says she'll go to Majorca alone – but in fact, she hides in her London flat. But when her friends, family, and even Callum seem so surprised and delighted at her single girl courage, Sophie decides to go all out and recreate the ultimate 'fake break' . . . with hilarious results.

Out now in paperback and ebook.

HODDER